Tell Me
How the Sun Rose

Theodore Clymer

Ruth Meyerson Stein
Doris Gates
Constance M. McCullough

Consultants

William E. Blanton

Milton D. Jacobson

Ken Johnson

Bonnie I. McCullough

Karen A. Scibinico

Roger W. Shuy

E. Paul Torrance

GINN AND COMPANY

ISBN: 0-7702-0578-X

Acknowledgments

Grateful acknowledgment is made to the following publishers, authors, and agents for permission to use and adapt copyrighted materials:

Atheneum Publishers, Inc., for "Mechido" by Giggy Lezra. Copyright © 1969 by Giggy Lezra. From *Mechido, Aziza and Ahmed.* Used by permission of Atheneum Publishers.

The Bobbs-Merrill Company, Inc., for "How the Birds Came to Have Their Many Colors," from *The Long-Tailed Bear and Other Indian Legends,* copyright © 1961, by Natalia M. Belting, reprinted by permission of the publisher. The Bobbs-Merrill Company, Inc.

Ruth Cantor, Literary Agent, for "The Creature in the Bush," adapted from *Taiwo and Her Twin* by Letta Schatz. Copyright © 1964 by Letta Schatz. Used by permission.

Collins + World for "The Maker of Ropes" by John Hampden, from *The Endless Treasure.* Reprinted by permission of the publisher.

Coward, McCann & Geoghegan, Inc. for the adaptation from *The Cave Dwellers.* Adaptation by permission of Coward, McCann & Geoghegan, Inc. from *The Cave Dwellers* by Richard M. Powers. Copyright © 1963 by Richard M. Powers.

Thomas Y. Crowell for the text of *The Seeing Stick* by Jane Yolen. Copyright © 1977 by Jane Yolen. By permission of Thomas Y. Crowell.

Curtis Brown, Ltd., for "Quiet Fishing" by Michael Freeman; "Gaining My First Goal" by Pamela McHenry; the selection beginning "The Football players run faster and faster..." by John Auerbach, all from *Journeys* by Richard Lewis.

The Dial Press for "Thi Kinh" from the book *The Beggar in the Blanket and Other Vietnamese Tales* by Gail B. Graham. Copyright © 1970 by Gail B. Graham. Used by permission of the Dial Press.

Dennis Dobson, Publishers, London, for the poem "The Brontosaurus" ("The Brontosaurus Had a Brain") from *Creatures Great and Small* by Michael Flanders and M. Minale. Used by permission of the publishers.

Doubleday & Company, Inc., for the poem "I go Forth to Move about the Earth" by Alonzo Lopez from the book *The Whispering Wind* copyright © 1972 by the Institute of American Indian Arts. Reprinted by permission of Doubleday & Company, Inc.

Little, Brown and Company, Boston for the adaptation from pages 42-53 "Lisa Faces a Crisis" from *The Wooden People* by Myra Paperny. Copyright © 1976 by Myra Paperny.

Farrar, Straus & Giroux, Inc. for "The New Boy" from *Pitcher and I* by Stephen Cole, Copyright © 1946, 1947, 1963 by Stephen Cole, Copyright 1946 by The Curtis Publishing Company, Copyright renewed 1974, 1975 by Stephen Cole.

Ernesto Galarza for the poems "the boa," "the elephant," "the giraffe," "the zebra," "the flamingos," "the vicuna," "the swan," and "the alligator," all from his book *Zoo-Fun,* published by Editorial Almaden, San Jose, California. Copyright 1971 by Ernesto Galarza. Used by permission of the author.

General Publishing Co. Ltd. for the story "The Legend of the Oriole" from *Tales of Nokomis* by Patronella Johnston. Used by permission of Musson Book Company, Don Mills, Ontario.

Peter Pauper Press, Inc. for "How the Milky Way Came to Be" and "Nature Cannot Be Changed," both from *African Folk Tales* by Charlotte and Wolf Leslau. Copyright © 1963 by The Peter Pauper Press. Used by permission of the publisher.

G. P. Putnam's Sons for the text from *When Great-Grandmother Was Young* by Maxine Kumin. Copyright © 1971 by Maxine Kumin. Reprinted by permission of G. P. Putnam's Sons.

Random House, Inc., for "The Ice Age," adapted by permission of Random House, Inc. from *All about the Ice Age,* by Patricia Lauber. Copyright © 1959 by Patricia Lauber. Also for "A Girl and the Altamira Cave," adapted by permission of Random House, Inc. from *All about Prehistoric Cave Men,* by Sam and Beryl Epstein. Copyright © 1959 by Sam and Beryl Epstein. Also for "Tragedy of the Tar Pits," adapted by permission of Random House, Inc. from *All about Strange Beasts of the Past,* by Roy Chapman Andrews. Copyright © 1969 by Roy Chapman Andrews. Also for the poem "My People" by Langston Hughes. Copyright 1926 by Alfred A. Knopf, Inc. and renewed 1954 by Langston Hughes. Reprinted from *Selected Poems,* by Langston Hughes, by permission of the publisher.

The Seabury Press for "The Children of Rain" retold by Elizabeth S. Helfman, adapted from her book *The Bushmen and Their Stories.* Copyright © 1971 by Elizabeth S. Helfman. Used by permission of The Seabury Press, Inc.

Virginia K. Smiley for "The Fuji Stick."

The Viking Press for "Andy and the Lion" and an illustration, from *Andy and the Lion* by James Daugherty. Copyright 1938, renewed © 1966 by James Daugherty. Reprinted by permission of the Viking Press. Also for "Sedna" from *Sedna: An Eskimo Myth* by Beverly Brodsky McDermott. Copyright © 1975 by Beverly Brodsky McDermott. Adapted by permission of The Viking Press.

A. P. Watt Ltd, London, for "The Maker of Ropes," adapted from *The Black Monkey* by John Hampden. Used by permission of A. P. Watt Ltd. and the author. Also for the galleys of "The Wasp in a Wig" by Lewis Carroll. "The Wasp in a Wig" copyright © Philip Jaques and Elisabeth Christie 1977 Trustees of the Estate of the late C. L. Dodgson. Reprinted by permission of the Trustees of the Estate of C. L. Dodgson, Clarkson Potter Inc. and Macmillan and Co. Ltd. and by courtesy of Mr. Norman Armour Junior and The Lewis Carroll Society of North America.

Illustrations were provided by the following: Angela Adams (348–363); Paul Blakey (78–97); Brenda Clark (170–181); Joshua Clark (76–77); Patricia Collins (303–311); Dave Cunningham (381–396); Jim Crowell (400–415); James Daugherty (138); Sam Dion (312–324); Len Ebert (238–243, 364–371); George Eisenberg (48–61); Helen Fox (64–75); John Freas (211–213, 244–249); Charles Freeman (294–299); Judy Sue Goodwin (417); Christa Keiffer (399); Harvey Kidder (372–379); Gordon Laite (250–258); Richard Loehie (26–44); Sal Murdocca (276–283); Jane Oka (380); Marianne Perlack (285); Jerry Pinkney (136–137, 153–168); Richard Powers (336–344); Jon Provost (24–25); Albert John Pucci (260–273); Jim Santiago (63); Miriam Schottland (206–207); Ralph Steadman © The Sunday Telegraph Magazine (144); Karl Stuecklen (101–115); Susan Swan (208–209); Phero Thomas (224–236); Kyuzo Tsugami (188–199).

Photographs were provided by the following: Holle Beldarchiv (328–329); Reproduced by permission of the British Library Board, Additional Ms. 46700, f. 46 v (142); Charles Michael Daugherty (139); William Finch (286–287, 290–291); Kevin Galvin (116–117, 182–183); Virginia Hamilton (100); Courtesy, Istituto Editoriale Italiano (326–327, 322–333); David Powers/Jeroboam, Inc. (130–135); Nicholas Krenitsky (142); Jock MacRae (118–129, 418–459); Stephen G. Maka (46–47); Terry McKoy (184–185); Peabody Museum, Harvard University-Photographs by Hillel Burger (214, 218–222); Herb Randle (216–217); Royal Danish Ministry for Foreign Affairs (154); Maureen Shaughnessy (188–199, 202–205); Mike Stammoulis (415); © Jean Vertut, Courtesy, Editions d'Art Lucien Mazenod, Paris from *Prehistorie de L'Art Occidental* (330–331); © Jean Vertut, Paris (334–335).

The cover and unit introduction pages were designed by Gregory Fossella Associates.

Contents

8

Tell Me
How the Sun Rose

Setting the Pace

In most stories the main characters solve problems of some kind. In doing so, they often learn important lessons, setting the pace for meeting new challenges in the future. The boys and girls in the stories of this unit also face problems. Perhaps these problems are like ones you and your friends are familiar with. As you read the stories, think about how you would act if you were in the same situations.

The Stein family is constantly moving from place to place so that Mr. Stein can "see the world." The year is 1927 and they have just settled in Chatko Falls, a remote Alberta village. Lisa Stein is looking after her younger brothers and sisters while their parents are in Edmonton buying supplies for the family store. With only the help of Lucy, a local hired maid, Lisa has to try to save her brother's life after an accident. How does she meet such a terrifying challenge?

Lisa Faces a Crisis

Lisa was happy that Teddy had finally found a friend. Late in the afternoon he had brought a quiet boy, his own age, upstairs and announced that they were going down the road to explore some streams.

When Lisa locked the store at six o'clock Teddy still hadn't appeared. "Lucy, it's late and that wind is whistling through the doors. Any idea what stream they could have gone to?"

Lucy, carrying plates to the table, shook her head. "The only stream I know around here is too swift for them to go in. It's near Wilders' farm."

"Where's Wilders' farm? Do you think I could find it myself? Teddy's never late like this."

"No, you'd never find it, especially now that it's getting dark."

"Well, there must be somebody who'd help me," Lisa replied.

"Well, you might go get Macnamara, he's the patrolman. But have your dinner first."

Lisa didn't wait for dinner but, with her open coat flying, dashed down the outdoor stairs to find him.

When she finally found him, Macnamara told her not to worry—although a frown creased his forehead. He wanted to walk her back to the store before beginning a search but she insisted on going with him. She trudged behind the shaky beam of the patrolman's flashlight.

"I never should have let him go. I just knew I was wrong. How long will it take to get there?"

"Maybe we'll stop and get a couple of fellows to help us in case they're lost." He shone his flashlight into the prairie ahead of them. Now shining snowflakes made it impossible to see clearly across the flat plain.

"Hey there, isn't that your brother down there?" Macnamara started to run in the direction of a small figure stumbling toward them.

"What's wrong with him? He looks wet or something," Lisa replied as she rushed toward the figure momentarily outlined by the beam of light. "Teddy, what happened? Where have you been?" she called.

Macnamara didn't waste any time on words as he dashed toward Teddy. "Darn fool kid, I bet you fell in that stream, that's what you did. You picked a miserable night for it too." Teddy just stood quivering with a tattered blanket around his shoulders.

13

"He looks like a wet rat," Macnamara continued, as they hustled Teddy toward the store. "Get him out of those duds fast, girl."

. . .

It was about four A.M. when she awoke to see little Mike standing at the bottom of her bed. Mike was still rubbing the sleep out of his eyes. "Teddy woke me up

Lisa. It's not my fault. He won't stop making terrible noises. I think something's wrong with him, Lisa."

Lisa didn't wait to hear any more. She jumped out of bed and rushed toward the boys' room with Mike trailing behind her. Teddy was sitting up in his bed with his hand over his chest. "My chest aches, Lisa, and when I cough, it's like I'm caught in the wringer of the washing machine. It hurts to breathe." Teddy clutched the eiderdown closely around him and bit his bottom lip. Lisa motioned Mike to go and awaken Lucy. She bent to feel Teddy's forehead.

By the time Lucy arrived with Mike, Lisa had already taken Teddy's temperature with the thermometer from Mama's medicine chest. Surely Lucy would know what to do next. She whispered to Lucy that the thermometer had registered forty point five degrees Celsius.

"He's like fire. He's so hot, Lucy. What shall we do now?"

"I don't know, Lisa. Maybe I should go out and pump some cold water. My mom always said herb tea cured anything. Maybe you should make some, but—but I don't remember the recipe. Mom always took care of everyone when they were sick."

"Then go get the doctor, Lucy." Lisa knew that whatever it was, Teddy was extremely ill, and Lucy obviously was not going to be of any great assistance. The doctor was the answer.

"There isn't a doctor in Chatko Falls, Lisa."

Lisa stared at Lucy in total shock. "There has to be

15

someone. His fever is dangerous, and he can't stay like this. What about a druggist?"

"The nearest doctor is in Edmonton or in Whistling Creek. You ought to know we don't have a drugstore."

Sending Lucy to pump some cold water, Lisa quickly applied compresses to Teddy's head. She then forced two aspirins down his throat and bundled flannel across his chest with Lucy's assistance. Teddy was now totally limp. Lisa then told Suzanne, who stood anxiously by the bed with Mike, to find Miss Wells, the telephone operator, and get her to open the telephone exchange so that she could phone her parents in Edmonton.

"But Miss Wells is sleeping by now," Lucy insisted.

"The two of you go and wake her up even if you have to pound and shout for an hour or break a window with a rock. It's an emergency. Then see if you can find Mr. Macnamara. He must know someone in town who can help us." Both girls rushed out the door. They were relieved to be given some direction.

Lisa forced another aspirin down Teddy's throat and changed the cool compress. She stared at all the bottles in her mother's kit. It was useless. What good was iodine, castor oil and Epsom salts? Teddy was so feverish now that he forcefully threw the covers on the floor. A few moments later he shivered, begging for a hot water bottle. His breath was labored. A dull rattling sound came when he coughed.

Four hours later Lisa sat dozing by the bed. She had finally reached Mama on the phone and her parents said they would soon be there with a doctor. She had

16

sponged Teddy with the alcohol and water combination Mama had told her about on the phone. Although she had repeated this process many times his fever always went up again. When she awoke from her brief nap to see Mike changing the compresses again, she didn't even bother to brush away the tears that slid down her face. Her most beloved brother was dying. She was certain. He lay very silent and quiet with the perspiration highlighting the dark tan face. If only she were a nurse like Florence Nightingale.

. . .

Now it was almost noon. Lisa and Lucy had sponged Teddy a dozen times more by the time Papa and Mama arrived with the doctor. They gently led Lisa out of the room as the doctor examined Teddy.

"Come on, Lisa, it wasn't your fault," Suzanne said as they all waited on the big horsehair sofa in the parlor. "There's no way you could have prevented Teddy from falling in the stream."

"He never would have gotten a chill if I'd made him stay here."

"Golly, Lisa, nobody would ever believe that snow comes so quickly to a place," Mike said.

. . .

Macnamara entered their home briefly to receive a prescription from Papa. It was to be filled at the drugstore in Whistling Creek. It seemed only minutes later when they heard the car return. Macnamara had driven so fast that puffs of dust remained on the street long after he had dashed back up the steps.

Lisa didn't know how long she had slept but a soft

touch on her arm brought her back from a dream where she had been chasing across a field after Teddy. The strange doctor, with his thin gray hair falling untidily across his face, was whispering to her. "You're a very brave and sensible girl, Lisa. Good head on your shoulders."

"But it was all my fault. I shouldn't have let him go." Lisa didn't dare ask him if Teddy would live. As long as she held back the fatal question he might be fine. "What is it?" she mumbled.

"Pneumonia, and there might be some other complications."

"We must take him to a hospital then," Papa said. Mama was weeping.

"The hospital is too far away. He still has a high fever and shortness of breath. I hope that with the medicine we now have the worst will soon be over. There are no miracle drugs for pneumonia, Mrs. Stein . . . perhaps someday. Your daughter did everything I myself would have prescribed. You have a good head, young lady." The kindly man absently patted her shoulder again.

Now she really couldn't hold back her tears any longer. Pneumonia was such a frightening word. Lisa threw her arms around Mama and buried her head in the familiar chest. Mama was still wearing her good city clothes and Lisa felt her lapel watch scratch her cheek.

Mama held her tightly and murmured something about her good girl. Suzanne and Mike burst through the door and also snuggled up to Mama. Their father sat down in a chair and stared through the picture hanging before him.

"This is a horrible nasty town. If we had stayed in our real home Teddy would be fine now," Suzanne shouted. "It's this wretched place that did it." Mama roughly clamped her hand over her younger daughter's mouth but it was too late and the room became silent.

Suddenly Lisa remembered the old nursery rhyme: "If wishes were horses, beggars would ride/If turnips were watches, I'd wear one at my side." Just wishing would not make Teddy better, and he was certainly not the first person to take sick in a town without doctors.

Papa remained sitting like a stone. Mama was too busy with the younger children to notice. Lisa realized that Papa might have been hurt by Suzanne's unthinking remark. Lisa always had been rather timid with her father, but somehow she knew she must now cross the wide room and do something to prevent him from blaming himself. Maybe it was some inner instinct, like that of a migratory bird, which forced him to move constantly from town to town. After all, birds had to go south in winter no matter what.

Lisa removed herself from the octopus of arms around Mama. Hesitantly she moved across the room. When she stood before her father she regretted her gesture. He hadn't noticed her. He slumped in his chair. "Papa, Teddy asked for you last night," she stammered.

"He really did?" Lisa nodded her head. But then another thought occurred to him. "And I wasn't there."

Had she made things worse by her remark? She could almost taste the bitterness in his voice. Quickly she continued. "He said what a wonderful fishing spot

20

he's found down by that stream and he'd like to tell
you about it."

Papa almost smiled then and rose from the chair.
"Hear that, Esther? He asked for me. There's something special about Teddy." Then, as if responding to
some preset signal, both parents left the room, Mama
to arrange dinner and Papa to check with his clerk.

Two hours later the doctor came from Teddy's room.
"He's a tough boy. He's going to make it. The fever is
dropping and his breathing is much better. He's got a
lot of courage, that boy of yours. He complains of pain
in his joints but he has fewer chest pains now."

When the doctor finally departed he suggested that
Lisa be allowed to see Teddy for a few moments. The

room was in semi-darkness with just a single light glowing from a corner lamp. Lisa leaned over a shadowy Teddy. He appeared to be asleep. While his face was waxy and drawn, no longer did his lips show a bluish discoloration. His silence made it difficult to accept the doctor's positive diagnosis. She leaned over, hoping to hear his heart beat. As she straightened up, his eyelids blinked open as rapidly as those of a china doll.

"You're some doctor," he barely whispered. Oh, he wasn't improved. He was still delirious. Now he thought she was the doctor.

"Doctor Lisa," Teddy croaked. He reached up for her fingers with his feverish hand. She was unable to utter a word so she kissed the top of his head. She wanted to express her great love but knew he'd scoff at her.

"It looks like you'll soon be running around chasing me again. You can't keep a wildcat down."

Painfully he managed a grimace. "It hurts to laugh." Then Mama entered the room and insisted that Teddy go to sleep. Shyly, blowing him a kiss as she had done when they were toddlers, Lisa retreated to the door, walking backward until she could see him no longer.

—Myra Paperny

22

Taking A Closer Look

1. How did Lisa feel about her brother? About her father? How do you know?

2. How did Lisa behave toward her brothers and sisters? Toward her mother? Toward her father? Why did she behave differently with each?

3. If Teddy had died despite Lisa's efforts, do you think the family would then have agreed with Lisa that it was all "her fault?" Why or why not?

4. What difference do you think this incident might have made to Mr. Stein and his future plans?

5. The author uses interesting words and phrases to describe events and characters in the story. How would you feel if:
    a. you felt "like I'm caught in the wringer of the washing machine".
    b. you were "sitting like a stone".
    c. you were surrounded by an "octopus of arms".

What Do You Think?

1. Why did it take courage for Lisa to decide what needed to be done for her sick brother?

2. Tell about a time when you, like Lisa, had to face a new and possibly frightening situation. How did you feel about it? What kinds of problems did you have to solve? What did you do about them?

I Go Forth to Move about the Earth

I go forth to move about the earth.
I go forth as the owl, wise and knowing.
I go forth as the eagle, powerful and bold.
I go forth as the dove, peaceful and gentle.
I go forth to move about the earth
  in wisdom, courage, and peace.

—*Alonzo Lopez*

Once, as if in a dream, Marra had met a seal named Nerea. Like many dreams, this one had faded by morning. Even the name Nerea was forgotten — until one day during the time of the full moon. What really happened that day? Was Nerea a dream or not? Is the full moon the key?

IS THE FULL MOON THE KEY?

One day during the summer vacation Alison and Marra were at loose ends. They had finished their chores and had no particular plans. It was Alison who suggested a picnic on the Cow and Calves, three small islands not more than forty minutes' row from the harbor. There were usually sheep on Cow Island and they thought there was a ram on Big Calf. They'd see when they got there. There was a small beach on Little Calf which might be best of all. It was scarcely more than a rock where the terns nested, but there were the ruins of the hermit's cabin to give it a sense of strangeness. No one quite knew who the hermit was or how long ago he had built his shelter or when he had died. There were just two walls of beach stones still standing under a single spruce tree. Most people thought he had been a pirate, so now and then children went out and dug for treasure, but no one had ever found a sign of it.

"What I wonder about was where he got his drinking water," someone would say.

"He could have had a catchment at the foot of that cliff," another would suggest, "or there may have been a little spring which has dried up since his time. I've known that to happen."

So there was something rather special about Little Calf even if you didn't believe in ghosts, and the girls told each other that they weren't scared of any old ghost.

"It's never done anyone any harm," said Alison. "It won't hurt us even if there is such a thing."

"No, I don't suppose so, but it is true that people have heard queer noises, and when Jerry Sinclair had been digging there a northeaster came up all of a sudden on the way back and nearly swamped his dory," said Marra.

"Well, we shan't dig." Alison was set on the picnic. The day was mild, with no wind or almost none. "Mother will let us make sandwiches. Why are you hanging back, Marra?"

It was true that Marra didn't feel very eager for the adventure, but she didn't know why. She had often longed to explore the islands but she didn't like to ask Pa to lend her his tender which he left tied up to his float when he took the lobster boat out. Now they would use the doctor's light new rowboat which was waiting at the pier. She didn't even have to ask Granny, who never cared where she was after the work which she nowadays did was finished.

"Scat!" Granny would say when the last chore had been done. "And don't let me see hide nor hair of you until the boats are in."

Granny didn't speak as fiercely as she used to. Sometimes her harshness seemed to be more from habit than from feeling, and Marra had been told by one or two of Granny's friends that Granny even said, "Some ways she's a little like my Aunt Lola."

She didn't say that to Marra and Marra knew better than to expect any kind word from her, but there was a general easing of the tension in the house. The fierce edge of Granny's hatred had worn down to dislike and even to tolerance. Still, Marra asked no favors from Granny and knew she would get none if she asked. But Alison was welcome to use her father's rowboat any time she wanted to, and they would put up the picnic at Alison's.

Still Marra hung back.

Something in her warned her, Don't go today, but she didn't know why. Not today, said her inner self, but outwardly it seemed exactly the right day. Pa had said that morning, "Should have a good day today. All signs point to it." But some sign in Marra didn't point to a good day. Yet here it was nearly noon and it was as fine as it had been at dawn.

"All right," said Marra, still a little hesitantly. "I've always wanted to explore Little Calf, and if we stay late we can come home by moonlight. Moon's at the full tonight."

31

They never reached the three islands. Marra rowed and Alison sat in the stern and handled the tiller. There was no sea running, just enough to bring the little wavelets to flower, and the flock of terns that seemed to follow them for a while seemed like flowers, too, against the sky, or so Marra thought, but Alison only laughed at her.

"We're getting very near," said Alison.

"Don't you want me to take the oars for a while? I'm not as good at rowing as you are, but you must be getting tired."

"I'm fine," said Marra, resting for a minute to turn her head and look at the islands they were approaching. There was Cow Island with a cliff and sheep feeding on the short turf, and Big Calf, and Little Calf circled by reefs. She even noticed the ruin of the pirate's house and some stones by the shore piled for a landing long ago. A glance showed her all this, but what her gaze steadied on was the sun. Surely it was not as bright as it should have been?

34

"Alison, isn't it cooler than it was?"

"Yes," said Alison comfortably. "It was too hot when we started out. Marra, what on earth are you doing?"

"I'm heading the boat for home," said Marra. "Help me, Alison. The fog is coming in. Look hard at our landing and try to steer for it even when you can't see it. The trouble is that everyone naturally rows harder with one hand than with the other, and a boat like this can be turned completely in the wrong direction in a fog without either of us knowing."

"But I can see our landing perfectly well."

"Now, you can," said Marra. "I hope you still can in ten minutes," and she began to row at a fast, steady pace. She had grown up hearing stories of dories and lobster boats, too, in heavy fogs carried out to sea by the tides. Some had been lost for days and some forever.

"You're making a lot out of nothing," said Alison uneasily.

"I hope so," said Marra. Alison was an inland girl. She might know the dangers of blizzards but she knew nothing of fogs nor of the danger of tides nor of their strength when the moon was full.

Marra went on rowing. Her back was to their destination, but already Cow Island and the Calves were blotted out by a thin veil of fog.

"I can still see the landing," said Alison. Her voice trembled a little, but she tried to hold it steady. Marra's fear had been communicated to her, Marra's courage, too, but she had plenty of her own.

It was almost as if the fog had heard her for now neither she, nor Marra, when she turned her head briefly to check her position, could see the landing on their own island nor its dwelling houses and trees and the fringe of fish houses and piers below them. The white moist presence of the fog drifted all about them, turning the sun into something like a small frantic moon and then wiping it out altogether. Now they moved through nothingness. Even sounds were strange. Somewhere far off a dog barked, a small familiar sound, but they could not tell whether it was ahead of them or to one side.

"Don't row too hard with your right oar," said Alison.

"I'm trying not to," said Marra. "Try to sit just as you were sitting before we lost sight of the landing place."

"I can't be sure!" wailed Alison.

There was a long, long silence while they moved through the dense white cocoon of the fog, and at last Alison said, "Marra, shouldn't we have reached the landing by now?

38

"I think so," said Marra. "I suppose we're going to land in Spain, and won't the Spaniards be surprised?"

If she had hoped to make Alison laugh, she succeeded. Alison gave a little snort of laughter and then, having once opened the door of her silence, burst into tears.

"Don't cry, Alison, don't cry. We may meet a lobster boat or something."

She was much more upset for Alison than for herself. Many people would miss Alison, but no one would miss her, or at least only a little. She didn't think about that, only felt her heart filled with a longing to protect Alison, her first friend. And with the sharpness of that emotion a forgotten memory awoke.

40

"Nerea!" she shouted. "Nerea! Nerea! Help us, Nerea!"

And almost at once, close beside them Nerea appeared, a gray seal this time with kind, mournful eyes. She nudged against the bow of the boat, turning it. "Don't try to steer, Alison," said Marra. "It will be easier for Nerea if you let her do it all."

The seal gave her a backward look, wise and loving.

"Oh, Nerea, we are so glad that you came!" Marra sighed. She went on rowing, slowly, so as not to get in the seal's way. Then, as the shape of the pier loomed more than life-sized out of the fog, Nerea gave Marra one long, last loving look and disappeared, taking all memory of herself and the rescue with her.

"Thank you," Marra began, but then forgot whom she was thanking. "Thank you, Alison, for steering us so well."

"I don't think I steered well," said Alison uncertainly, but she, too, had forgotten who or what it was that had brought them home. With stiff hands they fastened the painter of the boat to the float and climbed up its short, slippery ladder.

Only when on the pier they almost bumped into the small bent figure in a yellow slicker did they see Marra's granny. But she saw them before they saw her.

"Only a couple of fools wouldn't have known that a fog was coming in," she told them crossly. "The others think you're off in the woods for your picnic. But I knew better. I watched where you were off to from the kitchen window. Now come on up to the house! Come on, Alison, you too. I've got hot chocolate on the stove and fresh beaten biscuits in the oven waiting for you. No use wasting them, now you're here."

Marra was too surprised to answer, but Alison said at once, "Thank you, Granny. We're half frozen."

—Elizabeth Coatsworth

The full moon is the key
It opens the gates of night
It makes the dog howl
and the tides rise high on their beaches.
Shadows change
Breezes are aware
Owls move silently on feather-soft wings
Now is the moment when the powers of magic
Are at their strongest.
Pull down the shades of the house
Close the doors
Even the stars draw back
It is the hour of the full moon
And nothing is certain.

—Elizabeth Coatsworth

What Do You Think?

1. How do you think Marra and Alison were saved?
2. If you were Marra, would you have gone to the islands? Why or why not?
3. Who would you rather have as a friend, Marra or Alison? Why?

Taking A Closer Look

1. What was special about Little Calf Island?
2. How did Marra feel about going to the islands that summer day?
3. Why did Marra turn around before reaching the islands?
4. An artist—in paint or in words—often gives clues to meaning rather than stating something outright. How do the following expressions add meaning and interest to the story?
   a. fringe of fish houses
   b. like a small, frantic moon
   c. dense white cocoon
   d. the door of her silence
5. Why was Marra surprised to see Granny waiting for her on the dock?

NO OTHER SIGN

At a distance
The restless dunes,
Lonely, desolate, beckon
With their straggly reeds
Given motion
By the endless winds.
The roaring waves
Crash blindly
On the jetty
"Closed until the summer."
There is no other sign of life

—*Javier Honda*

46

The Milestone Group

In olden times wooden signposts marked distances from one town or city to another. Later, the miles were marked off by large stones set by the side of the road. These stones were called *milestones*. As you read this story, can you figure out another, newer meaning of this word?

48

The Plan

Mom seemed quite upset this evening, Lucy decided as she set the kitchen table. She put down four plates and slid four forks toward them. Mom turned from the stove with a steaming casserole in her hand. Lucy stepped back to let her serve the supper.

The kitchen was small. There wasn't room for all six of them to sit down together. But it didn't matter, really. Dad wouldn't be home from his night job until morning. And the boys ate almost on the run. Now they came noisily into the kitchen to gobble up their food before returning to the street.

"Dennis," said Mom. She held her eleven-year-old by the back of his shirt. "You go wash yourself. You too," she added, darting a look at Dennis' younger brother, Christopher. "Come, Bonnie," she said more gently to the small girl beside Lucy. "Come, baby. Time to eat."

Bonnie slid into a chair and pulled her plate toward her. Mom put the casserole back in the oven. She didn't join her children at the table. There was room for only four.

"Take my place, Mom," said Lucy suddenly. Mom worked in a small factory and she seemed very tired tonight.

"No," said Mom wearily. "You go ahead. I'm going to stretch out for a little while before I eat. Right now I'm just too downhearted to think about food."

Bonnie, with her fork almost to her mouth, suddenly put it down. She called to her mother, about to leave the kitchen.

"Look, Mom. Look here." She put two fingers into her mouth and took hold of a front tooth. "Look, Mom. It's loose. It'll come out any day now."

"Don't I know it," said Mom. "It's been bothering me day and night. I've been planning on a bright and smiling picture of my littlest. But by the time I get the money saved up, she'll be gap-toothed."

The boys laughed and Mom threw them an angry

stare. "Go right ahead and laugh," she told them. "I got pictures of you at her age. Lucy too. But not one picture of my Bonnie and she's my littlest."

Mom went heavily from the room. The four at the table looked at each other with sudden soberness. It was not like Mom to talk to them in this way. Sure she got tired and grumpy. But she never said mean things like that. Mom must be more upset than they knew.

Lucy listened to be sure Mom had gone into her bedroom. Then she said very low, "I've been thinking about something." The other three fastened interested eyes on their big sister. The boys stopped chewing to listen.

"Next month is Mom's birthday."

"I know," said Dennis. "I want to get her something real nice. But what? Everything nice costs so much money. Where can I get some money?"

"And this birthday is very important to Mom," Lucy continued. "She calls it a milestone. She says she plans to live until she's eighty and this birthday puts her halfway there. Forty! Right in the middle. A milestone!"

Mom forty! It seemed a great age. They thought about it in silence as they cleaned up their plates.

Finally Christopher said, "Are you planning something for Mom?"

Lucy nodded. "In a way," she said. "I have an idea, that's all." She looked around the table. "You want to come in on it?"

Dennis' eyes grew cautious. "What do you have in mind?"

"I want to have a picture taken of all of us together. I want it right now before Bonnie's tooth comes out."

"Do you have the money for that?" asked Christopher, whispering.

Lucy shook her head. "That's the trouble. We've got to get the picture first and the money later. Bonnie will lose her tooth before we can get the money."

"Why not just a picture of Bonnie by herself? It might not cost so much," suggested Dennis.

"No," said Lucy. "This is the milestone picture. I want Mom to have us together just the way we looked when she got to be forty. A 'Group.' That's what they call a picture with lots of people in it."

"The Milestone Group," said Dennis slowly. "I can see it on the wall now. Mom would like that. You have a good idea there, Lucy."

"Then you'll come in on it?"

"What do you mean 'come in on it'?"

"You'll help get the money to pay for it?"

"How?"

"There must be some way you can help," Lucy said. "Stop hanging around the schoolyard after school and running up and down the streets on Saturday. Go look for something to do. You'll find something if you look hard enough. Christopher can look along with you."

"What are you going to do?" asked Christopher.

"Oh, I've several good leads," said Lucy.

"I want to do something too!" said Bonnie in a loud voice that surely reached the bedroom.

"Shoosh," hissed Lucy. "You're only six. You can help me here at home so I can get to my jobs faster. Helping me is the same as helping at a regular job. See?"

Bonnie nodded a bit uncertainly. But then she seemed satisfied.

Before leaving the table, the children agreed they would have the picture taken. Then they picked up their plates and stacked them in the sink. They would get around to washing them later.

Next day Lucy hurried home from school. She took the three flights of stairs without a stop. Bonnie, she knew, would be there waiting for her. Lucy hoped she

53

would be bathed and in her best dress. The boys would be along soon. Lucy wanted to lay out clean shirts for them.

"Bonnie," she called guardedly, entering from the hall into the small living room. Dad was sleeping and she didn't want to wake him.

Bonnie came out of the other bedroom, grinning happily.

Lucy's face lit. "You still have it, Bonnie!"

Bonnie nodded, enjoying the sudden drama of her loose front tooth. She was dressed neatly in a pink cotton print.

"Let me braid your hair and put a ribbon on," said Lucy. "Then I'll change into my new blouse. The boys should be here by that time."

She had hardly finished with Bonnie's hair when the boys came in. "Your shirts are in the bedroom," Lucy told them. "Put them on quickly. We have a lot to do before Mom gets home."

Putting the Plan to Work

A few minutes later, the four excited children came down the stairs and went out into the street. Lucy let the boys go in front of her so that she could keep an eye on them. She took Bonnie by the hand. "It's Green's across the street in the next block," she said.

"We know," Dennis called over his shoulder. He and

Christopher were off, dodging in and out among the people on the crowded sidewalk. Lucy hurried after them, pulling Bonnie along with her.

A buzzer sounded as they opened the door of Green's Studio. Mr. Green himself came out into the small showroom where they stood. Behind him they could see lamps on tall stands surrounding a single chair.

Mr. Green was round — round bald head, round cheerful face, round belly, round-toed shoes on his feet, and round glasses over his eyes, which were round and dark and wise.

"Something I can do for you?" he asked. He looked from one serious face to the other.

Lucy drew in a long breath. "Do you ever take pictures on credit?"

Mr. Green smiled at her. "Not usually," he said gently.

Lucy pushed Bonnie in front of her. "Show him," she said. Bonnie wiggled her front tooth for Mr. Green.

"Did you come here to have me take out the tooth?" he asked in some surprise.

"No!" said Lucy. "But we're here because of the loose tooth." In a rush of words she explained about Mom's milestone and their great desire to have a group picture to present to her on that important day.

"Your mama sent you?" inquired Mr. Green.

"Oh, no," said Lucy. "It would spoil everything if she knew."

"I see," said Mr. Green, slowly, thoughtfully.

"And if I take this picture, how will you pay?"

"We'll all go out and find something to do. Already we have two baby-sitting jobs for next week. We can also wash cars, or run errands to the grocery store—oh, anything," explained Lucy.

"But how do I know you will pay for the picture?" Mr. Green went on. "Sometimes people get a picture and forget about the money."

Lucy shook her head. "You don't understand. We won't take the picture away. We'll leave it right here. Then every time we get a quarter, even a dime, we'll bring it in to you."

"Then why not save up the money and *then* have the picture taken?" Mr. Green flung out his hands as if he had discovered the only answer.

"We already told you," said Lucy, her voice rising. "We've got to get this picture before Bonnie's tooth comes out. Don't you see?" She shook Bonnie's shoulder. "Show him again, Bonnie." And Bonnie did.

A light dawned on Mr. Green's face and he lifted his eyes to the ceiling. "Ah, yes. Now all is clear. I didn't get it at first." Again he looked from one to the other as if trying to make up his mind. All four returned his look, their brows wrinkled with worry.

At last he whirled about.

"Come," he said. "Come in," and he led them toward the tall lights and the waiting chair.

The next few days were worrisome for Lucy. If the others felt the same way, they didn't let on. Her worry

was their father. What would he say? Had they dared too much? What would he do when he found out that they had paid fifteen dollars for a picture?

"We won't tell him. It will be better that way," said Lucy.

"You can say that again," returned Dennis. "He would skin us if he knew we were spending that much money."

It wasn't easy that first week. Only three dollars and a quarter went into the little box under the counter in Mr. Green's studio. Three weeks to go, about. It seemed a very short time in which to earn eleven dollars and seventy-five cents.

But the three were eager to work and the news got around. Slowly the value of the coins in the studio box grew. On the day before Mom's birthday, they added up to fourteen dollars and seventy-five cents. Just a quarter to go. It might as well have been a hundred dollars! What could they do?

That night at supper, Bonnie's tooth came out.

"Look, Mom," she said, holding it out on her small palm. "My tooth!"

Mom gave a startled look at Bonnie's hand, then at her gap-toothed mouth. She burst into tears. "It happened!" she cried. "It happened just like I knew it would. My baby's tooth is gone and I never got a bright and smiling picture."

The children looked at one another. They were pleased that Mom was too upset to notice their secret smiles.

Then their faces sobered. Tomorrow was Mom's birthday. Since it was a Saturday, they would be free to find jobs. But they couldn't be sure they would get the needed quarter.

The next morning, Bonnie sprung her surprise. Dad had already eaten and gone to bed. Mom had picked up her string bag and gone out to do the weekly shopping.

"I got something to show you," she whispered as the four gathered together in the living room.

"What?" asked Christopher.

Again, as on the night before, Bonnie held her hand out straight. On her palm lay a shiny quarter!

"I put my tooth under the pillow last night and this morning the tooth fairy took it and left me a quarter."

"You're kidding?" asked Dennis.

Bonnie shook her head. "It happened to a girl at school, and now it's happened to me."

"How come the tooth fairy knew about *your* tooth?" asked Lucy. She had never found a quarter under her pillow.

Bonnie shrugged. "Maybe Dad told her."

The others looked at one another.

"Did you tell Dad about the tooth fairy?" asked Lucy.

Bonnie nodded. "When he started to bed, I followed him and I showed him my tooth. I told him I needed a quarter for Mom's birthday present. I said maybe the tooth fairy would leave it. And he said the tooth fairy wouldn't leave anything if I stood around. So I went away. When I came back, the tooth was gone and the quarter was under my pillow."

"Then you gave away our secret," said Lucy. "Did you tell about the Group?"

"No," said Bonnie. "When Dad asked me how much we spent on Mom's birthday, I told him. I said we all worked together. And he said what could a little kid like me do? And I said nothing until my tooth came out. But I could get a quarter with it, maybe. And so I did."

"And didn't Dad get upset because we spent so much money?" asked Dennis.

"No, he didn't," said Bonnie. "He just said we were good to remember Mom's birthday. And then he gave me a hug."

Lucy's face lit with joy. Now she knew Mom really

would be surprised. "Come on," she said, still remembering not to wake up Dad. "Let's hurry and get The Milestone Group."

Moving quietly, they made for the door.

—*Doris Gates*

What Do You Think?

1. Mom said that her fortieth birthday was important, a *milestone*. What other events in the story might also be called milestones? What are some milestones in your life?
2. Bonnie's loose tooth caused the problem, but it also saved the day. Explain how it did both.
3. If this were your story, how would you end it? Why do you suppose the author ended it the way she did?

Taking A Closer Look

1. You sometimes can read people's feelings by the way they act. How do you think each of the other children felt about Lucy's plan? How can you tell?
2. You never meet Dad directly in the story. From what the children say about him, what kind of person do you think he is?
3. Why do you think Mr. Green agreed to take the picture on credit?
4. Which part of Lucy's plan seemed the most difficult to carry out? Who do you think helped the most? Explain your answer.
5. Tell about a time when you worked hard to do something special for somebody.

MY PEOPLE

The night is beautiful,
So the faces of my people.

The stars are beautiful,
So the eyes of my people.

Beautiful, also, is the sun.
Beautiful, also, are the souls of my people.

—Langston Hughes

63

Billy lives on a farm in Alberta with his parents and younger brother. He has made an important decision which leads to unexpected events. Instead of getting on the school bus, he is going to run away from home. Then he meets a man named Bill who helps him to change his mind.

Billy's Award

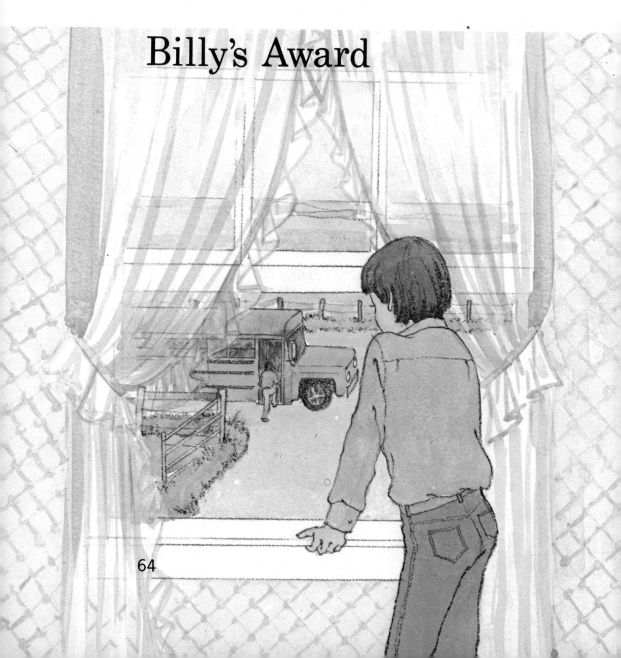

"Promise you won't tell! Promise!"

"Okay, okay! I promise. Cross my heart and spit."

"All right, then." Billy rose from his younger brother's stomach and Mark scrambled up from their bedroom floor. "Now, here's what you do," went on Billy. "Tell the bus driver I'm not going to school today. Say good-by to Mom and don't stop to talk. Dad's down to the pasture. He won't notice."

Mark looked worried. "I wish you didn't have to run away," he said. "Which way are you going?"

"Over the south hill. I'll hitch a ride to one of those big cattle ranches and get a job. When I'm rich, I'll come home and help Dad build a new barn. Now, scram!"

Through the window they saw the big, yellow Alberta school bus slowing down to a stop at the gate. Mark clattered down the stairs. He shouted "Bye, Mom!" over the whine of the vacuum cleaner.

Billy watched as his brother climbed on the bus. The door closed and the bus drove away. Billy sighed with relief. The first part of his plan had worked. Mark was a great kid but next year they would be in the same grade if Billy failed his reading. Billy shook his head. The thought was unthinkable.

He tiptoed into the closet and sat on the floor, hidden by clothes. The next part was waiting till Mom and Dad had gone off to their early morning meeting about the August Fair. It was too bad he wouldn't be able to show his calf. This was Billy's first year in 4-H and Bub was a good calf.

Downstairs the vacuum cleaner droned to a stop. Billy heard the lock of the cleaning cupboard snap shut. Dishes clinked and clanked into the sink. Water gushed out of the tap. He could hear his own breathing. Sounds of footsteps tumbled over one another as his mother rushed up the stairs. They stopped at the bedroom door. Billy stopped breathing.

He had made the bed. Were *all* the clothes hung up? The footsteps moved away. Billy breathed again. Soon his Mom went down the stairs. The kitchen door slammed. Finally, Billy heard the sound he was waiting for — the burp and roar of the truck starting.

He ran to the window and waited until the old, red truck disappeared along the road to town. "I'll buy them a new one when I get back," he promised.

In a hurry now, he rolled his quilt into an awkward bundle and tied it with binder twine. With it he ran down to the pantry where he grabbed cans off the shelves and threw them into a large, green garbage bag. Half a loaf of bread and a tub of margarine followed the cans. The runaway boy twisted the top of the bag into a knot, and heaved it on to his shoulder. He tucked his bundle under his arm and headed for the barn for a last good-by to his precious calf.

"Mark will take good care of you," he whispered in Bub's ear. He was rewarded with a moist lick. Bub returned to his feeding.

Billy wrinkled his freckled nose as he left the barn. There was an odd smell in the barn. It wasn't a good barn smell. Billy forgot about it as he started to climb the south hill.

His straight, brown hair was sticking to his forehead in moist clumps by the time he reached the top of the hill. He was glad to put down his bulky packages and stop for a rest. He looked down at the square, two-story house that had been home for all of his nine years. It looked lonesome. The old barn was sway-backed, like the mare he and Mark used to ride, till she died of old age. Wait! Wasn't that a little curl of smoke swirling out from the hayloft end?

Billy couldn't believe his eyes! Then he remembered the funny smell. Cigarette smoke. How could that be? Bub! Bub was in there! That thought sent Billy flying down the hill.

The barn was full of smoke. Billy soft-talked Bub out of the barn. He put him in the little corral. Luckily the wind was blowing the smoke away from the corral, not towards it. All the other animals were down in the pasture.

Billy dashed back into the barn to see what else he could save. He heard a moaning sound. Of course! Cigarette smoke meant some person must have been sleeping in the barn.

The smoke make Billy's eyes sting. Coughing and choking, he groped his way towards the smoldering hay. A man lay there in a crumpled heap.

Tears were streaming from Billy's eyes, but he set his teeth and grabbed the man by the arms. He dragged and jerked him along the floor. After what seemed hours, they reached the door, and fresh air.

Panting, Billy drew in gulps of it and began to feel better. The man on the ground stirred. He sat up, rubbing his eyes. He caught sight of the tiny lick of flame at the top of the barn.

"WOW!" he cried as he leaped to his feet and hustled Billy out of harm's way. He was only about a head and a half taller than Billy. "What's going on here?"

"Your cigarette set the barn on fire," replied Billy.

"Oh no!" exclaimed the man. "You're right. I did light one. I must have fallen asleep again. Lucky you were home. You saved my life. No time for thanks now. You'd better phone for help. I'll get some water."

Billy's face turned as red as a turkey's wattles. He did not move.

"What's the matter? You do have a phone, don't you?"

There was no way out. "I can't read," blurted the boy.

"In that case, let's run," said the man, briskly. Just as they reached the house, they heard a loud S-SWOOSH! as smoke burst into flame. They phoned the village fire chief, found buckets, and raced for the pump by the corral. The din was deafening now. Flames crackled and snapped. Black smoke hissed out of the cracks. Bits of wood splintered off and cinders flew in all directions.

They threw pail after pail of water on the sizzling building. Soon their faces were streaked with soot and sweat. As they pumped and carried the water, the man talked to Billy.

"My name is Bill," he said. "What's yours?"

"Same as yours, but they call me Billy. You running away from home, too?"

"Something like that. Why? Were you running away?" The man smiled in such a friendly way that, suddenly, the whole story tumbled out.

He shouted it out in short bursts of words, because they were pumping and hurrying to the barn, and throwing the water at the same time.

"I just can't get the hang of reading — the teacher says I might have to do the year over. I wouldn't mind only Mark, that's my brother, will be in my class then, I couldn't stand that. I was running away when I saw the smoke. I had to come back."

"I'm glad you did," said Bill. "Don't worry. We'll work something out. I caused this mess. I'll have to do something about it. You are a fine young fellow. I'm proud to know you. You stayed calm. You remembered to do all the right things. That is just as important as reading. I just bet you can conquer reading, too."

Billy felt better right away. When the firemen came with Mom and Dad and half the townsfolk to help, the fire was almost out. Everyone set to work to finish the job.

Later, over coffee and food for Bill, and milk for Billy, Mom and Dad heard both stories.

"The whole thing was my fault," confessed Bill. "It was about two in the morning when I decided I couldn't walk any farther. I'm a school teacher. I'd been sick and I was hiking across the province to get back into shape. I was going to come to the house in the morning to explain. Billy saved my life."

"That's all very well," said Dad, "but what am I going to do about my barn?"

"Let me rebuild your barn," replied Bill. "I have some experience as a carpenter."

Dad looked doubtful. "I could not pay you anything."

Bill laughed. "Some of this good cooking would suit me fine. Billy can help me and, in return I'll work with him on his reading problem. How's that?"

So, it was settled. Billy's teacher promised to wait till September before deciding about his reading.

All summer Bill and Billy worked hard. They talked and read; they hammered and nailed. One day the barn was finished; another day the words on the page came alive for Billy. In between times, Billy fed and groomed Bub.

At last the day of the Fair arrived. Everyone in the village and district seemed to be there.

Billy saw his teacher. "I can read now," he told her, proudly. And then Billy had two surpises.

The first was a Blue Ribbon for Bub. "Hurray for Bub," he shouted. The second was a medal for bravery for Billy.

"Hurray for Billy!" yelled the crowd. Everyone wanted to shake Billy's hand.

"How does it feel to be a hero?" asked the *Times* reporter.

"I feel so proud," replied Billy, beaming. "But, it sure is hard on the hands."

— *Margaret B. Kay*

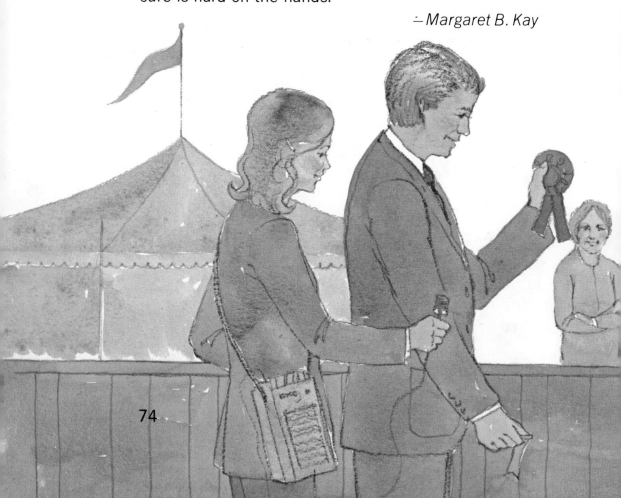

What Do You Think?

1. What would you do if you had Billy's reading problem?
2. Do you think Billy's decision to run away was the right one? Why or why not?
3. How did Billy show his bravery?

Taking A Closer Look

1. What do you think would have happened to Billy if he had actually run away?
2. What kind of person is Bill the teacher? What do his actions tell you?
3. What does the story tell you about farm life in Alberta?
4. Why is reading so important? What could you not do if you couldn't read?

MEDIA LUNA

La luna va por el agua.
¡Cómo está el cielo tranquilo!
Va segando lentamente
el temblor viejo del río
mientras que una rana joven
la toma por espejito.

—*Federico García Lorca*

HALF MOON

The moon goes over the water.
How tranquil the sky is!
She goes scything slowly
the old shimmer from the river;
meanwhile a young frog
takes her for a little mirror.

—*Federico García Lorca*
Translated by W. S. Merwin

Boarding school can be fun, but sometimes a new student can have a hard time getting into the swing of things. In this story Robby Armstrong tells you in his own words about a new boy at his boarding school.

PITCHER

The New Boy

When boarding school opens in the fall, the smart thing to do is to get there early. Then you can grab the best bureau and the lower bed in your room. You just pile your stuff on them and they're yours for the year. Then spend the rest of the day fooling around with the other old boys, watching the scared new ones come in. I hope I didn't look lost and lonely the way they did when I was a new boy. But maybe I did.

Anyway, last fall we—that's me and Monk and Horse-face and Geezil[1] and a few other guys—were sitting on the stone wall in front of the dormitory watching the new boys come in. They walked past us, stiff and shy,

[1] Geezil (GEE-zəl)

in clothes you could tell were new and uncomfortable. All of them were carrying suitcases. They wouldn't really look at us except out of the corners of their eyes. And they hurried past us into the building. We'd sit there and keep quiet while they walked by. But after they'd gone inside, we'd talk about them. We'd try to decide what kind of people they would turn out to be.

In the middle of the afternoon, a funny little character walked up the path. He wore great big glasses perched on a nose that looked kind of punched in. His ears stuck out like flags. Only he didn't hurry past us like the others. In front of us he put his suitcase down and smiled. It was a stiff smile, like the ones people had in pictures taken about forty years ago. But it was a smile. I guess he was trying to be friendly.

79

"Hello," he said.

"Hello," said Monk, without much interest.

The new boy smiled wider. "Hello," he said again. Then he waved his arm around. It was the longest and skinniest arm I've ever seen on a boy his age. "I guess this is the school." He bobbed his head and batted his eyes when he said it. You could tell that he really knew it was the school. He was only trying to be nice. But Monk's too sharp to let a simple remark like that get past him.

"The school?" Monk rubbed his chin. "What school?"

"Why, *the* school." When this new boy wrinkled his forehead, he looked more like a bewildered owl than before. "The school where you all go."

Monk scratched his head and turned to us. "Do you fellows go to school?"

"I haven't been to school today," said Horseface. That wasn't exactly a lie.

"And neither have I," said Geezil. "Do you go to school, son?"

The new boy laughed. It was a squeaky sound and showed he knew he was being kidded. "You fellows sure are funny," he said. "I think I'm going to like it here." With that he picked up his suitcase. "So long. See you later." At the foot of the steps he turned to wave his hand. But that was a mistake. I can see him now, smiling under his glasses. He was looking at us while his foot reached for the steps behind him. Then, he fell right up the stairs.

80

"Somebody's in for a bad time," Monk said.

"What?" I asked.

"Somebody has to room with him, you clown," he explained.

"That's right," I agreed. "Say, I wonder when my roommate is going to show up. It's beginning to get late."

Monk gave me his glassy stare that makes you think he's a moron. That's until you learn that he's as sharp as the next guy. "Maybe he has," he said.

"What?" I said again.

Monk nodded his head toward the door. "That last character rooms with *somebody* in there," he said. "You might be the lucky one."

"Oh!" I said, and I got up. A few seconds later I was standing in the doorway of my room. Monk was right.

The new boy had his coat and shirt off by now. He was over in front of the long mirror, trying to make a muscle with his left arm. His back was to me, so for a minute he didn't see me. I could see the smile on his face in the mirror. He stood there with one arm bent at

81

the elbow. It had the poorest excuse for a muscle in it that I've ever seen. Then he caught sight of me in the mirror. Even through the dust on the glass I could see him blush. But when he turned around, he was still smiling.

"Dynamic tension," he said.

Really, I didn't laugh. Right then I think I liked him for trying to carry it off with a laugh on himself. I think I was glad he was going to be my roommate. All the same I did a mean thing. I went to the window and stuck my head out. Then I signaled Monk and Horseface and Geezil to come up. They sure came running. I hardly had my head back in again before they were in the room.

"Why, hello again," said the new boy. "Come on in."

"Thanks," said Monk. By his tone of voice any fool could see that he was in already. He sat down on the bed. "What's your name, kid?"

"My name's Robert," said the new boy. He smiled all over.

Monk shook his head. "It won't do," he said. "That's Robby Armstrong's name." He pointed to me. "And he was here first." He turned to us. "Anyone got any ideas?"

"Handsome?" Horseface offered. The new boy winced, but smiled.

"Four-eyes," said Geezil. The new boy blinked, still smiling.

Monk snorted. "You clowns have no imagination."

82

"Of course you could do better," said Horseface.

"Sure," said Monk. "I named *you,* didn't I? Let's call him Pitcher."

Geezil nodded. "Turn your head, son," he said to Pitcher.

Pitcher showed us his profile. To this day I am still not used to his nose and his flappy ears.

"See what I mean?" asked Monk. "You know, little pitchers have big ears. Maybe someday he'll be a great baseball pitcher too. Or even a star on the football team. Who knows? Funny things happen."

"Right," said Geezil. "Well, what are we waiting for? Let's initiate him."

So we put Pitcher into the shower the way we do with all the new boys around here. Pitcher didn't mind it a bit. He smiled all the time, except when he slipped over the soap and fell flat on the floor. Then he laughed. He was such a good sport that I began to feel mean. I was glad when the guys got tired and left to look for some more new boys. I wanted to get Pitcher alone so I could talk with him. You see, already I was coming to like him!

When the first bell rang, I took him to the dining hall right away. That way I'd have ten minutes to show him the ropes. By that I mean where to get water and milk in case his table ran out. On the way we bumped into Coach. So I introduced Pitch.

"Coach, this is Pitcher," I said. They shook hands, both smiling.

"It's a good name, don't you think?" Pitcher asked. He put his hands over his ears.

"Yes. . . ." said Coach slowly. "And I'm glad you like it, because that helps." Then he asked, "Are you coming out for football tomorrow?"

Pitcher's eyebrows went up. "Me?"

"Certainly. Why not?"

"Well, I didn't know that I could. I mean, I'm not very big. . . ."

Coach put his hand on Pitcher's shoulder. "We have teams here for the smaller boys," he said. "We've noticed that they don't stay small very long. How about sitting at my table tonight? We'll talk about football."

"Gee, can I?" Pitch looked as pleased as a boy can be.

"Sure," I put in, maybe to show that I knew my way around. "On the first night you can sit anywhere. After that they assign you a table."

So we sat at Coach's table, Pitch on his right and me on his left. We talked football. Coach was telling Pitch how everybody in school is almost as interested in the Brat team (that's what they call us) as in the varsity. All the students come down to cheer the Brat games even louder than they cheer the big team.

Well, Pitch was able to live through the first night of school with all its troubles. The next afternoon we all went out for football. If Pitcher had been a big athlete he wouldn't have made such a bad start. But the trouble was, he was just the opposite. He was terrible, as we soon learned. He tried harder than anyone I ever saw. But he couldn't do anything right. He missed more tackles than all the rest of us put together. He'd dive at the ball carrier—dive like crazy. But the ball carrier would be long gone. When he ran interference for me—I'm quarterback—half the time he'd get caught in his own feet. He'd fall down just in the right place for me to fall over him.

I lost my cool a few times over things like that. After all, a guy wants to have his team win. You can't hate me for liking to make a few good plays myself now and then. But the other Brats were worse than I was toward him. Because, after all, I liked Pitcher. The others didn't, and they kept riding him. I don't need to tell you how they did it. You know how boys can be when they've found somebody to pick on.

Of course, I could tell from the way Pitcher acted in our room that his unpopularity was beginning to get under his skin. But it was nearly a month before I learned just how badly he felt. I'll say this for Pitch. He could keep his feelings to himself. It wasn't until I woke up one night and heard him crying that I had any idea of how much he'd been hurt inside. I listened to him for a while. I kept wondering what I could do to make it easier for him. Then he started to moan and talk out loud.

He gasped words out. Then I heard him beating his fist on his pillow. "I can't take it! I can't take it another day!" The way his voice sounded made my hair stand on end. Then he went on. "And I can't run away. I just can't quit and run away, that's all. What'll I do. . .?"

But I didn't hear any more. I stuck my fingers in my ears.

Coach Takes Over

The very next afternoon I went down to see Coach. I wanted to tell him the whole story. Coach listened. He didn't interrupt once. Toward the end he got up and stuck his hands in his pockets. Then he started looking for his pipe over behind where I was sitting. When I got through, he sat down quietly for a few minutes. He kept looking out the window and blowing smoke rings the way he does when he's got something on his mind. After a while he laid down his pipe suddenly. He put his hands on his knees, and looked hard at me.

"Go get Pitcher," he said.

"Yes, sir," I said. I got out of there without asking any questions. Lots of times with Coach you don't ask any questions out loud. But you can be sure I was wondering plenty while I ran to the room.

When we got back, Coach had a football in his hands. He turned it over once or twice before he said anything.

"Pitcher," he said at last. "I sent Robby for you because I want you and him to learn a private play. A play that nobody else is going to hear about until we use it in your Brat game this Saturday."

"Yes, sir," said Pitcher. His voice sounded kind of eager, and sad too.

Coach turned to me. "You understand me, Robby? Nobody is to know this play but you and Pitch."

I nodded. The Coach was up to something.

"It's simple," Coach said. "So simple that it might do the trick. Especially against boys who haven't played much football. Robby, who plays right end against your team?"

"Monk does," I said.

"Perfect!" Coach smiled happily. "If we have to make a fool of somebody, it might as well be. . . ." All of a sudden he got serious. "Well, let's get down to business. Robby, you take the ball." He tossed it to me. "Now bend over and move to the right as if you were going on an end run. Get set exactly as you do in play eighteen. That's right. Now, Pitch, stand over here in the wingback spot. Right. Now Robby. Come over in this direction again on your end run. Give the ball to Pitcher as you go by him. He'll be starting in your direction.''

"Yes, sir," I said.

As I remember, we practiced that play for half an hour. Finally we had our timing perfect. Pitch almost never dropped the ball when I put it in his hands. That is very good for Pitch. Coach stood there watching us and coaching us. He had me bend over farther and slip the ball to Pitch. Finally I hardly knew myself that I had given it to him as he went past me. He had Pitch hold the ball behind his hip with one hand, until you couldn't see it from the front. I think he worked over us harder than he does with the big team. At last he seemed satisfied. He tossed me the ball again and sat down.

"Do any of the varsity backfield men live up in your dormitory?" he asked me.

"Yes, sir," I said. "Washburn lives on the first floor. And Star Collins lives on the second, right down the hall from us."

"Collins is the man," Coach said, sort of to himself. He looked at us. "I'm going to change my mind about no one knowing this play but you two. I want Star to help you practice. After all, both of you are rather inexperienced."

"Yes, sir," I said. That suited me fine, because Star is a good guy. Besides, he is a great backfield man.

"So take this ball to your room and keep things quiet," Coach told us. "Every night this week you two are to practice that play. Star will be watching you. I'll tell him myself what I want him to look for. Get that play perfect, understand?"

"Yes, sir," said Pitch. I nodded.

"Then Friday you'll come down here for a last work-out with me. If I can see that ball pass between you, or if Pitch drops it, I'll skin you both alive. Understand?"

"Yes, sir," I said. Pitch nodded. You can tell when Coach means what he says.

Well, we practiced with Star watching us. We practiced up in our room in front of our mirror. Before long even we couldn't see that ball slip out of my arms into Pitcher's. And we didn't say anything to anyone. Then on Friday we showed our stuff to Coach and he was satisfied. When we had done it for him several times without a slip, he made us sit down. Then he told us what to do in the game the next day.

You should have seen that game! Of course, the whole school was there, the way they always are for Brat games. And of course they were cheering and yelling the way they always do. The first half was full of good football too. I mean, as good as we can play. And it was plenty exciting. Most of the time our two teams rolled back and forth, up and down the field. But finally Monk, the captain of the Blue team, caught a pass and scored. But they didn't convert. So, when I slipped around right end later on and scored, we had them tied. We didn't convert either. So the half ended 6-6.

All this time the students in the bleachers were yelling and shouting and giving advice. Coach was sitting quietly on the bench. Pitcher was beside him, not saying a word. Once, during a time-out, I noticed that Pitch was biting his nails. Except for that he seemed all right. Even at the half he didn't say anything except, "Nice going, fellows. Let's beat them this half." Only no one noticed him. I'm afraid most of the fellows were hoping Coach would never send him into the game. They figured with him in the game we'd never beat

90

Monk's team. Maybe I felt the same way myself, even with that secret trick play. I began to wonder whether Pitch would hold on to the ball if we had a chance to try the trick in a real game. Then the second half started. Now I had to use all my wondering to figure what Monk's team would pull next.

Halfway through the last quarter the score was still tied. We took over the ball on our forty-yard line. I was trying to decide what plays to use when I saw Pitch come running out on the field. So did the rest of my team back there in the huddle. They all groaned.

"There goes the ball game," said Horseface.

"And how," said Geezil.

Then Pitch tripped over the grass or something and fell flat on his face before he was halfway to us. No one said anything more.

Even I was feeling worried until Monk called across to us. "Oh, you lucky fellows!" When I looked up and saw him laughing at me, I made up my mind to fix his wagon.

So, the way Coach had told me, I called play eighteen. That's a right-end run, with me carrying the ball and Pitch on the wing. It didn't work worth a darn, because I fell over Pitch on the line of scrimmage. But that was all right because it wasn't supposed to work. Back in the huddle I called the same play again. This time it went for two yards, because I was able to get out of Pitcher's way. In the huddle I yelled "Eighteen!" again, good and loud.

"Quiet, you dope, they'll hear you!" Horseface whispered to me.

"Well, let's run it anyway," I said. I didn't even smile. Horseface didn't know that the idea was to have Monk hear me call the play.

So we ran it, and how I got creamed! Even Monk was in on the tackle. He'd run behind the line of scrimmage all the way around from his end to get me. Which was what Coach had figured he would do.

"Play eighteen," I said in the huddle, good and loud.

"Have you gone crazy, Robby!" Horseface was part mad, part worried too. "Are you out of your mind or something?"

"Eighteen!" I said again, loud and clear.

"It's third down," said Geezil. "Coach will kill you if you don't kick."

"Eighteen!" I yelled once more. "Me in the tailback, Pitch on the wing."

"Buddy, you asked for it," said Horseface. He walked up to the scrimmage line. He knew that Coach gets mighty sore if anyone but the quarterback tries to run the team. But I had an idea he was planning to kill me after we lost the game. I was kind of worried myself. But then the ball came back at me and, I stopped worrying and got down to business.

It was as if we were in our room practicing in front of the mirror. I started off to the right and Pitch started toward me. We passed each other behind our right tackle. Even I didn't know when I slipped Pitch the ball. It went so smooth and easy. I was still doubled up, as if I had the ball, when Monk sailed into me from the side. He knocked me out of bounds. But I got up again as if I'd been made out of rubber. I wanted to see if our trick play was going to work. Brother, I saw!

Way out there across the field Pitch was galloping toward the goal line. He held the ball off behind his hip exactly the way Coach had taught him. Not a soul was near him. Even the safety on Monk's team had pulled way over to the right to get me. Coach's reverse play had worked.

It had worked so fine that even the crowd in the stands had not followed the play. You could tell because they didn't make a sound. They were just looking all over for the ball. And then they found it. Boy, you should have heard the yelling!

"Pitch has it!"

"Pitch has the ball!"

"Look at the boy run!"

"How did he get it?"

"Run, Pitch! Run with that ball, Pitch!"

I've heard noise on a ball field, but none like that. I've seen crowds stamp their feet and jump up and down and throw their hats in the air. Not the way they did that day when Pitcher went racing down the left sideline. He hugged the ball to his chest now, the way Coach had told him. And no one was near him. Everybody was screaming, "Pitch! Pitcher!" and pounding each other's back.

Mind you, I wasn't sitting on the ground with Monk in my lap all this time. As soon as I could, I'd pushed him away and taken off after Pitch. Not that there was any blocking to do. I just wanted to be around when he crossed the goal line. Even running as hard as I could, I heard the shouts for him. I could see his white teeth flashing the world's widest smile.

And then, of course, he tripped. On the two-yard line he caught one toe behind his ankle and went sprawling. So did the ball. It slipped out of his hands like wet soap. That didn't matter. It bounced over the goal line, and I was there to fall on it. That counts six points in any league.

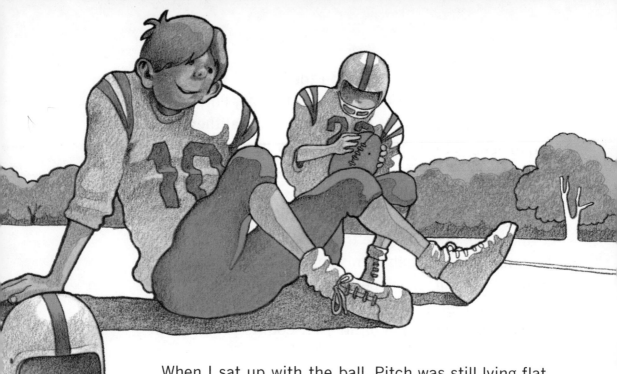

When I sat up with the ball, Pitch was still lying flat on the ground.

"Hey, Pitch!" I yelled. I was worried. "Are you all right?"

Pitch sat up then and batted his eyes. He looked at the other players on the team running toward him. They were shouting and clapping and laughing. He listened to the crowd in the stands screaming his name while they jumped up and down. Then he smiled, the biggest smile I've ever seen on anyone his size.

"I'm all right," he said as he got up. He took a deep breath and smiled wider. Just before the team swamped him to beat him on the back, I heard him say, "I'm the happiest boy in all the world!"

—*Stephen Cole*

What Do You Think?

1. In what ways do you like or admire Pitcher?
2. Did you find a deeper meaning in this story? What do you think the author wanted you to think about?

Taking A Closer Look

1. What was Pitcher's problem and how was it solved?
2. Why did the other students pick on Pitcher during that first month of school?
3. How do you think Monk and the other students treated Pitcher during the rest of the school year? Explain your answer.
4. Try to explain what happens in the reverse play.
5. How does the author make you think the story was written by Robby Armstrong?

97

Where Do Stories Come From?

Where do stories come from? Many writers get their ideas from the people and events they know and remember best. Some authors look to the past and try to imagine what might have happened at a certain time and place. Others eye the future and try to describe what is yet to come. Still others add a special touch to an old tale, creating a new one. And there are some storytellers who pick their thoughts right out of the air!

Lee Edward loved the way Mama Luka[1] told him time-ago tales of Jahdu.[2] But who is Jadhu, and how does Mama Luka know so much about him? Can you figure it out?

HOW JAHDU FOUND HIS POWER

Mama Luka liked to sit in her tight little room in a fine, good place called Toronto. She liked to sit with the window blinds drawn against the sunlight. And Mama Luka did, every day.

Mama Luka had black skin and a nose as curved as the beak of a parrot. She wore her hair in one long pigtail down her back. She called the pigtail her plait, and she could sit on it. She sat on it whenever she felt like telling tales.

Mama Luka took care of Lee Edward after his school was out for the day and until his mother came home from work. And Mama Luka sat all the while in her little room in the good place, telling Jahdu stories to Lee Edward. She told them slow and she told them easy. And Lee Edward listened. He sat on the floor with his eyes tight shut, which was the best way for him to imagine Jahdu.

[1]Luka (LOO-kah)　[2]Jahdu (JAH-doo)

Lee Edward loved Mama Luka. She sometimes called him Little Brother just like his own mama did. And he loved his own mama and papa, too. Lee Edward loved Jahdu and Jahdu stories. And he loved the way Mama Luka told them like any child would.

"Now here we go, Little Brother," Mama Luka said one day.

"There are many a-thousand Jahdu stories," she told Lee Edward. "I know about two hundred of them. I've told you a roomful of Jahdu stories. So that leaves one more roomful of Jahdu stories to tell. Now, you pick out of the air in this room one more Jahdu story."

Lee Edward looked around the room. At last he pointed to an empty space just above Mama Luka's head.

"That one," Lee Edward said.

Mama Luka reached above her head. She cupped her hands around the place Lee Edward had pointed out in the air. And she brought her hands down slowly to her face. Mama Luka opened her mouth and swallowed what had been in her hands.

"Lee Edward, you picked a time-ago story out of the air," she said. "It has a strong taste to it, for it tells how Jahdu found out he had magic power."

"So tell it," Lee Edward said to Mama Luka.

"So I'm getting myself ready," said Mama Luka.

"Lee Edward," began Mama Luka, "the story you picked is about a time not long after Jahdu had been born. He had not much shape then and not much

size. And only his face was clear. Jahdu didn't know
he had any magic at all.

"Lee Edward in that time-ago," said Mama Luka,
"Jahdu wasn't as tall as you."

"What did his face look like?" asked Lee Edward. He
hoped to catch Mama Luka before she had time to
think. But Mama Luka wasn't to be caught this day or
any other day. No, she wasn't.

"Little Brother, don't you try to trick me," said Mama
Luka. "I know better than to talk about the face of
Jahdu."

"Just give me a hint," said Lee Edward.

"Child, nobody who has seen the face of Jahdu will
tell you what his face looks like. And I have seen it,"
said Mama Luka, "and I can't tell."

"Well then, get on with the story," said Lee Edward.

"Here it comes," said Mama Luka.

THIS IS THE JAHDU STORY WITH A STRONG TASTE THAT MAMA LUKA TOLD TO LEE EDWARD.

Jahdu was running along. He was two feet tall. Yes, he was. And he had been in the world one year.

Jahdu lived high atop the Mountain of Paths. He made his home in the only black gum tupelo tree in the pine forest covering the mountain. From his tree, Jahdu could see all the paths to the valley below. He could see which paths the animal children who lived on the mountain walked along.

Jahdu believed the paths the animal children walked along were good and safe. And only these good and safe paths would Jahdu run along.

But Jahdu was only a year in the world. He did not yet know everything. No, he didn't. One day Jahdu was running along a path behind some animal children. All at once the animal children stopped still.

A bandicoot rat fell to the ground. He grew stiff and he screamed and cried loudly for his mother.

A brown bear cub stood up on one hind leg. He hopped in circles, bumping into a fawn and stepping on a baby otter. The brown bear cub sang a wordless song. The young woodchuck, the raccoon girl, and the wolf child wandered away into the pine wood and were lost. Some of the other animal children sat down on the path, moaning to themselves and trembling all over.

It took Jahdu an hour to gather all of the animal children on the path again. Then he tied a rope around all of them and led them to another path he knew to be good and safe. There, he let them loose.

"I'd better go back to that first path," Jahdu said. "I'd better find out as fast as I can what caused those animal children to stop still and hop around and fall down and act silly."

Jahdu found the path on which the animal children had stopped still. As he went running down the path, something he couldn't see tried to catch him. But Jahdu was stronger than whatever it was that tried to stop him. He kept right on running along.

"Woogily!" whispered Jahdu to himself. "There are baneberries growing on both sides of this path. Everybody knows baneberries can make animal children sick. I'd better keep on this path to find out what it is that tries to catch me. I'd better find out why baneberries grow on both sides of a good and safe path."

Jahdu stayed on the path. Yes, he did: All at once Jahdu fell into a hole full of thorns.

"Ouch!" said Jahdu. "Thorns have points to hurt Jahdu!" Jahdu jumped out of the hole and bounced into a soft bed of sweet-smelling leaves.

"Woogily!" said Jahdu. "This funny path has good and bad about it. But it surely isn't safe for animal children to walk along."

Jahdu kept right on the good and bad path with baneberries on both sides of it, full of thorn holes and soft beds of sweet-smelling leaves. He ran and he ran until he came to a stream. He sat down in the middle of the stream to cool himself. Suddenly thirteen crawfish started pinching Jahdu. He leaped out of the water.

"Woogily!" said Jahdu. "That's a nice little stream so fresh and cold. But it has thirteen crawfish that can pinch the paws of little animals. I'd better hurry and find out where this funny path ends."

106

So Jahdu kept on hurrying along the good and bad path with baneberries on both sides, with thorn holes and soft beds of sweet-smelling leaves, and a stream across it with thirteen crawfish.

All at once Jahdu ran smack into a banyan tree at the end of the path. He bounced clear around the banyan tree. Yes, he did. He started running again and ran smack into the banyan tree once more.

"Woogily!" cried Jahdu. "How in the world did a banyan tree get into these pine woods on the Mountain of Paths? Running into banyan trees doesn't feel very good. Little animals will hurt themselves if they go walking into banyan trees!"

Up in the banyan tree was an animal who had a round, sweet face and a bell on its head. And up in the banyan tree was another animal who had a square, mean face and no bell anywhere. Both animals lay side by side peering down at Jahdu.

"I've never seen animals such as you," said Jahdu. "What in the world are you called?"

The animal with a bell on its head spoke first to Jahdu. "I'm called Sweetdream," it said in a soft, sweet voice.

"And I'm Nightmare," said the other animal in a harsh, mean voice. "You're Jahdu and we don't like you."

"Oh, for goodness sake!" said Jahdu. "Like me or not, I'm here to stay. And please tell me why there's a banyan tree at the end of a path on which little animals might walk."

"Because it's here," said Nightmare in a mean voice, "just as Sweetdream and I are here and the path is here, so there!"

"When the bell on my head tinkles," said Sweetdream, "Nightmare and I know little animals are walking along our path."

"Then we use our charms to get them," said Nightmare. "It's such fun watching our spells work on them."

"Just how do your spells work on the little animals?" asked Jahdu.

"Well," said Sweetdream, "my spell makes the animals stop still, then hop around and sing sweet songs, and do and say whatever sweet things are in their heads when my spell strikes them."

"And my spell makes them grow stiff," said Nightmare. "They fall to the ground and scream and cry. Or they moan and tremble all over and do whatever bad things are in their thoughts when my spell strikes them."

108

"Little animals ought to be able to walk along and do as they wish," said Jahdu. "I don't think it's right to use spells on them."

"I don't care what you think," said Sweetdream sweetly. "I do as I please."

"There's nothing you can do to stop *me*," said Nightmare, "so you better go on your way."

Jahdu was angry. He ran to the banyan tree and shook it as hard as he could.

"Come down from that banyan tree, you awful things!" Jahdu yelled. "Come down and I'll surely take care of you!"

Jahdu shook and shook the banyan tree until both animals sitting in it turned purple all over.

"Stop it!" said Sweetdream and Nightmare. "You're making us dizzy and sick!"

"Then come down," said Jahdu, "so Jahdu can take care of you."

"We can't come down," said Sweetdream. "We're attached to this banyan, we can't ever come down!"

Then Jahdu saw that the two animals were growing like figs on the banyan's branches.

"Woogily!" he said. "Now Jahdu's caught you for sure!"

Jahdu ran around and around the banyan tree as fast as he could. He was showing off for the two tree-grown animals. Yes, he was. And he ran so fast he shook the dust right out of himself.

Jahdu's dust rose up into the banyan tree. It settled

on Sweetdream and Nightmare and they fell fast asleep.

Jahdu stopped running.

"Woogily!" he said. "Did I do that? Did my dust put Sweetdream and Nightmare to sleep?"

Wherever the Jahdu dust fell, it put things to sleep. A spider walking along the banyan tree trunk got Jahdu dust on him and fell asleep. A bluebird flying low near the banyan tree got a whiff of the Jahdu dust and had to land in the tree. As the Jahdu dust settled on the bluebird, it fell asleep.

"Woogily!" said Jahdu. "I've got me some magic! I can put things to sleep! Maybe I have more magic. Let me see."

Jahdu tried wishing there was no good and bad path, no Sweetdream and Nightmare and no banyan tree. But

110

this didn't work. No, it didn't. For the path stayed. So did the banyan tree and the sleeping Sweetdream and Nightmare.

Jahdu had another idea. He started running around the banyan tree. Jahdu ran slower and slower and ever so slowly.

The Jahdu dust rose off the two animals up the banyan tree. It rose off the tree trunk and the spider, off the bluebird and off everything. Then the Jahdu dust fell back into Jahdu. All that had been asleep woke up. Sweetdream and Nightmare yawned and stared down at Jahdu.

"Woogily!" said Jahdu. "I can wake things up. I've got me another magic!"

"You shouldn't have put us to sleep," said Sweetdream. "We have to work in the daytime so we can watch the fun."

"You won't watch the fun anymore," said Jahdu, "for I'm going to make you work at night."

"You can't make us do anything we don't want to do," said Nightmare.

"If you don't do what I want you to do, I'll put you to sleep for a week," Jahdu told Nightmare.

"Oh, no," said Sweetdream. "Please don't put him to sleep for a week."

"A month," said Jahdu, feeling good all over.

"All right, you have us," said Nightmare. "Just don't get carried away."

Jahdu drew himself up as tall as he could. Yes, he did. And he told Sweetdream and Nightmare what he was going to make them do.

"Nightmare will sleep from daylight to nightfall," said Jahdu. "He will work his spell only at night and only on sleeping animals. And if I ever catch him playing around with his spell when it's daylight, I'll put him to sleep for a year!"

Nightmare looked glum but he didn't say a word. He still felt sick from Jahdu's shaking the banyan tree.

"As for Sweetdream," said Jahdu, "she'll work her spell in the daytime only on those little animals who sleep by day. And then only once in a very long while. The rest of her work she will do at night and on sleeping animals, just the same as Nightmare."

Sweetdream smiled sweetly but said nothing.

"I'll never have any fun again watching my spell work," muttered Nightmare.

"That's the truth," said Jahdu. "I'm getting rid of that awful path, too. I'll put it to sleep for the rest of time!"

And so Jahdu did. He ran up and down the path as fast as he could go. Jahdu dust rose from Jahdu and fell all over the path. At once the path was fast asleep. The baneberries on both sides of the path dried up and slept, too. All kinds of forest plants started growing over the path.

Jahdu stood where once the path had begun. Now, young pine saplings started growing there. Jahdu shouted down the path at Sweetdream and Nightmare.

"Your path is gone," Jahdu shouted. "No little animals will come along here! Now you'll have to send your charms out on the night air. Your spells will never again be very strong. For the night air is so light it can carry only a little of your charms at a time!"

Jahdu went running along. Yes, he did. He could run very fast and he could run very slow. He could shake Jahdu dust out of himself and cause it to fall back into himself again. With his magic he could wake things up and put things to sleep.

THIS IS THE END OF THE JAHDU STORY WITH A STRONG TASTE THAT MAMA LUKA TOLD TO LEE EDWARD.

—*Virginia Hamilton*

What Do You Think?

1. When Lee Edward shut his eyes to hear the Jahdu stories, he might have imagined how Jahdu looked. How do you imagine Jahdu to look?
2. Do you think Mama Luka liked to tell Jahdu stories to Lee Edward? How do you know?
3. Mama Luka tells Lee Edward that this Jahdu story "has a strong taste to it." What is meant by this phrase?

Taking A Closer Look

1. Why do you think Lee Edward liked Mama Luka's stories about Jahdu so much?
2. What could Mama Luka have meant when she said the story was "a time-ago story"?
3. Why do you suppose Mama Luka would not describe Jahdu to Lee Edward?
4. One of Jahdu's favorite expressions is "Woogily!" What do you think "woogily" means? What word or words could you substitute for "woogily"?
5. "How Jahdu Found His Power" is a story-within-a-story. How is Mama Luka's story about Jahdu different from the story about Mama Luka and Lee Edward?

115

What I Would Like to Be

I think that I should like to be a tree.
Planted by some lonely stream to grow
and grow so green, so tall, so fresh
  and nice
to have some man, woman, or a child
stop beneath my green branches
to be comforted in the shade which my
  branches cast.
I think that I would like to be a tree
to brighten some yard or some lonely
  countryside
And then at some late summer day
to shed my leaves, to fall asleep
and awake at another season
to become so green, so tall and so
  nice
and to brighten someone's day.

—*Deidre Harris*

116

This story takes us to Nova Scotia, back to a time and way of life that have gone forever. Was life better then?

When Great-Grandmother Was Young

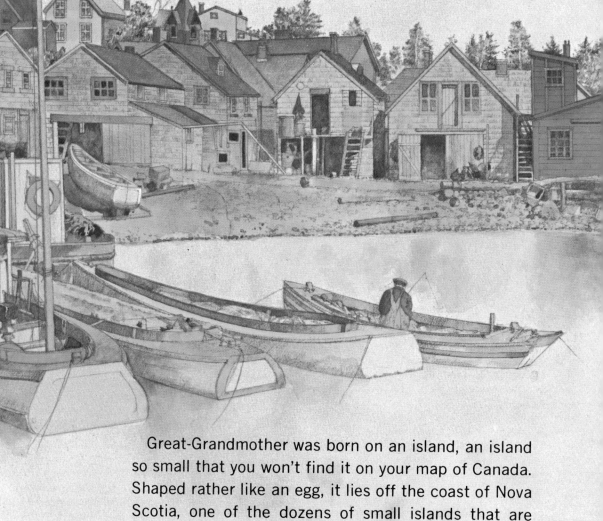

Great-Grandmother was born on an island, an island so small that you won't find it on your map of Canada. Shaped rather like an egg, it lies off the coast of Nova Scotia, one of the dozens of small islands that are sprinkled along the eastern shore. Gerrard's Island is its name.

Today only one couple lives there. Many of the barns have fallen down, and the schoolhouse is empty.

But when Great-Grammy was little, thirty families lived in a village on the harbor side, and twenty-two children of all sizes sat together in the funny, square, one-room schoolhouse.

All the island menfolk went to sea, some for fish and some for seals. Herring and cod, haddock and lobsters were the biggest catches.

Great-Grammy's father was a sea captain and carried cargo of all kinds up and down the coast of Nova Scotia in his sailing ship. In his spare time, he too cast his nets for herring.

Twice a year the family would steam a potful of those tiny, bony, slippery fish with onions and potatoes over a fire on the beach.

"Be sure to tell what a fine and smelly party that was!" says Great-Grammy. For she and her sister and her two big brothers were proud to be called by that old Nova Scotia nickname, "herring-chokers."

From Gerrard's Island you can see the mainland easily on a clear day. In the summer the stretch of open water seems simple and quiet. But in the spring, when the tides are the highest, and in the fall, when the storms are fiercest, it is still a splashy, roller-coaster trip across to Pope's Harbor or up the coast to the nearest mainland town of Tangier.

The tides are the same that wash into the Bay of Fundy. They are the highest in the world.

Life is still lived here according to the tides. Clams

are to be gathered at low tide, and big ships put out to sea when the tide reaches its fullest.

Great-Grammy loved to go at low tide into secret coves where long-ago pirates might have buried their treasure. "Captain Kidd's hideaway is somewhere near there," she says. She and her friends dug and poked and sifted through the sand, but they never found anything more secret than Indian arrowheads.

When Great-Grammy was little, fall was a busy gathering-in time for everyone. Berries were picked and made into jam. Crops were brought in, hams and slabs of bacon hung to be smoked. Mothers made sausages and potfuls of headcheese. The island people put in store-bought supplies for the winter.

Flour and sugar in large barrels were hauled to the island on great flat scows. There was always a keg of molasses and wooden boxes of spices such as cinnamon, cloves, and nutmeg. There were fat tubs of raisins for winter nibbling, coffee and tea for the grown-ups, and a precious can of cocoa for the children. In the root cellar where they would not freeze, Father packed homegrown potatoes and onions, carrots, and turnips, in layers of straw. "And of course apples," says Great-Grammy. For apples are her earliest memory.

As soon as she was old enough to hold a big needle threaded with string, Great-Grandmother was given her first important chore. Her mother pared and cored fresh-picked apples. Big sister sliced them. Great-Grammy sat by the kitchen stove and strung

120

crisp apple slices for winter cooking. As they worked,
they sang old sad songs about the sea. The ballad of
the *Atlantic*, a shipwreck of 1873, was their favorite.

When she had a string as long as she was tall, she
tied the ends together to make a giant necklace, and
Mother hung each strand in the attic to dry. How
good the attic smelled! Winter and spring were spicy
with applesauce, apple cakes, pandowdy, and pie.

The families on Gerrard's Island farmed, as well as
fished. Everyone had a vegetable garden, and children
always helped. Great-Grammy grumbles, "Don't ask
about the weeding." But hauling water from the well
to sprinkle the seedlings was a cool and pleasant job.

Pump, splash! Pump, splash! she loved to dawdle,
leaning on the handle. Once when she looked down
deep into the well, a frog looked back up at Great-
Grammy.

Almost every family had a cow — and a pig and a few sheep too. Oxen did most of the heavy work. Pairs yoked together hauled logs out of the woods. In the springtime these great patient animals easily pulled the plows across the fields. Their broad horns curved upward from the yoke, and their astonishing loose neck skin hung beneath the bows.

"Horses!" scolds Great-Grammy, who never cared much for oxen. "You were going to forget to tell about the horses." For this was long before automobiles and mail trucks and paved roads came to the island. Long, long before television and telephones and even radios. When friends had something to say to one another, they wrote letters or came to visit. Every barn had an empty stall with a manger full of hay saved for the visitor's horse. Sundays after church was a favorite visiting time.

On the island, any family that had a buggy with a canopy over it was considered well-to-do. But there was always a farm cart and a steady old horse to pull it.

Letters went by stage. The stagecoach companies in Nova Scotia used draft horses. Two famous black stallions pulled the stage from Halifax to Windsor when Great-Grammy was a girl.

The roads were so bad that the horses had to be especially strong. In spring the dirt turned to mud as thick as melted chocolate and the wagon wheels sank in up to their axles. In winter the roads humped up with snow. The horses needed special shoes with metal prongs to grip the ice.

Great-Grandmother remembers their horse's name. It was Queen Elizabeth, but they called her Bess. And Bess was the most perfect, agreeable, all-round horse any family ever had, except for one thing. Bess was afraid of the ocean. Not many horses had to worry about the Atlantic Ocean, and most horses never even see a wave or a whitecap, but poor Bess did. She had to go to the blacksmith every fall for her winter shoes, and the blacksmith lived on the mainland in Tangier.

Father and the two boys would coax and plead and push and pull Bess onto a big flat-bottom scow. The two boys would tie their rowboats on either side of the scow and row hard for the mainland. Father would stand at Bess's head, patting and soothing her and distracting her with a peck of windfall apples.

One mild October day of the yearly crossing, Great-Grammy came along for the ride in her brother's rowboat. Just when everything was going well, a little paddleboat crossed in front of the scow and tooted its horn in greeting. Bess had heard and ignored louder noises than that, but this day she acted as if a hundred yellow hornets had stung her at once. She reared, yanking her halter out of Father's grip. A snort, a whinny, and over went Bess, nose first into the chilly ocean.

Father kicked off his boots and dived in after her. "I cried and covered my eyes," said Great-Grammy. She knew that Father could swim, but she was sure her good dear Bess would drown. The boys howled with dismay and rowed harder than ever. At last Great-Grammy dared to peek. Side by side swam Bess and Father, Bess making wet noises of displeasure, and Father talking crossly to her between arm strokes.

Man and horse touched bottom in the harbor at about the same moment. By the time the boys had docked the boats, there was Father, calmly leading Bess up the path toward the blacksmith's shop. Water ran out of his trouser legs. Every few steps Bess stopped and shook herself like a dog. Father decided to board Bess with the blacksmith until winter. She would not have to cross that strip of ocean again by boat. Usually the harbor was frozen over by Christmas and on good days the islanders could cross back and forth to the mainland on the ice.

First the menfolk sawed through the ice in several places to make sure it was thick enough. Then whole families crowded out onto this new frozen land. People traveled by sleigh and on skates and even by sailboat fastened on a pair of old sleigh runners.

On New Year's Day, Great-Grandmother's older brother strapped on his Norwegian skates with their curling elves' toes and skated across to Tangier. Back he came riding a fat and frisky Bess.

Bess's vacation on the mainland had cost Father fifty bales of hay. But the next fall, Bess could not see the deep blue ocean. She wore an apron for a blindfold and rode across peacefully on the scow. "As peacefully," said Great-Grammy, "as a queen on a royal barge."

"Toot Toot"

When Great-Grandmother was fourteen years old she left Gerrard's Island and traveled to Halifax to go to school. It was an all-day journey by buggy from Tangier. What a noisy and bustling place the city was to this brave but frightened explorer! Everyone was a stranger. Everyone was in a hurry.

For the first time in her life, Great-Grammy lived in a house that had water inside for cooking and cleaning. There was a special room for bathing, and it had a toilet called a water closet. Overhead, a tank stored water, and a long pull chain hung down from it. It was much, much nicer than an outdoor privy.

For the first time in her life, Great-Grammy rode in a strange new buggy which did not need a horse to pull it. There were several such automobiles on the broad, paved streets of the city. Here too she saw her

126

first policeman. At night, winking gas streetlamps cast yellow pools on every corner, and many of the houses had gas lamps inside on the walls. They were much easier to tend than the hand lamps that burned kerosene at home.

At the seminary with fifty other young ladies, Great-Grammy missed the one-room school on the island. She was homesick for the sound of girls and boys saying lessons aloud. But she was getting her high school education, a rare thing for girls in her day.

For the first time in her life, she wore a dress bought in a store, and not sewn at home. "Pale yellow, with tiny ruffles," Great-Grammy remembers. "And button shoes fastened with a button hook."

But Great-Grammy would rather remember earlier days—those days when she was the youngest child by the driftwood fire. And she did go back again.

Great-Grammy was only twenty when she put on a beautiful white dress she had made herself. It had enormous balloon sleeves and a wide, frothy white train. Rows of lace marched around and around the skirt.

She and Great-Grandfather got into the buggy, and old Bess slowly pulled them through the village. The island church was full of flowers. The organ played the wedding march. "I was born and raised and married on the island," says Great-Grammy. "And proud to be a herring-choker."

—*Maxine Kumin*

128

What Do You Think?

1. Did you like this story? Why, or why not? Which part did you like best? Why?
2. How do you suppose the name "herring-chokers" originated? Can you find clues in the fifth paragraph on page 119?
3. What did Great-Grandmother do for fun when she was a little girl?
4. What chores did Great-Grammy do?
5. How did Great-Grandmother get her education? What was special about Great-Grammy's going to the seminary in Halifax?
6. Is schooling today similar to Great-Grammy's or different? How?

Taking A Closer Look

1. Do you think Great-Grammy's family was a happy one? What in the story makes you think so?
2. How did the sea influence the lives of the people on Gerrard's Island?
3. What special difficulties did living on an island cause?
4. Would you like to have lived on Gerrard's Island in Great-Grandmother's day? What would you like about it? What would you dislike?
5. Why do you suppose most people finally left Gerrard's Island?

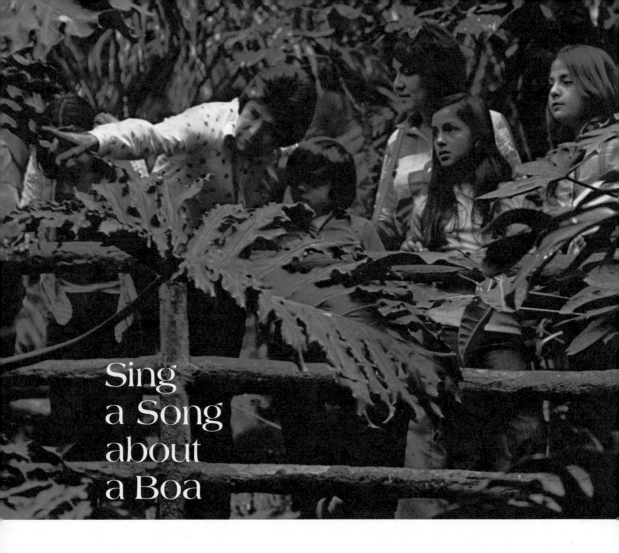

Sing
a Song
about
a Boa

Things you enjoy can be fun to write about. Ernesto Galarza visited a zoo and wrote poems about the animals he saw there. Read about the animals in his zoo and see what funny ideas they gave him.

Could you write a poem or two
About the animals in a zoo?

the boa

Sing a song
about a boa who was eight feet long.
His name was Bo-ab-dil.
But nearly everyone who knew him
  around the zoo
called him simply
Bill!

the elephant

If you had a trunk instead of a nose
you could swish it around like a garden hose.
If you had a trunk where your nose should be
you could pick up a log or even a tree.
If you had a trunk attached to your jaw
you could sip a soda without a straw.
If you want to know the reason you can't
it's because you are **not** an elephant.

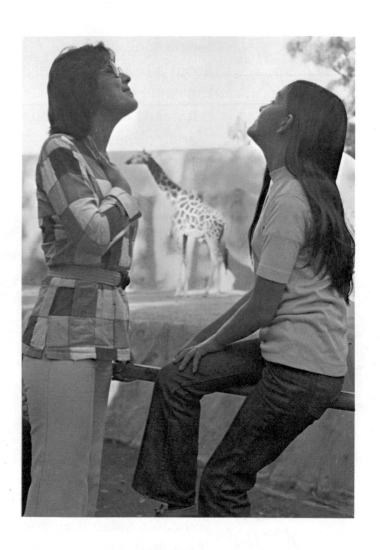

the giraffe

I have a friend whose name was Titus.
Once he was sick with laryngitis.
By day he'd cough, by night he'd kaff,
just like any sick giraffe,
until he became a nervous wreck
from such a pain in such a neck.

the zebra

The zebra puzzle for today
is easy, if you're bright.
The two-tone stripes he wears, are they
white on black, or black on white?
The answer ought to make you laugh:
the two-tone stripes are half-and-half.

 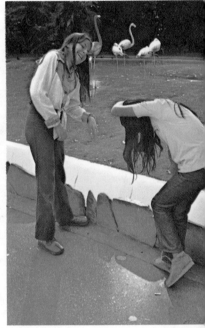

the flamingos

Flamingos are an elegant lot
with legs like stilts, which they are not.
They sleep on one as easy as pie
and hang the other one out to dry.

the vicuña[1]

The softest thing that you can touch
— like fuzz and fur and
fog and such —
is the vicuña. How do I know?
Because the vicuña says it's so.

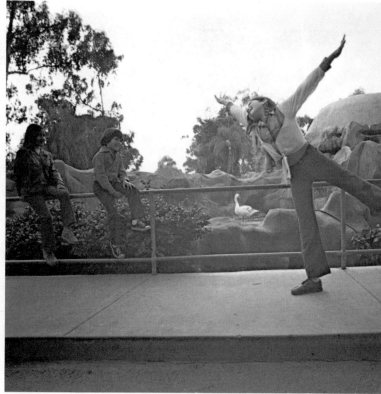

the swan

Oh my, Oh me,
how beautifully
we glide across the pond.
Who would not want to be
a swan?

[1]vicuña (və-KOON-yə)

the alligator

When you observe an alligator grin
he may be saying: "Please come in."
Just tell him: "Thank you, Mr. Alligator.
I'll be around a little later."

— *Ernesto Galarza*

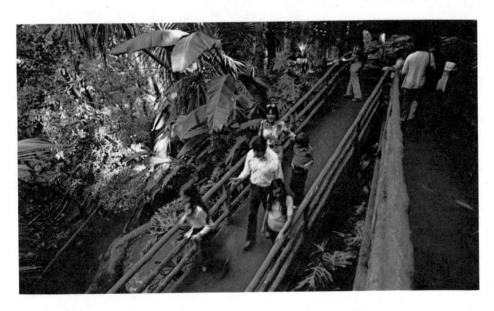

The next two stories are related. The first is an old
Greek tale told almost 2,000 years ago. If you've never
heard the story, you are in for a surprise. The second
story is a modern tale. Can you tell where the author of
"Andy and the Lion" got the idea for his story?

Androcles and the Lion

Androcles,[1] a runaway slave, had escaped to a forest for safety. He had not been there long when he saw a lion groaning with pain. He started to run, but then saw that the lion did not follow him. The lion only kept on groaning. Androcles turned and went to it. The lion, instead of rushing at him, put out a torn and bleeding paw. Androcles, seeing the poor beast in pain, wanted to help it. He went up and took its paw. Discovering a large thorn, Androcles pulled it out and so relieved the pain. The grateful lion in return took Androcles to its cave and every day brought him food.

Sometime later both were captured and taken to Rome. Androcles was sentenced to be killed by being thrown to a lion. The lion had not had food for several days. Androcles was led into the arena before the Emperor and his court. At the same time the lion was let go. It came running toward its prey. But when it came near Androcles, it did not attack him. Instead, it jumped up and fawned upon him like a friendly dog. The Emperor, much surprised, ordered that Androcles be brought before him to tell his story.

The Emperor freed both the slave and the lion. He thought such kindness and such gratitude were deserving of reward.

—*An Old Fable*

[1]Androcles (AN-drǝ-kleez)

Andy and the Lion

written and illustrated by James Daugherty

It was a bright day with just enough wind to float a flag. Andy started down to the library to get a book about lions. He took the book home and read and read. Andy read all through supper and he read all evening and just before bedtime his grandfather told him some tall stories about hunting lions in Africa. Every story ended with "and then I gave him both bar-r-r-e-l-l-s!" That night Andy dreamed all night long that he was in Africa hunting lions. When at last morning came Andy woke up. The sun was looking in at the window and Prince was tugging at the bed clothes. The lions had left but Andy kept thinking about them. Andy was still thinking lions after breakfast when his mother gave his hair a final brush and Andy started off to school.

Andy walked along swinging his books and whistling a tune. As he came to the turn in the road he noticed something sticking out from behind the big rock just at the bend. It looked very queer so Andy and Prince crept up cautiously to investigate. It moved! It was a lion! At this moment Andy thought he'd better be going and the lion thought so too. They ran and ran around the rock. Whichever way that Andy ran — there was the lion. Whichever way the lion ran — there was Andy. At last they both stopped for breath. The lion held out his paw to show Andy what was the matter. It was a big thorn stuck in his paw. But Andy had an idea. He told the lion to just be patient and they'd have that thorn out in no time. Fortunately Andy always carried his pliers in the back pocket of his overalls.

He took them out and got a tight grip. Then Andy braced one foot against the lion's paw and pulled with all his might until the thorn came out. The grateful lion licked Andy's face to show how pleased he was. But it was time to part. So they waved good-by. Andy went on to school and the lion went off about the business of being a lion.

In the spring the circus came to town. Of course Andy went. He wanted to see the famous lion act. Right in the middle of the act the biggest lion jumped out of the high steel cage and with a terrible roar dashed straight toward the people. They ran for their lives and in the scramble Andy found himself right in the lion's path. He thought his last moment had come. But then who should it be but Andy's own lion. They recognized each other and danced for joy. When the crowd came back ready to fight the lion and capture him, Andy stood in front of the lion and shouted to the angry people: "Do not hurt this lion. He's a friend of mine." Then the next day Andy led the lion and all the people in a grand parade down Main Street to City Hall. There the Mayor presented Andy with a medal for bravery. And the lion was very much pleased. And the next day Andy took the book back to the library.

—*James Daugherty*

140

What Do You Think?

1. Name as many features as you can that are the same in "Androcles and the Lion" and "Andy and the Lion." In what ways are the two stories different?

2. Is the lesson taught in Mr. Daugherty's story the same as the lesson in the Androcles story? Explain your answer by using examples from both stories.

Taking A Closer Look

1. What surprised you in these stories? Do you think the events in both stories could have really happened? Why or why not?

2. Which story do you think is funnier? Give reasons to support your answer.

3. Make up a modern-day fable that teaches a lesson. Your story can be funny or serious.

The Real Alice

Would you have guessed that a picnic and a girl named Alice were the beginnings of a famous story? Behind the make-believe character of Alice in *Alice's Adventures in Wonderland* was a real Alice.

On July 4, 1862, young Alice Pleasance Liddell and her two sisters went on a picnic with some of their parents' friends. One of these friends was Charles Lutwidge Dodgson, who later wrote under the pen name Lewis Carroll. At the picnic, Dodgson entertained the real Alice with stories about another adventuresome Alice. The lively Alice of the stories was very much like Alice Liddell herself, but what strange adventures she had!

Alice Liddell begged Dodgson to write down the Alice tales. Some months later, a hand-printed book called *Alice's Adventures Under Ground* arrived at Alice Liddell's home—and in the back was a picture of herself, the real Alice.

Later, additions to the story Charles Dodgson had begun that summer day were published for all to read in *Through the Looking-Glass*. The poem on the next page is from that book and tells about the picnic at which the first stories were told. Can you see Lewis Carroll's clue to the real Alice?

A boat, beneath a sunny sky
Lingering onward dreamily
In an evening of July—

Children three that nestle near,
Eager eye and willing ear,
Pleased a simple tale to hear—

Long has paled that sunny sky:
Echoes fade and memories die:
Autumn frosts have slain July.

Still she haunts me, phantomwise,
Alice moving under skies
Never seen by waking eyes.

Children yet, the tale to hear,
Eager eye and willing ear,
Lovingly shall nestle near.

In a Wonderland they lie,
Dreaming as the days go by,
Dreaming as the summers die:

Ever drifting down the stream—
Lingering in the golden gleam—
Life, what is it but a dream?

Not all of the story Charles Dodgson told Alice Liddell was in the final published book. After the printer set the following episode in type, Dodgson cut it out of the book. Why? Because the artist doing the pictures for *Through the Looking-Glass* claimed that a wasp in a wig was impossible to draw. Only in recent times has the Wasp been drawn successfully as in the picture above.

On the next pages are copies of some galley proof for *Through the Looking-Glass*. Galley proofs, called "slips" in those days, are long, numbered sheets of paper with all the text of a book printed on them. Authors make their final corrections on this proof before the book is arranged in pages. Here, just as the author marked them, are the "slips" for "The Wasp in a Wig."

Alice has just reached the edge of a brook.

The Wasp in a Wig

and she was just going to spring over, when she heard a deep sigh, which seemed to come from the wood behind her.

"There's somebody *very* unhappy there," she thought, ~~and she went a little way~~ *looking anxiously* back ~~again~~ to see what was the matter. Something like a very old man (only that his face was more like a wasp) was sitting on the ground, leaning against a tree, all huddled up together, and shivering as if he were very cold.

Omit to middle of Slip 68 —

64

"I don't *think* I can be of any use to him," was Alice's first thought, as she turned to spring over the brook :——"but I'll just ask him what's the matter," she added, checking herself on the very edge. "If I once jump over, everything will change, and then I can't help him."

145

So she went back to the Wasp——rather unwillingly, for she was *very* anxious to be a Queen.

"Oh, my old bones, my old bones!" he was grumbling on, as Alice came up to him.

"It's rheumatism, I should think," Alice said to herself, and she stooped over him, and said very kindly, "I hope you're not in much pain?"

The Wasp only shook his shoulders, and turned his head away. "Ah, deary me!" he said to himself.

"Can I do anything for you?" Alice went on. "Aren't you rather cold here?"

"How you go on!" the Wasp said in a peevish tone. "Worrity, worrity! There never was such a child!"

Alice felt rather offended at this answer, and was very nearly walking on and leaving him, but she thought to herself "Perhaps it's only pain that makes him so cross." So she tried once more.

"Won't you let me help you round to the other side? You'll be out of the cold wind there."

The Wasp took her arm, and let her help him round the tree, but when he got settled down again he only said, as before, "Worrity, worrity! Can't you leave a body alone?"

146

"Would you like me to read you a bit of this?" Alice went on, as she picked up a newspaper which had been lying at his feet.

"You may read it if you've a mind to," the Wasp said, rather sulkily. "Nobody's hindering you, that *I* know of."

So Alice sat down by him, and spread out the paper on her knees, and began. "*Latest News. The Exploring Party have made another tour in the Pantry, and have found five new lumps of white sugar, large and in fine condition. In coming back——*"

"Any brown sugar?" the Wasp interrupted.

65

Alice hastily ran her eye down the paper and said "No. It says nothing about brown."

"No brown sugar!" grumbled the Wasp. "A nice exploring party!"

"*In coming back,*" Alice went on reading, "*they found a lake of treacle. The banks of the lake were blue and white, and looked like china. While tasting the treacle, they had a sad accident: two of their party were engulphed——*"

"Were *what?*" the Wasp asked in a very cross voice.

"En-gulph-ed," Alice repeated, dividing the word into syllables.

"There's no such word in the language!" said the Wasp.

"It's in this newspaper˄ though," Alice said a little timidly.

"Let it stop there!" said the Wasp, fretfully turning away his head.

Alice put down the newspaper. "I'm afraid you're not well," she said in a soothing tone. "Can't I do anything for you?"

"It's all along of the wig," the Wasp said in a much gentler voice.

"Along of the wig?" Alice repeated, quite pleased to find that he was recovering his temper.

"You'd be cross too, if you'd a wig like mine," the Wasp went on. "They jokes at one. And they worrits one. And then I gets cross. And I gets cold. And I gets under a tree. And I gets a yellow handkerchief. And I ties up my face——as at the present."

Alice looked pityingly at him. "Tying up the face is very good for the toothache," she said.

"And it's very good for the conceit," added the Wasp.

Alice didn't catch the word exactly. "Is that a kind of toothache?" she asked.

The Wasp considered a little. "Well, no,"

he said : " it 's when you hold up your head——
so——without bending your neck."

" Oh, you mean stiff-neck," said Alice.

The Wasp said " That's a new-fangled name.
They called it conceit in my time."

" Conceit isn't a disease at all," Alice re-
marked.

66

" It is though," said the Wasp : "wait till
you have it, and then you'll know.   And when
you catches it, just try tying a yellow handkerchief round your face.   It'll cure you in no
time !"

He untied the handkerchief as he spoke,
and Alice looked at his wig in great surprise.
It was bright yellow like the handkerchief, and
all tangled and tumbled about like a heap of
sea-weed.   " You could make your wig much
neater," she said, " if only you had a comb."

" What, you're a Bee, are you ? " the Wasp
said, looking at her with more interest.   " And
you've got a comb.   Much honey ? "

" It isn't that kind," Alice hastily explained.
" It's to comb hair with——your wig's so *very*
rough, you know."

" I'll tell you how I came to wear it," the
Wasp said.   " When I was young, you know,
my ringlets used to wave——"

149

A curious idea came into Alice's head. Almost every one she had met had repeated poetry to her, and she thought she would try if the Wasp couldn't do it too. "Would you mind saying it in rhyme?" she asked very politely.

"It aint what I'm used to," said the Wasp: "however I'll try; wait a bit." He was silent for a few moments, and then began again—

" When I was young, my ringlets waved
　　And curled and crinkled on my head:
　And then they said 'You should be shaved,
　　And wear a yellow wig instead.'

"But when I followed their advice,
　　And they had noticed the effect,
　They said I did not look so nice
　　As they had ventured to expect.

"They said it did not fit, and so
　　It made me look extremely plain:
　But what was I to do, you know?
　　My ringlets would not grow again.

"So now that I am old and gray,
　　And all my hair is nearly gone,
　They take my wig from me and say
　　' How can you put such rubbish on?'

150

"And still, whenever I appear,.
  They hoot at me and call me ' Pig !'
And that is why they do it, dear,
  Because I wear a yellow wig."

" I'm very sorry for you," Alice said heartily : " and I think if your wig fitted a little better, they wouldn't tease you quite so much."

" *Your* wig fits very well," the Wasp murmured, looking at her with an expression of admiration : " it's the shape of your head as does it. Your jaws aint well shaped, though—— I should think you couldn't bite well ? "

Alice began with a little scream of laughing, which she turned into a cough as well as she could At last she managed to say gravely "I can bite anything I want,"

" Not with a mouth as small as that," the Wasp persisted. " If you was a-fighting, now ——could you get hold of the other one by the back of the neck ? "

" I'm afraid not," said Alice.

" Well, that's because your jaws are too short," the Wasp went on : " but the top of your head is nice and round." He took off his own wig as he spoke, and stretched out one claw towards Alice, as if he wished to do the same for her, but she kept out of reach, and would not take the hint. So he went on with his criticisms.

"Then your eyes——they're too much in front, no doubt. One would have done as well as two, if you *must* have them so close——"

Alice did not like having so many personal remarks made on her, and as the Wasp had quite recovered his spirits, and was getting very talkative, she thought she might safely leave him. "I think I must be going on now," she said. "Good-bye."

"Good-bye, and thank-ye," said the Wasp, and Alice tripped down the hill again, quite pleased that she had gone back and given a few minutes to making the poor old creature comfortable.

What Do You Think?

1. In what ways was the Wasp strange? In what ways was he like people you might know?
2. Was the Wasp the kind of person you would like to have around? Why or why not?
3. Do you think Alice really helped the Wasp? Explain your answer.

Taking A Closer Look

1. What was Alice about to do when she decided to help the Wasp?
2. What did Alice do to help the Wasp forget his troubles?
3. How do you know that the Wasp was a complainer?
4. Why did the Wasp tell his story in the form of a poem?
5. What did the Wasp think was the main cause of his unhappiness?
6. In what ways does the Wasp find Alice "strangely shaped"?

The Real Ugly Duckling

More than a hundred years ago in Odense, Denmark, lived a boy named Hans Christian Andersen. Too poor to go to school, young Hans Christian spent his days in his imagination. He listened wide-eyed to the old tales of magic and adventure his grandmother told him. Then he acted them out in his toy theater. Not satisfied with only cardboard actors, he began to train himself. One day he would be a famous actor, he told everyone. To prove it, he would recite poetry, sing, and dance for anyone who would listen.

Unfortunately, all the practice in the world could not help Hans Christian. He was a homely child with a large nose and a long, sad face. Besides, he had no talent at all for acting. When he performed, he tripped over his clumsy legs and big feet. His audiences broke up with laughter. The boy's dream of becoming famous seemed foolish. Only his mother believed in him.

When Hans Christian grew older, he left Odense for Copenhagen. Here, he was certain, would be great chances to become an actor. There were, indeed, more opportunities, but not for Hans Christian. No one in Copenhagen appreciated his dancing or singing. Poor, hungry, and ragged, he became discouraged. Yet still he held to one idea: "First you suffer a great deal, then you become famous."

Then two things happened to change Hans Christian's fortune. First, he made an important decision. Since he couldn't be a successful actor or singer, he would become a great writer. Second, he caught the attention of a wealthy man who sent him to school. At sixteen, the tall, awkward Hans Christian sat with small children to learn. Again people laughed at him, but he held fast to his new dream.

After long years of schooling, Hans Christian began to write plays and books, and soon he turned to tales of magic and adventure. Some were his own tales. Others he borrowed from his grandmother's stories. One by one his fairy tales appeared, and finally they were all published in one book.

Finally Hans Christian had become famous. His tales were different from anything people had read before. Children and grownups alike loved them! Once people had laughed at him. Now even the kings of Europe admired him. He had suffered, but now he was famous.

Later, when Hans Christian Andersen wrote the story of his life, he said that it had been like a fairy tale. And indeed it had. The poor young dreamer had become the friend of kings.

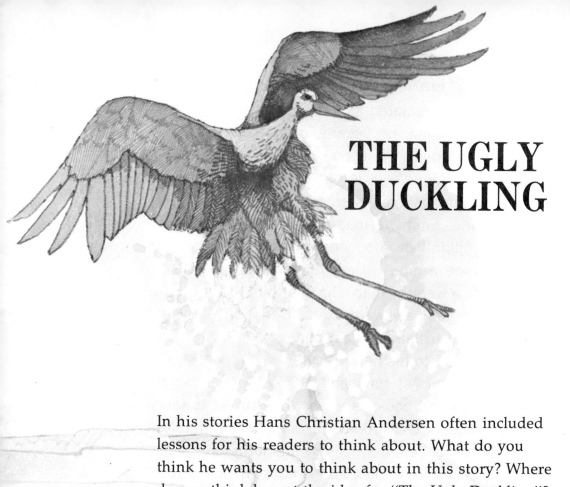

THE UGLY DUCKLING

In his stories Hans Christian Andersen often included lessons for his readers to think about. What do you think he wants you to think about in this story? Where do you think he got the idea for "The Ugly Duckling"?

The country was lovely then. It was summer. The cornfields were yellow. The oats were green. The hay had been put in bundles in the green fields. The stork went about on his long red legs and chattered Egyptian.[1] This was the language he had learned from his good mother. All around the fields were great forests. In the middle of these forests lay deep lakes. Yes, it was beautiful out in the country.

In the sunniest spot there stood an old house with deep water all around it. Great leaves grew from the walls of the house down to the water's edge. Some were so high that little children could stand up under them. Here, hidden among the leaves, a duck sat upon her nest. She was waiting to hatch her ducklings. No one had visited her for a long time. The other ducks would rather swim about in the water than sit and talk with her.

At last one eggshell after another broke open. From all the eggs little heads stuck out.

"Peep! Peep!" they said. And they all came tumbling out as fast as they could. They looked all around them among the green leaves. Their mother let them look as much as they wanted. For green is good for the eyes.

"How big the world is!" said all the young ones. They certainly had more room here than in the eggs.

[1] Egyptian (i-JIP-shən)

"Do you think this is all the world?" said the mother. "It stretches far across the other side of the garden. But I have never been that far yet. I hope you are all here now." And she stood up. "No, one of you is missing. The largest egg still lies there. I wish it would hatch soon. I am very tired of waiting." And she sat down again.

"Well, how goes it?" asked an old duck who had come to pay her a visit.

"Well, that one egg is taking a long time," said the mother duck. "It will not crack. Now, look at the others. They are the finest little ducks I have ever seen!"

"Let me see the egg that will not hatch," said the old visitor. "You may be sure it is a turkey's egg. I was once cheated in that way. My young ones were afraid of the water. I hate to tell you, but I couldn't get them to go in. I quacked and quacked, but it was no use. Let me see that egg. Yes, it is a turkey's egg. Let it lie there while you teach the other children to swim."

"I think I will sit on it a little longer," said the duck. "I've sat so long now that I can sit a few days more."

At last the great egg broke. "Peep! Peep!" said the duckling as it came out. It was very large and very ugly. The duck looked at it.

"What a large duckling," said she. "None of the others look like that. Can it really be a turkey chick? Well, we shall soon find out. It must go into the water, even if I have to push it."

The next day was bright and beautiful. The sun shone on all the green leaves. The mother duck went down to the water with all her family. Splash! She jumped in. "Quack! Quack!" she said, and one duckling after another plunged in. The water closed over their heads. Then, in a moment, they came up and swam like their mother. The big ugly gray one swam with them.

"No, that is no turkey," said the mother duck. "See how well it uses its legs. And see how straight it holds itself. It is my own chick! On the whole, it's quite pretty if one looks at it properly. Quack! Quack! Come with me. I'll lead you out into the great world and present you in the duck yard. But keep close to me so that no one will step on you. And watch out for the cat!"

And so they came into the duck yard. A terrible row was going on there. Two families were quarreling over an eel's head. And in the end the cat got it.

"See how it goes in the world," said the mother duck. She licked her bill, for she too wanted the eel's head. "Now, use your legs. Shake yourselves and don't turn in your toes. A proper duck turns its toes out, just like father and mother—so! Now bend your necks and say, 'Quack!'"

And they did. But the other ducks looked at them angrily. They said, "Look there. Now we're to have these ducklings hanging on. There are enough of us already! And—ugh—how ugly that duckling yonder looks. We won't stand that!" And one duck flew up at the ugly duckling and bit it in the neck.

"Let it alone," said the mother. "It is not harming anyone."

"Yes, but it's too large and strange," said the duck who had bitten it. "It should be put down."

"Those are pretty children," said an old duck with a rag around her leg. The rag meant that she was very special. "They are all pretty but the big one. I wish the mother could hatch it over again."

"That cannot be done, my lady," replied the mother duck. "The big duckling isn't pretty, but it has a good disposition. Besides, it swims as well as any other. Yes, I may even say it swims better. I think it will grow up pretty, and perhaps even become smaller in time." Then she patted the ugly duckling's neck and smoothed its feathers. "Besides, it is a drake," she said. "His appearance is not so important. I think he will be very strong. He will make his way in the world."

"The other ducklings are pretty enough," said the old duck. "Make yourselves at home. And if you find an eel's head, you may bring it to me."

Now they all felt at home, all except the ugly duckling. Everyone looked down on him. He was made fun of, as much by the ducks as by the chickens. "He is too big," they all said.

Then a turkey nearby blew himself up like a ship in full sail. He came running straight at the ugly duckling. He gobbled and gobbled and grew quite red in the face. The poor duckling did not know which way to turn. He felt sad because he looked so ugly. He was the joke of the whole duck yard.

So it went on the first day. And afterwards things grew worse and worse. The poor duckling was attacked by everyone. Even his brothers and sisters were quite angry with him. They said, "If only the cat would catch you, you ugly creature." And the mother said, "If only you were far away." The ducks bit him. The chickens pecked at him.

Then he ran off and flew over the fence. The little birds in the bushes flew up in fear.

"They hate me because I am so ugly," thought the duckling. And he shut his eyes and ran farther on. Soon he reached the great marsh where the wild ducks lived. Here he lay a long while, weary and sad.

Toward evening he left the marsh. Wandering on, he came to a poor old cottage. It looked as though it was ready to fall. A storm was coming up and the wind whistled around the duckling. The poor thing could hardly stand against it. The wind blew harder and harder. Then the duckling noticed that one of the hinges of the door was loose. There was a small opening where the door was hanging. He saw he could slip through the crack into the room. And that is what he did.

A woman lived here with her cat and her hen. The cat could arch his back and purr. When anyone patted him the wrong way, his fur gave off sparks. The hen had tiny short legs. But she laid good eggs. The woman loved the hen as if she were her own child.

In the morning the cat and the hen noticed the strange duckling. The cat began to purr and the hen to cluck.

"What is this?" said the woman looking all around. But she could not see well. She thought the duckling was a fat duck that was lost. "What an unusual prize!" she said. "Now I shall have duck's eggs. I hope it is not a drake."

She let the duckling stay on trial for three weeks. But no eggs came. The cat was still master of the house and the hen was the lady. They always said, "We and the world." They thought they were half the world, and by far the better half. The duckling had different ideas, but the hen would not hear of them.

"Can you lay eggs?" she asked.

"No."

"Then will you hold your tongue?"

And the cat said, "Can you arch your back and purr and give off sparks?"

"No."

"Then you will please say nothing when people with sense are speaking."

And the duckling sat in a corner and was very sad. Then one day the fresh air and the sunshine streamed in. The duckling wanted to float on the water. He felt he should speak of his longing to the hen.

"What are you thinking of?" cried the hen. "You have nothing to do. That is why you have these fancy ideas. Lay eggs or purr and these foolish thoughts will go away."

"But it is such a pleasure to float on the water," said the duckling. "It feels so good to let it close over your head when you dive to the bottom."

"Yes, that must be a great pleasure," said the hen. "I think you have gone crazy. Ask the cat about it. He's the cleverest animal I know. Ask him if he likes to float on the water or to dive down. I won't speak about myself!"

"You don't understand me," said the duckling.

"We don't understand you? Then who is to understand you? You surely don't pretend to be cleverer than the cat. I won't say anything of myself. Don't make a fool of yourself. And be thankful for all the kindness you have received. You have a warm room, don't you? And you have us wiser ones to learn something from, don't you? But you are always chattering. It is not pleasant to have you around. Believe me, I speak for your own good. I tell you these things so that you may know I'm your friend. Just learn to lay eggs, or to purr, or to give off sparks!"

"I think I will go out into the wide world," said the duckling.

"Yes, do go," replied the hen.

And so the duckling went away. He floated on the water and dived. Still no one paid attention to him because he was so ugly.

Now came the autumn. The leaves in the forest turned yellow and brown. The wind caught them so that they danced about. Up in the air it was very cold. The clouds hung low, heavy with snow and hail. The poor little duckling did not have an easy time of it.

One evening—the sun was just setting—a whole flock of great, handsome birds came out of the bushes. They were very white, with long necks. They were swans. They gave out a peculiar cry and spread their great broad wings. They flew away from that cold place to warmer lands and open seas. They flew so high that the duckling felt quite strange as he watched them. He turned round and round in the water like a wheel. He let out such a strange, loud cry that he frightened himself.

Soon he could see the handsome birds no longer. He dived down to the very bottom of the pond. When he came up again, he was quite beside himself. Oh, he could not forget those beautiful, happy birds. He did not know their name or where they were flying. But he loved them more than he had ever loved anyone. He did not envy them at all. How could he think of wishing for such loveliness as they had? He would have been glad if only the ducks would have put up with him—the poor ugly creature!

The winter grew cold, very cold. It would be too sad to tell all the trouble the duckling had to go through during the hard winter.

But at long last spring arrived. The duckling lay among the marsh reeds in the sun. The weather began to get warm again and the larks began to sing.

All at once the duckling could flap his wings. They beat the air more strongly than ever before. Then suddenly they took him away. Before he knew where he was, he found himself in a great garden. Trees bent their long branches down to the shores of a lake. Oh, here it was so beautiful, the joy of spring! Suddenly, from the thicket came three lovely white swans. They shook their wings and swam lightly over the water. The duckling knew the wonderful birds at once. He was filled with a sudden strange feeling of sadness.

"I will fly to them, to the royal birds. They will beat me because I, who am so ugly, dare to come near them. But it is better to be killed by *them* than to be snapped at by ducks, pecked at by chickens, or suffer hunger in winter!"

He flew out into the water and swam toward the beautiful swans. They looked at him. They came sailing down upon him, their wings spread wide.

"Kill me!" he cried. He bent his head down upon the water, expecting nothing but death. But what did he see in the clear water? It was himself. But he was no longer a clumsy, gray bird, ugly to look at. He was a — swan!

It does not matter if one is born in a duck yard. It only matters if one has come out of a swan's egg.

The ugly duckling forgot all the trouble he had been through. Now he realized his happiness. The great swans swam round him and stroked him with their bills.

Into the garden came little children who threw bread and corn into the water. The youngest cried, "There is a new one!" And the other children shouted with joy. "Yes, a new one has come." They clapped their hands and danced about. They threw bread and cake into the water for all the swans. And they all said, "The new swan is the most beautiful of all. He is so young and handsome!" And the old swans all bowed their heads before him.

He felt quite shy now and hid his head under his wing. He did not know what to think. He was so happy and yet not at all proud. He thought how he had been attacked and hated. And now he heard them all saying that he was the most beautiful of all birds. Even the trees bent their branches straight down into the water before him. The sun shone warm on his back. He shook his wings and lifted his long neck. Happily he cried out, "I never dreamed of so much happiness when I was the Ugly Duckling."

—Hans Christian Andersen

What Do You Think?

1. Why were Hans Christian Andersen and the ugly duckling unhappy at first? How did they both find happiness?
2. Where do you think Hans Christian Andersen got his idea for "The Ugly Duckling"? Who was the real ugly duckling?
3. Why didn't the ugly duckling have confidence in himself at first? How did he find confidence?

Taking A Closer Look

1. Tell how the ducks and chickens in the duck yard treated the ugly duckling. Why did they treat him in this way?
2. To help us understand how humans behave, Andersen makes the animals talk and act like people. Name five different animals in the story and tell in what ways each animal talks and acts like a person.
3. In your opinion, what was the happiest part of this tale? What was the saddest part? Explain your answers.
4. "What you are inside is more important than how you look or where you come from." Why do you think this saying is true of the ugly duckling? Think of an example to show what this saying means to you.

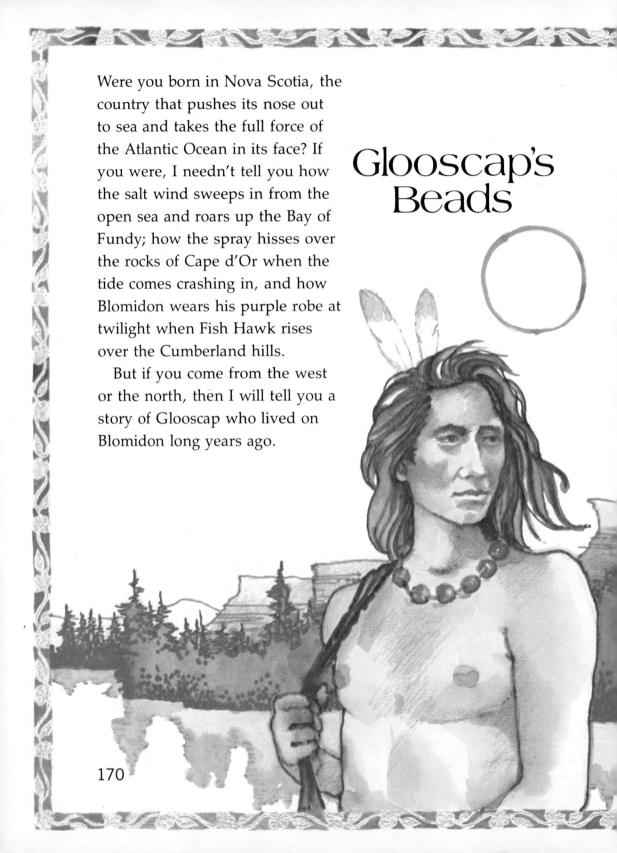

Were you born in Nova Scotia, the country that pushes its nose out to sea and takes the full force of the Atlantic Ocean in its face? If you were, I needn't tell you how the salt wind sweeps in from the open sea and roars up the Bay of Fundy; how the spray hisses over the rocks of Cape d'Or when the tide comes crashing in, and how Blomidon wears his purple robe at twilight when Fish Hawk rises over the Cumberland hills.

But if you come from the west or the north, then I will tell you a story of Glooscap who lived on Blomidon long years ago.

Glooscap's Beads

170

Glooscap was the Big Man of the Micmacs, the Indians who lived in Nova Scotia before the white men came, and whose descendants are there today. The Great Spirit made Glooscap and gave him to the Micmacs to be their friend and teacher. He taught them the names of the stars and the trees and the flowers, where to find the biggest game and the finest fish, how to store food, and cultivate their gardens.

Now Glooscap had an enemy, Guyadunsque[1] the Beaver. When Glooscap brought the animals down from Skyland to live on the earth, the beaver was the last to be called, and he had borne a grudge against Glooscap ever since.

Glooscap tried all sorts of plans to win Guyadunsque's friendship. All his kindness did no good whatever. The beavers went on just as they had done before. They threw trees into the rivers where the people fished, dammed up the water so that it flooded their gardens, and kept the whole Minas Basin so untidy that Glooscap was ashamed to invite his friends to visit him.

Glooscap lived a very busy life. But there was one thing he never neglected, no matter how much work he had to do, and that was his garden. It was a very beautiful place, built in a curve of the shore at Advocate, opposite Blomidon, the great blue mountain where Glooscap had his wigwam. In this garden grew the brightest flowers, the tallest corn, and the finest roots and herbs in the country; for Glooscap was a wise medicine man, and cured sickness with his magic salves and potions.

1 Guyadunsque (gigh-a-DUNSK)

One day, as Guyadunsque was swimming along past Advocate, he saw Glooscap working in his garden. The beaver pushed up to the shore and hailed the Big Man, "What are you working at, Master?"

Glooscap answered politely as he always did. "I am weeding pumpkins, my son."

"Pumpkins?" said Guyadunsque scornfully. "Why don't you grow young birches or some nice red willow? Pumpkins have no taste at all."

"That's what you think," said the Big Man cheerfully. "Myself, I am fond of pumpkins."

He went back to his weeding, and as he stooped over it Guyadunsque noticed that he was wearing a fine necklace of purple stones. Certainly the Master had not worn these before, he thought to himself. I have never seen anything so beautiful.

When Guyadunsque got home he called to him a young beaver who was known to be a bit of a gossip.

"Keeseegoo, you hear much. Do you know where the Master got his purple beads?"

"Purple beads? The Master has no purple beads."

"You're no use to me," said Guyadunsque, and went out again. Sitting on a rock in the stream he called down Culloo, the great eagle.

"Culloo, you know everything. Do you know how the Master got his purple beads?"

But Culloo knew no more than Keeseegoo. He suggested that the beaver ask Blinker the Whale. When Guyadunsque found the whale and asked his question, Blinker did not know.

"I can tell you how to find out, though," said the old fellow.

Blinker said that if Guyadunsque would go to the point of Cape d'Or at the rise of the moon he might see something that would explain the purple beads.

Guyadunsque swam home wondering whether Blinker had told him a story to get rid of him. However, he was really very curious about the beads; so that night when the big white star Fish Hawk rose over Blomidon, the beaver went softly out of his lodge and paddled down the shore.

Guyadunsque strained his eyes through the darkness and saw something moving towards him over the water. The gentle splashing drew nearer, and now the beaver lay very still, flattening himself against the rock, for he saw who was coming. The canoe was hollowed out of pure stone, white and unearthly in the moonlight, and at the paddle sat Glooscap, the Master of Blomidon.

The canoe beached at the foot of the bluff, and the Master got out and came towards the cove. When Glooscap's footsteps had passed Guyadunsque looked into the cove.

What was the Master at? First he used the axe briskly, with short strong strokes; then he stooped and lifted up a slab of rock that had come loose. Underneath the slab was quite a deep hole, and into this the Master dug his axe with long, swinging blows.

Standing on tiptoe the beaver could just see the bottom of the pit. The Master stooped down and was picking little pieces of rock out of the hole. Only they were not rocks, but big purple stones.

Soon after this Glooscap went away visiting on the neighboring island to the north, which we know as Prince Edward Island, but which the Indians called Epagweit, "Cradled-on-the-Wave." He left his wigwam in charge of his grandmother, who kept house for him, and his niece Marten. Before he went he warned them not to let anyone use his gardening tools.

174

One night Marten and the old grandmother sat by the fire making moccasins for Glooscap. After Grandmother dropped off to sleep there came a soft scratching at the doorway of the wigwam. Marten went to see who was there, and found Keeseegoo outside.

"It's a fine warm night, Marten," said he. "Won't you come out for a walk?"

Who would know, thought Marten, if she slipped out for a few minutes? She pulled the flap across the doorway of the wigwam, fastened it securely, and crept down the path beside Keeseegoo.

"What bright eyes you have, Marten!" said the young beaver. "They're like fireflies in the dark!"

Marten was pleased, because no one had ever paid her compliments before.

"And how fine your hair is, Marten! It is as smooth as the tassels on the corn in the moon of the harvest. You are very beautiful, Marten!"

175

The foolish girl was flattered, and smiled and tossed her long black braids, for no one had ever said such grand things to her.

"Marten," said Keeseegoo as they went along, "would you like me to give you a present?"

She said, "Yes, Keeseegoo, I should like a present very much."

"Then you must get me the Master's long hammer," said Keeseegoo, "the one that has the two points, one sharp and one wedge-shaped. He won't mind if I borrow it."

But Marten said she couldn't possibly do that.

"I can't bring you the present if you don't give me the hammer," said Keeseegoo, walking away.

Marten ran after him.

"Wait, Keeseegoo. If you promise not to tell anyone, I will get you the hammer."

Marten went down the mountainside until she came to the little cave where Glooscap kept his gardening tools. The pickaxe was leaning by itself in a corner. Marten ran out with it quickly, afraid that someone might see her and tell the Master.

"Here it is," she said, thrusting it at the beaver, "but promise me you won't let anyone see it."

Keeseegoo promised, seized the pickaxe in his teeth, and hurried off.

Marten called out, "When will you bring it back?"

Keeseegoo answered without stopping, "Tomorrow when Oaklahdahbun rises over Blomidon."

"I will be here," said Marten. "Don't be late, or

Grandmother will wake up and I shall be scolded."

When Keeseegoo left Marten he went as fast as his feet would carry him to the beavers' lodge. Guyadunsque sat outside waiting for him.

The next day as Marten went about her housework Grandmother said to her, "What is there in your belt that shines so brightly, my granddaughter?"

Marten replied, "It is a new flower I picked on the mountainside, Granny."

A little later the old woman said, "What is that on your forehead that sparkles so gaily, my granddaughter?"

And Marten replied, "It is a bright pebble I found on the beach, Granny."

But Marten lied; for in her belt and on the band about her hair she wore the two purple stones Keeseegoo had brought her.

The next day Glooscap came home; and Marten hid her purple stones in a box and put it under the deerskin that covered her at night. The first thing the Master did was to visit his garden, and he stopped on the way for his tools. When he returned he said to Marten, "Has anyone been in the tool shed since I went away?"

Marten became very busy putting wood on the fire, but she answered promptly, "Not that I know of, uncle."

"Someone has been in," said Glooscap. "My tools are not where I left them."

Now when Marten put the pickaxe back in the cave after Keeseegoo had returned it to her, she had quite forgotten which corner she had taken it from. She was frightened, for Glooscap loved to have things neat and kept each tool in its own place. However, she could not remember although she tried; so she put it in the northeast corner, and murmured a prayer to the Great Spirit that it might be the right one.

Glooscap said no more about the misplaced tools, and Marten hoped the danger was past. But the next morning there was trouble.

Marten heard of it from Culloo the Eagle.

"Do you know that the Master's beads have been stolen?" asked he, flapping down to sit on the center pole of the wigwam.

"Who stole them?" she asked.

But Culloo only wagged his head and flew off, saying, "Ask Guyadunsque."

By nightfall every man, bird, and beast on Blomidon knew that the Master's bead quarry at Cape d'Or had been broken into and that the beavers did it.

178

Marten had taken the purple stones down to the beavers' lodge and left them there, hoping that the Master would never know she had had them. But one day he said to her, "Why did you give away the purple stones, my daughter?"

Then, because he looked at her so kindly, Marten began to cry, and sobbed out the whole story, which was the best thing she could have done. Glooscap listened quietly until she had finished, and then he said, "Flattery belongs to the powers of darkness, my daughter. They will steal the sparkle from your eyes and the smile from your lips, because those who listen to the Evil One cannot laugh. Keep the laws of the Great Spirit in your heart, so that you may be free and happy."

The rest of the tale is soon told. Glooscap set a trap below Blomidon for the beavers, for he felt they needed a lesson; but Keeseegoo hid in the bushes and saw what was done, and then ran to warn Guyadunsque. That night the beavers built a great dam of felled trees and broken bark across the Minas Basin from Blomidon to the Cumberland shore; and in the morning the waters overflowed and poured into the Master's garden. The corn was laid low, the pumpkins were washed into the sea, the neat rows of herbs and precious plants were torn up by the force of the water, and all the beautiful pebbles and shells that Glooscap had gathered to decorate his flower bed went rolling down the cove and lay tumbled and broken along the shore.

Then Glooscap rose up in majesty and strode down to the seashore. He took his great bow and broke the dam in pieces; some of them he hurled across the Basin to Advocate, where they lie to this day; but he dropped one piece where he stood, and it has been called Cape Split ever since. Glooscap's anger shook the rocks in the sea and swayed Blomidon like a leaf in the wind; thunderclouds roared in the sky, and jagged lightnings leaped upon the hills. All living creatures crept into their holes and dwelling places, and for a night and a day no creature dared stir abroad. Then the Big Man's anger melted, as snow melts in the warm winds of spring; the sun shone, the skies became blue, the little animals went about their business, and life again took up its daily tasks. The beavers never repeated their evil trick. Moreover, they behaved themselves from that day forward.

Sometimes amethysts are found in Glooscap's cove today; but if you get one and show it to an Indian he will ask you not to keep it.

"Put it back," he will say. "Those are Glooscap's beads, and when he comes he'll want them."

For the spirit of Glooscap still breathes on Blomidon, although the Master has long gone to the Happy Hunting Grounds to make a home for his people. Perhaps you'll see him if you walk at moonrise on the rocks of Cape d'Or when Blomidon wears his purple robe at twilight and Fish Hawk rises over the Cumberland hills.

—Hilda Mary Hooke

What Do You Think?

1. Where did the author get her inspiration for this tale?
2. Do you feel that Glooscap treated the Beaver fairly? Why or why not?
3. What lessons does this story teach?

Taking A Closer Look

1. In this story animals talk and act like people, as they do in "The Ugly Duckling." What other animal fables do you know?
2. How does Glooscap show his kindness in his dealings with the animals?
3. Describe how you think Glooscap might have looked.
4. What were Glooscap's duties in life? What did he have to do after life, in the Happy Hunting Grounds?
5. List the Micmac names for animals, stars, and places used in the story.

181

Here are four stories written by young people about your age. The stories are as different from one another as are the authors themselves. As you read these stories, can you guess where the young writers may have gotten their ideas?

Quiet Fishing

My float was silent and still, and its yellow and white markings gleamed in my ever fading eyes. The gentle fall of distant water could be heard as it pounded the stream. My mind went with the water, up and down, in and out, moving forward as it went. You let your mind run away, as if swept away by the stream.

—*Michael Freeman*

182

Gaining My First Goal

Up, up, up and oh help. Why didn't it go in like it should have? It should go up and in so very perfectly, and it's got to. Up, up, ah, it's going, going, gone. Blast it. I know I'm standing wrongly and yes, um Barbara always says, "The sun's in my eyes." Well, "The sun's in my eyes." But it can't be, I'm inside.

I know, maybe I'm better at long shots. When Barbara takes them she stands 3 m away, and I'm 4 years younger and 18 cm smaller, so 18 divided by 3 is 6 and 6 take away 4 is 2. Therefore I stand 2 m away.

Hey this looks better, just right. Oh, not again it can't miss. But it's not, it's going to go in.

Oh help, aren't I just so good.

—Pamela McHenry

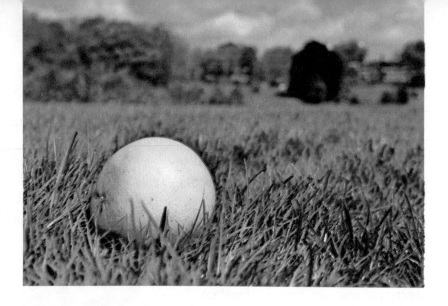

The football players run faster and faster when suddenly whirling colors appear on the field. The football players are dancing now. They begin running again but they are running in slow motion. The football is thrown and in mid air it turns into a whirling colorful grapefruit. Suddenly a siren-like sound comes from the spinning grapefruit. The pitch of the sound gets higher and it becomes piercing. It still gets higher until it is a deafening, screeching shrill. Then it stops! The grapefruit hits the ground but does not bounce up from the ground the slightest amount. But there are no football players rushing for this still grapefruit. The field is lone and empty. The only thing on the field is this one grapefruit. It begins shrinking and getting smaller and smaller. If one listens carefully one can hear a faint song which has no source.

—John Auerbach,

Why They Changed Their Minds

At the first of the year my so-called friends called me "Too Tall Irma." That really made me angry because I couldn't help it. The story changed when we played baseball and they all wanted me on their team. I could run, I could catch, and I could really hit the ball.

—*Irma Hernandez*

185

Everywhere Tales

In all parts of the world there have been storytellers
who could hold their listeners spellbound with tales of
wonder and adventure. Often these tales spoke of
natural events people feared or could not understand.
Sometimes stories of mighty heroes and heroines were
created to give courage and comfort to people. And
once in a while a good tale was told just for fun. The
old tales of this unit were told and retold for hundreds
of years before they were written down.

This is a legend of Tse-Shat people, Indians living in British Columbia. The first seven lines tell what life was like without fire.

How the Human People Got the First Fire

Long, long time ago the human people had no fire.
There was no fire to cook the food,
The people ate their food cold.
There was no fire to dry their clothes,
No fire to warm them at winter time.
There was no fire to give them light when the moon would not.

It has been said there was no fire at all amongst the human people. No one had fire, except the Wolf people. The Wolf people were the most dreaded people in all the land.

"No other people shall ever have our fire," they would say, and they guarded it with care, for they alone owned the precious fire.

"No one shall have it," they declared.

The human people wanted and needed the fire very much. Great chiefs and their wise councilors would sit and make plans, and more plans to find a way in which to capture the wondrous fire. "Let us call all the strong and brave men," the wise men would say.

So the great chiefs from all the land would command that all men come forward and try to capture the fire. The strongest would boast that he would go forth to the land of the Wolf people and force his way into their village and bring the fire back. He was strong. The brave knew no fear. He would go forth and capture the fire.

The wise one would say, "I will find a way to win the fire. I am wise."

The fastest would boast, "I will run off with the fire and bring it here to you all. I am fast."

One by one they would go out to capture the fire, and one by one they would come back with the same story. It cannot be done!

The strongest would say, "I could not even get near the village of the dreadful Wolves. They have guards all over the place of the fire. No one can ever enter their village. We can never have the fire."

The fastest would say, "I got so close to their village that I could smell the food roasting in their great fires, but I could not enter their great house."

The wise old one would say, "I'll think of a way."

The great chief was very sad. His best men had failed him and all the people of the land.

"What shall we do? What can we do? We shall be cold again this winter. We shall eat cold, raw food. We shall be blind by night when the moon will not give us light, and there is no fire to light the way. We must have the fire!" cried the great chief in despair.

No one spoke. No one moved. All had tried and all had failed. All the people were very sad indeed.

But there was really no great need for sadness, for all the while the great council had met — the many trials to capture the fire — young Ah-tush-mit, Son of Deer, had the real secret of how to procure the fire from the Wolf people.

All throughout the great struggle for the possession of the fire Ah-tush-mit had been gamboling about the beach, racing, leaping and hopping about on his long, spindly legs. He had seemingly paid no heed to all the great fuss about the fire.

He was racing past the people, as he had done so many times before, when suddenly he stopped directly in front of the chief and announced very simply in a small, small voice, "I'll get you the fire."

"You will what? What did that little boy say?" There was anger in the loud queries from the great braves and the strong men.

Then from the foolhardy ones a loud hee-haw went up — "Ho-ho-ho-ho-ho-ho."

"I'll get you the fire," the small boy repeated quite unabashed and not a bit frightened of the braves and the strong men, for he knew they had all tried and had failed to capture the fire.

The little boy stood there, so small, so tiny and foolish looking among the great strong men. The wise chief was solemn while the others chuckled and laughed.

Ah-tush-mit, the Son of Deer, began twitching his long, long ears and rolling his big eyes as he looked this way and that way — but still he held his ground.

"I'll get you the fire," he persisted.

At last the great chief looked up and said, "Choo — all right — Ah-tush-mit, my strongest, bravest, fastest and wisest have all failed. Do the best you can."

Ah-tush-mit called the womenfolk together.

"Make me the most colorful costume you can," he said. "I am going to dance for the Great Wolf chief."

"Dance? Who wants to dance at a time like this?" all the women wanted to know. "The boy is really foolish. He is wasting our time," they all declared.

"Obey and do everything Ah-tush-mit says," the wise old chief commanded his people. "Let the boy try. Give him a chance as I did to all of you."

Thus the womenfolk made him a headband, a sash for his belt, bands for his knees and elbows, and for his ankles too. All these were made from the inner bark of the cedar tree, and dyed the color of the young cohoe salmon — as red as red can be.

Ah-tush-mit fitted and worked with his regalia until it was just right. He paid special attention to the bands for his knees. He kept remarking these kneebands had to fit exactly right — not too tight, not too loose — just right so that he could dance well.

While he was paying special attention to the kneebands no one noticed that he tucked something into them between the bark and the skin. He worked with the kneebands and finally they were smooth.

"Now I want the best drummers and singers," he announced. "Come with me to the outskirts of the Wolf village. Do not enter with me. When I give the signal you must all run back home as fast as you can.

"We shall go before dark so that you can reach your homes before the night blinds you," he assured the brave men and women drummers and singers who were to risk their very lives to accompany him to the outskirts of the Wolf village.

At last everything was in readiness. Evening came. Ah-tush-mit sallied forth to capture the fire for the human people from the most dreaded Wolf people.

"Show yourselves. Do not hide or sneak in any manner," he warned. "The Wolf people are wise and cunning. They would be sure to see us anyway, even if we were to try and sneak in by the dark of the night."

So the odd little company sang and beat their drums with all their might and main. The Wolf people heard them from a long distance off they sang so lustily. One strange thing took place. Ah-tush-mit did not take the lead as everyone had expected. Instead he hid himself behind the company of drummers.

Finally the group of singers and drummers reached the outskirts of the great village of the dreaded Wolves. The huge doors of the house opened slowly, and the biggest, fiercest-looking Wolves bounded out to see what all the noise and din was about.

The humans could see the large fire burning and blazing inside the great house of the Wolves. They could almost feel the heat and the smoke smelled so sweet as they inhaled with all their might, for they had never before seen or smelled the fire.

What a wondrous beautiful sight! Great sparks

burst and escaped through the smoke hole on the top of the great roof. What a wonderful thing! So bright and beautiful in the gathering gloom of the dark night. These were the thoughts that ran through the minds of the awe-stricken humans.

Suddenly Ah-tush-mit sprang forward from his place of concealment. He was on all fours as he began his dance. He sidled towards the door of the great Wolf house. It was fast getting dark. The flickering light from the fire reached out to him and cast pleasing shadows all around as he danced and sprang about on his four spindly legs. Suddenly, he made the signal and the singers and drummers stopped their din abruptly and fled for home.

Little Ah-tush-mit was left all alone with the fire and the fierce Wolves. There were no more drums nor singers to give him courage, and he was very frightened. He was very, very frightened indeed.

He could hear the Wolf chief asking, "What is all the noise about?"

A Wolf guard answered, "It is only young Ah-tush-mit dancing."

"Send him away," the chief growled.

"Ah, what a jolly little boy! Bring him in. Do let him in," the Wolf chief's wife called out.

"Let us see him dance for awhile, then send him home," the chief agreed.

Ah-tush-mit increased the pace of his dance. Towards the great doors he pranced, hopping straight up and down, with no bend to his knees. Hop, hop, hop, hop, he went, sidling ever closer to the opening of the doorway, and as he circled around he sang a rollicking ditty:

Kiyaaa tlin, tlin, tlin, tlin,
Kiyaaa tlin, tlin, tlin, tlin,
Ooo nootl sahshh keeyah-qwa-yup qwatlin,
Hee yah ahh haaa ya-yaulk tah khaus ti-nah-is,
Kiyaaa, tlin, tlin, tlin, tlin,
Kiyaaa, tlin, tlin, tlin, tlin,
Break, crack, crack, crack, crack,
Break, crack, crack, crack, crack,
Do I break yon stakes with these I wear?
My flints, my sandstone hooves,
Break, crack, crack, crack, crack,
Break, crack, crack, crack, crack,

Ah-tush-mit's voice was small, but he sang with all his heart. He sang with all his might. He was singing to capture a spark. He was singing for his life!

Hop, hop, hop, hop, stiff-legged, he entered the doors. Once inside he could see the fire burning brightly and all about it was a bed of stakes made of broken bones implanted into the earth, as sharp as mussel shells they were. This was what his little song was all about.

Ah-tush-mit danced with all his heart. He danced as he had never danced before. He danced so he might capture a tiny spark. Ah-tush-mit danced for his life!

"Kiyaaa tlin, tlin, tlin, tlin," he sang as he sidled ever closer towards the awful trap made with broken bones. Skirting its edges in a half circle, he danced towards a far corner, closer to the fire, but where the bones were neither so large nor too plentiful.

Suddenly he had arrived at his chosen spot and with a mighty leap he was among the broken bones, hopping higher and ever higher as he picked his way among the sharp spear-like bones. His sharp little feet seemed to fit around and pass between the dangerous bones harmlessly. His long shanks and slim legs kept his plump little body safely away from the sharp, sharp points and thus he was saved from being torn to shreds.

"Do I break yon stakes of bones with these I wear? My flints, my sandstone hooves?" he sang.

The Wolf people were completely fascinated. Their big and awful jaws hung open in wonderment. Ah-tush-mit had won the cheers of the Wolf people.

The little fellow's bright costume glowed in the firelight.

"Break, crack, crack, crack, crack," his little song floated over the great fire. "With these I wear my flints, my sandstone hooves," he caroled as he suddenly sprang right beside the great fire.

Ah-tush-mit sang louder and louder, he leaped higher and ever higher; he was dancing to capture a spark; he was dancing for his very life.

"Ah, what a jolly little boy! He is a dancer, a good dancer," the mama Wolf beamed.

Then it happened—as quick as a flash—before your eyes could blink. Ah-tush-mit had turned towards the roaring fire and with a mighty leap he sailed into the air—right over the roaring fire sailed he.

"Ho-ho-ho-ho-ho," roared the Wolves. "Ah-tush-mit is on fire. Ho-ho-ho-ho-ho."

Ah-tush-mit had indeed caught on fire. His little legs smoldered between the knees. He stopped his dancing and bounded through the great doors with a mighty leap. Once clear of the great Wolf house he raced for his life towards home as fast as he could.

All around the leaping, roaring fire the Wolves sat bemused. The whole action of little Ah-tush-mit had happened so quickly and seemingly without intent that they were taken completely by surprise. Before they realized what had occurred Ah-tush-mit was well away from the Wolf village. Ah-tush-mit, the Son of Deer, the fleetest of them all, had outsmarted the Wolves, the most dreaded people of the land.

With a spark smoldering between his knees he had captured the fire! With his sharp pointed feet, his flints and sandstone hooves he had successfully run the sharp broken stakes of bones.

Yes, indeed, with his colorful costume, his captivating dance, he had outwitted the most cunning people of the land. Ah-tush-mit, son of Deer, the small one, had captured the fire for the human people.

The secret something Ah-tush-mit had tucked between his knees had been a small bundle of very dry sticks he had gathered from the undermost branches of the spruce tree. It was this that had caught fire since it was dry as dry can be, and even some of the spruce gum still stuck to the twigs. When the sticks caught fire the cedar bark bands had smoldered until he reached home with the tiny sparks of fire. This was where the tinder had come from and where the human people first came to know about fire.

But Ah-tush-mit had burned himself. The inside of his knees was badly scorched. Thus it is to this day that the inside of all deers' knees is singed black. That is how the human people got their first fire.

In the growing season, when all living things burst out in bloom
Sit in the glade of the wood at eventide.
If your own heart be open to love be there for Ah-tush-mit
You will hear the thump and the beat of his little song:
Thump, thump, thump, thump.

George Clutesi
British Columbia

What Do You Think?

1. Why do you think a folk tale about the source of fire was told?
2. What does the story tell you about the way of life of the human people? The Wolf people?
3. Think of another title for this story and tell why you think your title is a good one.

Taking A Closer Look

1. Ah-tush-mit seems to be both boy and deer. What is there in the story to support this theory?
2. Why was Ah-tush-mit gamboling and running on the beach all the time the braves were trying to get fire?
3. What lesson would this folk tale teach?
4. Can you think of any other way that the human people might have got fire from the Wolf people?
5. Can you think of other folk tales in which a small hero outwits a large enemy?

"The Legend of the Oriole" and Other Tales of How and Why

Do you ever wonder how the sun rose, or how the Milky Way came to be, or why the sun is brighter than the moon? From earliest times such wonders of nature have amazed and puzzled people in all parts of the world. Often stories have been told to help "explain" how and why things are the way they are.

The Legend of the Oriole

A tale told by the Ojibwa Indians

Nokomis[1] loved the warm summer days. She was an old woman, and the cold made her ache all over.

But now it was summer, and the sky was very blue. The sun was bright, and the little ripples on the lake sparkled like small drops of dew. The birds of the forest were singing all at once, and the leaves of the trees were rustling in the wind.

Nokomis was going for a walk with her grandchildren. Today they were going to the big hill, about a kilometre away from camp. Bedabin[2] wanted to look for flowers, and Tawa[3] wanted to find lots of berries. Both of them wanted to watch the birds.

Tawa and Bedabin especially wished to watch the oriole. They had spent many hours lying flat on the ground beneath an elm tree, as still as possible, to see these beautiful birds build their long nests and feed their young. The male bird was especially beautiful, for he had a bright orange breast and a deep black back.

[1]Nokomis (no - KO - mis)   [2]Bedabin (bed - ah - BIN)   [3]Tawa (TAH - waw)

202

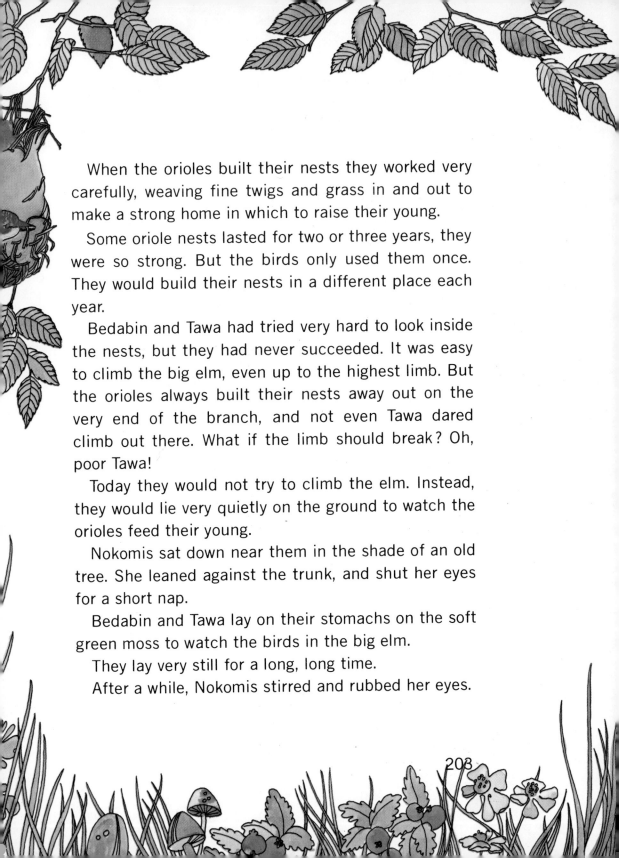

When the orioles built their nests they worked very carefully, weaving fine twigs and grass in and out to make a strong home in which to raise their young.

Some oriole nests lasted for two or three years, they were so strong. But the birds only used them once. They would build their nests in a different place each year.

Bedabin and Tawa had tried very hard to look inside the nests, but they had never succeeded. It was easy to climb the big elm, even up to the highest limb. But the orioles always built their nests away out on the very end of the branch, and not even Tawa dared climb out there. What if the limb should break? Oh, poor Tawa!

Today they would not try to climb the elm. Instead, they would lie very quietly on the ground to watch the orioles feed their young.

Nokomis sat down near them in the shade of an old tree. She leaned against the trunk, and shut her eyes for a short nap.

Bedabin and Tawa lay on their stomachs on the soft green moss to watch the birds in the big elm.

They lay very still for a long, long time.

After a while, Nokomis stirred and rubbed her eyes.

"Do you know why the oriole is such a beautiful bird?" she asked with a smile.

"Weren't they always this lovely?" Tawa wanted to know.

"Oh, no," said Nokomis.

At one time the oriole was a plain, gray little bird. His coat of gray was very dull. But he had a beautiful voice, and every morning he sang a song to greet the Sun as he came up over the edge of the forest.

All the other birds ignored the plain little oriole. The poor bird felt quite lonely. But he kept on singing to the Sun each day.

Sun loved the oriole very much for the beautiful melody with which he was greeted each morning. It made Sun feel very joyous, and he shone even more brightly than usual.

One morning, after oriole had sung his song, Sun said to him, "I wish to do something for you, because you have been so friendly. I will grant you one wish. Think hard before you make it, because there can be only one."

"I wish to be beautiful," oriole said at once. All his life he had wanted this, and he had known right away what to say.

Sun said no more, but went on his way further up the sky.

Later in the day, when Sun was almost directly overhead, the oriole flew over a pond. He looked into the still water, and saw a beautiful orange and black bird.

How surprised he was, and how full of joy. He could hardly stop singing.

"Now all the other birds will play with me, and I won't be lonely any more," he sang joyfully.

The next morning, because he was so grateful, he sang all the harder to greet the Sun.

Sun was pleased at the small bird's joy, and happy that oriole had remembered to say thank you. He smiled warmly, and said, "You are now beautiful on the outside, but your beautiful song and your beautiful soul give me even more pleasure. You will always remain lovely, as long as you continue to sing your song to the world.

"I will teach you how to build your nests in safe places out on the highest limbs, and no one will ever learn the secret of how you weave them there. In this way I will know that there will always be orioles to greet the sunrise."

—Retold by Patronella Johnston
Ontario

Why the Sun Is Brighter
Than the Moon

A tale told by the Lilloet[1] Indians

Once the sun was pale, as pale as the moon.

The sun saw a boy fishing. The boy wore a garment of feathers, and the feathers were bright. The sun said to himself, "If I had such a garment, I would be more splendid than the moon."

The sun came down to the boy. "Give me your feather robe," he said. "And I will give you my goatskin blanket for it."

The boy looked at the plain goatskin blanket. He looked at the feather cloak. "My grandmother made this for me," he said. "I cannot give it to you."

"But you can say that the sun gave this blanket to you. Is there anyone else who has a blanket from the sun?"

"My grandmother was long in making this robe," the boy said. "And longer in getting the feathers for it."

"Your grandmother can look into the sky every day and see her feather robe if you give it to me."

[1] *Lilloet* (LIL-ə-wət)

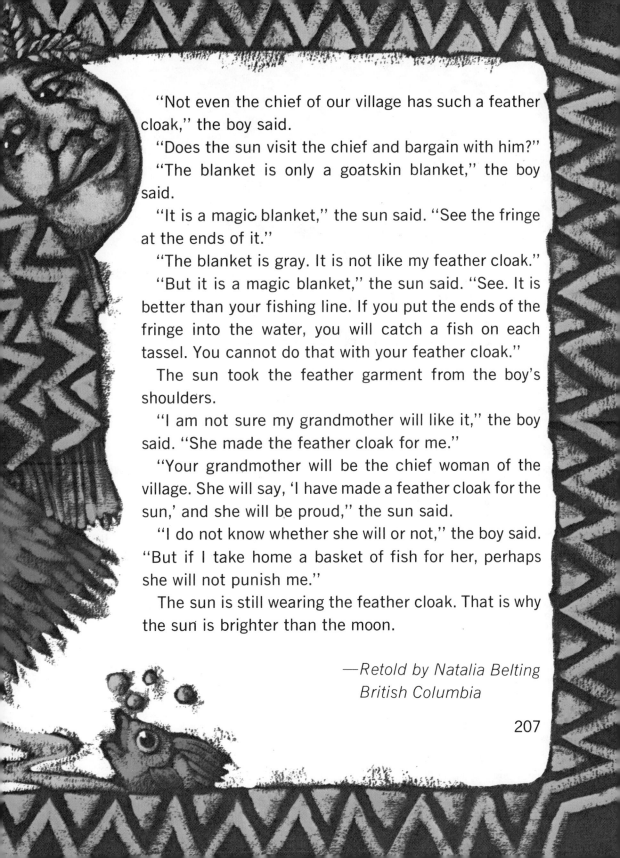

"Not even the chief of our village has such a feather cloak," the boy said.

"Does the sun visit the chief and bargain with him?"

"The blanket is only a goatskin blanket," the boy said.

"It is a magic blanket," the sun said. "See the fringe at the ends of it."

"The blanket is gray. It is not like my feather cloak."

"But it is a magic blanket," the sun said. "See. It is better than your fishing line. If you put the ends of the fringe into the water, you will catch a fish on each tassel. You cannot do that with your feather cloak."

The sun took the feather garment from the boy's shoulders.

"I am not sure my grandmother will like it," the boy said. "She made the feather cloak for me."

"Your grandmother will be the chief woman of the village. She will say, 'I have made a feather cloak for the sun,' and she will be proud," the sun said.

"I do not know whether she will or not," the boy said. "But if I take home a basket of fish for her, perhaps she will not punish me."

The sun is still wearing the feather cloak. That is why the sun is brighter than the moon.

—Retold by Natalia Belting
British Columbia

207

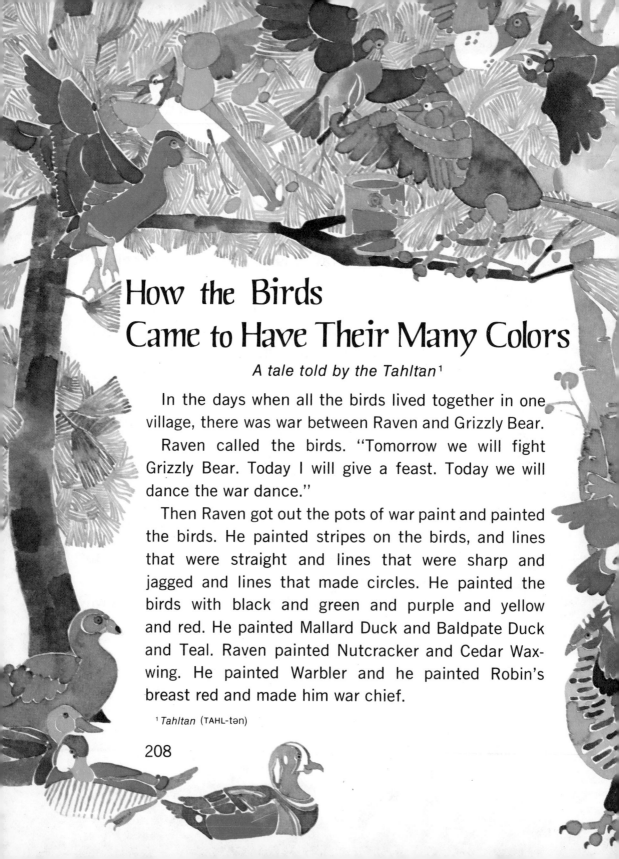

How the Birds
Came to Have Their Many Colors

A tale told by the Tahltan[1]

In the days when all the birds lived together in one village, there was war between Raven and Grizzly Bear.

Raven called the birds. "Tomorrow we will fight Grizzly Bear. Today I will give a feast. Today we will dance the war dance."

Then Raven got out the pots of war paint and painted the birds. He painted stripes on the birds, and lines that were straight and lines that were sharp and jagged and lines that made circles. He painted the birds with black and green and purple and yellow and red. He painted Mallard Duck and Baldpate Duck and Teal. Raven painted Nutcracker and Cedar Waxwing. He painted Warbler and he painted Robin's breast red and made him war chief.

[1] *Tahltan* (TAHL-tən)

208

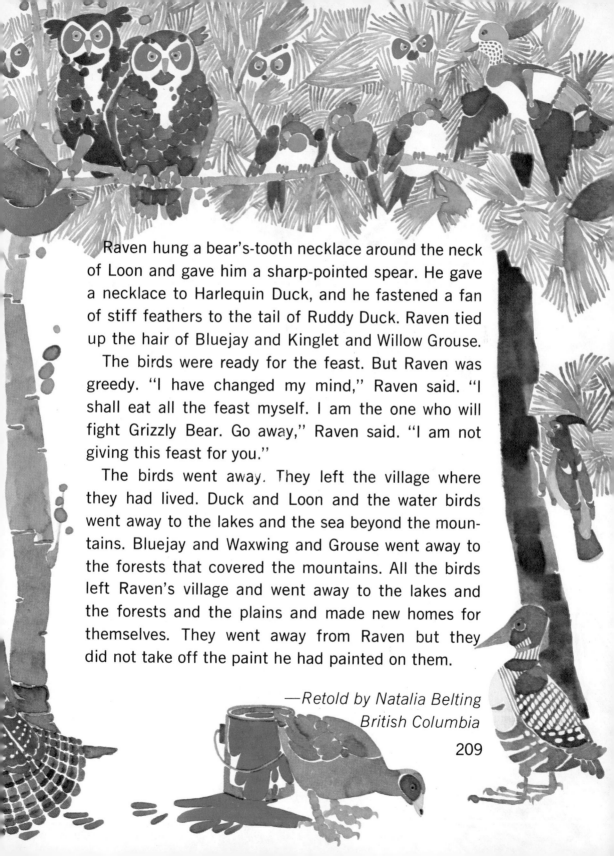

Raven hung a bear's-tooth necklace around the neck of Loon and gave him a sharp-pointed spear. He gave a necklace to Harlequin Duck, and he fastened a fan of stiff feathers to the tail of Ruddy Duck. Raven tied up the hair of Bluejay and Kinglet and Willow Grouse.

The birds were ready for the feast. But Raven was greedy. "I have changed my mind," Raven said. "I shall eat all the feast myself. I am the one who will fight Grizzly Bear. Go away," Raven said. "I am not giving this feast for you."

The birds went away. They left the village where they had lived. Duck and Loon and the water birds went away to the lakes and the sea beyond the mountains. Bluejay and Waxwing and Grouse went away to the forests that covered the mountains. All the birds left Raven's village and went away to the lakes and the forests and the plains and made new homes for themselves. They went away from Raven but they did not take off the paint he had painted on them.

—Retold by Natalia Belting
British Columbia

209

Nature Cannot Be Changed

One day, a rabbit and a monkey were talking together. However, while talking, each of them constantly gave in to his own bad habit. The monkey, of
course, kept scratching himself with his paw. The
rabbit, fearing to be attacked by an enemy, kept turning his head about in all directions. The two animals
were not able to keep still.

"It's really amazing," said the rabbit to the monkey,
"that you cannot stop scratching yourself even for a
moment."

"It's not more amazing than to see you always turning your head for no good reason," answered the
monkey.

"Oh, I could easily stop doing that," said the rabbit,
"if I only wanted to."

"Very well! Let's see if you can. Let's both try, you
and I, to keep still. The one who moves first will lose
the bet."

The rabbit agreed. And so they both watched to see if the other moved.

Soon it became impossible for both of them. The monkey itched all over. Never in his life had he itched so badly. The rabbit, on the other hand, was sure that some enemy was going to jump on him from behind.

Finally, when the rabbit could stand it no longer, he said, "Our bet did not mean that we could not tell each other stories to pass the time. Or did it?" "It did not," answered the monkey, foreseeing some trick on the part of the rabbit. The monkey was planning to use the same trick himself. "All right then, I'll start," said the rabbit. "Imagine, one day when I was in an open field, I was in terrible danger. . . ." "Strangely enough the same thing happened to me one day," interrupted the monkey. "Oh really?" continued the rabbit. "I saw dogs jumping through the field in all directions. They came from the left, from the right, from the front, from behind. I turned my head this way, that way. . . . You see? Like this. . . ." To make his point, the rabbit turned his head in all the directions he had mentioned in his story.

Of course the monkey too had a story to tell. "That day," he said, "I was bothered by a group of children who kept throwing stones at me. They threw one here, and another there. . . ." With each place he mentioned in the story, he gave himself a good thump with his paw to stop the itching.

The rabbit, who knew why the monkey was doing that, burst out laughing. Then he said to his friend, "Let us be frank. As much as we would like to, we cannot change our natures. This proves it. Neither of us has won the bet, nor lost it."

—Retold by Charlotte and Wolf Leslau
Sierra Leone

What Do You Think?

1. Which of these tales did you enjoy the most? Tell why.
2. Do you agree that nature cannot be changed? For example, could you change your own nature in any way if you wanted to? Tell why or why not.
3. What event of nature is the most amazing or puzzling to you? Create your own tale to "explain" this event of nature.

Taking A Closer Look

1. What questions does the tale "The Legend of the Oriole" try to answer?
2. What is the Milky Way? Try to imagine another explanation of how the Milky Way came to be.
3. When the boy came back to his grandmother with a goatskin blanket instead of her feather cloak, how do you think she acted? What might have happened?
4. Why do you suppose the birds didn't change back to the way they looked before Raven gave them their many colors?
5. Did the monkey and the rabbit really want to change their ways? How can you tell?

213

The Inuit, people of the arctic plain, were sick and hungry. They depended on Sedna to save them. But Sedna, spirit of the sea, had troubles of her own.

SEDNA

Winter's darkness cast
her shadow over the arctic plain.
The Inuit were hungry and sick.
They longed to fill their stomachs
with the tender meat
of the seal and walrus.

Day after day the hunters
waited for Sedna,
the powerful sea spirit,
to release her animals.

The Inuit called to the Angakok
to work his special magic.
"Please help our people.
Ask the sea spirit to
send forth her gifts."

When the Angakok
chanted his magic song,
the earth trembled
and the sea churned.

As he listened to the troubled sea,
Sedna rose from the waves.
She paid no attention to the pleas of the Angakok.
Instead she told a story
to the man of magic.

"When I was young and beautiful,
I was wooed by many men.
But I loved only one.
His song was so enchanting
that I agreed to become his wife.

"Much later I discovered
that he was a cunning spirit,
a sea bird who had changed him
into a man. To take on human shape
he had shed his feathers
and removed his beak.

"We lived among the petrels, and their
constant chatter was like the cries of
a thousand winds. Oh, how frightened
and confused I became.
I longed for the peace of my village.

"One day I left the cliff nest
and returned to my people.
I begged them to save me.

"But the bird spirit was too powerful.
He made the dogs howl and caused
huge waves to swallow the huts.
Many people and animals died.

"'You must return Sedna to me,'
the bird spirit warned. But my
father did not listen. We climbed
into an oomyak to escape. 'Return Sedna,'
demanded the petrel, once again.

217

"My father shivered when he looked up
and saw the sky grow black.
Helpless against the fierce bird spirit,
he threw me into the icy waters.
I struggled to breathe
and clung to the boat.

"To save himself my father struck
at my hands.

"My fingers broke into little pieces
and fell into the sea.

"As I watched, I saw my fingers become
shiny seals, fat walruses, and great
whales. And so I became mother of
all sea beasts. Now I live beneath
the sea. I am a powerful spirit,"
she sighed, "but I am clumsy.
I cannot plait my hair."

The Angakok was moved
by Sedna's sad story.
He knew what he must do.

Quickly he plunged
past the ice floes
and followed Sedna
to the bottom of the sea.

He found Sedna in a dark hut.
The entrance was guarded by a giant dog.
Sedna was covered with seaweed,
and little animals crawled in her hair.
In a bitter tone she demanded:
"Plait my hair and rid me
of these animals."

The Angakok replied:
"Yes, I will do so.
But you must promise to send
your gifts of food to our people.
Drive the seal and walrus
toward us so that we may live!"

220

Sedna agreed.
She guided the seals up
through the breathing holes,
letting the hunters trap them.
The women prepared the seals
and cut off large chunks of meat
for the hungry people.
Joy came to the Inuit.
They gave thanks
before the great feast.

The sea was calm once more,
for the powerful mother
of all sea beasts was pleased.
She was grateful to the Angakok
for arranging her hair
and satisfied that the people
had shown respect for her bounty.

The Inuit know that
whenever there is
hunger and sickness
it is because the spirits
of the dead are unhappy.
The living must never forget them.

—*Adapted by Beverly Brodsky McDermott*

What Do You Think?

1. Do you think Sedna really helped the Inuit? Why or why not?
2. The story of Sedna is written like poetry. Is this a good way to tell this story? Explain your answer.

Taking A Closer Look

1. Why did the Inuit need Sedna's help?
2. Who had Sedna married?
3. Why did Sedna's father decide to return her to the bird spirit?
4. Where did seals, walruses, and whales come from?
5. Why was Sedna unhappy as the spirit of the sea?
6. How did the Angakok help Sedna?
7. What did Sedna do in return for the Angakok's help?

WHY the Sea is Salt

This old Norwegian folk tale, rewritten as a play, explains a mystery that puzzled people long ago. According to this play, why is the sea salt?

CHARACTERS:

STORYTELLER

RICH BROTHER

POOR BROTHER

OLD BEGGAR

POOR BROTHER'S WIFE

1ST VISITOR

2ND VISITOR

3RD VISITOR

4TH VISITOR

5TH VISITOR

6TH VISITOR

SEA CAPTAIN

MEMBERS OF HIS CREW

(The curtain is down. Storyteller strolls to center stage from left carrying a guitar. At center stage Storyteller makes a deep bow to the audience over the guitar, which is held in place.)

224

STORYTELLER:

There were two brothers as
you shall hear,

And one was rich and one
was poor.

The poor one stands at the
rich one's door,

A-begging of food and nothing more.

*(Storyteller returns to the left
side of the stage and sits
cross-legged on the floor as
the curtain rises . . . .)*

SCENE I

TIME: *Long ago*

PLACE: *A wood with the terrace of a house just visible
at right of stage. (The Rich
Brother and the Poor Brother
are talking. The Rich Brother,
richly dressed, stands on his
terrace, his back to his front
door. The Poor Brother is in
rags and stands facing his
brother, but in such a way
that the audience can see his
face, which wears a pleading
expression.)*

RICH BROTHER: This is the
fourth time you've come
begging, and I say I have
had enough. Begone and
don't bother me again!

POOR BROTHER: But, Brother,
I beseech you. My wife and
I are without a morsel to
eat. Help me this *one* time
and I will bother you no
more.

RICH BROTHER: *(Hesitates,
scowls, then throws up his
hands.)* Very well then. But
this is the last time. *(He
enters the house and reap-
pears with two loaves of
bread and a side of bacon.)*
Here, take this and begone.
*(He goes quickly back into
the house.)*

*(Poor Brother turns from the
terrace and walks down the
path through the wood. From
stage left, an old beggar*

enters and meets him on the path.)

OLD BEGGAR: In the name of charity, give a poor old starving man a morsel to eat.

POOR BROTHER: I have just been a-begging myself and yet I am not so poor that I can't help someone who is worse off than I. At least I have food and you have none. Here, take this. *(He hands over the two loaves and is about to cut the side of bacon in half when the beggar stops him.)*

OLD BEGGAR: Oh enough, enough! Do not cut the bacon. Keep it for now and your generosity will be rewarded.

POOR BROTHER: And how will that be? Surely you are hardly in a position to reward me.

OLD BEGGAR: I will tell you something. *(He draws close to Poor Brother as if to share a secret.)* Not far from here is the entrance to the underground home of the dwarfs. Go there with the bacon. They love bacon and I happen to know they have none, so they will want yours. But don't give it to them until they agree to give you in return a little hand mill, which they keep hidden behind the door. When you have it, meet me here and I will tell you how to use it.

POOR BROTHER: Thank you, good man. Now tell me how to find the entrance to the dwarfs' home.

OLD BEGGAR: *(Turning to point down stage left, while Poor Brother bends to follow the direction in which he is pointing.)* You follow that path until you come to a large stone and then . . .

CURTAIN FALLS

(Storyteller strolls to center stage as before.)

STORYTELLER: So the Poor Brother found the home of the dwarfs where they live down among the roots of these very trees. *(Gesturing.)* They wanted the bacon, just as the old man said they would, and they offered many fine things in exchange for it. But the Poor Brother wouldn't trade unless they gave him the mill. So at last they did.

(Storyteller returns to the left side of the stage and sits cross-legged on the floor as the curtain rises. . . .)

SCENE II

TIME: *A little later*
PLACE: *The path in the wood. (Poor Brother hurries toward the Old Beggar, who has been waiting for him. Poor Brother is carrying the mill.)*

OLD BEGGAR: Good, good! I see you have it.

POOR BROTHER: *(Grinning happily.)* That I have, and I am eager to know how it works, for surely this is a magic mill.

OLD BEGGAR: It is a magic mill. You have only to ask it for whatever you want and it will grind out your wish. It will keep on grinding until you say, "Good little mill, I thank you for enough." *(He shakes his finger under Poor Brother's nose.)* Now don't forget those words. "Good little mill, I thank you for enough."

POOR BROTHER: You can be sure I won't. And thank you, kind sir. This is my lucky day! *(He turns and hurries along the way he has come as the . . .)*

CURTAIN FALLS

(Storyteller strolls to center stage as before.)

SCENE III

STORYTELLER: Now the Poor Brother ran home to his wife. He could hardly wait to show her the wonderful mill. Besides, he himself was eager to see what it could do, for don't forget, he was very, very hungry.

(Storyteller returns to the left side of the stage and sits cross-legged on the floor as the curtain rises. . . .)

TIME: *A little later*

PLACE: *Inside the Poor Brother's cottage. There is a window without any curtain over it, a bare table with a drawer in it, and some rough, straight chairs. There is a door at right. All has an air of poverty and want. (Poor Brother's wife is sitting in front of an empty, cold fireplace.)*

POOR BROTHER: *(Rushing in.)* Look, Wife. Just see what I have here. This is our lucky day!

WIFE: *(Looking around, but not leaving the chair.)* I see nothing but a little hand mill. What has taken you so long? I am cold and I am hungry. Where is the food you went to get?

POOR BROTHER: *(Placing the mill on the table.)* It is all here. This is a magic mill. It will grind whatever you want. Speak, Wife, what would you like to eat?

WIFE: *(Getting slowly out of her chair and approaching the table.)* Sausages. I'd like some sausages and some good white bread.

POOR BROTHER: *(Leaning over the mill.)* Grind sausages and white bread!

(There is a grinding noise. There should be a drawer in the table which the Poor Brother now opens. The drawer should be facing away

from the audience. From the drawer the Poor Brother draws a long string of sausages, pretending it comes from the mill. Next he lifts out some loaves of white bread.)

POOR BROTHER: Look at this, Wife. (*He holds up the string of sausages as the grinding noise continues.*) And just look at this. (*He shows her the loaves of white bread.*) Didn't I say this was our lucky day?

WIFE: (*Overjoyed.*) Husband, husband, you are right! This is our lucky day! What a fine husband you are.

POOR BROTHER: (*Loudly over the grinding noise.*) Good little mill, thank you for enough. (*The grinding noise stops.*)

(*Poor Brother and Wife look at one another with joy, then they join hands and dance around the table as the . . .*)

CURTAIN FALLS

(*Storyteller strolls to center stage as before.*)

STORYTELLER: Now that they knew how to get all the food they wanted, the Poor Brother and his wife planned a feast for all the poor people of the town.

When the Rich Brother heard about this, he hurried over to the Poor Brother's house to find out where he had gotten the money to pay for so much food.

(Storyteller returns to the left side of the stage and sits cross-legged on the floor as the curtain rises. . . .)

SCENE IV

TIME: *A little later*

PLACE: *Inside the Poor Brother's cottage as before. Now there is a white cloth on the table. (Three couples besides Poor Brother and his wife are standing around the table helping themselves to the feast spread there.)*

1ST VISITOR: *(Popping berries in his mouth.)* What wonderful strawberries!

2ND VISITOR: *(Smacking his lips.)* Taste this roast beef.

3RD VISITOR: *(Smelling and then eating the cheese.)* I never ate such delicious cheese.

4TH VISITOR: *(Wiping her mouth.)* Nor I such wonderful cake.

5TH VISITOR: *(Reaching across the table greedily.)* I must have one of those jelly tarts.

6TH VISITOR: *(Grabbing up the plate.)* No you don't. There are just enough for me.

WIFE: *(Hurrying over.)* Let her have them. The mill will grind as many more as we want.

1ST VISITOR: Will it grind *anything* you want? Even money?

5TH VISITOR: Of course, silly. Didn't you hear them say it is a magic mill?

1ST VISITOR: *(Taking Poor Brother by the arm.)* Ask it to grind money, enough money for us all.

231

POOR BROTHER: A fine idea. *(He starts toward the shelf where the mill is sitting, when there comes a loud knock on the door.)*

WIFE: *(Opening door.)* Why, Brother! What brings you to our humble house? Come in, come in. You are welcome!

RICH BROTHER: *(Entering and approaching the table, too astonished to answer her greeting. Visitors step back as he draws near.)* What is this? What is this? How did you come by all this wonderful food? I gave you only bacon and bread.

POOR BROTHER: *(Approaching with the mill in his hands.)* By means of this, Brother. This is a magic mill. It will grind anything we wish.

RICH BROTHER: *(Reaching for the mill.)* Then I must have it. You must let me borrow it. I promise to bring it back. Yes, yes. I must have it! *(He seizes the mill and starts out the door.)* I promise to bring it back. *(He runs out.)*

POOR BROTHER: *(Running out after him.)* Stop, stop! There is something you must know. Come back! *(He stops in doorway and shakes his head.)* He must think I want to take the mill from him. See how fast he is running.

WIFE: Let him go. We can get the mill later if he does not bring it back.

POOR BROTHER: *(Turning to her.)* You don't understand. He doesn't know how to make the mill stop.

(Everyone stares from one to another, shaking their heads, as the . . .)

CURTAIN FALLS

(Storyteller strolls to center stage as before.)

232

STORYTELLER: *(Striking some chords and chanting.)*
The Rich Brother took the mill on the run
For he thought that now he'd have some fun.
But he couldn't make it stop with pleading or swearing,
So he's up to his neck in soup and herring.
(Storyteller returns to the left side of the stage and sits cross-legged on the floor as the curtain rises. . . .)

SCENE V

TIME: *A few minutes later*
PLACE: *Inside Poor Brother's cottage as before. (Villagers have gone and Poor Brother and Wife are seated at the table licking their fingers and looking well-fed, when the door bursts open and Rich Brother rushes in. He is wet and bedraggled and highly excited.)*

RICH BROTHER: Come, come quickly! It's the mill; it's your *miserable* mill. How I wish I had never heard of it! You played a trick on me, that's what you did. Now, come and untrick me!

POOR BROTHER: *(Rising from his chair.)* What happened? What did you ask the mill to grind?

RICH BROTHER: Soup, you fool. Seeing all the good food here made me hungry. So as soon as I got home, I asked the mill to grind soup and serve up herring. Now my house is awash in soup, my garden is flooded, and there are herring all over the house.

WIFE: *(Starts laughing as Rich Brother talks, then throws her apron over her face and rocks back and forth in a fit of merriment.)*
(Rich Brother and Poor Brother run out of the house as the. . .)

CURTAIN FALLS

(Storyteller strolls to center stage as before.)

STORYTELLER: The next one to hear about the magic mill was a sea captain who traveled back and forth across the ocean bringing shiploads of salt to his countrymen. He thought it would be a good thing to borrow the mill and have it grind salt. Then he wouldn't have to go a-sailing for a good long time.
(Storyteller returns to the left side of the stage and sits cross-legged on the floor as the curtain rises. . . .)

SCENE VI

TIME: *Some weeks later*
PLACE: *Inside Poor Brother's*

cottage. But what a change! There is a white, fluffy curtain at the window. There is a picture above the hearth and a fire glowing within it. (In a comfortable rocker sits the Wife wearing a fine gown and a lace cap on her head. Her back is to Poor Brother and the Sea Captain who are sitting on a sofa, legs crossed and at ease.)

SEA CAPTAIN: As I was saying, if you would let me borrow the mill, I could fill my ship with salt here and sail home instead of having to go to a very distant port each trip.

POOR BROTHER: You would be sure to bring the mill back to me.

SEA CAPTAIN: Of course I would. I'm an honest man.

POOR BROTHER: Very well, then. You may borrow the mill. *(He goes across the room to where the mill sits on its shelf.)* Here you are,

only there is one thing you must remember . . .

SEA CAPTAIN: *(Grabbing the mill out of Poor Brother's hands and not waiting for him to finish his sentence.)* Don't you worry, I'll remember to bring it back. I'll remember. *(He rushes out of the room as if he were afraid Poor Brother might change his mind as the . . .)*

CURTAIN FALLS

(Storyteller strolls to center stage as before.)

STORYTELLER: But the Sea Captain wasn't an honest man. No sooner did he have the mill aboard his ship than he ordered his crew to weigh anchor and set sail for home. And as soon as the ship was under way, he ordered the mill to grind salt. It began to grind and soon all the sacks were full and then the hold began to

235

fill. But the Sea Captain couldn't make the mill stop grinding.

(Storyteller returns to the left side of the stage and sits cross-legged on the floor as the curtain rises. . . .)

SCENE VII

TIME: *A few minutes later*
PLACE: *The deck of a sailing ship. (Sailors appear at right as the Sea Captain comes running onto center stage from left.)*

SEA CAPTAIN: Man the boats! Man the boats! The ship is filling with salt. It will sink; it *is* sinking. We shall all be drowned! *(They all go running off right as the . . .)*

CURTAIN FALLS

(Storyteller strolls to center stage as before.)

STORYTELLER:
The ship *did* sink to the
bottom of the sea,
And the mill kept grinding
as busy as could be.
It has kept on grinding with
never a halt,
And that is the reason why
the sea is salt.
(Storyteller plays a few chords on the guitar, then bows deeply and exits.)

—*Norwegian Folk Tale Retold*

What Do You Think?

1. Which characters in the play were greedy? In what ways were they punished for being greedy?
2. How does the play explain why the sea is salt? Try to find a scientific answer to this question.
3. Who is your favorite character in this play? Why do you like this character?

Taking A Closer Look

1. Do you think Rich Brother and Poor Brother were selfish? Do you think either of them was generous? Why?
2. The play doesn't tell, but why do you think Rich Brother was rich and Poor Brother was poor?
3. There is a saying, "A fool and his money are soon parted." Put the word *mill* in place of the word *money* in this saying. Now tell how the play proves this new saying to be true.
4. An actor should use his face and voice to show how a character feels. Say each line below and show with your face and voice how the character felt.
   a. Rich Brother: "Begone and don't bother me again!"
   b. Poor Brother: "Help me this one time and I will bother you no more."
   c. Wife: "This is our lucky day!"
   d. Sea Captain: "The ship is filling with salt. It will sink; it *is* sinking. We shall all be drowned!"

Tales of Wit and Wisdom

The wise person and the witty
person have always been
popular characters in folk tales.
As you read the three tales
that follow—from Viet Nam,
Africa, and China—decide
which character you admire the
most, and why.

THI KINH

Thi Kinh[1] was very beautiful. Her black hair was long and fragrant, and her big, dark eyes sparkled like living stars when she spoke or laughed. Young men for kilometres around had begged for her hand in marriage, but Thi Kinh refused them all, preferring to marry a poor and simple man from her own village.

Thi Kinh worked in the rice fields by day and attended to her household chores at night. It was a hard life, but Thi Kinh didn't mind the endless toil. Because she loved her home and her husband with all her heart she was content.

One afternoon Thi Kinh was sitting outdoors shelling shrimp for the evening meal, while her husband napped in a hammock.

Thi Kinh gazed fondly at her husband. And then she noticed that one of the hairs in his beard was growing in the wrong direction. She went into the hut and got a

[1]Thi Kinh (TIGH kin)

239

sharp knife. Then Thi Kinh tiptoed over to where her husband lay and bent over him, intending to shave off the hair while he slept.

Just then Thi Kinh's husband stirred in his sleep. The knife slipped and scratched his cheek, and he awoke with a start. When he saw Thi Kinh standing over him and holding a knife, he leaped to his feet in alarm.

"You were trying to murder me!" he screamed at the astonished Thi Kinh. "Murderess! Leave my house at once!"

Thi Kinh was so surprised by her husband's angry words that she was unable to speak. But several neighbors heard the commotion and came running to see what was the matter.

"Thi Kinh tried to kill me!" her husband told them. "Look at the knife! There's blood on it!"

Shamed by her husband's awful accusation, Thi Kinh bowed her head and began to weep. Her silence and her tears seemed to prove that what her husband was saying was indeed the truth, and Thi Kinh was told to leave the village and never to return.

Homeless and friendless, Thi Kinh trudged through the countryside. She did not know where she ought to go or what she ought to do. When she could walk no longer, she lay down beneath a tree and wept until she fell asleep.

The next day Thi Kinh came upon an old pagoda which had become a monastery. Thi Kinh stood very still and watched the brown-robed monks go about their business of meditation and prayer. The peace and the beauty of life in the monastery soothed Thi Kinh's aching heart, and she decided to disguise herself as a man and seek refuge within the monastery's walls.

She cut off her long hair, rubbed her smooth face with dirt, and rearranged her clothes. Then she went to the gates of the monastery and begged for admittance. Not realizing that she was a woman, the Superior of the monastery welcomed her and bade her stay as long as she wished.

Life was slow and peaceful within the monastery. As the days passed, Thi Kinh began to forget the trouble and heartbreak that had brought her to the monastery. She kept to herself and never spoke. None of the other monks suspected that she was a woman.

Several years later a baby was left upon the steps of the pagoda. The baby's mother was so poor that she could no longer afford to care for the child, so she had wrapped it in a ragged blanket and abandoned it to the charity of the monks.

When the motherless infant opened its eyes and saw the cluster of brown-robed monks peering down at it, it began to cry. Thi Kinh alone understood that the baby was frightened of the monks and wanted its mother. She knelt and cradled the child in her arms, crooning to it until it stopped crying and nestled against her shoulder.

The other monks stared at her in horror for now they realized that she was a woman.

The Superior of the monastery was very angry at having been tricked by Thi Kinh. He ordered her to take the baby and leave the monastery within the hour. Thi Kinh had no choice but to obey.

Although Thi Kinh was so unhappy that she no longer cared what became of her, she knew that the baby depended upon her for its food and shelter. And she did all that she could. She trudged from village to village, working in the fields, gathering firewood, and sometimes begging from door to door so as to get enough food for the child.

The long weeks of hunger, worry, grief, and wandering took their toll. Thi Kinh's beauty faded. Her lustrous black hair became gray. Her smooth cheeks and forehead were lined. Her once-sparkling eyes grew dull. She was thin and ragged.

At last her roaming brought her to the outskirts of the village where she had lived with her husband years ago. She was so changed that no one recognized her as she walked slowly down the street, holding a begging-bowl in one hand and the baby in the other.

A man came forward and dropped several coins into the bowl.

"You remind me of someone I loved," he said sadly, when Thi Kinh thanked him for his generosity. "I give you this in her name."

Thi Kinh stared at him. She knew the man at once. It was her husband!

"I had a wife named Thi Kinh," he continued. "I drove her away with my false accusations, and I have regretted it ever since. Oh, what I wouldn't give to see her again!"

Tears filled Thi Kinh's eyes, and her hands shook so that she could hardly hold the bowl. In a halting voice she told her husband who she was and all that had happened since she'd left the village.

When she had finished, her husband took the begging-bowl from her hands and smashed it to the ground.

"You will never have to beg again," he told her.

For at last Thi Kinh had come home.

Many years later Thi Kinh's story reached the ears of the King. He was so impressed by her courage and her goodness that he bestowed upon her the title of Quan-Am Tong-Tu,[1] which means The Compassionate Protector of Children.

And so she is remembered to this day.

—*Retold by Gail B. Graham*

[1] Quan-Am Tong-Tu (KWAHN-ahm TAWNG-too)

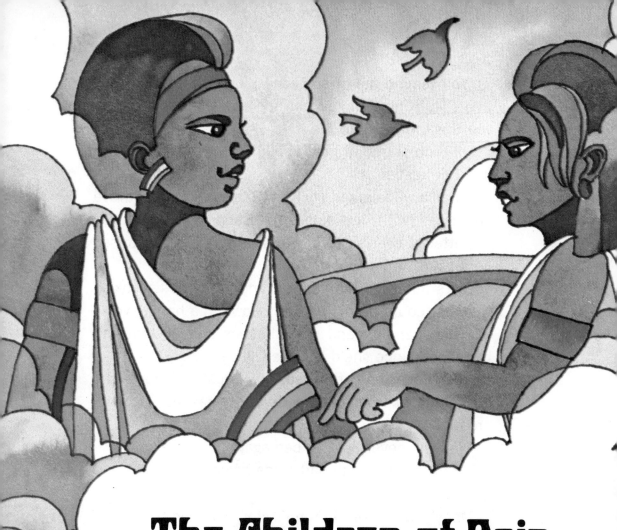

The Children of Rain

Rain was a beautiful woman who lived long ago where the sky grows rosy before the sunrise. She wore a rainbow about her waist.

Rain married a man and they had three daughters. When the eldest was grown up, she decided to visit the people on earth.

244

Rain said, "When you go to the earth you will find good people and bad people. Beware of the bad ones."

The daughter went to the earth, fell in love, and married there. So from that time on she lived among the people of the earth.

In time her mother in the sky had a fourth child, a boy named Son-eib. The eldest sister on earth did not know about this son.

Years passed. The two younger girls missed their sister. One day they said to their mother, "We would like to visit our sister on earth."

Son-eib wanted to go, too. But Rain was afraid to let all her children go. "You might get lost," she said.

Wolf was then living in the sky. He heard what the mother said and he approached her. "I will go with your daughters and your son and show them the way," he said. "I know the earth people."

So Wolf and the children all set out together.

But Wolf had evil plans. As they traveled along, Son-eib could feel that something was wrong. He was worried. When Wolf and his sisters were not looking, he caught a pretty red bird and hid it under his belt.

They walked for a long time, many days and many nights. Finally they came to a large village where good and bad people lived. A woman approached. She looked Son-eib up and down. "This boy's eyebrows are so like my mother's," she said. "How can this be?"

Wolf was annoyed. "Don't pay any attention to him," he said. "He is not a human being, he's just a thing. We don't even give him food."

Son-eib was very angry when he heard this, but he said nothing. When the villagers brought food for the travelers, Son-eib did not eat.

Towards evening the same woman came again and said, "This boy has my mother's eyebrows. Let him sleep in my house."

Wolf was angry, and he shouted, "You don't know what you are talking about! He is just a thing. He must sleep in a hut by himself."

246

There were bad people in the village who listened to Wolf. They shut Son-eib up in a hut outside the village and fastened the door on the outside.

At last it was dark. The woman and all the other good people of the village were asleep. Wolf and the bad people crept up to the hut where Son-eib was sleeping and set it on fire. Tall flames rose to the sky. Son-eib perished in the flames. But a beautiful red bird rose up from the flames and flew through the clouds.

The bird flew to where Rain lived and sat in a tree beside her. "Son-eib's sister did not know him," the bird sang. "Son-eib is dead. He perished in the fire."

Rain called to her husband, "Come and hear what the bird has to tell!"

He came and listened. "What shall we do?" he asked.

Rain was angry. "Why ask *me* what to do? Your name is Fire! I am only Rain." And they walked away from each other.

A little later a small cloud came floating through the sky. It moved towards the village where Son-eib had died in the fire. Around the cloud was a rainbow. It grew bigger and bigger.

The people in the village were very much afraid when they saw this. They ran towards their huts. But there was no use in hiding. Out of the rainbow fire flashed down to earth. This was a special fire from the sky and it killed only Wolf and the bad people.

The rainbow then stretched wide over the earth, and a mighty voice was heard coming from the sky. "Do not kill the children of the sky!"

Ever since that time, the Bushmen say, people have been afraid of the rainbow. When they see it in the sky, they take two pieces of wood, strike them together, and shout: "Go away! Do not burn me! Go away!"

—Retold by Elizabeth S. Helfman

The Young Head
of the Cheng Family

In the Cheng family, there were a father, three sons, and two young daughters-in-law. Plum Blossom and Peony were brides of the elder brothers, and they had but recently been brought into the household. Both girls came from a village a few miles beyond the Cheng farm, and they both grew homesick frequently. Since they had no mother-in-law living, they had to ask their father-in-law for permission to visit their parents. This became quite a bother to the old man.

The next time they begged to visit their mothers, he said, "You may go, but only on one condition. When you return, you must bring me things I want. You, Plum Blossom, must bring me some fire wrapped in paper. And you, Peony, bring me some wind on a paper. If you fail to get these things for me, you are never to come back here."

Old Cheng thought that the girls would not accept these conditions for their visit. But they were so eager to get away, they would have promised him anything.

It was a long, hot walk to their native village. After a while, they sat down to rest by the roadside. When they began to think of their promises to their father-in-law, some of their happiness drained away. Before long, both girls were weeping noisily.

As they sat there rocking and crying, a young girl rode out of a field on the back of a big water buffalo. "Are you in trouble?" she asked.

"*Ai-yee, ai-yee!*" wailed the girls, and they told her of the promises they had made to their father-in-law.

Instead of grieving with them, the girl, whose name was Precious Jade, laughed. "Dry your tears!" she said. "Come home with me. I will show you how to bring your father-in-law exactly what he wants. And then you can go and have a happy visit with your mothers."

When they reached her family's house, Precious Jade gave Plum Blossom a paper lantern. "When you light the candle inside this lantern, your father-in-law will have his fire wrapped in paper," she said. To Peony, she gave a paper fan. "Wave the fan. There is some wind on paper!" she exclaimed.

The two young wives thanked Precious Jade again and again. Then they fairly flew to the homes of their mothers. There, they had a glorious visit with their little sisters and brothers, and they returned to their father-in-law happily.

252

"What!" he shouted. "You have dared to come back without the things I commanded you to bring me?"

"Oh, no, Most Honorable Father-in-Law!" exclaimed the young wives. "Here are the things you wanted."

The old man was astonished when he saw the lantern and the fan. He wondered how his flighty young daughters-in-law could suddenly have become so clever. He did not have to wonder long, because the girls soon told him about Precious Jade.

"What a remarkable young person!" he thought, stroking his wispy gray beard. "I should like to have her in the family."

At once, Old Cheng engaged the services of a go-between. Before long, a marriage was arranged, and Cheng's youngest son married Precious Jade.

When the wedding festivities were over, Old Cheng made Precious Jade the female head of the household. She was to take charge of everything.

Before the young sons returned to their work in the fields, they went to Precious Jade for instructions, as their father had ordered. She told them never to go to or from the fields empty-handed. When they went to the fields, they were to carry tools or seed or fertilizers. When they returned, they were to bring bundles of sticks for firewood. Her instructions were sensible, and the men followed them faithfully. So the sons kept the farm in fine condition. They gathered so much fuel that it was not necessary to buy even one stick of firewood that whole winter.

253

In the spring, Precious Jade told the men to gather up all the stones in the field and to heap them in the courtyard near the house.

One day, Yu Kai,[1] a man who went about the countryside to buy precious stones, passed the great pile of stones in the Chengs' yard. He had no more than glanced at the heap when he saw a large piece of precious green jade. In order to get a bargain, Yu Kai pretended that he wanted the stones to build a bridge. He offered to buy the whole heap for a trifling sum. But Precious Jade became suspicious of the stranger. Instead of agreeing to his price, she asked an unreasonably large sum for the pile. She refused to consider anything less. To her surprise, the stranger agreed to the high price she had set. He told Precious Jade he would return in two days to remove the stones and bring her the money.

[1] Yu Kai (YOH KIGH)

254

When the stranger left, Precious Jade looked thoughtfully at the pile of stones. They appeared to be quite ordinary, and yet she realized that there must be something of great value in them. Could it be that there was a gem in that heap of rocks?

The next day, Precious Jade sent her father-in-law to invite Yu Kai to a feast. She advised the men of her household to serve the best wine to their guest. Before dinner, she asked her father-in-law to bring the conversation around to precious stones, and to ask their guest just how one could recognize a gem among ordinary rocks.

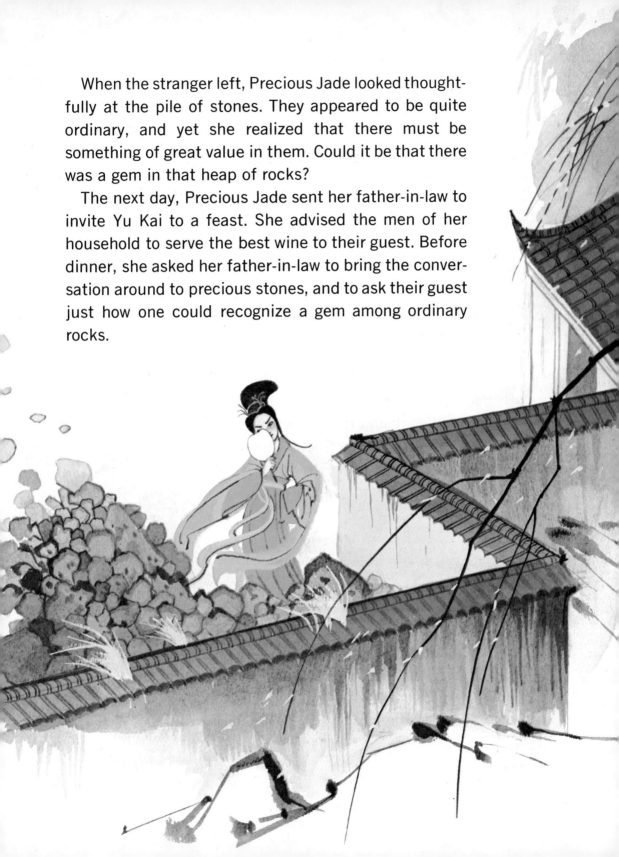

Everything was done as she instructed. And their guest proved himself to be very fond of good wine. After the feast the ladies left the room, and the men continued drinking and talking. Precious Jade hid behind a screen. When their guest had gotten pleasantly tipsy, his tongue loosened. In no time at all, the girl learned what she needed to know.

As soon as it was light Precious Jade hastened to the rock pile. She found the piece of jade and removed it from the heap.

When Yu Kai came to collect his pile of rocks, he saw that the value had departed from his purchase. He went to see Precious Jade again. This time, she bargained so shrewdly that she was able to get from him not only the original high price for the rock pile, but an additional sum for the jade stone.

Before this, the Cheng family had been well-off. Now they were wealthy. They built a splendid ancestral hall, and over the entrance Precious Jade had inscribed the words *No Sorrow*.

没 有 憂 愁

One day, a mandarin passed that way and noticed the remarkable inscription. He ordered his sedan chair set down before the Cheng door, and he sent for the head of the family.

When Precious Jade appeared, he was astonished. "Yours is a most unusual family," he declared. "Never before have I seen one without sorrow. Nor have I ever seen a family with such a young head. You are much too bold. Therefore, I will make you pay a fine. You must weave for me a piece of cloth as long as this road."

Precious Jade put her hands together and bowed respectfully before the great man. "I will begin weaving the moment Your Excellency tells me exactly how long this road is," she told him.

The mandarin gave her a long hard look. "I will also fine you as much oil as there is water in the Eastern Sea," he told her.

Again Precious Jade bowed respectfully. "Excellency, if you will measure the sea and tell me exactly how much water it contains, I will begin at once to press the oil from my beans."

"Indeed!" gasped the mandarin. "Since you are so clever, perhaps you will tell me what I am thinking. If you do, I will give you no more fines. In my hand is my pet quail. Tell me, do I mean to hold on to it or to set it free?"

"Your Excellency," Precious Jade said calmly, "I am an ordinary girl, and you are a mandarin, a great magistrate. If, sir, you know no more of these matters than I do, you have no right to fine me at all. Observe that I stand with one foot on one side of the threshold and the other foot on the other side. Tell me, do I mean to go into the house or to come out of it? If you cannot guess my riddle—you who are so great and wise—you should not ask me to guess yours."

The mandarin glared at the clever young head of the Cheng family. His eyes sparkled, and he laughed. "I can now understand the inscription above your doorway," he said. "The spirits of sorrow would not dare to pass over your threshold, for then they would have *you* to deal with!" Still laughing, he ordered his bearers to pick up his sedan chair and move on. And the Cheng family continued to prosper.

—Robert Wyndham

258

What Do You Think?

1. Which character in this group of stories do you think is the wisest? Give reasons for your choice.
2. Do you think any of the characters were *not* very wise or witty? What might you have done in that character's place?
3. If Thi Kinh and Precious Jade could have changed places, how might their stories have been different?

Taking A Closer Look

1. Why do you believe Thi Kinh deserved the title "The Compassionate Protector of Children"? What other title might the King have given her?
2. Rain warns her children to watch for good and bad people on earth. Which character in the story do you think was the most "good"? the most "bad"? Explain your answer.
3. Why do you think Precious Jade chose the inscription "No Sorrow"?
4. Find some of the riddles in "The Young Head of the Cheng Family." Can you think of some other puzzling requests the father-in-law or the mandarin could have made?
5. Which one of these stories could also be thought of as a "how" or a "why" tale? Explain your choice.

How does a rich person become a rich person? Is it by work, or by chance? Saadi[1] and Saad[2] cannot agree on an answer. And so they decide to put the question to a test.

The Maker of Ropes

In the wonderful city of Baghdad,[3] the city of peace, there lived two friends named Saadi and Saad. Saadi was very rich. He always said that no one could be really happy unless he was rich. But his friend Saad laughed at this, saying, "I am not rich. Yet no one in Baghdad is happier than I am!"

One day they were walking together down the long line of shops in the bazaar. They were having a great argument. Saadi said, "Anyone can become rich by working hard, if there is enough money to get started. But a person must have money and must work."

"That is the best way, and the most certain way," said Saad. "But it is not the only way. Some people get rich by chance."

[1] Saadi (SAH-dee)   [2] Saad (SAD)   [3] Baghdad (BAG-dad)

They went on arguing, until Saadi said, "Let us put it to the test."

They stopped outside a very small shop. A rope-maker, who looked very poor, was hard at work inside.

"What is your name, my friend?" asked Saadi.

"My lord," answered the man, "my name is Hassan."[1] He bowed politely to his important visitors.

"And you make ropes, I see. Are they good ropes?"

"Indeed they are," answered Hassan quickly. "There are none better in Baghdad. Fishermen and captains of ships come to my shop to buy them."

"Then, why are you so poor?"

"I have no money, my lord," said Hassan very sadly. "I work hard all day long, but I earn very little. I have only enough to buy rice for my wife Ayesha[2] and our four children, charcoal for the stove, and oil for the lamp. I can never save enough to buy all the hemp I need. Without hemp I cannot make my business grow."

"This is just the person we want," said Saadi to Saad. Then he gave a purse to Hassan, saying, "Here are two hundred gold dinars. I give them to you in the name of Allah.[3] I hope your business will now prosper."

Hassan was so surprised that he could not speak. He fell on his knees and kissed the hem of Saadi's long silk robe. Then the two friends said goodbye and left him holding his riches.

His first thought was, "Where can I put all this money to keep it safe?" There was no safe place for it in his

[1]Hassan (ha-SAN)   [2]Ayesha (AH-ee-shə)   [3]Allah (AL-ə)

little shop. At last he put ten gold dinars in his pocket. He took off his turban and hid the purse under the long folds of cloth.

Then he went out. With six dinars he bought some hemp. Then he bought grapes, oranges, and a large piece of meat. His family had had nothing but rice to eat for many a day. Then a terrible thing happened. As he was walking along the street a hungry vulture swooped down from the sky. It tried to grab the meat from Hassan. He struggled so hard that his turban fell off. At once the vulture leaped down on it and carried it away.

He screamed at the bird, and everyone in the street joined in. But it took no notice. Bird and turban were soon out of sight in the sky.

Poor Hassan! He had to buy a new turban, which left him with very little money. Then he went home sadly to Ayesha to tell her the story. She ranted and raved, but he took it more quietly. "It is the will of Allah," he said very sadly. "I must not complain. I must get on with my work."

A few months later Saad and Saadi paid Hassan another visit. They were surprised to find him working as before. He told them what had happened.

262

"What!" cried Saadi angrily. "Do you expect us to believe that? Who ever heard of a vulture carrying off a turban? What have you done with the money?"

"By Allah, it is true, my lord," said Hassan sadly. "You can ask along the street. Many people saw it happen."

"There are many strange stories of vultures," said Saad. Saadi, a kindly man, soon forgot that he was angry.

Taking out his purse, he counted two hundred gold dinars onto Hassan's bench. "There," he said. "Let us try again and hope for better fortune." He would not wait for Hassan's thanks. Taking Saad's arm he went quickly away.

Hassan stared at the gold, hardly able to believe his eyes. "How can I keep it safe?" he asked himself. "I will take it home and find a safe hiding place."

So he tied the coins in a large piece of rag. With great care he carried them home. Ayesha and all the children were out. He looked around carefully. There were no hiding places. He had only a table and stools and cooking pots, and straw beds on the floor. The only possible place was an old pot full of bran which had stood in a dark corner for months. He hid the gold deep in the bran and went back to his work.

Soon after his family came home, a peddler went from house to house selling washing balls. Ayesha wanted to buy some, but she had no money at all. She looked wildly around the house for something which could be spared. Then she said to the peddler, "How many washing balls would you give me for this pot of bran?"

"Four," he answered.

"Oh," she said. "This is a very good bran and a very good, strong pot. Could you not give me six?"

"Five," he answered.

He carried away the pot, while Ayesha set to work to cook rice for the family supper.

Very soon Hassan came home. He went straight to the dark corner where the pot had stood. It was gone!

"Ayesha," he cried in horror, "where is the pot of bran?"

"Oh, that old thing!" she answered. "I gave it to a peddler for five washing balls which I wanted badly."

"Who is he?" shouted her husband. "Where does he live? How can I find him?"

"I don't know," she answered, stirring the rice. "I've never seen him before."

Hassan pulled at his hair and his beard, and beat his breast. Then he told Ayesha about the two hundred gold dinars. She immediately got angry. "You fool! You should have told me," she wailed. "You should have told me they were there!" And all the children burst out crying.

"They are gone," groaned Hassan. "There is no hope. It is the will of Allah that we should be poor." And next morning he went off sadly to his work.

Six months later Saad and Saadi once again passed that way. They stopped at Hassan's shop. He was so frightened that he made believe he did not see them. Then Saadi spoke to him.

"Well," asked Saadi, "how is it with you, Hassan? Have you begun to grow rich?"

Hassan fell on his knees and in tears told them about the pot of bran.

"Stand up, man!" cried Saadi angrily. "How dare you tell me such lies? What have you done with the money?"

"In the name of Allah, it is true!" sobbed Hassan, beating his breast.

"I believe you," said Saad. "Many accidents more strange than that have happened."

He set to work to calm his friend. Then Saadi said, "Well, I have done. Now, Saad, perhaps you can show me how this unhappy man can get rich by accident. Money does not help him."

Saad took out of his pocket a piece of lead. He gave it to Hassan, saying, "I found this in the street just now. How much is it worth?"

"Nothing," answered Hassan.

"Then keep it carefully until you have a use for it. Perhaps it will bring you good fortune."

Hassan put it into his pocket and the two friends went away.

Late that night there came a loud knocking at the door. When Ayesha opened it she saw a woman whom she and Hassan knew. The visitor said, "My husband has lost the piece of lead which holds down his net. If he can't go fishing tonight, our family shall have nothing to eat tomorrow. The shops are all shut. I have asked all our other neighbors, but no one has one. You are our last hope. Can you lend us a piece of lead?"

"Very gladly," answered Hassan. He searched about in the dark until he found it and gave it to her.

"Thank you a thousand times," she cried. "My husband will give you all the fish he catches in the first throw of his net tonight." And she went away happy.

Next morning she came back, carrying a very fine large fish. "This was the only one he caught in his first throw," she said. "But it is the largest he has ever caught. It is yours for your kindness."

Thanking her warmly, Ayesha took the fish and cut it up for cooking. Inside it she found what she thought was a large smooth piece of glass. She gave this to her children to play with and went on with her work.

The children, who had no toys, played with the piece of glass all day. After dark they found that it gave out a beautiful light. Soon they began to quarrel over it. They made such a noise that Hassan stopped them to find out what it was all about. He told his wife to put out the oil lamp. To his surprise, the glass shone so brightly that it lit the hut.

"See how lucky we are!" cried Hassan. "This piece of glass will save us from having to buy any more oil for the lamp."

The children were so excited that they made a great noise. At last their father sent them to bed.

Now in the hut next door there lived a jeweler. He was too miserly to live in a good house, even though he was rich. Next morning his wife Rachel came to complain about the great noise the children had made the night before.

"I am very sorry," said Ayesha. "It won't happen again. I hope you will forgive us. They got so excited over this piece of glass which I found in a fish. It's pretty, isn't it?"

"Yes, it is," said Rachel. "And do you know I've got a piece very like it. They would make a nice pair. Would you like to sell it to me?"

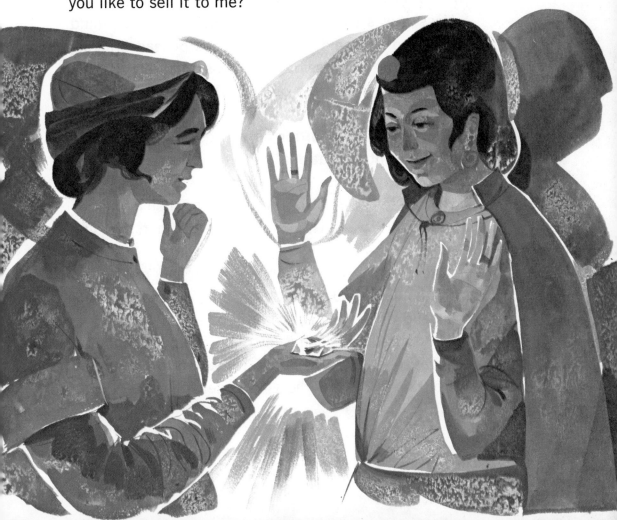

But the children, who had heard all this, did not want to lose their toy. They began to cry, begging their mother not to sell it. So to quiet them she said, "No, thank you, Rachel." The jeweler's wife went away.

She went straight to her husband's shop in the bazaar to tell him about the piece of glass. Then she went back to Ayesha. She called her out of the hut so that they could talk without the children hearing.

"Ayesha," said she, "will you sell me that piece of glass for twenty gold dinars?"

At that moment Hassan came home for dinner. Ayesha asked what he thought of Rachel's offer.

Hassan was silent. He was turning over in his mind what Saad had said about the piece of lead bringing him good fortune. Seeing him look so doubtful, Rachel said to him quickly, too quickly, "Would you take fifty dinars?"

"No," he answered, for he was growing very suspicious. "I want a great deal more than that."

"A hundred dinars," said Rachel.

Now he felt sure. "No," he said. "For such a fine diamond as this I want a hundred thousand dinars. Nothing else."

"Oh, that's an impossible price," she cried. "No stone could be worth it. Come, neighbor, take twenty thousand while you can. You will be a rich man."

"A hundred thousand is my price," said he, "and that is because you are a neighbor. If I take it to a jeweler in the bazaar I shall ask more—and get it."

"Fifty thousand dinars," she said.

"No," he answered.

She sighed. "I cannot offer you more for this stone," she said. And away she went.

It was not long before the jewler himself appeared. "Good neighbor," he said, "will you show me this diamond of yours?"

He examined it lovingly. At last he said, Rachel offered you fifty thousand gold dinars. I will give you twenty thousand more."

"No," said Hassan. "My price is one hundred thousand."

The jeweler argued and argued, but it was no good. Hassan would not change his mind. Finally the jeweler agreed. That night he gave Hassan ten leather bags. Each contained ten thousand gold dinars.

Ayesha fell into Hassan's arms, weeping for joy. The children all laughed and cried too, though they only half understood. "Let us give thanks to Allah," said Hassan. "I was wrong. He does not want us to stay poor."

Hassan would have gone on his knees before Saad and Saadi. He wanted to thank them, but he had no idea where they lived. He gave a large gift of gold dinars to the fisherman. Then he set to work to build up his business. He went to see all the best ropemakers in Baghdad to buy all the rope they could make. He promised to pay them quickly, and this pleased them very much. He built a large warehouse to store the rope, with a shop where people could buy it. He also added fine rooms for his family to live in. Very soon everyone in Baghdad knew him for his honesty and his riches. Now he and Ayesha and their children had fine clothes and enough to eat.

Some time after this Saad and Saadi called at his little shop in the bazaar to see how he was getting on. They found the shop empty. But some people told them where to find him. At once they set out for his new home and warehouse.

Hassan saw them coming. He ran to meet them and would have bent down to kiss their robes. They would not let him. Instead, they both embraced him. After he had thanked them most warmly, he led them into his fine house. Hassan seated them in the place of honor. He sent for sweetmeats, and for sherbet, and for drinks that were scented with rose water. Then Hassan told them his story.

"This is a fine tale," said Saadi. "But I do not believe it any more than your tales of the vulture flying off with your turban, or your wife's giving away the pot of bran. I am sure that it was the four hundred dinars I gave you which have made you rich. But never mind. All that matters is that you have succeeded. I am very glad."

"Nonsense!" cried Saad, with a laugh. "I am sure that all three stories are true. It was my piece of lead which brought him good fortune."

"My lords," said Hassan, "it is now growing late. If you would honor my poor house by staying the night, I

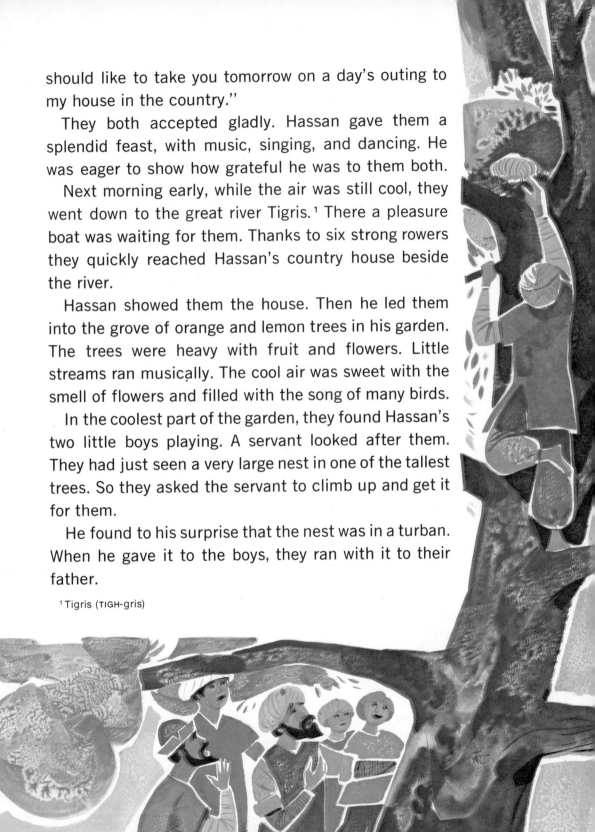

should like to take you tomorrow on a day's outing to my house in the country.''

They both accepted gladly. Hassan gave them a splendid feast, with music, singing, and dancing. He was eager to show how grateful he was to them both.

Next morning early, while the air was still cool, they went down to the great river Tigris.[1] There a pleasure boat was waiting for them. Thanks to six strong rowers they quickly reached Hassan's country house beside the river.

Hassan showed them the house. Then he led them into the grove of orange and lemon trees in his garden. The trees were heavy with fruit and flowers. Little streams ran musically. The cool air was sweet with the smell of flowers and filled with the song of many birds.

In the coolest part of the garden, they found Hassan's two little boys playing. A servant looked after them. They had just seen a very large nest in one of the tallest trees. So they asked the servant to climb up and get it for them.

He found to his surprise that the nest was in a turban. When he gave it to the boys, they ran with it to their father.

₁ Tigris (TIGH-gris)

Hassan knew it at once. He showed it to his two guests. "My lords," he said. "Do you think this turban has been long in that tree?"

"It looks as though it has been there for many months," answered Saadi. "And the nest inside it is an old one."

"Let us sit down," said Hassan. He led them to a stone seat. There he took out the nest, while they watched. He unwound the cloth of the turban until a large purse fell out of it. It was the same large purse which Saadi had given him on his first visit.

Hassan emptied the purse on the bench. Then he asked Saadi to count the coins. There were a hundred and ninety gold dinars.

"This," said Hassan, "is the turban which the vulture flew away with."

"There can be no question about it," said Saadi. "You have shown us, friend Hassan, that your first tale was true. I believe now that the other tales were true also. I hope you will forgive me for not having believed you."

"I will gladly," answered Hassan. "For I owe all my good fortune to you and Saad."

Saadi turned to Saad and said with a smile, "This has shown that I was wrong and you were right. A person may sometimes get rich by a lucky chance."

—John Hampden

What Do You Think?

1. Would you pick Saad or Saadi for a friend? Give reasons for your choice.
2. Which saying do you agree with more: "Some people get rich by chance" or "Anyone can become rich by working hard"? Explain your answer.
3. Do you believe Hassan's good fortune changed his nature? Explain your answer.

Taking A Closer Look

1. Find parts of the story that show it takes place in another country.
2. Name some ways fishermen and captains of ships could use the ropes Hassan made.
3. Which of the three stories Hassan told Saadi and Saad would you find the hardest to believe? Why?
4. How did the piece of lead help Hassan to become rich?
5. Compare the way the members of Hassan's family lived at the beginning of the story with the way they lived at the end. In what ways do you think the new wealth made the most difference to Hassan's family?

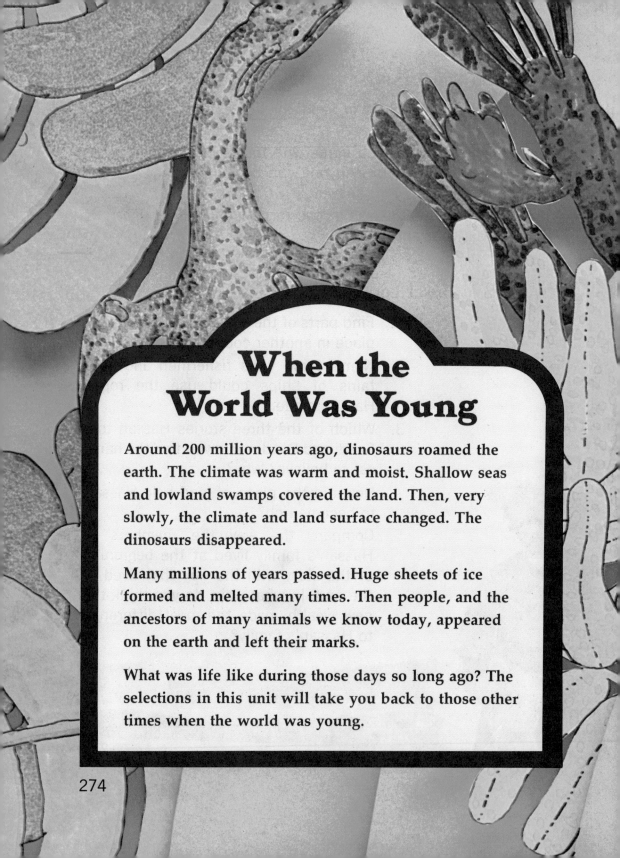

When the World Was Young

Around 200 million years ago, dinosaurs roamed the earth. The climate was warm and moist. Shallow seas and lowland swamps covered the land. Then, very slowly, the climate and land surface changed. The dinosaurs disappeared.

Many millions of years passed. Huge sheets of ice formed and melted many times. Then people, and the ancestors of many animals we know today, appeared on the earth and left their marks.

What was life like during those days so long ago? The selections in this unit will take you back to those other times when the world was young.

The dinosaurs ruled the earth for a longer period of time than any other creatures. Some dinosaurs were the most powerful animals ever to live on this planet. Then why do we not see dinosaurs today? Why did they disappear from the earth? Perhaps in this story you will find some clues to an answer.

The Battle of the Dinosaurs

Triceratops[1]

"Three-Horned Face" really describes this great ugly beast. It was the last of the horned dinosaurs, and a powerful fighter.

Triceratops was sometimes over 9 m long. Its legs were heavy and strong, with the hind legs longer than the front ones. It stood about 2.5 m high at the hips. But its head was the thing to fear most. With it the dinosaur could drive a punishing wound into its enemies.

Three-Horns' head was almost one third the length of its body. A frill fanned out over neck and shoulders like a curved shield of bone. Jutting out from this shield were long pointed horns. They grew straight out from

[1]*Triceratops* (trigh-SEHR-ə-tops)

above the eyes. A smaller, thicker horn grew above the nose. Below that was a beak, like a parrot's, but much larger.

Though Three-Horns ate plants, it was far from a gentle animal. Nature had given Three-Horns wonderful weapons. And it was quick to use them. Some of its fossil bones show many scars. You can see that this was an animal who lived to fight another day.

Triceratops must have had a frightening charge, rather like the rhinoceros of today. Its neck muscles were powerful, its body and legs massive. When Three-Horns matched its swordlike horns against the dagger teeth of *Tyrannosaurus*,[1] there must have been a battle that shook the earth!

[1]*Tyrannosaurus* (ti-ran-ə-SAWR-uhss)

Tyrannosaurus Rex

"King of the Tyrant Lizards" is the name given to the greatest and strongest meat-eating animal that has ever walked the land. Lions and tigers are as gentle as pussycats when compared to this monster.

When you see *Tyrannosaurus*, you understand why the other dinosaurs had developed strange armor. Some had grown queer snorkels that would allow them to hide out in the deepest water. This giant, striding across the earth on two powerful legs, meant death to all others. *Tyrannosaurus* feared no one.

The Tyrant King was 14 m long. It was 6 m high when it walked among its subjects. The giant's hind legs were massive and clawed. *Tyrannosaurus* had a heavy tail with which it kept balance. Its little arms had become so tiny that they just hung uselessly. The two small claws on each "hand" were too weak to help the beast hold food and too short to reach its mouth.

278

This was a beast of such great appetite that it didn't even eat with its hands! *Tyrannosaurus* just snapped at food with its mouth. The giant would destroy and devour with that one mighty weapon.

Never was there a skull built to attack and feed on other giants like *Tyrannosaurus* ! In the first place, that skull itself was over 1 m long! The powerful jaws were hinged so they could open wide. And the jaws were armed with curved teeth that had sharp edges. They were like the blade of a saw. Some of these teeth were 15 cm long.

Tyrannosaurus could bite through the thickest hide and crush the most powerful bones. It hunted the smaller meat-eaters and the giant plant-eaters, even the armored ones. There were few dinosaurs who could escape those terrible jaws. Let us imagine what one of these prehistoric battles might have been like.

Fight to the Finish

The long summer of the dinosaurs is drawing to a close. Volcanoes rumble and there is smoke in the distance. These are warning signs of changes soon to take place on the earth. But the strange beasts who rule the earth know only that there are green plants to be eaten, and living enemies to escape from.

They clump through ferns and flowering plants. They move slowly, chewing on juicy leaves, enjoying the warm air. The world is a fine place for dinosaurs. And then there is a sudden stir. A few of the smaller, swifter, two-legged dinosaurs hurry past. They are running from something still unseen. A dinosaur with a duck bill pounds by on her heavy hind legs. She leans well forward as she tries to reach the nearby lake quickly.

Triceratops lifts her head slowly, and stops chewing. She, too, decides to move, clumsily, slowly. Only *Ankylosaurus*[1] stays where he is. Safe under his curved armor, he lies low, hoping the danger will pass.

And then the cause of all this stir appears. *Tyrannosaurus* comes crashing through a grove of young oak trees, towering as tall as some of them. His great jaws are open and ready as he strides heavily across the green ground.

His little eyes catch sight of *Ankylosaurus*. He bounds over toward him, his jaws opening wider. The

[1]*Ankylosaurus* (ANG-ki-loh-sor-əs)

280

Tyrant King's tiny arms are useless. So he lowers his great head and prepares to attack with his teeth.

The huge sharp teeth strike the armored back of *Ankylosaurus*. But they make no mark on this fortress of bone. Instead, *Ankylosaurus* swings his heavy club of a tail. There is a sharp crack as it connects with the Tyrant's jaw. A tooth breaks, and the great animal backs off. He grunts in pain and anger. *Ankylosaurus* is evidently not good to eat!

The little red eyes look for other game. They glow as they see *Triceratops* moving behind a bush. Three giant strides of *Tyrannosaurus*' huge legs and he is almost upon Three-Horns. But Three-Horns knows better than to try to run away. Her strong point is not speed.

Triceratops turns to face her towering enemy. There stands *Tyrannosaurus*, more than twice as tall as *Triceratops*. He has dined on many of Three-Horns' kind. Yet even the Tyrant King can be defeated sometimes by a desperate fighter.

Triceratops thrusts her heavy head forward. Her huge collar stands up like a shield above her neck and shoulders. But the rest of her is all too easy to attack. The Tyrant King swings his great jaws open. He starts to drop down for the attack. But *Triceratops* stands firm on her heavy legs and thrusts forward.

The long, pointed horns find a soft spot in the giant's underside. The earth shakes as the two great bodies clash. *Tyrannosaurus* stabs at Three-Horns' back with his teeth. But he does not get a firm hold. Three-Horns lumbers backward and gets ready to charge again.

There is a hush over the land as the two dinosaurs fight it out. The tall palm trees shudder as the earth shakes beneath them. But everything else is still. The plants are trampled flat by the heavy feet and tails of these beasts. And they are stained bright red where the beasts have spilled their blood.

The Tyrant King is badly wounded and his breath comes in gasps. But he cannot turn and run for his life. He is a slave to his hunger. Instinct tells him he must get meat in his jaws.

Once again, *Tyrannosaurus* snaps at the back of *Triceratops*. Once again, the long teeth cut to the bone. But *Triceratops* makes one last painful charge. The

282

three horns go deep. The terrible giant shudders and thrashes as he falls to the ground. *Tyrannosaurus* has fought his last fight.

This is a rare victory for *Triceratops*. Usually *Tyrannosaurus* gets what he goes after. But this day a lucky *Triceratops* limps away from the battle. She will carry the scars of her victory for the rest of her life. And millions of years later, her fossil bones in a museum will tell her story to us.

As the plant-eaters began to die out, *Tyrannosaurus* had fewer animals on whom to feed. And finally, even the mighty king died out too. His size and strength and terrible jaws were of no use to him in a changing world where he could find no food. In the end, the king was no greater than his subjects.

—*Darlene Geis*

What Do You Think?

1. Name four reasons why the author would call dinosaurs "strange beasts."
2. If you did not already know the outcome of this
battle, which dinosaur would you have picked as
the winner in the "fight to the finish"? Give reasons
for your choice.
3. How can the fossil bones of *Triceratops* in a museum
tell you anything about this dinosaur?

Taking A Closer Look

1. How do the animals fit their names: *Tyrannosaurus Rex*
("Tyrant King") and *Triceratops* ("Three-Horned Face")?
From their descriptions in the story, make up some other
good names for them.
2. List some facts that describe the earth when the age of the
dinosaurs was drawing to a close.
3. Scientists do not have all the facts about the disappearance of the dinosaurs. Using clues from this story and from
other books you have read, name some possible reasons
for their disappearance.
4. Why didn't the Tyrant King run for his life after being
wounded so badly?
5. Reread the last sentence in the story. What do you think it
means?

The Brontosaurus

The Brontosaurus[1]
Had a brain
No bigger than
A crisp;

The Dodo
Had a stammer
And the Mammoth
Had a lisp;

The Auk
Was just too Aukward—
Now they're none of them
Alive.

Each one,
(Like Man),
Had shown himself
Unfitted to survive.

[1] Brontosaurus (BRAHN-tə-sor-əs)

This story
Points a moral:
Now it's
We
Who wear the pants;

The extinction
Of these species
Holds a lesson
For us
ANTS.

—*Michael Flanders*

285

Was there really an "Ice Age"? Was there really a time when many parts of the land surface of the world were covered by fields of thick ice? And were there people and animals living in those days? How can we possibly know anything about a time so long ago?

THE ICE AGE

THE SECRETS OF THE WINTRY PAST

Slowly—centimetre by centimetre, metre by metre—the ice crept forward. From the far north great sheets of ice spread out, swallowing the land. From the high mountains rivers of ice reached down and filled the valleys.

All things gave way before the ice.

Ice ground up rock. It carved the sides of mountains. It dug great hollows in the earth. It scooped up dirt, gravel, stones, and boulders. Whole forests fell, trees snapping like toothpicks before the flow of ice.

287

There was snow, driven by howling winds. There was rain that fell and froze. The ice grew thousands of metres thick. And growing, it pushed farther south. Year after year it flowed on, covering meadows, lakes, and hills.

The ice was felt far away, for winds sweeping across it carried the cold of winter to the land ahead. All living things fled before the cold—or died.

And this went on for thousands of years.

Sometimes the ice would melt at the edges and shrink back. Then the forward flow would start again. Creeping, grinding, carving, scraping, the ice of ever-winter would swallow the land.

Finally the great tongues of ice, the great sheets of ice, drew back for good, leaving behind their floods of melt-water.

In time, life came back to the land, for the ice was gone. It had drawn back to the far north, back to the mountain heights.

The land, of course, was changed. There were new lakes and rivers born of melting ice. Ice had carved out hills and valleys. There was land scraped bare of soil. There was land made rich by soil the ice had dropped.

On this ice-free land, plants grew and spread. Animals came to live on it. And people followed the animals.

Thousands of years passed. People made the land theirs. They grazed herds, planted crops, and built cities where once sheets of ice had glittered in the sun. And no one guessed the wintry secrets of the past.

THE SECRETS ARE UNLOCKED

The earth holds many secrets of its past. For thousands of years the Ice Age, the time of ever-winter, was one of those secrets. Only two hundred years ago people still did not dream that thick sheets of ice had once covered a third of the earth's land.

In the places where people lived, there was no year-round ice. In winter snow might fall and water freeze. But the spring sun melted the snow and ice and called the land to life, making it green with plants. This same thing happened year after year.

In some parts of the world there were glaciers, big masses of ice that did not melt away in summer. But glaciers were found only in the far, cold places — in polar lands and in the high mountains. There the glaciers were, and there they stayed.

The only people who had ever known about the ice were those who lived during the Ice Age. Some saw the ice. Some fled the floods when the glaciers began to shrink and melt. But these were early people who could not write, and they left no record of the ice or floods. What they had seen and known became forgotten. People who lived later did not learn of it.

And so it happened that two hundred years ago the Ice Age was still a secret. No one knew that it had taken place. Yet the story of the Ice Age had been written. It had been written, not by people, but by the ice itself. Where the ice had been, it left its marks upon the land. By learning to read these marks, scientists discovered the Ice Age.

There were, for example, many puzzling boulders. These boulders were puzzling because they did not match any kind of rock in the place where they were found. It was clear that something must have carried them kilometres from the place where they had formed.

Scientists had wondered about these boulders for years. Most scientists thought that a great and sudden flood must have carried and dropped the boulders. Then, in the early 1800's, a new idea was put forward. Perhaps, some scientists said, glaciers had carried the boulders. Perhaps these glaciers once reached down from the mountains, scooping up rocks and carrying them along. When the glaciers melted and shrank, they dropped the rocks and left them behind.

Was this new idea true? To find out, daring Swiss scientists climbed the Alps. They camped on glaciers and studied them. And they made several discoveries. One was that glaciers move. In time, ice from the upper end of a glacier flows to the lower end, where it melts. Moving, the ice leaves its mark on rocky, mountain walls. It polishes some rock smooth. It makes deep scratches in other rocks.

The marks of modern glaciers were found in the Alps. The same kinds of marks were found in many

other places where there are no glaciers today. That was how scientists started to read the secret of the Ice Age, as written in the earth. That was how they learned of a time when sheets of ice and rivers of ice flowed over lands that are now green and free of ice.

Since that time of discovery, scientists have learned much more. They now know that the earth has had several ice ages. The older ones took place hundreds of millions of years ago. Their marks are very faint, but they can still be read. The last ice age is the one we call the Ice Age.

No one yet knows when the Ice Age began, but some scientists think it started some ten or twenty million years ago. It did not come suddenly upon the earth as a huge snowstorm. Instead, it began as a slow cooling of the air. As time passed, the air grew cooler and cooler, and the oceans also cooled. In faraway places, more snow fell in winter than the summer sun could melt. Year after year the snows fell and piled up. The weight of new snows packed the old snow into ice. The ice grew thicker and thicker.

With their great weight of ice and snow, the glaciers began to flow. Rivers of ice crept down from the mountains. Sheets of ice spread out over polar lands. Only an ocean could stop the ice, for glaciers are land ice and do not form over water. Where glaciers met an ocean, their tongues broke off and floated away as icebergs. But on land the glaciers flowed on and on, over mountains, hills, and plains. New snows fell on this ice and made it even thicker. The ice flowed on, covering large parts of Asia, Europe, and North America. In North America the ice reached as far south as where St. Louis is today.

Then something happened, and the glaciers stopped growing. They melted and shrank back, back to the far places of the earth. After a time they began to grow again. Once more ice covered once-green lands. And this happened four times during the Ice Age. Four times the great glaciers reached down. Four times they melted and shrank back. The last started to draw back about 19,000 years ago. By 6,000 years ago most of the land was once more free of ice. The land was beginning to look very much as it does today.

In the past 150 years scientists have learned much about the Ice Age, but there are some secrets they have not yet discovered. What caused the cooling and made the glaciers grow? What stopped them from growing and made them shrink? Why did they grow and shrink four times? Has the Ice Age ended, or will the glaciers grow a fifth time? Many scientists have ideas about these questions, but no one can answer them for sure.

Over the years scientists have also asked many questions about life in the Ice Age. They have wondered about the animals that lived during the Ice Age. Why did some kinds die out, while others did not? Why did some kinds live through the Ice Age but die out at its end? And what about early people? Did they keep away from the ice? Or did they find a way to live near the wall of ice and hunt the cold-loving animals? Some of the answers to these questions have been found, as you will see in the next part of the story. But you will also discover that many mysteries still remain about "Life in the Ice Age."

LIFE IN THE ICE AGE

There was a time when elephants crashed through the forests of North America, when camels lived upon the land along with horses, deer, and mammoths. Huge herds of bison, or buffalo, roamed the plains. Saber-toothed tigers sprang from hiding at passing horses or deer. Giant, shaggy-coated ground sloths uprooted trees and ate their leaves. The land was alive with wolves, lions, wild pigs, bears, and dozens of other kinds of animals.

Then the ice came. By the end of the Ice Age, three-fourths of all these animals had disappeared from North America. Some are still found in other lands, but some are long gone from the earth.

The Ice Age made itself felt in many ways.

To begin with, there was the ice, creeping forward, covering the land, and making whole forests fall. Where the ice lay thick upon the land for thousands of years, there could be no life at all.

Then there was the cold that moved ahead of the ice, carried by winds that swept the glaciers. Because of the cold, plants of the north kept spreading south, while southern plants spread farther south. At times when the ice melted and drew back, the plants spread slowly north again.

The shifting of plant life was important because plants are the basic form of food on earth. Many animals eat plants. Other animals eat the animals that eat plants. And people eat both plants and animals.

So when plant life moved, animal life also moved. In the last part of the Ice Age, whole groups of people moved too. These people were herders and hunters. Where the animals went, the people followed. And the animals followed the plants.

Of these animals, some kinds survived the Ice Age.

Some kinds survived in one place and died out in another. Still other kinds died out everywhere.

The saber-toothed tiger was one of the animals that died out everywhere. A big, fierce killer, the saber-tooth ruled wherever it lived. No other animal was its match. Yet the ice wiped it out, while animals that served the saber-tooth as food survived.

The giant ground sloth also died out. There is reason to think that early people tamed the sloths, which were harmless plant-eaters. The people survived, but the sloths did not.

The end of the mammoths is even more puzzling. Mammoths were huge animals of the elephant family. As cold spread over the land, some mammoths grew thick, shaggy fur. They became cold-loving animals that hugged the northern borders of the land. When the Ice Age ended, mammoths changed again. They survived the flood and the warmer times. Then they died out. Perhaps they were killed off by early hunters, who killed herds of animals by driving them over cliffs. Perhaps something else happened. No one knows.

To many people the greatest mystery of all has to do with horses. During the Ice Age, big herds of horses grazed the plains of North America, Europe, and Asia. In Europe and Asia horses survived both the Ice Age and its end. In America they did not. Yet American bison grazed the same plains as the horses, and the bison survived. No one knows what happened to the horses. But there were no more horses in the Americas until, long after, explorers and settlers brought them in from Europe.

There are also great gaps in what we know about the people who lived during the Ice Age. So far we do not know whether people came to North America during the Ice Age or only as it was ending. We do know, though, that 20,000 years ago there were people living in Europe. These people were cave dwellers, and they were skilled hunters and herders. They could not write, but they drew pictures on the walls of their caves, and they made carvings. Their paintings, like their carvings, tell a story of animals. To these people, animals were both food and clothing.

On the walls of the caves, long-dead animals parade. There are woolly rhinoceroses. There are mammoths and bison and horses. There are lions, bears, hyenas, and saber-toothed tigers.

A whole Ice Age village has been uncovered in Czechoslovakia.[1] Here Ice Age hunters camped. They made shelters and warmed themselves with fires. Piles

[1] Czechoslovakia (chek-ə-sloh-VAH-kee-ə)

of bones show that they hunted mammoths, rhinoceroses, lions, horses, arctic foxes, and reindeer. They killed small animals with spears. They trapped big animals by digging deep pits and covering these over. When a mammoth or a rhinoceros fell into the pit, the hunters killed it with huge stones.

Most Ice Age people lived well south of the glaciers. Some hunted near the edge of the glaciers. Perhaps some even lived near the edge of the ice. Certainly, they *could* have.

They had fire, which they would have needed for warmth. They would have found animals, which they needed for food. From the same animals they could have gotten warm furs for robes and clothing. With their tools of bone and hard stone, the people could have made clothing like that worn today by Eskimos.

Fire, food, clothing. The people would have needed one more thing—shelter. There were some caves, but not enough. Still, the people had the skills and tools to make tents. They could have felled and trimmed poles. They could have skinned animals, dressed the skins, and laced the skins around tent poles. There are tribes in cold parts of the world that use such tents today.

Did these people live near the edge of the glaciers? Did they see the ice move forward or shrink back? We do not know, but we are still learning. Perhaps the surprising thing is that we know so much.

—*Patricia Lauber*

What Do You Think?

1. What were the titles of the three sections in "The Ice Age"? Which section did you find the most interesting? Why?

2. Choose one of the mysteries that still remain about the Ice Age. Think of some answers that might explain it.

3. Skim the first section of "The Ice Age." Find some words and phrases that describe what the ice did as it slowly crept forward. Which words or phrases do you like the best? Why?

Taking A Closer Look

1. Think about this sentence: "The Ice Age made itself felt in many ways." Reread the first part of the section titled "The Secrets of the Wintry Past," and find four facts that explain this statement.

2. In the section titled "The Secrets Are Unlocked," find two of the marks that the glaciers left upon the land.

3. Are we living in the Ice Age today? Explain your answer. Then check what you have said by reading the last three paragraphs in "The Secrets Are Unlocked".

4. Skim the last two pages of the selection and find the things the Ice Age people would have needed to live near the edge of the glaciers. Do you think you could ever live near a glacier? Explain your answer.

5. The people who lived during the Ice Age did not write. How did they leave their story?

During the Ice Age, the area that is now the city of Los Angeles in California was warmer than the lands to the north, just as it is today. Animals living during that period came to this area for protection from the terrible cold. Some of the animals, however, did not fare so well, as you will see.

TRAGEDY OF THE TAR PITS

Imagine time turned back almost a million years. That was the beginning of the Ice Age in America. Great fields of ice covered much of the northern part of the continent.

The country near Los Angeles, California, looked much as it does today. In the wide valley at Rancho La Brea, trees and bushes were scattered through tall grass.

To the east, the thread of a river could be seen. Nearby lay several strange pools. Around each was a bare black patch of ground on which nothing could grow. The pools were half-liquid asphalt, or tar. Through them broke bubbles of oil and smelly gas. After a rain the surface may have been covered with a few inches of water. It was not good water, but one could drink it.

During dry weather a film of dust made the tar look like hard ground. The pools, the valley, and distant mountains shimmered in the hot summer sun.

A saber-toothed "tiger," just rising from sleep, looked over the valley. She stood at the top of a shaded hill. She was a powerful beast, the most feared killer of the country. She had a short tail and large front limbs. From either side of her upper jaw, two long teeth pointed downward. They were nine inches long, curved like sabers, and very sharp. No animal could stand against her. She wasn't really a tiger. She looked so much like one, however, that tiger is what she is usually called.

The saber-toothed tiger was ruler of the country. All of it belonged to her by right of strength and her terrible teeth. She stretched like a giant house cat and yawned. The lower jaw dropped, lying almost flat against her neck. This allowed her mouth to open widely. It gave her free use of her teeth as knives or daggers. Those teeth could cut through skin, flesh, and even bone.

The saber-tooth was hungry, but the sun beat down with blazing heat. Food in plenty moved about in front of her. She had only to select. But the day was hot, and she didn't want to push herself. A herd of mammoths lumbered along the skyline. They were like our living elephants, but larger. Their great ivory tusks, curving inward, were like bars of polished steel.

But mammoths were not favorites of the saber-toothed tiger. They were too big, their skins too thick, their strength too great. At any time they would give a powerful fight. Only a baby mammoth was worth the trouble.

At one side, camels were feeding among the bushes and small trees. They were big animals, larger than camels of today. Their hair was thick. But they had no humps of tissue and fat on their backs.

The saber-tooth looked at them without interest. It would take effort to track one down and make the kill. She wasn't hungry enough. It was a lazy day. A little more sleep would be very good. She stretched out on the rock. Her eyes closed, and her chin rested on her paws.

Half an hour later she waked suddenly. Some strange instinct brought her to her feet. In the valley below, her eye saw something move. Two huge, golden-brown animals were pushing through the brush.

Instantly the tiger's body stiffened. Her yellow eyes blazed. This was her favorite prey — the big, slow ground sloths. They were cousins of the small sloths living today in South America. Today's sloths hang with hooked claws beneath tree branches.

These ground sloths were larger than a grizzly bear. All through their skins were little pieces of bone. It gave them a kind of armor. Also, the hair was very thick and long. And they had great curved claws.

The sloths moved about, sure that they were safe. They were safe enough from most animals, but not from the saber-tooth. She could cut through their skin with blows of her sharp teeth. She must be careful of their claws, but that wasn't hard. The ground sloths were too slow to worry her. But their flesh was very good.

The beasts were working their way toward the black pools. They were thirsty. Water from the rain of the night before shone in the sun. They crossed the bare, black ground around the largest pool. Then they splashed in to drink. For a few moments nothing happened. Then slowly the bottom began to give way. Their feet sank into sticky tar. Struggling in fear, they tried to pull themselves out. But their hind legs only went deeper and deeper into the black tar. Escape was impossible.

The saber-toothed tiger had left her hill. She crept silently through the brush. Belly down, chin almost touching the grass, her body seemed to flow across the ground. It was like the smooth movement of a snake. With eyes blazing she watched the great beasts stuck in the pool. The time had come. In one jump, she leaped on the back of the nearest sloth. With a sharp turn the animal threw her off. She rolled over in the asphalt. Roaring, the saber-tooth turned to bite the neck beside her. But she couldn't raise her feet. The sticky tar held them in a clutch of death. For the first time in her life, fear gripped her heart. She tried to drag herself out. But it was too late. She was sucked down slowly into the deep black pool.

In the bare branches of a tree waited half a dozen great black vultures. They were watching the tragedy taking place below them. Huge birds they were, with bare red heads, large beaks, and wings 3 m wide. They were like the California condor that lives today.

Like all vultures, they fed on dead flesh or helpless animals. They didn't kill as eagles and hawks do. They waited until an animal died or had been caught.

While the sloths were still struggling, the vultures circled over them. One dropped down upon the surface of the pool. Then another and another. Croaking, they gathered around the exhausted beasts. In a moment their great beaks would tear out pieces of living flesh. But as each bird tried to move, the sticky tar gripped its feet. Like insects on flypaper, their wings and feathers were caught. Soon the vultures were only black balls of tar. Long before the sun went down, all trace of birds and beasts had gone. The pools shone like silver. The traps were ready for new victims.

The story you have just read is true. It is imaginative only in details. We know it is true because of the bones buried in the asphalt. Also because we can see the same tar traps today. The pits are not so large as they were a million years ago.

One morning I stood on the edge of one of the La Brea pools. A rabbit and a heron were struggling in the black tar. A hawk circled overhead, coming lower and lower. I watched it dive for the rabbit. It sank its claws in the animal's body and tried to lift it out. In two minutes the bird itself was caught. Such has been the fate of many animals and birds through the years. Often cattle, horses, and dogs have been caught. Some were dragged out with ropes. Others, not seen in time, died.

308

By this time the pits have been shut off so that animals cannot be trapped by the deadly tar.

The pools were first formed by oil that rose up from the earth in springs. Around the springs the tar remains soft. Elsewhere it becomes hard when mixed with earth and dust. In the Ice Age, the oil springs were more active than now.

Then people began to take asphalt out of the La Brea pits to make roads. They discovered thousands of bones buried in the tar. For a time, little was done about it. Then scientists at the University of California began to study the strange bones. Thousands of skulls and tens of thousands of other bones have been dug out. The bones are filled with asphalt, but they have changed very little. Of course, nothing remains of the flesh, skin, horns, and hoofs. The bones are mixed up so that the skeletons are never together.

The La Brea tar pits are the richest fossil deposit ever discovered anywhere. Nowhere else are found the remains of so many different kinds of animals. Nowhere else are the bones so well preserved. Nowhere else are they so easy to dig out and study.

In studying the La Brea fossils, people have discovered more than fifty different kinds of birds. They have found at least that many kinds of mammals, too. There are remains of elephants, camels, and sloths; of deer, bison, horses, and wild pigs. Three thousand skulls of the "grim wolf," and two thousand of the saber-toothed tigers, have been found. Also there are

309

bones of bears and lions and other beasts. Most of these animals have been extinct for thousands of years.

Most of the bones are those of flesh-eating mammals, birds of prey, and wading birds. The story of the saber-toothed tiger, the sloths, and the vultures gives the reason. The larger animals, caught in the asphalt, set the trap. They drew the others into the tar. Day after day this has gone on for a million years.

The remains of ducks, geese, and herons are numerous. Perhaps they were fooled by the sheets of shimmering water on the tar. They may have thought these were pools in which to swim.

The La Brea tar pits tell a wonderful story about the animals that lived in southern California during the Ice Age. It is a whole chapter in the past life on this earth, written in black asphalt tar.

—*Roy Chapman Andrews*

What Do You Think?

1. How does the word "tragedy" apply to this story?
2. There are two parts to this selection. One is completely factual. The other is partly imaginative. If the author didn't tell you, how would you know the difference? Think up good titles for the two different sections.

Taking A Closer Look

1. How was the Ice Age in Europe, as described in "The Ice Age," the same or different from the way it was at the La Brea tar pits in California?
2. Do you agree or disagree with the author when he calls the saber-toothed tiger the "ruler of the country"? Why?
3. Name four prehistoric animals and four modern animals that may be compared to one another. How are the pairs of animals alike? How are they different?
4. How were the tar pits formed? How are they different now from the way they were a million years ago? Why are they different today?
5. Find three reasons why scientists call the La Brea tar pits the richest fossil deposit anywhere.

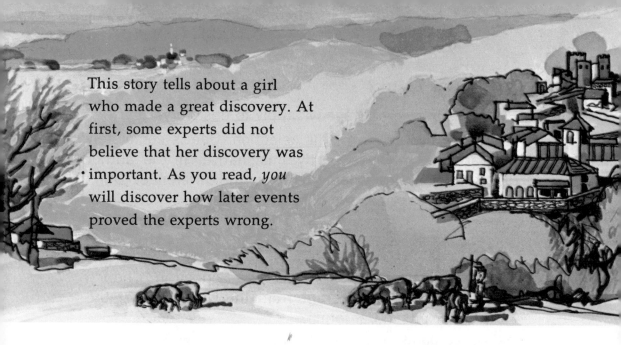

This story tells about a girl who made a great discovery. At first, some experts did not believe that her discovery was important. As you read, *you* will discover how later events proved the experts wrong.

A Girl and the Altamira¹ Cave

A girl only five years old discovered the amazing paintings in the Altamira Cave. This cave, in Northern Spain, holds important clues about prehistoric cave people. The story of how it was discovered is a famous and interesting one.

The girl's name was Maria. She was a daughter of Spanish nobility. Her family lived in a gray stone castle in the tiny village of Santillana del Mar.² The village is among the limestone hills that rise up along the Bay of Biscay.

The story really begins in 1878, when Maria's father, Don Marcelino de Sautuola,³ visited Paris. There he

¹Altamira (ahl-tah-MEE-rah)
²Santillana del Mar (sahn-tee-YAH-nah del MAHR)
³Don Marcelino de Sautuola (dawn mar-say-LEEN-oh day SOW-TWOH-lah)

312

tools and carved antlers found in France. He was so interested that he decided to search himself for clues about cave people. He also decided that a cave near his own castle would be a good place to begin. Northern Spain was near a place in France where many cave homes had already been discovered .

Before Don Marcelino left Paris, he asked about the proper way to explore a cave. He learned that he might have to dig through many metres of earth before reaching any signs of a cave home. He was told to dig very carefully. He must sift every bit of soil. He must be sure not to miss the tiniest scrap of bone or the smallest bit of chipped stone. Don Marcelino returned home determined to follow the directions carefully. He would be proud if he could find even a few stone tools or bits of bone. Then he would be adding to the world's knowledge of our prehistoric ancestors.

There was only one entrance to the cave Don Marcelino had chosen. It was a narrow crack in the earth in a rocky meadow. No one had known about the crack, or the cave, until a few years before. A hunter's dog had fallen into it and was not seen again. The crack was covered over so that children could not crawl in and be hurt or lost.

But now, when Don Marcelino reached home, he opened up the old cave. He went down a sloping passage. At the foot of it was a cave room of fairly good size. A passage a little more than 1 m high led off the room. The passage was too low to work in. So Don Marcelino started digging slowly away at the floor at the front of the cave.

Months went by. He was beginning to think he had made a poor guess. Perhaps no prehistoric people had ever lived in that cave. But one day in November, 1879, he found several interesting stones. They were neatly chipped into the shape of spearheads. That night he hurried home to show the stones to his family.

Little Maria saw the spearheads too. She couldn't understand why everybody thought the stones were so important. But she could see that her father was very excited. She decided that the cave must be a wonderful place. She told Don Marcelino she wanted to go with him.

At first Don Marcelino shook his head. He felt sure Maria would quickly grow tired of playing in a dark cave. But he was very fond of his little daughter. It was hard for him to refuse her anything. So he finally agreed to take her into the cave. She must promise, however, not to disturb him at his work.

Maria was disappointed in the cave, as her father had known she would be. There was nothing to play with. It wasn't much fun to watch her father scraping away in the dirt. After a time, with a candle in her hand, she crept into the low passage.

Soon the little tunnel grew broader. But it was still very low. Even a small child like Maria had to be careful. She might bump her head on the rough ceiling as she moved along.

314

Suddenly, glancing up at that ceiling, Maria stopped still. The candle wavered in her hand. All around her, in the flickering yellow light, there seemed to be animals. She thought she saw huge beasts with curving horns and staring eyes.

"Father!" Maria screamed. "Bulls! Bulls!"

Her voice echoed against the stone.

Don Marcelino dropped his tools, grabbed a candle, and crawled into the tunnel.

"I'm coming, Maria!" he called. "Don't be frightened."

But when he saw Maria, he knew she was quite safe. She was not frightened at all. She was pointing at the ceiling.

"Look, Father!" she cried. "Look!"

At first Don Marcelino couldn't understand what he was supposed to look at. He turned about to look up at the ceiling. It was very close above his own head. He could see at first only some black lines, and some splotches of red and yellow.

Then slowly, one after the other, the splotches and lines took on shape. He turned this way and that. Finally, he was lying flat on his back to see more clearly. Don Marcelino now knew why Maria had shouted out the word "Bulls!" Some of the shapes did look like bulls. They were huge staring beasts with curving horns.

Don Marcelino blinked his eyes. The more he stared, the more real the animals seemed. He could see that the paintings were skillfully done. The red and black and yellow creatures appeared to be alive.

There was one great beast with head down and hind legs bent under it. It looked as if the huge animal had been struck a mortal blow just before Don Marcelino first saw it.

Not far away was a red horse with a black mane and a black tail. It looked as if it had just touched the ground after a long leap.

Amazed, Don Marcelino looked from one picture to another. Red animals had been painted over animals outlined in black. A red creature was half covered up by another animal. The second one was painted in black and yellow. Its legs were set as if it were about to spring.

How had these paintings come to be made? The ceiling was so low that an adult couldn't sit up straight in it. Who had made the paintings? And when? Don Marcelino knew that only he and a few of his workers had entered the cave since he had opened it.

He tried to puzzle out an explanation for the figures leaping and striding across the rock ceiling. He began to see that the ones that looked like bulls were not bulls at all. He studied them more carefully. Suddenly he caught his breath. The bull-like animals were really bison. Bison were horned and humped animals that had disappeared from Europe thousands of years before.

317

The other figures on the ceiling were prehistoric animals too. There were wild horses, reindeer with long antlers, and huge wild boars. The animals were of a kind no living person had ever laid eyes on.

That was when Don Marcelino saw how important little Maria's discovery was. That very evening he wrote a long letter about the cave paintings. He sent the letter to scientists in the Spanish capital, Madrid.

He wrote that the paint on the ceiling of the cave looked fresh and new. He noted that some red even came off on his finger when he touched it. But, he said, no one skillful enough to paint these figures had entered the cave since it was discovered. And it was discovered only a few years earlier. Besides, he wrote, the animals were prehistoric animals. None of Don Marcelino's neighbors knew what such animals looked like. He felt sure that the pictures had been painted when there were bison in the Spanish hills. They had been painted, he said, by the same people who hunted those bison. They had been painted by the cave people of prehistoric times.

His letter brought a geologist hurrying to the little village of Santillana del Mar. He wanted to see the cave, which Don Marcelino called Altamira. At first the geologist thought Don Marcelino must be playing a joke on him. No prehistoric people, he said, could have painted those pictures. But when he questioned Don Marcelino, the geologist began to change his mind. When he saw the cave himself, he found some more of

318

the chipped stones Don Marcelino had found. He also found some bones of prehistoric animals. So the expert decided the amateur was right. At once he returned to Madrid to make a public announcement of Maria's discovery.

Maria and the little village in which she lived became famous. Every day people came to visit the Altamira cave. Even the King of Spain arrived to admire the paintings. He wished to praise the little girl who had found them. Copies of the paintings were prepared for a great meeting of scientists from all over the world. The meeting was soon to be held in Lisbon,[1] Portugal. Those coming to the Lisbon meeting were invited to visit Altamira.

[1] Lisbon (LIZ-bən)

Then that meeting took place, and suddenly everything changed. The scientists in Lisbon said they didn't even have to look at the pictures. They were sure that the story of Altamira was a hoax.

Once more Santillana del Mar became a quiet village. No one came to visit it after the experts had their say. The newspapers that had been praising Don Marcelino and his little daughter now made fun of them. Experts refused to answer Don Marcelino's letters. They also refused to let him attend their meetings to tell them about Altamira.

Finally Don Marcelino sealed up the opening to the cave.

Years passed. Maria de Sautuola grew up. After Don Marcelino died, she was one of the few people who even remembered the cave. She was also among the few who remembered when Altamira had been the pride of Spain.

In the meantime, French prehistorians were exploring caves in their country. They were discovering more and more about cave people. They dug down through the layers of debris that filled some of the caves. There they found hundreds of bones and stone tools. Sometimes their digging even exposed drawings on the walls. But the drawings were so simple that they could have been made only by cave people. In fact, these drawings were exactly what most people expected of cave people. Nobody connected them with the paintings the King of Spain had admired as works of art.

Then, in 1901, French experts began to clear the debris from two caves close to the village of Cro-Magnon.[1] This is the village where young Louis Lartet[2] first found the five skeletons of Cro-Magnon man. Each centimetre of soil revealed another centimetre of cave wall. In time they reached the original floors of the two caves. They had dug away debris that had been undisturbed for thousands of years. The walls they now saw had been covered up all that time. And the walls were decorated!

On the walls of the Les Combarelles[3] cave were hundreds of figures of prehistoric animals. These figures were carved into the rock. The animals seemed to run and leap like living beasts.

On the walls of the Font-de-Gaume[4] cave, there were only a few paintings in red and black. But everybody agreed that the red rhinoceros and the black-and-red reindeer looked alive too.

Many experts had been present while the caves were being cleared. They knew that the decorations had been put on the walls before the caves became filled up. The had to face the fact that those painted and carved walls proved two things.

They proved that the cave people had discovered the idea behind all art. That idea is that lines and colors, on a flat surface, can give the impression of an animal, or of some other real thing.

[1]Cro-Magnon (kroh-MAG-non)   [2]Louis Lartet (loo-EE-lahr-TAY)
[3]Les Combarelles (lay kawm-bah-REL)   [4]Font-de-Gaume (FOHN-də-GOHM)

The paintings and drawings also proved that the cave people were really good artists. Some pictures were so simple they looked like the work of a small child. But in almost every case the animals on the cave walls seemed alive. Only a skillful artist can give the appearance of life to lines and splotches of color.

One expert who saw the works of art in the French caves was Emil Cartailhac.[1] He was a well known French paleontologist. As he stood before them he remembered something he had done almost twenty-five years earlier. He had refused to visit a certain Spanish cave called Altamira. He had refused because he couldn't believe that what its discoverer said was true. Now Cartailhac knew that the Spanish amateur must have been right.

Cartailhac was an honorable person. He blamed himself for having questioned Don Marcelino's word without even seeing the Altamira paintings. Then he packed his bags and set out for Spain.

[1] Emil Cartailhac (ay-MEEL kahr-tay-YAK)

A few days later Maria de Sautuola met the Frenchman. She led him up to the sealed opening of Altamira. She turned the key in the rusty lock, pushed the door open, and took him inside. Quietly she lit candles. She then showed him the pictures she had first seen when she was five years old.

Cartailhac could hardly believe his eyes. The paintings had been so well preserved in the cool cave! They looked as if they had been made only an hour before. But Cartailhac knew at once their true age. And he knew that they were by far the greatest example he had ever seen of prehistoric art.

323

From that day on, the village of Santillana del Mar again became a famous place. It was always crowded with eager visitors. Experts came from every quarter of the world. Those who couldn't come asked that copies of the pictures be made. Then they too could see the paintings that had suddenly become so famous.

A book was published showing all the drawings and paintings on the Altamira ceiling. The floor of the cave was dug away so that the works of art could be better seen. In time the Spanish government took over responsibility for the cave. Now its paintings, one of Spain's greatest art treasures, would always be protected. Every year, Altamira becomes more famous. More people go there to admire the pictures little Maria de Sautuola first saw by the light of her candle.

Maria de Sautuola lived to hear all the experts admit that her father had been right. She lived to hear her own name spoken in praise all over the world. She had discovered the clue proving that some of the greatest artists of all time were cave people. These were the people who lived among bison and mammoths during the Ice Age.

—Sam and Beryl Epstein

What Do You Think?

1. Pretend you are deep in the cave with Maria when her candle flickers on the ceiling. Tell what you see and how you feel.

2. What could have been Don Marcelino's feelings as he sealed up the cave? How would Maria have felt twenty-five years later when the cave was reopened?

3. If Don Marcelino had not searched for prehistoric tools, do you think the Altamira paintings would ever have been discovered? Explain your answer.

Taking A Closer Look

1. List the directions for the proper way to explore a cave. How do you know that Don Marcelino did or did not follow them correctly?

2. Name two other caves besides Altamira that are mentioned in this story. Where are they? What has been found in each one?

3. Why were the experts so sure the Altamira paintings were a hoax? If you had been in Lisbon, what would you have thought about the cave?

4. How did Cartailhac show he was an honorable person?

5. What has been done to the Altamira cave to make it easier to see the paintings? Why was this necessary?

CAVE ART FROM THE ICE AGE

Deep, deep in caverns, in places almost impossible to find or reach, cave artists of the Ice Age decorated rock walls and ceilings with paintings of animals they saw and hunted. Many of these creatures have long since disappeared from the earth. For tens of thousands of years the magnificent Ice Age paintings have been sealed up and preserved by nature in the cool caves. Until they were discovered only a century ago, perhaps no one, except the cave dwellers themselves, ever knew they existed. How fortunate we are today to be able to see these great art treasures from so long ago!

As you look at some of the colorful cave paintings, try to imagine how the cave artists might have created them. What tools do you think they used? How do you think they created the different colors? Try also to picture in your mind what the daily life of the cave dwellers might have been like. Do you find any clues in these paintings?

Young Maria might have seen this red and black bison
when she looked up at the ceiling in the Altamira cave.

One of the most beautiful of the animal murals in the Altamira cave is in the Picture Gallery. Animals are painted life-size on a part of the roof.

Here is a painting of part of a hind, which is a kind of deer. The entire hind is painted in the Altamira Picture Gallery.

Here is another bison from Altamira. The roof has many rocky bulges. The cave painters used these bumps to make animals seem real. Some parts of the bison seem to stand out.

329

In 1920 a child climbed down an underground passage and broke into the cave at Pêche-Merle,[1] France. Two years later the hall with pictures was discovered.

In this picture you see one of the ten paintings of mammoths found at Pêche-Merle. Notice the long hairs covering the trunk and legs of the mammoth.

[1] Pêche Merle (PESH MAIRL)

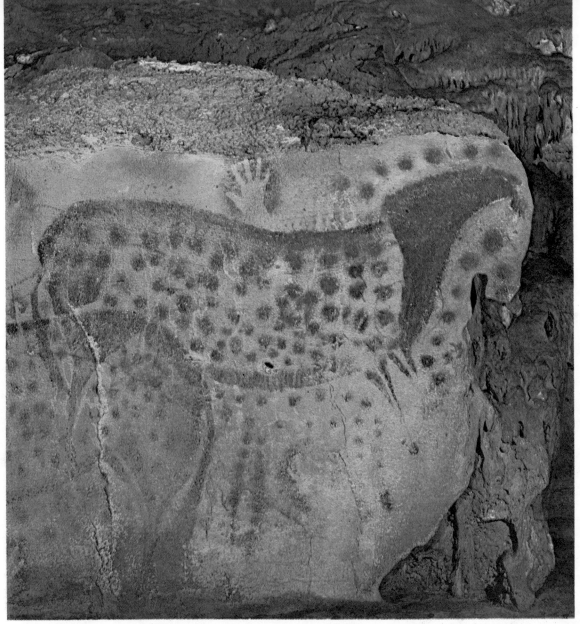

Almost opposite the paintings of the mammoths is a room with pictures of polka-dotted horses and outlines of hands. These are painted on rock walls. Do you see the hand in this picture? How do you think the cave painters made prints of their hands?

331

Some of the most famous of the Ice Age paintings are in the caves of Lascaux,[1] France. These were discovered in 1940 by four boys chasing a dog down a hole in the ground. After going down a 6 m tunnel, they found themselves in a big hall whose walls were covered with paintings. Passages from this cavern led to other rooms with murals.

Here is a picture of a wall painting at Lascaux. A leaping cow is shown with little horses underneath. The box-like figure near the cow's head may be a fence or trap.

[1]Lascaux (las-KOH)

The heads of cows and a horse are grouped on the ceiling. Notice the "trap" in the middle.

A large bull is painted over an earlier figure.

334

This painting seems to tell a story. It is at the bottom of a deep pit at the end of a passage at Lascaux. A bison is seen with horns lowered and eyes wide open. A spear has gone through its body. Nearby is a simple drawing of a person who appears to be lying on the ground or falling backwards. On the other side is a bird on a stick. Is this a hunting scene, or is it a dance of the hunt with people in masks? What story do you see in this strange painting?

335

Failure in the hunt would mean no food for the tribe of cave dwellers. But the hunt this day brings unexpected adventure for Marek[1]-son. As you read this story, what do you learn about how the cave people hunted, and how they may have lived?

THE GREAT HUNT

A hunting party is following a path down from its cave to the valley below. At the head of the line of hunters is Marek, the shaman.[2] Right behind him is his young son, Marek-son.

By late morning, the hunting party has reached the other side of the valley. The party comes to a pass leading into a land of plains and hills. This is a grazing land. Here game can be found in good times.

The sun, which was pale at dawn, is now partly hidden by clouds. A wet, raw wind bites into the faces of the hunters.

As the weather gets worse, Marek studies the sky. He knows that the sudden storms of spring can be most dangerous.

And now, in the rugged pass, the storm breaks upon the hunters.

Hurriedly they seek cover, climbing up the steep walls of the ravine. They seek places high enough to be safe

[1]Marek (MAR-ek)   [2]shaman (SHAH-mən)

from the flash flood. The flood, they know, will soon come rushing upon them.

A loud rumble of thunder echoes in the ravine. Lightning flashes against the low clouds. Gusts of wet, icy wind lash against the hunters, hidden behind the rocks.

The clouds burst. A wall of water roars down the narrow pass. Trees, rocks, and trapped animals are carried along in the rushing stream. It is well that the cave dwellers have chosen high places in the storm.

Now, as suddenly as it came, the storm is over. Marek has left his place of safety. The others climb down from the rocks. Only a trickle of water runs along the floor of the ravine.

Carefully Marek leads the party ahead. Suddenly, just in time, he stops them. A huge rock hanging out from the cliff comes crashing down. Swiftly the hunters draw back, but only for a moment. When the small rocks and mud have stopped falling, they move forward.

Marek-son climbs to the top of the ravine and studies the landslide. He looks all about him. He looks back to the way the party has come and ahead to the flatlands. He hopes bison will be grazing there. Far off, across the plains, he can see black specks growing smaller. He strains his keen eyes to make them out.

Something has frightened the game. The storm? The coming of the hunters? It is true that bison become harder to track the more often they are hunted. But this is the first time Marek-son has found the prairie bare of game.

This, he knows, means failure for the hunters and for his father. His eyes narrow as he carefully searches out the answer.

There is something strange out in the middle distance. One huge form seems to lean against a grove of trees. Forgetting the hunters still below him, Marek-son sets out to see this strangeness. Moving down to the flatlands, the boy

loses sight of it. But his sure sense of direction takes him toward one grove of trees.

His sense of smell, sharp as an animal's, adds to his excitement. There is a strong, musky smell in the air. It grows stronger as he nears the grove.

Marek-son knows he must come near any game only with much care. All animals are alert. They are easy to anger, and can be dangerous. His nose tells him this is no animal he has seen before. He moves toward the grove more carefully than usual.

As he enters the grove, he nearly bumps into a living mountain of flesh. He can't believe that a thing so huge can be alive. He knows that if he makes a mistake, he will die.

Now a sudden excitement shakes the hairy creature. It towers into the branches of the trees around him. The beast roars with anger as it senses Marek-son in the grove. Its huge head comes down almost in reach of the young hunter. Something like a snake reaches toward him. Long tusks root wildly in the earth.

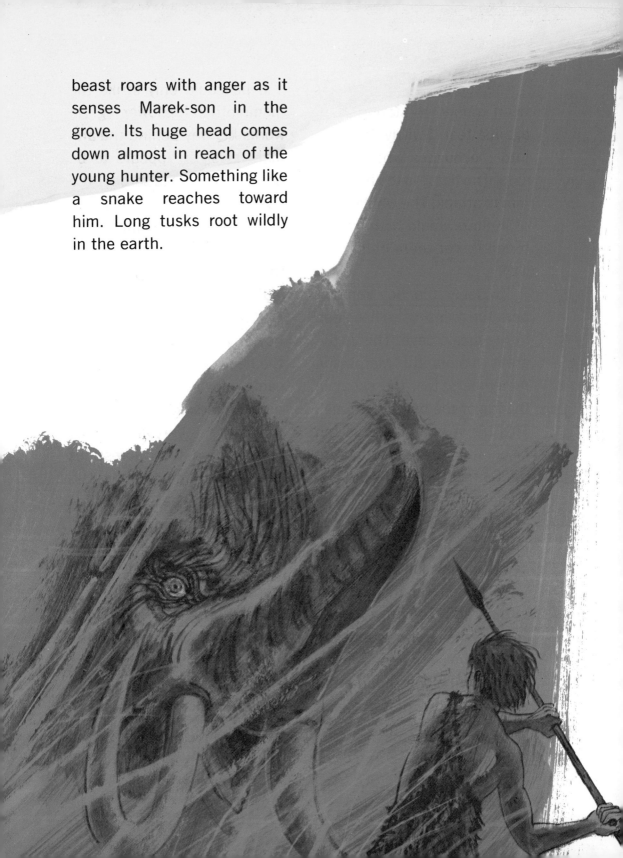

The son of the shaman has been trained to stand strong against fear. Swiftly, he darts into the bushes where he is safe. The beast is too huge for him to attack. The whole party of hunters would be hard put to kill it. Yet there must be a way.

Suddenly the boy remembers the painting he has seen in the magic cave. This is the great mammoth! Marek-son remembers, too, the spear in the leg of the painted animal. This beast is as huge as ten bison. If it can be killed, there will be food for all his people. If he can only wound the beast! Then, perhaps the hunters, when they come up, can somehow kill it.

Marek-son weighs his spear in his hand. To throw it here among the trees would do little harm to such a huge beast. Yet he does not dare to leave the grove that protects him.

If he could only strike the mammoth in the lower leg! He works his way behind the animal. Its sight appears to be poor. It continues to beat the bushes the hunter has just left. Marek-son comes very close to the beast. He can see the bugs crawling in its long, matted hair.

With all his strength, the boy drives his spear deep into the heavy leg. Almost with the same movement, he throws himself back into the bushes. But at that very instant he feels a hard blow across his back. For a moment, Marek-son feels as if he is part of the landslide back in the ravine. He feels as if he is being thrown down a long rocky slope.

The hunters arriving from the ravine have come near the grove. They can hear the roars of the big beast as it fights to get at Marek-son. They speed up their steps to a run. When

340

they reach the grove, they immediately attack the mammoth. All afternoon they fight it. Some throw their spears, then watch their chance to rush in and grab their weapons. They draw their spears out of the beast's flesh as it whirls to face yet another attacker. Now the sky grows dark. But the mammoth stands at bay near the edge of the plain. It seems as powerful as ever.

As the day ends, the hunters are growing desperate. They may lose this prize if night falls before they have killed it. Their attacks become more daring. Yet the great beast fights back with its powerful trunk.

Marek has remained in the grove with his son. Marek-son moves restlessly in pain. Marek has cleaned the boy's wounds. He has covered the red streak across his back with a comforting herb.

The shaman, like the hunters, is worried about the coming of night. It is his task to bring the hunt to a successful end. Even more than the hunters, he knows that the dark is full of danger. It can mean escape for the beast.

He bends over his son. The boy's eyes, still dull with shock and pain, meet his father's. Suddenly Marek-son remembers something, something very important. Painfully, he speaks the word for "landslide."

The landslide! The falling rock had left a gaping pit at the edge of the cliff.

Marek understands what his son means and his face brightens. He places a spear beside the boy for protection against animals. Then he leaves quickly, for he must return to the hunt.

He comes again to where the hunters are still fighting the mammoth. They all shout with joy as they see their shaman. Most of them do not have weapons now. They can only throw rocks at the great beast.

Quickly Marek tells the hunters of his plan. He sends half the party on ahead. Next he makes a small fire with flint and leaves. The others make torches out of branches and grasses.

Then, waving their flaming torches overhead, the hunt-

ers frighten the mammoth with fire. It roars wildly in great terror. Of all the weapons of the hunters, fire is the one most feared.

Night comes quickly now. Moving clumsily in the dark, the beast climbs toward the top of the ravine. It is hurried on by the burning torches on all sides. Reaching the top, it turns to face the hunters. They cannot come near it from below. But Marek grabs a flaming branch and throws it into the woolly face of the beast.

Roaring loudly, its hair burning, the mammoth steps back.

The hunters who have gone ahead have lined a path with fires. The others drive the beast along the path with their torches. At the end of the path the pit has been hidden with brush. On the edge of the pit, the mammoth stands for a long moment. Its feet seek firm ground. But the earth crumbles away beneath its great weight. With a loud roar, it slides into the hole. There is an earthshaking thud. A howl of victory goes up from the hunters.

The great mammoth is theirs!

The sun has risen and set three times over the valley. And now it is evening again. There has been a long line of men, women, and children bearing back the meat from the mammoth. There has been a funeral for two hunters killed in the hunt. There have been both joy and sadness in these three days.

The torches light the magic room where Marek-son lies. His spear, brought from the battle, has been placed beside him. Marek has taken care of him during these long days and nights. Now the shaman raises a torch to light the ceiling above his son. The boy's eyes grow wider. For the first time his attention seems caught. In his eyes a gleam of health tells the father that his boy will recover.

It is something above the young hunter that holds his attention. It is there on the ceiling of the magic cave. Painted on the ancient drawing is a figure driving a spear into the mammoth. In that figure Marek-son sees with growing pride his part in the hunt. The painting tells him all he needs to know about the outcome of the great hunt of his people. His people are the cave dwellers of thirty thousand years ago.

—*Richard M. Powers*

What Do You Think?

1. What part of the hunt do you think the most exciting? Tell about it as if you were there at the time.
2. What two important facts did the cave painting tell Marek-son? How was each of these facts important to the great hunt?
3. Tell at least three facts you learned about cave dwellers from this story. Which fact was the most interesting to you? Why?

Taking A Closer Look

1. Tell two important ways Marek-son helped in the great hunt.
2. Pretend you are Marek, the shaman, and explain to the hunters your plan for killing the mammoth.
3. Why was the landslide important to Marek's plan for capturing the mammoth?
4. Why do you think the word *magic* was used to describe the room where Marek-son saw the painting of the mammoth?
5. Look back to the next to the last page in the story. Find the sentence, "The sun has risen and set three times. . . ." What does the sentence tell you?

346

Under One Sun

You are about to take a trip to other lands, with stops in Morocco, Nigeria, Mexico, Japan, and China. Though the boys and girls you will meet have different customs from you own, they, like you, face problems, have adventures, and dream dreams.

347

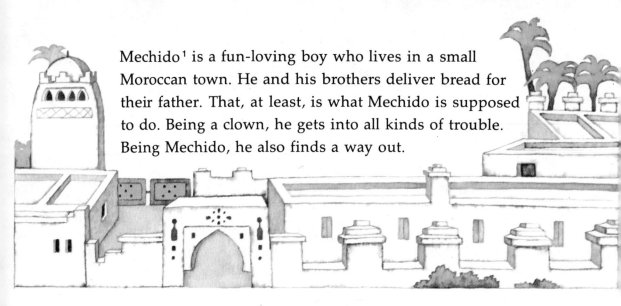

Mechido[1] is a fun-loving boy who lives in a small Moroccan town. He and his brothers deliver bread for their father. That, at least, is what Mechido is supposed to do. Being a clown, he gets into all kinds of trouble. Being Mechido, he also finds a way out.

MECHIDO

Mechido lived in a small Moroccan town. When he was nine, the time had come for him to go to work, as his older brothers had done, delivering bread for their father. Their father was a baker. He owned a small oven in the town.

"He has finished his training," said his brother Mohammed. "He can make his way home blindfolded."

"Can he balance the breadboard on his head?" asked their father.

"Yes. And he can come around corners without letting it fall."

"Good," said his father. "And can he climb up and down stairs and still keep it on his head?"

"Yes," said the brothers, and winked at each other.

"Then he is ready. And if he is ready, why are you laughing?" Mechido's brothers were laughing very hard.

[1] Mechido (mə-SHEE-doh)

348

"Stop laughing at once and answer," commanded their father.

"Mechido is a clown," said his brother Driz. "I am weak thinking of the trouble he will cause."

Mechido hung his head in chagrin.

And everyone became serious. They all stood around him in a little circle, staring, his brothers solemn and a massive frown on the father's face. Mechido wilted.

He began work the next day. From then on he was called the Tarah,[1] as all Moorish boys are called who deliver dough to the oven. The women make their batter at home; and it is the Tarah's job to run with the breadboard from house to house, collect the dough and uncooked pastries and, balancing them all on the breadboard, carry them to the oven. When they are baked, it is the Tarah who delivers them again from house to house. Morning and afternoon the women bang their door knockers and call, "Tarah!", and the Tarah goes running.

Mechido's father had his oven in a semicellar. A long slanting chute opened into the cellar from the street. It was here that Mechido would send the loaded breadboard sliding down to his father. It was here, craning his neck up the chute to listen, that Mechido waited that first morning for the first woman to call.

But it was not a glad Mechido. He felt apprehensive, more than anything else because of his father. Mechido's father had once been a wrestler, and he still had plenty of muscle. He also had a close, black beard. When he was dressed in his best burnoose and fez, Mechido thought the beard made him look like a prince. But somehow, it had a different effect in the

[1] Tarah (tə-RAH)

cellar. There he wore only full white pants. Seeing him with the long bread paddle in his hand and those old wrestling muscles shining, his face glowing from the heat and that little beard glistening, Mechido thought he looked very much like someone to be feared.

"Tarah!" There it was. Mechido grabbed the breadboard.

"Tarah!" Mechido darted into the street.

"Tarah!" Mechido dashed up a stairway, burst through a door and fell into a pair of floury arms.

That first day, the hardest thing for him to get used to was the piercing cries of "Tarah" that followed him everywhere. He was in such a state of alarm that every time he heard the call, he fell down.

Around a corner he came with two dozen cakes on his head. "Tarah!" He stumbled and two dozen cakes took off in the air.

He sped through a hall with eight loaves of bread piled up on his head. "Tarah!" A shadowy figure swelled out on a wall. He leaped and eight loaves rolled away.

He tore past a fountain. "Tarah!" from above. "Allah!" from Mechido, and sixteen sweet cakes lit in the water.

This happened near the close of the day, and it was almost too much for Mechido. It had already been a very bad day. He tried to fish out the cakes but they were sinking fast. Unhappily, he watched them settle on the bottom. His father! What was he going to tell his father?

That was something he could not understand about grown-ups. Why were they so earnest? So drastic! They hardly ever saw the bright side of things. Mechido could not see why. He often wondered about it.

The cakes were disintegrating. What had shortly before been so crisp was now so flabby. Mechido was sure his father would not take this well.

It was too depressing to think about. A few minutes later, to cheer himself up, with twenty-four rolls of fresh dough on his board, he slid down three flights of bannisters backward. He did not see the woman waiting at the foot of the stairs.

"Tarah," she hissed in his ear as he sailed to the bottom.

"Ay!" he cried, threw his hands in the air, and the breadboard fell over flat.

"Smashed," said his father when he saw the twenty-four rolls of dough. "Sit down, Mechido, my son. Let us take the toll."

There was a cloudy look in his eyes.

"Out of thirty-five deliveries today, my son," began his father, "thirty-one were incomplete and four were not made at all. What happened, my son?"

"It is their voices, my father," answered Mechido. "Such shrieks! Such screams! I drop everything."

351

His father took two pieces of dough and put them in Mechido's ears.

"Tarah!" he thundered. "Can you hear that?"

"Yes. But it is not piercing."

There was a snort from Mechido's father. It was plain that he was not long on patience.

"You will plug your ears every day," he said in a thick voice. "That is one thing. Here is another thing. Where are your Aunt Zorah's[1] cinnamon wafers? Can you answer me that?"

Mechido felt more and more apprehensive.

"There is a wall in front of Abdelkrim[2] the candlemaker's house," he began cautiously. "Do you know that wall?"

His father grunted.

"It's not high. I was walking on top of it with the wafers on my head. I was walking on it, sir, as the scarecrows walk at night, with their eyes tight closed. I did not see the end of the wall. I fell."

"You fell. And the wafers?"

[1] Zorah (zə-RAH) [2] Abdelkrim (AHB-dəl-kə-REEM)

Mechido bit his lip. "In Abdelkrim's pigpen."

The cloudy look in his father's eyes had grown to a storm.

Then followed a scolding. But there were so many scoldings in Mechido's career as bread boy, I think it's kinder to leave them out.

That night, from his bed, Mechido could hear his parents' voices in the front room, next to his. His father was raging.

"...down a bannister..."

Mechido's eyes danced.

"...into a fountain..."

Mechido's stomach was heaving.

"...and over a wall..."

Mechido held his sides and wheezed.

That was only the first night. His father went on in a similar way night, after night, after night.

As the days passed, Mechido got into so much more trouble, his brother took over the job of Tarah.

It was a very contrite Mechido who appeared before his father one night.

"I beg," said Mechido, "for one more chance."

Mechido's father was unmoved.

"Your last chance," he said somberly, "your last chance is gone. Finished and gone."

"Oh, my father, only one more chance, I beg of you."

"Finished and gone. I am *almost* finished and gone," said Mechido's father, and he pounded the table.

Mechido pressed his knees together, took a deep breath, and said in a rush, "There is something I want to do, and it will take only a week. You will not see me during that week, and if at the end of it you like what I have done, perhaps you will forgive me and allow me to be Tarah again. That is all I beg of you, my father."

His father brightened visibly. "If it means that I shall not lay eyes on you for one week, yes! One thousand times, yes!"

And the next day, and the next, and the next, not a hair of Mechido's curly head was seen. At night, he came home to climb into bed after everyone else had eaten, and in the morning he left before breakfast.

"Where does Mechido spend his time?" his father asked at the dinner table.

No one knew.

"Where does he eat?"

No one knew.

"But is he eating?" his father demanded.

"I heard him counting his money last night," said his brother Driz. "He was saying, 'Oranges, nuts, and cheese,' and I heard his money clink."

"I think," said Mohammed, "he is buying his own food with the coins he took as tips while he was Tarah."

"Mohammed," announced his father at the end of the meal, "tomorrow you will find out where Mechido goes."

"I have seen him!" Mohammed exclaimed at dinner the following night.

Their father's eyes gleamed.

"He was at Abdul[1] the cabinetmaker's; and I saw him there as I was on the way to Aunt Zorah's with bread. He was sitting

[1] Abdul (AHB-dəl)

354

at Abdul's workbench, sandpapering something. He had his tongue clenched between his teeth. On the way back from Aunt Zorah's he was hammering something. I called him, but he jumped up and looked very angry and closed the door."

Their father said nothing. The next morning, on the pretext of an errand, he left his son Driz at the oven and went by the cabinetmaker's. Through a window he could see Mechido bent over a sheet of tin. He was honing the edges and measuring them, sliding them back and forth over something. Mechido's father stepped away from the window and puffed out his chest.

"My poor little Mechido," said his mother at dinner, looking at his empty place. "And what is it that he is doing?" she asked.

"One of his pranks, you'll see," said Driz.

"I belive it is not a prank," his father said proudly. "Perhaps Mechido is not the dunce you think," he said in rolling tones. "Two days more, Driz, my son, and you shall see."

The evening of the seventh day, at the end of dinner, Mechido ran into the room. His cheeks were flushed and his eyes were shining. In his hands he carried a box.

"It's finished!" he cried. "Look what I have made!" And he set it on the table for them to see.

It was rather long, just over 1 m, and .05 m or so high. The sides were made of fine, thin sheets of wood, and on one end of it was a little door with hinges and a small latch. It was quite plain, except for the little door, which had inlays of different colored pieces of wood arranged in the pattern of a star. "Look inside!"

Mechido's father and mother and his two brothers crowded around while Mechido unlatched the door. Inside were three shelves of bright tin. "You see," explained Mechido, "they slide in and out." He slid each of the shelves out and in again.

"Do you like it? Isn't it beautiful!" Mechido hugged himself. "Isn't it just the most beautiful thing?"

"It is very nice, Mechido," said his father. "But what is it?"

"It is," said Mechido, "a breadbox."

"What, Mechido, my son, do you mean?" his father said slowly.

"I mean, it is a breadbox for carrying bread. Instead of a board, you see. It is very light, much lighter than the board." He put it on his head. "And it balances." He tipped it from side to side. "And nothing, nothing can ever happen to the bread again. If I fall in the street, let me fall! The bread is safe. No more garbage in the dough. If they throw mud at me, let them throw! The bread is safe. Look. I go to Aisha's[1] house." He walked around the table. "She piles on the dough. Whisk, I go to Abdelkrim's, more dough. Then to Aunt Zorah's for more." He marched back around the table. "And off to the oven, all baked at once!" Mechido clapped his hands. "And the best is this. When I deliver the bread again, it will still be hot!"

[1] Aisha (AH-ee-shə)

Driz and Mohammed stared first at their brother and then at the box and then at their brother again. Who would have guessed that such a clown could make such a box?

"Oh, my dearest Mechido." His mother swept him into her arms and covered him with kisses. "How hard you have worked! See the tiny nails you drove in. How many times you must have hammered your little fingers!" She kissed him again.

"Not once!" cried Mechido. "Oh, I did it very well. It's the most wonderful work in the world. It is the most exciting thing I have ever done. I would rather do that than any—" He stopped short. He was afraid he had offended his father.

But Mechido's father stood silent. There was something stubborn in the set of his shoulders.

"No, Mechido, my son." He spoke stiffly, "It cannot be. The art of the Tarah is in his board. The way he handles it. That is his merit; that is his skill. There will be no breadbox. It was not a good idea."

357

"But, Father! It is better. It has three shelves. It carries far more than a board. And now the bread will be safe!" Mechido's voice was rising. "Now there can be no mistakes. The bread will not fly off into the fountain. The bread will not fall to the pigs."

"No. No. One thousand times no!" His father's face had turned a dark red. "For seven generations the boys of this family have carried a simple board. I will not have my son parading around town with a fancy box on his head. A box with a door! No."

"Father—" Mechido's throat was closing—"the bread will still be hot."

"No!" said his father and brought his hands palm down on the breadbox.

Mechido made a choking sound and fled from the room. He did not want his brothers to see him cry.

From his bed he heard his mother berating his father. It was the only time in his life that he had heard them fight on his account, but it did not console him at all.

"You are cruel," he heard her cry out. "Obstinate and cruel. And you have broken his heart. It is a beautiful box. I would like to see you try to make such a box."

For once Mechido did not hear his father shout. He answered something in such a low rumble that Mechido could not make it out.

He sat on his bed with his cheeks flaming.

"It is not just," he said to himself again and again. Tonight he did not care to peek through the hole. And, "Tomorrow I am going to fill the hole with putty. I will never look at my father again. So help me, I will never even look into his eyes again." At that sad thought, tears welled over and down his hot cheeks.

He was about to give over into sobs when he heard a murmur in the next room. It was Abdul the cabinetmaker's voice. Abdul had been very kind to him; this might be worth seeing after all. Mechido dried his face, lifted the poster, and looked through the hole.

Abdul was crossing the room. He was a big clumsy man who shuffled when he walked. He had heavy, sloping eyes that were full of humor, and when he was amused they seemed to slide down the sides of his face. Mechido thought that was a marvelous sight, and during his week with Abdul he had tried to say all kinds of funny things, just so he could watch what happened to Abdul's eyes.

Abdul bowed a deep bow. "I see you have the box," he said with a smile.

"We have it," answered Mechido's father.

"I have come to congratulate you," said the kindly Abdul, "on your remarkable son. A man is blessed to have such a son."

Mechido's father was immediately on guard. He observed Abdul with veiled eyes.

Abdul rubbed his fingers over the top of Mechido's box. "Never have I seen a boy work so hard. Such devotion and such concentration! Do you know, my friend, that your son sat for six hours at a stretch, morning and afternoon, without stirring?"

"That is interesting," said Mechido's father. "Very interesting."

"Look at the workmanship." Abdul bent over the box. "He has sanded it like satin. The shelves are measured to a fraction of a fraction. This is a nine-year-old boy! Do you realize that? Never have I seen a boy with such a gift. And the inlays in the door—they require the craft of a grown man." Abdul folded his arms across his stomach and rocked slowly on his feet. "My friend, your son Mechido could become a master cabinetmaker and I would consider it an honor if you would allow him to become my apprentice."

Mechido gave a start. "It's too good," he whispered into the wall.

Mechido's father apparently could not find his tongue.

At last he said, "Is it so fine a box as that?"

"For a nine-year-old boy, it is an extraordinary box," said the genial Abdul.

"But, Abdul, you have an apprentice. Your own son is your apprentice."

Abdul's jovial smile faded. "My son. My own son is the night-mare of my life. My son!" Abdul clutched his stomach. Then he clutched Mechido's father by the nape of his burnoose. "My own son wants to be a juggler. Or a weight lifter. The bane of my life is my own son. Do you know—no, how can you know—what he does when I leave the workshop? He piles everything on his head—planks, blocks of wood, tools, as many things as he can, the more the better. My half-made cabinets on top of the planks, sideboards on top of that, and when I come back I find him walking up and down the stairs, balancing it all on his head, all my beautiful work piled up, and with his hands he is throwing nails into the air and catching them. Oh, my own son, the bane of my life!" Abdul drooped.

Mechido's father was fascinated. "He likes to carry things on his head?"

A dejected nod from Abdul.

"The more the better?"

"Yes." A sigh.

"And does he not often drop the things?"

"Drop my cabinets! Should he dare, indeed that would be too much." The more Abdul sagged the more pleased Mechido's father grew.

"Surely he must get into trouble in the streets?"

"Who, Hamed?[1] Have you never seen my large son, Hamed? He walks like an ox." Abdul wagged his head sadly from side to side. "Woe to him who goes near Hamed in the streets."

"Rejoice, my friend! Hamed has found his destiny!" Mechido's father gave a sudden cry and embraced him. "If ever there was

[1] Hamed (hah-MED)

361

a born bread boy, Hamed is he. He will be my apprentice! And Mechido will be yours!"

Mechido smothered a shout.

Abdul's sunken frame rose back into shape. "My greatest friend!" he cried, and they embraced again. "I am doubly honored. It will be a privilege and a pleasure. What's more—" through the hole Mechido saw to his delight that Abdul's eyes were beginning to slide—"apart from his skill, Mechido amuses me. The jokes he makes. He is a nice boy."

Mechido's father smiled. There was an expression in his face that Mechido had never seen before, something fond and deeply tender.

"Yes, there is no one like Mechido," he said softly. "My Mechido, he is a very fine boy."

And Mechido felt his cheeks grow hot again, but this time from joy.

—Giggy Lezra

What Do You Think?

1. When people say someone is like "a square peg in a round hole," what do you think they mean? How might any of the characters in "Mechido" be called "a square peg in a round hole"?

2. Describe in your own words each of the characters given below.

    Mechido   Mechido's father   Abdul

    Mechido's mother   Hamed

3. When Mechido left home during the daytime hours for a week, why did he not tell his family where he was going and what he was doing?

Taking A Closer Look

1. Many accidents happened to Mechido on his first day as Tarah. Name some of them. Which accident do you think mattered most to his father?

2. In what ways did Mechido's parents feel differently from one another about the breadbox Mechido made?

3. Write a help-wanted ad for an apprentice to a baker or a cabinetmaker. Be sure to list the tasks to be done and the skills needed for the job.

4. How did Mechidos father act, and what did he say, while talking with Abdul? How do his actions and words at that time prepare you for the end of the story?

Taiwo[1] and her twin brother Kehinde[2] live in Nigeria. One day, as they go out into the bush looking for palm nuts, they suddenly hear a strange sound. What can it be?

The Creature in the Bush

One afternoon, Taiwo went to the bush to hunt for palm nuts. But she was not alone, for Kehinde, her twin brother, went with her.

They frisked through the bush as free as young goats, Taiwo this way, Kehinde that way, calling out to each other as they went. Each claimed boastfully to have found more nuts than the other. The bush was so shady and pleasantly cool.

Suddenly Taiwo heard a loud rustling sound. Some big creature was pushing through the bush. It sounded very close.

Taiwo stiffened. Still as a stone, she listened. What could it be? Goats and sheep did not wander so far from the village. It sounded too big to be a rat or rabbit or bird.

[1] Taiwo (TIGH-woh)   [2] Kehinde (KAY-in-day)

Then she heard a cry, a strange scolding cry, coming from the same direction as the rustling. Taiwo remembered the fearful tales she had heard about the bush.

"Kehinde!" she called. "KEHINDE!"

Kehinde was searching around a palm tree not far from Taiwo's. At the sound of Taiwo's cry, he ran quickly to see what the trouble could be.

"Listen, Kehinde!" Taiwo's voice was all trembly. "Do you hear it?"

Kehinde listened. He too heard the loud rustling. He too heard the scolding cry. But the cry did not sound strange to Kehinde. In fact, it sounded very familiar.

"That is very odd," Kehinde answered, looking quite puzzled. "Surely it sounds exactly like the Bale's[1] turkey. But how would the turkey come to be here in the bush?"

Taiwo did not answer. If it was indeed a turkey, how silly Kehinde would think her if he knew how frightened she had been.

Kehinde pushed through the bush toward the noise. "It is the turkey!" he shouted back. "It has broken its string again. Come, help me catch it!"

Taiwo ran toward her brother's voice. And there indeed was the turkey, flapping through the bush with the end of string dangling behind it. Kehinde was thrashing and crashing after it.

"Come!" he called again. "Help me catch it!"

The twins chased and chased, but they were no match for that turkey. Their crashing and thrashing

[1] Bale (BAH-lay)

frightened it and made it quite frantic. They could not get close, for when they did, the turkey rose from the ground and flapped away out of reach. Soon they were stinging with countless scratches and puffing for breath, and still no closer to catching the turkey.

"Wait! Let us stop a bit," Taiwo puffed. "I just cannot run any more."

"Oh, no," Kehinde protested. "If we stop, then he will run away!"

Taiwo dropped to the ground. "Run away!" she exclaimed, leaning her back against a tree trunk and trying to catch her breath. "Run away! What is he doing now? Sleeping?" Taiwo shook her head. "We will have to think of a better way to catch him. We are just frightening him and tiring ourselves."

Kehinde shrugged his shoulders and dropped down beside Taiwo. He was quite as breathless as she. It did feel good to sit back against the tree. It was so pleasant and quiet. Very quiet.

Each of the twins realized the same thing at the same time. The turkey was no longer flapping about. When they had stopped chasing, he had stopped fleeing. He was probably as tired as they were. And hungry too. They could hear him scratching about in the bush nearby.

Thinking of the turkey's hunger reminded Kehinde that he was hungry too. "I wish I were a turkey and could scratch for my food," he said. "How I would like something to eat now!"

"My head is surely empty today," Taiwo said. "I brought some *eko*[1] for us to eat and forgot all about it."

Taiwo pulled the leaf-wrapped packets from their hiding place in her wrapper. Kehinde reached eagerly for his. Already he could taste the smooth corn porridge sliding over his tongue and into his empty stomach.

But, just as Taiwo was handing the packet of *eko* to Kehinde, the idea came to her. Of course! This was the way! In Taiwo's excitement, the words came sputtering out.

"Listen, Kehinde! We must not eat it! We must not eat the *eko*! We can use it for bait. For turkey bait. I have a plan that . . ."

"Not eat it!" Kehinde protested, the tempting green packet practically in his hands. "Turkey bait? Whatever are you raving about?"

[1] *eko* (EK-KAW)

"It is such a good plan. Just listen. You will see."

Kehinde looked very doubtful, but he listened nonetheless.

Taiwo explained her plan carefully. "When we ran after the turkey and made much noise, he just got frightened and ran away. But if we go slowly and quietly, perhaps we can make him come after us instead of us going after him. This is what we must do . . . ."

The more Kehinde listened, the less doubtful he looked. It did sound like a very good plan.

Kehinde stayed where he was, crouched very still near the trunk of the tree.

Taiwo crept quietly toward the turkey. She moved slowly and cautiously, careful not to let twigs snap or branches slap. At last only a small shrub was between her and the great black bird. She could almost reach out and touch him.

Her fingers broke off a small bit of the pasty corn porridge. Slowly, careful not to rustle the bush by her movement, she threw the small ball of corn porridge toward the bird. The *eko* landed near the turkey's head.

Peck! Peck! With a pick and a peck and a shake of his head, the turkey gobbled up the *eko*. Then he scratched eagerly about, turning his head this way and that, searching for more of this treat.

Quickly Taiwo broke off another piece of *eko* and threw it to the turkey. Again the gobbler gobbled it up and hunted about for more. Taiwo threw the third piece, but so gently that it landed quite close to her feet. The bird pushed eagerly through the brush to get it.

Taiwo moved slowly away from him, back toward the tree where her brother was crouching. Every few steps she dropped a small piece of *eko* to the ground.

The turkey followed the trail of *eko*. He came nearer and nearer to Taiwo. The string dangled from his leg so temptingly! Taiwo could have bent down and grabbed it so easily! But she knew that this would not do. The turkey would only pull away.

The first portion of *eko* was almost finished. Thank goodness! Here was the tree where Kehinde waited. Taiwo stopped. She crumbled the last of the *eko* and dropped the crumbs in a small heap near the base of the tree.

Such a feast! The great bird pecked and swallowed, pecked and swallowed. Here a crumb, there a crumb, everywhere crumbs. The turkey paid no attention to Taiwo, standing there so still. He did not notice Kehinde reach out quietly from behind the tree and take hold of the end of the dangling string.

Now it was Kehinde's turn to move quietly and cautiously. He pulled the string gently toward him — very gently. He must be sure not to tug on it or he would alarm the bird. Now! He had hold of enough string. Quickly Kehinde wrapped the string around the trunk of a small sturdy sapling that grew beside the big tree. Once around. Twice around. Quickly he tied the string with the tightest knots he could. At last! The turkey was their prisoner.

Some villagers, out searching for the turkey, helped the twins return it to the Bale, the chief of the village. He was so pleased, he rewarded Taiwo and Kehinde for their good work.

—Letta Schatz

370

What Do You Think?

1. How well do you think the twins get along with one another? Which sentences in the story make you think so?
2. Why do you suppose the twins bothered to catch the turkey instead of letting it go? How do you think the bird got into the bush in the first place?

Taking A Closer Look

1. When Taiwo said, "My head is surely empty today," what do you think she meant? Think of other ways to express the same idea.
2. Look up the word *eko* in the Glossary. How do you think *eko* would taste? In what way is it like some of the foods you have eaten? Try to describe *eko* to someone who has never heard of it.
3. "If at first you don't succeed, try, try again." How does this saying apply to the twins? What could have been wrong with their first plan? Why did they finally succeed?

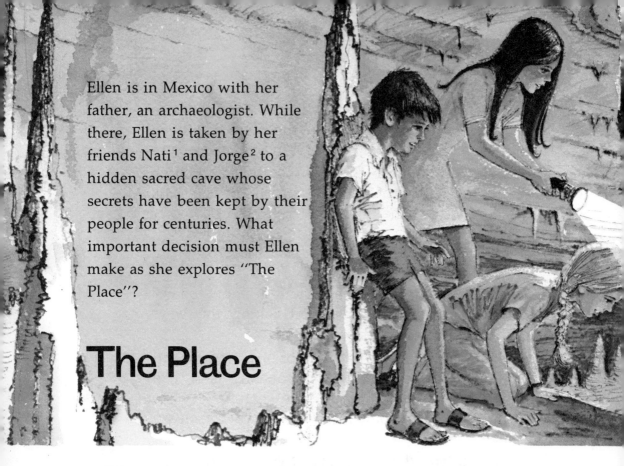

Ellen is in Mexico with her father, an archaeologist. While there, Ellen is taken by her friends Nati[1] and Jorge[2] to a hidden sacred cave whose secrets have been kept by their people for centuries. What important decision must Ellen make as she explores "The Place"?

The Place

"Keep close to the wall," whispered Jorge. "The water's deep here, and the path is slippery."

Ellen obeyed and walked with one hand touching the limestone surface beside her. It was wet and slimy under her fingers.

"Hold the torch down a moment and let me see the water," she begged Nati, who stopped, a little impatiently, and threw a circle of light into the stream below them. There were fish there, very small fish which paid no attention to the glare, but went on swimming about. Ellen sat down on her heels, so that she could see them better. One rose to the surface for a drowning midge.

[1] Nati (NAH-TEE)   [2] Jorge (HOR-hay)

"Look," she whispered. "Look! It has no eyes! It must know there's something to eat near it by the vibration in the water."

"Didn't I tell you this is a wonderful place?" Jorge answered, delighted by Ellen's surprise, but Nati murmured urgently, "Come along!" and started off again with the torch and Ellen had to follow.

The air grew colder and colder and the stale odor of bats grew stronger. When Nati for a moment swept the light upwards, bats' eyes glared back, studding the roof above them. Ellen knew she had nothing to fear from bats, but suppose a jaguar had a den somewhere in the cave? Suppose the next eyes that shone in the beam of their light should be a jaguar's eyes?

But if Nati dared lead the way, Ellen would follow. On down the narrow passage they went and into another great chamber filled with more strange shapes, and always the air grew colder, as they went deeper and deeper into the earth. By now they must have come nearly 1 km, Ellen thought.

"I love it," she said, between chattering teeth. "It's wonderful, but let's go back now."

"No," whispered Nati. "This is not yet the Place. There is nothing to hurt you here."

Ellen gritted her teeth. She wouldn't suggest going back again. It was Jorge who murmured excitedly,

"We're almost there."

Again a man-made wall appeared to side of the cave and the passage which they entered was very winding, while the ground sometimes rose steeply underfoot. They had left the stream behind them, and there were no bats here to hang like fungus from the roof. Once, in a quick spurt of light, Ellen saw hollows in the stone wall, made to hold pitch-pine torches, for the limestone above them was blackened with old smoke stains.

And then they came to the Place.

Once more there was a man-made wall and a narrow entrance. This time it was not a cavern they entered, but a room floored by flagstones, with plastered walls reaching up to the natural ceiling. There were the remains of frescoes on these walls, where the damp had not destroyed them. Priests and warriors and women formed a procession towards an altar, or so Ellen thought in the glimpse she had, before Nati directed the light to the center of the cave, from which rose what appeared to be a shining seated figure, at least 3 m high.

It was a stalagmite like the others they had seen, but instead of having taken the shape of a mushroom, tower, or animal,

374

it was like a human with bent head and arms close to the sides of the body. There seemed even to be hands laid in the lap. And all this shone and glistened, in white darkening to amber, like a moist and living thing.

While Ellen stared, the other two children dropped to the ground, crouching, rather than kneeling, before the figure. They were praying, but in their own language. Their prayers seemed to be earlier prayers than any said in the village church. Jorge was repeating the same words, over and over, like a lesson, but Nati, Ellen guessed, was begging for forgiveness for having brought a stranger into this holy place.

When Nati had finished, she went forward on her hands and knees to put some copal[1] in an earthenware incense bowl standing on a stone altar before the god. She must have broken it from the lump she had bought for her mother at the market. There wasn't much, but there was enough. Nati lighted a match and held it to the copal, but for a moment the incense refused to catch fire; then, at last, it slowly began to burn and the fragrant smoke drifted into the air.

Nati, satisfied, sat back on her heels.

"It's all right," she said to Ellen in quite an everyday voice. "The god is satisfied and has accepted my offering. But you'd better make one, too. Why don't you offer your watch?"

Ellen's silver watch was the only thing of any value she had with her, but she didn't hesitate. As, lighted by the torch, she and her shadow were stooping a little to lay the watch on the stone slab, she saw that all around her were ancient bowls and jars, such as her father and his workers sometimes dug up, but

[1]copal (KOH-pəl)

these were unbroken and sat in a thick circle, facing the god.
There were jars shaped like chiefs, and some like market
women with their little children. There were laughing cripples,
and old men, and prisoners with their arms tied behind their
backs. There were parrots and doves, and a jaguar with white
eyes, and a fat pot-bellied puppy, on four wheels like a toy. There
were toads and snakes and a baby playing with its toes and tall

376

ears of corn. A few of the jars held large jade beads. All faced towards the image, as they must have faced for hundreds and hundreds of years, ever since they were first brought to the Place as offerings.

And the god? The cavern itself had made the image from limestone, drop by heavy drop, as it had made the columns and chandeliers and waving curtains.

And suddenly the jaguar spoke, not from the shadows of the shrine, but from its den in Ellen's heart. If only she had not promised! In all her father's explorations, he had never found anything like this. If he should write an account of the Place for some scientific magazine, he would be famous among archaeologists, and everyone would know that it was his daughter, Ellen, who had brought him here, so she would be famous, too. Better still, she would be given the reward, which the Society offered for new archaeological sites. And that meant she could buy Centavo,[1] the red horse!

Centavo and the Place! The Place and Centavo! Almost from the beginning, the two had combined to fill her heart with longing. Two things which she had supposed could never be hers. And now . . .

Ellen shook her head until her braids stung her cheeks.

No!

She had sworn on her life to tell no one and to bring no one here, but even if she had not sworn, she would never, never never take from these people the last secret which bound them to their ancestors. Smiling, they dug out old temple foundations for her father; politely, they took him to forgotten terraces.

[1] Centavo (sen-TAH-voh)

Hoping to please him, they brought him the beautiful things they had found in their fields. But this they did not show him, although they all knew about it. This was theirs and theirs alone! What would be left of its mystery after the frescoes had been photographed? When the jars and bowls had been taken away to museums? When the figure had been measured and copied, perhaps even chipped from its foundation? No! No! No! No! Jorge was right. The Place was the most wonderful place in the world and it should remain so! What did she and Centavo or even her father matter compared to these people and this old god, hidden away in the depths of the earth?

"I'll never tell," Ellen promised the figure. The air was so still that she could hear her watch ticking, the sound echoing back from the stone altar. For a little while it would go on and then the hands would stop. But what was time to a limestone deity created, drop by drop, over so many centuries?

Nati touched her arm.

"We must go now, Ellen," she said out loud. From the moment the copal had begun to burn, Nati had been at ease, as though the image and she understood one another.

"Snap on the torch again, please, Nati," Ellen begged. "Let me see everything: the pictures and the jars and the god. I want to remember the Place as long as I live."

"I told you it was the most wonderful place in the world," said Jorge. "Wasn't I right, Ellen?"

"Yes," said Ellen. "It's the most wonderful place in all the world."

—*Elizabeth Coatsworth*

378

What Do You Think?

1. How might the information about the Place be of value to Ellen's father? Do you agree with her decision not to tell him about it? Explain your answer.
2. Why do you think the Place is considered sacred by Nati and Jorge's people? Why do you think they kept the Place a secret from outsiders?
3. Jorge and Ellen describe the Place as "the most wonderful place in all the world." What place would you describe in this way? Explain why you would choose that place.

Taking A Closer Look

1. List in two columns some of the things Ellen saw in the Place. In the first column list the things that were made by people. In the second column list things that were formed naturally.
2. What are some of the different kinds of jars and bowls in the Place? Why do you suppose they are in different shapes?
3. Explain the following sentence in the story: "And suddenly the jaguar spoke, not from the shadows of the shrine, but from its den in Ellen's heart."
4. Compare Ellen's feelings about the Place at the beginning of the story with her feelings at the end.
5. Tell what you have learned in this story about the work of archaeologists.

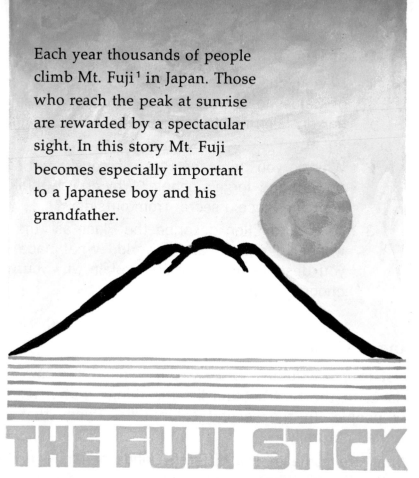

Each year thousands of people climb Mt. Fuji[1] in Japan. Those who reach the peak at sunrise are rewarded by a spectacular sight. In this story Mt. Fuji becomes especially important to a Japanese boy and his grandfather.

THE FUJI STICK

Fujio pushed his bowl of rice away from him and put down his chopsticks, his dark eyes thoughtful. The evening meal was usually a happy time in the Toyama[2] home. The family sat on the *tatami*[3] covered floor around a low table and Mama-san served the rice from a large wooden bowl. The tea was strong and hot, and the talk around the table was good. Usually. But today Fujio's forehead creased in a frown—today there was something wrong.

[1]Fuji (FOO-jee)   [2]Toyama (TOH-YAH-MAH)   [3]*tatami* (Tə-TAH-MEE)

380

He looked around the table. Mama-san smiled her same gentle smile as she ladled rice into their bowls and poured the tea. Papa-san sat straight and proud, smacking his lips as he enjoyed the rice in his bowl. Obaa-san[1] sat primly, as a grandmother might, nibbled her rice and sipped her tea in silence. And small sister Michiko,[2] with her bobbed black hair and impish black eyes, pushed the rice around in her bowl with the ends of her chopsticks. Now and then she giggled at the way the tiny bits of rice skidded around the slippery china and found their way down into her lap.

[1] Obaa-san (oh-BAH-ah-sahn)   [2] Michiko (MEE-chee-koh)

At last Fujio's glance fell upon his aged grandfather. His dark eyes narrowed. That was where the trouble was! Ojii-san[1] wore his old, mended kimono instead of his newest one. He sat with his balding head bowed to his chest. His rice sat untouched in his bowl. The bitter green tea he usually loved cooled in the cup in front of him. Fujio scowled. What was the matter with Grandfather? Couldn't the others see that he was acting strangely?

At last Grandfather raised his head and looked around. His black eyes seemed narrower than usual. It was then that the family knew he wished to speak. Immediately everyone was silent.

"My birthday is two days from now," he announced. "Seventy-two years have passed by swiftly. There is much I want to do before I become tired and stiff. I have one very strong wish, and that is to climb to the top of the great mountain." Now his eyes seemed to hold a vision. Fujio felt his own heart thump faster at Grandfather's words. He leaned forward to hear the old man. "I want to stand proudly at the top of Fuji-san and greet the sunrise as my own honored father once did. I wish to look down upon my beautiful country and see the blue lakes and the green valleys and the mountains."

Fujio's own eyes widened as he watched the effect of his grandfather's words upon Mama-san and Papa-san. "You are too old to climb so high," Papa-san said. "Climbing is for the young."

[1]Ojii-san (oh-JEE-ee-sahn)

The old man shook his shiny head. "Some of the pilgrims who climb the sacred mountain are as ancient as I. If they can do it, I can do it!" His jaw was set in determination. Fujio watched his grandfather shake his head indignantly. "I have listened too long now to my friends talk about climbing the mountain," the old man said. "And too many times I have had to look upon the seals of Fuji-san on their walking sticks. Soon I will be much too old to climb. I must do it now!"

Grandmother nodded and smiled in agreement. Fujio found himself nodding too. Surely the family would understand Grandfather's wish. It was very clear to him.

But no more was said about it then. Silence fell over the table like a cloud. When the meal had ended, Grandfather placed his cushion-like *zabuton*[1] on the floor in front of the television and prepared to watch an American western. Fujio sat on his heels beside the old man. He felt a tingle of excitement go up his back as he spoke.

"Ojii-san . . . I wish to talk to you about your dream to climb Fuji-san." He spoke as quietly as he could. "I have this same dream. Some of my older friends have already seen Lake Kawaguchi[2] from the top of the mountain. They make fun of me because I have only seen the lake from the foot of the great mountain. They say I am too small to climb—a baby! I have been thinking. We could climb to the top together. We would

---

[1] *zabuton* (zah-BOO-TON)   [2] Kawaguchi (KAH-WAH-GOO-CHEE)

show everyone that you are not too old—and I am not too young."

He sat back, waiting breathlessly for his grandfather's reply. The old man stared at the bright television screen for a long time. Fujio rocked on his heels, frowning. Hadn't his grandfather heard him? He opened his mouth to repeat his words, but his grandfather nodded.

"I think your idea is good, Fujio. You were named for the great mountain. It is right that you climb to the top while you are young. Yes . . ." he nodded again. "It is a good idea. We will help each other and enjoy the climb together. The family will see our dreams come true when we show them the seals of the great mountain on our walking sticks." He sat taller. "We must make our plans. Perhaps it can be a secret journey." A smile spread over his wrinkled face. "Do you think so?"

Fujio bounced on his heels, holding back a shout of joy. "Oh, yes! We will climb to the top the very day of your birthday. Tomorrow we will plan what clothes to wear on our journey up the mountain."

Grandfather slapped his knee in happiness. "We will need strong walking sticks—and a camera to take many pictures."

"And rice cakes to eat when we get hungry!" Fujio jumped to his feet, wishing he could spin around the room to show how good he felt. But this was not allowed in the house.

384

He went out the open door to the garden. There, beside the pool, he spun around. The stones tickled his feet, reminding him that he was still in his soft cotton *tabi*[1] and had forgotten to put on his sandals to come outside. It didn't matter! Nothing mattered now. He and Grandfather were really going to climb to the top of Mt. Fuji! The day after tomorrow! Nothing would spoil their dream now.

He stepped across the pool on the large flat stones and stood beside the stone lantern at the edge of the path. Little Michiko toddled into the garden, scuffing her wooden *geta*[2] as she walked. She carried her favorite *kokeshi*[3] doll clutched tightly in her small fist. When she reached Fujio, she held the armless wooden doll out to him. "See what Mama-san bought for me from the doll peddler on the street."

[1] *tabi* (TAH-bee)   [2] *geta* (gay-TAH)   [3] *kokeshi* (koh-KAY-shee)

385

Fujio nodded, sighing in disgust. He had seen the wooden doll with the painted face endless times. He couldn't be bothered about dolls now. Now he wanted only to think about the journey to Mt. Fuji.

Michiko's small mouth pouted. "I heard," she said impishly. "You and Ojii-san will climb the mountain."

Fujio whirled to face her, his eyes showing his alarm. "It is a secret, Michiko."

She shook her dark head and turned back to the house. Fujio watched her go. She was little. Perhaps she didn't understand about secrets, he told himself. Perhaps if he gave her a present, she would forget. His eyes darted about the garden. What would she like? "Michiko . . ." he called softly, "come back . . ."

And as Michiko turned back, Fujio's eyes came to rest on the small cage beside the bench near the path. Of course! He hurried over to the bench and picked up the tiny cage, peering inside. "Hello, my happy singer," he greeted his pet cricket. "I think you will soon have a new owner. . . ." He motioned to Michiko. "I will give you my cricket if you keep the secret."

Michiko's dark eyes looked at the insect in the cage. Her tiny nose wrinkled and she shook her head. "No! I do not want your bug!" With that, she clip-clopped over the path toward the house.

A frown creased Fujio's forehead. Now Mama-san and Papa-san would know the secret he and Grandfather shared. Would they forbid him to go on the journey up the mountain? The cricket in the cage chirped and

Fujio sighed. "I am not sure this is the time to sing, my friend."

He stayed in the garden until Mama-san's soft voice called to him. "It is time for bed, Fujio."

Fujio hung the cricket cage on a tree branch and went inside. Mama-san and Grandmother closed the sliding doors, dividing the big room in two for the night. Mama-san spread the heavy quilt-like *futon*[1] on the floor—one for each to sleep on and one to cover with. Fujio slept in the same room as Grandfather and Grand-mother. Michiko slept in the second room with Mama-san and Papa-san. There was no time to talk to Grand-father alone. No one metioned Mt. Fuji again that night. Fujio sighed. They would have to talk about it in the morning—before breakfast, when Grandmother and Mama-san put the beds away in the closets,

[1]*futon* (fə-TON)

opened the sliding doors, and cleaned the house. Papa-san would go off to work in the bakery. Then he and Grandfather could walk in the garden and talk. And they would know if Michiko had told their secret.

Fujio snuggled down under his quilt and stared up at the ceiling. Grandfather's snores filled the room. "How could he sleep?" Fujio wondered. In another day they would journey to the foot of the great mountain! They would start their climb! No matter what anyone said, they would get to the top! Butterflies danced in his stomach at the very thought.

The next morning when the family gathered around the table for their breakfast of soybean soup and rice, Fujio had the feeling again that something was wrong. This time he looked straight at his grandfather. Ojii-san's bald head was again bowed. The silence in the room made Fujio shudder. He looked at Michiko. She grinned impishly at him. "I have told about your trip," she said sweetly.

"We do not like the idea, Fujio. It would be too long a climb for your grandfather's tired legs—and too long a climb for your short legs." Mama-san shook her dark head.

Grandfather looked up. His dark eyes were glowing. "I *must* go up the mountain. How many more years will I be able to climb? Would you have me the only aged one in all Japan who hasn't seen the sunrise from the top of Fuji-san?"

Fujio watched his mother and father look at each

388

other. Papa-san shrugged his shoulders. "Honored Father, if you feel that strongly about it, you must certainly try to climb the mountain. With a strong stick, and Fujio to help you, you might reach the summit."

Fujio felt his heart speed up. "Thank you Papa-son."

"I will drive you to the foot of the mountain tomorrow morning. It will take you all that day and night to climb. But if you tire, you must come back down. Agreed?"

Fujio and his grandfather both nodded. "Agreed!" Fujio exclaimed. And he began to count the hours until the next morning.

Early the next day Papa-san drove Fujio and his grandfather across the many kilometres to Mt. Fuji. He helped them adjust their packs on their backs and then said good-by.

"And much luck in your climb," he told them. As he gazed up the slope to the top of the mountain towering in the clouds, he shook his head. "You will not do it," he muttered. "It is too far to climb."

Fujio saw his grandfather straighten up as tall as his thin frame could go. "We will! You go home now, my son, and work in the bakery. Return tomorrow and you will see our seals of Fuji-san."

Fujio watched his father drive off. Then they started up the mountain. The trail wove up gently up the slope and many people walked upward. Now and then Fujio saw a pair of worn straw sandals by the side of the trail. He pointed toward one of the pairs. "Someone has lost his shoes, Grandfather."

The old man shook his head. "The pilgrims who climb the sacred mountain carry many pairs of sandals. They throw them aside when they become worn and they put on a new pair." He pointed to another pair of the straw sandals farther up the slope. "They mark the trail for climbers."

Bells tinkled ahead and behind them. Fujio saw the pilgrims dressed in white. For them, the summit of the sacred mountain was a shrine, a place to visit and worship. He saw that they had bells tied to the ropes which they wore around their waists to help pull each other up the slopes. Each climber had a lantern. "I am glad we have flashlights," he told his grandfather.

Onward up the slope they walked, slowly on the uneven parts. When they reached a small temple, they bought strong walking sticks to help them on their climb. There were many climbers. Young people passed by Fujio and Grandfather. Climbers the age of Papa-san walked more slowly, Fujio noticed. Wives and husbands climbed beside each other. But Fujio did not see anyone as ancient as Grandfather. And he didn't see another child as young as himself.

Now and then they had to stop along the path to rest. Grandfather shaded his eyes and looked upward toward the summit. "It is still a long way to the top, Fujio."

How tired Grandfather sounded! Fujio's dark eyes showed his concern. "Perhaps we were wrong to come after all, Grandfather. We can turn back."

Grandfather stood tall and straight. "We will go to the very top and see the sunrise from there in the early morning."

Fujio slipped his pack off his back and took out the rice cakes Mama-san had packed for them. "Here. We will eat, Grandfather. Then we can go on."

As they sat beside the trail, other climbers went by them. Some sang happy songs. The people wound along the path as far up the slope as Fujio could see. He watched Grandfather eat the rice cake. Could the old man go on to the top? He sighed. Could *he* go on? Even now his legs ached. He brushed dust off his heavy shoes. He could go back down and climb again another year when he was taller and stronger. But Grandfather's bones were already stiff with age. If he went down now, he might never be able to say that he had climbed the great mountain. Grandfather would be ashamed to tell his friends that he could not climb the mountain. That must not happen!

Grandfather got slowly to his feet, using his walking stick to push himself up. "We must go on, Fujio. We will almost reach the top by dark."

Fujio nodded. At least Grandfather had not given up. Up and up they went, more and more slowly with each step. Fujio found himself breathing hard. He watched his grandfather closely. Now and then the old man stopped to take a deep breath and mop his forehead. Fujio's legs throbbed from the climb. He watched his grandfather in wonder. How could one so old climb so well? What a strong man his grandfather was!

They climbed through the long afternoon and stopped again to eat. The sun began to set and the climbers put on heavier clothing and lit their lanterns. Fujio took their flashlights out of the pack to light the path ahead of them. Soon the slope was twinkling with hundreds of lights. Fujio heard his grandfather puffing. Once the old man stumbled and fell to his knees. Fujio helped him to his feet. On they went. Now Fujio put his arm around Grandfather's waist to help him along the darkened path. The old man's footsteps became slower and slower. Fear clutched at Fujio. How far could they go? "We should have listened to Mama-san and Papa-san," he thought.

At last they reached a hut near the top of the mountain. Many of the climbers went in and stretched out on the floor to sleep. Grandfather motioned Fujio inside and they too stretched out on the floor. Soon

Grandfather was snoring. Fujio sighed and closed his eyes. Now they were too far to return home. So of course they would go on. He smiled in the darkness. In the morning they would be standing on top of the world!

Shuffling feet and hushed voices woke Fujio. The first faint light of dawn filtered into the open doorway of the hut. Quickly he shook his grandfather. "It is almost morning, Ojii-san. We must go on."

Grandfather tried to rise, but fell back to the floor. "I cannot get up!" he moaned. "Your mother and father were right. Old bones were not meant to climb mountains."

Fujio's heart pounded. If Grandfather couldn't go up, he couldn't go down either! What would become of them? He looked anxiously at Ojii-san.

The old man looked sad. "If you want to see the sunrise, go on without me," he told Fujio.

Fujio shook his head. "I will not go on without you, Grandfather. Come, I will help you. Your dream to go to the top of the mountain will come true. It will!"

He took his grandfather's thin arm and pulled him to his feet. The old man leaned on Fujio, and on his heavy walking stick. "I will try," he said finally. And slowly they started out, up the slope of the mountain.

Grandfather's weight seemed to push Fujio down. The mountain air was thinner than that below. He puffed for breath. Each step became painful. Ojii-san's feet dragged. Often he would stop, mop his forehead, and sigh. "I will wait for you here, beside the path," he said.

Stubbornly, Fujio shook his head. "No! We have come this far. We will go on together." As he spoke, Fujio tripped on a loose stone. He felt a sharp pain in his ankle as it turned. He cried out as he sank to the ground. Grandfather bent to help him to his feet. Fujio gasped, "My ankle! I twisted it."

Ojii-san pushed Fujio gently to a rock. "Then we must sit here and rest," he said. "I am afraid we have come as far as we can. This great mountain is too much for us." He rubbed his grandson's ankle as he spoke. They sat quietly, neither one speaking. The light in the eastern sky was beginning to brighten. Fujio could see the pink and gold sunlight peeking through the clouds. In just a few more minutes the sun would be up. He saw his grandfather's eyes searching the sky. How much he wanted to see that sunrise! They must get to the top before the sun rose.

With an effort, Fujio got to his feet. "Come, let us go on, Grandfather. Now I must lean upon you. We won't give up now. We are near the top and the sun is coming up."

His grandfather nodded. He put his arm around Fujio. Suddenly his fading strength seemed renewed. Up they went. Slowly . . . very slowly. Soon they could hear chanting voices and shouts of joy ahead of them. The end of the trail was near! On they went. Fujio's ankle hurt. Grandfather moaned under his breath. But—they were there!

The sun slid out from under a cloud blanket and rose, a giant red ball in the sky. Fujio shouted a loud hurrah, and Grandfather's eyes filled with tears. They stood together, quietly watching the beautiful sight before them. "We have done it!" Grandfather exclaimed. "We will get a seal of the mountains to put on our walking sticks. Those waiting for us below will want to see them."

Fujio nodded. His heart throbbed with happiness. "The way down is easier, Grandfather. We can go slowly and ask for help if we need it. We will have no trouble." He sighed and breathed the clear air. It was, he thought, like standing on top of the whole world. He clutched his walking stick tightly. "We climbed well, Grandfather. And we will have the proof."

—*Virginia K. Smiley*

What Do You Think?

1. Explain why you would agree or disagree with this saying: "One who climbs Mt. Fuji once is wise; one who climbs it twice is a fool."

2. Why do you think Grandfather hadn't climbed Mt. Fuji as a young man? Why couldn't he wait any longer?

3. What did the Fuji stick stand for? If you had earned a Fuji stick, what would it mean to you?

Taking A Closer Look

1. What problems did Fujio and Grandfather have to solve before they could climb Mt. Fuji? How did each show his determination to succeed?

2. Find four ways the author tells you the story takes place in Japan. What clues tell you it happens in modern Japan?

3. Fujio's father said, "Climbing is for the young." Tell why you agree or disagree with him.

4. Think of a word or phrase to describe how each person in these sentences felt.
   a. Butterflies danced in Fujio's stomach.
   b. Grandfather's jaw was set.
   c. Fujio's heart thumped faster.
   d. Grandfather's rice sat untouched in his bowl.

5. Tell about a time when you were determined to do something that others felt you were too young to try? Did you succeed?

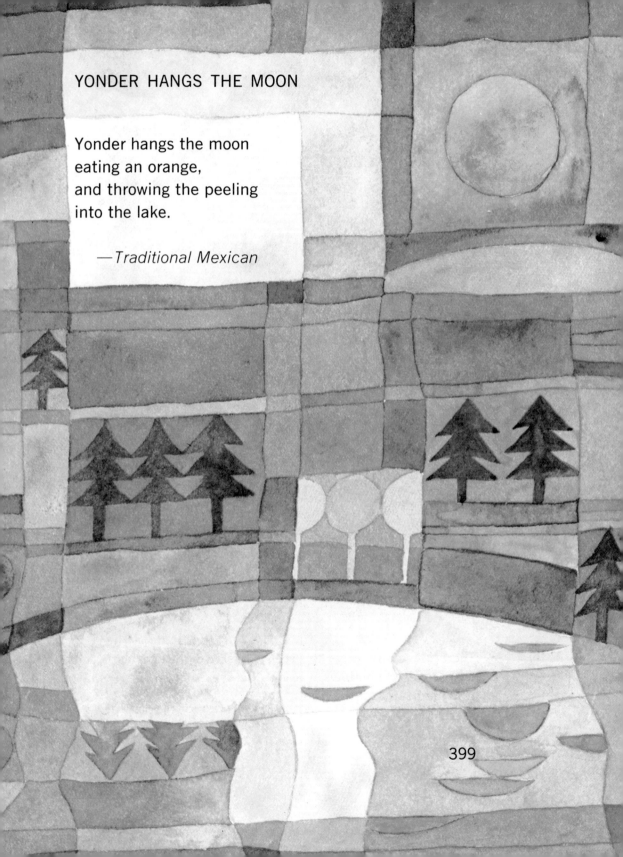

YONDER HANGS THE MOON

Yonder hangs the moon
eating an orange,
and throwing the peeling
into the lake.

—*Traditional Mexican*

399

There are many ways to "see" — as Hwei Ming was quick
to discover. Sometimes it is not the eyes that see best of all.
It is the heart and the mind.

400

The Seeing Stick

Once in the ancient walled citadel of Peking
there lived an emperor who had only one daughter,
and her name was Hwei Ming.[1]
Now this daughter had carved ivory combs
to smooth back her long black hair.
Her tiny feet were encased in embroidered slippers,
and her robes were woven of the finest silks.
But rather than making her happy,
such possessions made her sad.
For Hwei Ming was blind,
and all the beautiful handcrafts in the kingdom
brought her no pleasure at all.
Her father was also sad
that his only daughter was blind,
but he could not cry for her.
He was the emperor after all,
and had given up weeping over such things
when he ascended the throne.
Yet still he had hope
that one day Hwei Ming might be able to see.
So he resolved that if someone could help her,
such a person would be rewarded
with a fortune in jewels.

[1]Hwei Ming (WAY MING)

401

He sent word of his offer
to the inner and outer cities of Peking
and to all the towns and villages
for hundred of kilometres around.
Monks came, of course,
with their prayers and prayer wheels,
for they thought in this way
to help Hwei Ming see.
Magician-priests came, of course,
with their incantations and spells,
for they thought in this way
to help Hwei Ming see.
Physicians came, of course,
with their potions and pins,
for they thought in this way
to help Hwei Ming see.
But nothing could help..
Hwei Ming had been blind from the day of her birth,
and no one could effect a cure.

402

Now one day
an old man, who lived far away
in the south country,
heard tales of the blind princess.
He heard of the emperor's offer.
And so he took his few possessions—
a long walking stick,
made from a single piece of golden wood,
and his whittling knife—
and started up the road.
The sun rose hot on his right side
and the sun set cool on his left
as he made his way north to Peking
to help the princess see.

At last the old man,
his clothes tattered by his travels,
stopped by the gate of the Outer City.
The guards at the gate
did not want to let such a ragged old man in.
"Grandfather, go home.
There is nothing here for such as you," they said.
The old man touched their faces in turn
with his rough fingers.
"So young," he said,
"and already so old."
He turned as if to go.
Then he propped his walking stick
against his side
and reached into his shirt
for his whittling knife.
"What are you doing, grandfather?"
called out one of the guards
when he saw the old man bring out the knife.
"I am going to show you my stick,"
said the old man.
"For it is a stick that sees."
"Grandfather, that is nonsense,"
said the second guard.
"That stick can see no farther
than can the emperor's daughter."

404

"Just so, just so,"
said the old man.
"But stranger things have happened."
And so saying,
he picked up the stick
and stropped the knife blade back and forth
three times to sharpen its edge.
As the guards watched
from the gate in the wall,
the old man told them
how he had walked the many kilometres
through village and towns
till he came with his seeing stick
to the walls of Peking.
And as he told them his tale,
he pointed to the pictures in the stick:
an old man,
his home,
the long walk,
the walls of Peking.
And as they watched further,
he began to cut their portraits into the wood.
The two guards looked at each other
in amazement and delight.
They were flattered at their likenesses
on the old man's stick.
Indeed, they had never witnessed such carving skill.

"Surely this is something
the guards at the wall
of the Inner City should see," they said.
So, taking the old man by the arm,
they guided him
through the streets of the Outer City,
past flower peddlers and rice sellers,
past silk weavers and jewel merchants,
up to the great stone walls.
When the guards of the Inner City
saw the seeing stick,
they were surprised and delighted.
"Carve our faces, too,"
they begged like children.
And laughing,
and touching their faces
as any fond grandfather would,
the old man did as they bid.
In no time at all,
the guards of the Inner City took the old man by his arm
and led him to the wall of the Innermost City
and in through the gate
to the great wooden doors of the Imperial Palace.

Now when the guards arrived
in the throne room of the Imperial Palace
leading the old man by the arm,
it happened that the emperor's blind daughter,
Hwei Ming,
was sitting by his side,
her hands clasped before her,
silent, sightless, and still.
As the guards finished telling
of the wonderful pictures carved on the golden stick,
the princess clapped her hands.
"Oh, I wish I could see that wondrous stick," she said.
"Just so, just so," said the old man.
"And I will show it to you.
For it is no ordinary piece of wood,
but a stick that sees."
"What nonsense," said her father
in a voice so low it was almost a growl.
But the princess did not hear him.
She had already bent toward
the sound of the old man's voice.
"A seeing stick?"

The old man did not say anything for a moment.
Then he leaned forward
and petted Hwei Ming's head
and caressed her cheek.
For though she was a princess,
she was still a child.
Then the old man began to tell again
the story of his long journey to Peking.
He introduced each character and object—
the old man,
the guards,
the great walls,
the Innermost City.
And then he carved the wooden doors,
the Imperial Palace,
the princess, into the golden wood.

408

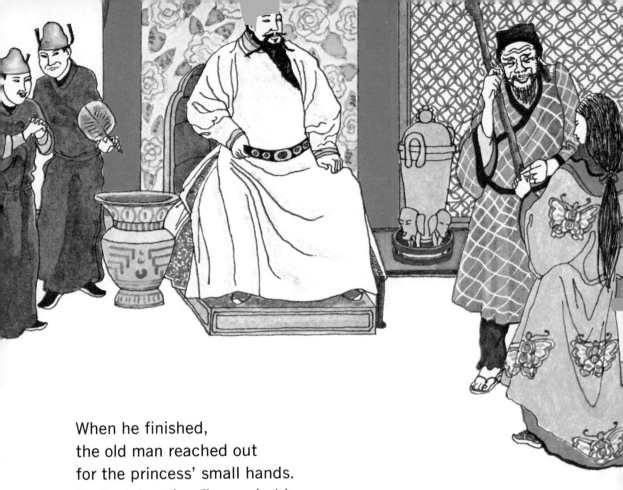

When he finished,
the old man reached out
for the princess' small hands.
He took her tiny fingers in his
and placed them on the stick.
Finger on finger,
he helped her trace the likenesses.
"Feel the long flowing hair of the princess,"
the old man said.
"Grown as she herself has grown,
straight and true."
And Hwei Ming touched the carved stick.
"Now feel your own long hair," he said.
And she did.

"Feel the lines in the old man's face," he said.
"From years of worry and years of joy."
He thrust the stick into her hands again.
And the princess' slim fingers
felt the carved stick.
Then he put her fingers onto his face
and traced the same lines there.
It was the first time
the princess had touched another person's face
since she was a very small girl.
The princess jumped up from her throne
and thrust her hands before her.
"Guards, O guards," she cried out.
"Come here to me."
And the guards lifted up their faces
to the Princess Hwei Ming's hands.
Her fingers,
like little breezes,
brushed their eyes and noses and mouths,
and then found each one on the carved stick.

Hwei Ming turned to her father,
the emperor,
who sat straight and tall
and unmoving on his great throne.
She reached out
and her fingers ran eagerly
through his hair
and down his nose and cheek
and rested curiously on a tear they found there.
And that was strange, indeed,
for had not the emperor
given up crying over such things
when he ascended the throne?

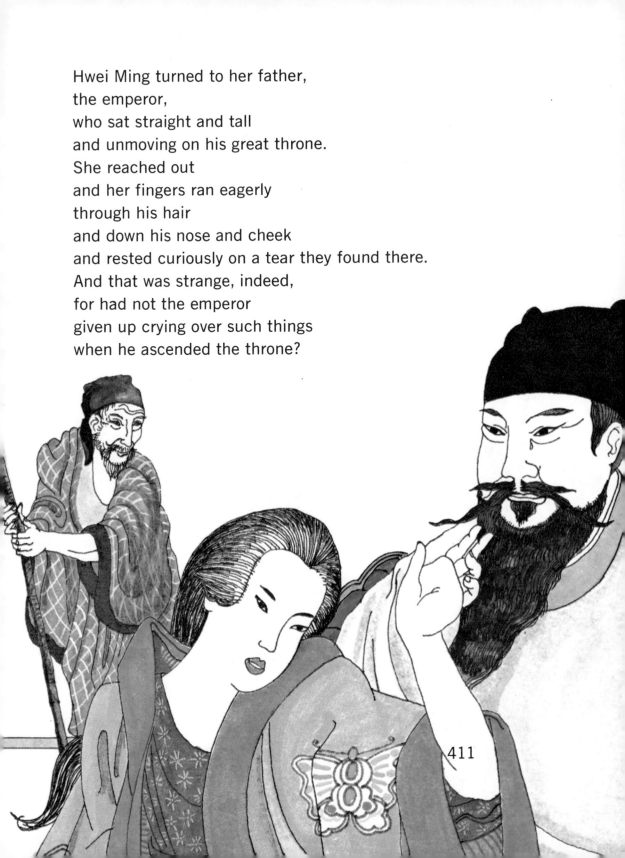

411

They brought her
through the streets of the city, then,
the emperor in the lead.
And Princess Hwei Ming
touched men and women
and children as they passed.
Till at last
she stood before the great walls of Peking
and felt the stones themselves.
Then she turned to the old man.
Her voice was bright
and full of laughter.
"Tell me another tale," she said.
"Tomorrow, if you wish," he replied.

412

For each tomorrow
as long as he lived,
the old man dwelt
in the Innermost City,
where only the royal family stays.
The emperor rewarded him
with a fortune in jewels,
but the old man gave them all away.
Every day
he told the princess a story.
Some were tales as ancient
as the city itself.
Some were as new
as the events of the day.
And each time
he carved wonderful images
in the stick of golden wood.
As the princess listened,
she grew eyes
on the tips of her fingers.
As least that is what
she told the other blind children
whom she taught to see as she saw.
Certainly it was as true
as saying she had a seeing stick.
But the blind Princess Hwei Ming
believed that both things were true.
And so did all the blind children
in her city of Peking.

414

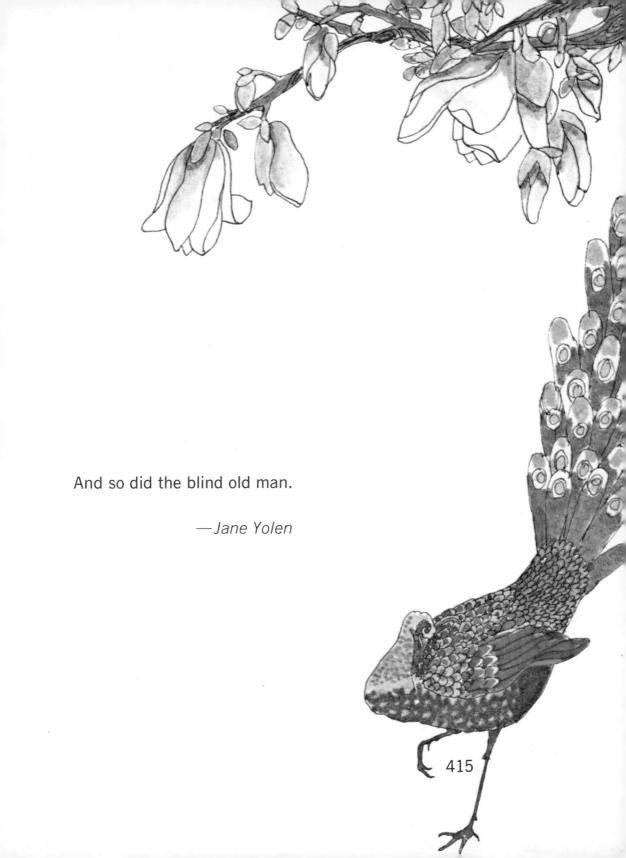

And so did the blind old man.

—*Jane Yolen*

415

What Do You Think?

1. Why do you think the old man came so far to see Hwei Ming?
2. In what ways did the old man's carved stick "see"? Did it only tell a story, or did it tell more than just facts? Explain your answer.
3. Do you think Hwei Ming could "see" as well as the sighted people around her? Why or why not?

Taking A Closer Look

1. What was the emperor's greatest hope?
2. Who tried and failed to cure Hwei Ming?
3. What did the palace guards think of the old man at first? What changed their minds?
4. How did the Seeing Stick teach Hwei Ming to see?
5. How did Hwei Ming show her eagerness to learn?
6. How did Hwei Ming help other blind children?
7. Why did the old man seem to have a special understanding of Hwei Ming?

THE SUN THAT WARMS YOU

Is it not so, brother?

The sun that warms you

        warms me,

The fate that forms me

        forms you,

The irk that frets you

        frets me,

The rain that wets me

        wets you,

The hour that tries you

        tries me,

But the sun that dries me

        dries you.

It is so, brother.

—*Eleanor Farjeon*

Tikta'liktak
An Eskimo Legend
by James Houston

Tikta'liktak drove his long sharp chisel into a crack and pulled himself up to the top of the jagged ice. From this height, he looked east and west along the rough barrier ice forced against the coastline as far as he could see.

He looked back along his trail of footprints across the snow-covered shore to his father's igloo, now almost hidden by the three hills that protected it from the howling winds that rushed over their island.

Tikta'liktak's people were sea hunters, singers, carvers, builders of sleek kayaks, masters of swift dog teams, whale hunters, listeners at the breathing places in the ice.

Because his father had always been a clever hunter, Tikta'liktak had grown up knowing only good times in the house of his family. There had always been great sea beasts for feasting, fat red trout, snow geese, and

420

sometimes meat from the swift herds of caribou that roved beyond the mountains on the inland plain.

There had also been singing and laughter in the house of his father, and hunters from distant camps had come to visit, bringing with them their whole families.

But at the end of this winter, the animals had fled from the plain. The birds had not yet returned from the south, and the fish remained locked beneath the frozen lakes.

The wind had blown in the wrong direction during the moons of February and March, holding masses of loose ice against the shores so that no man could travel or hunt on the sea. It was a time for starving.

Tikta'liktak thought of his family lying in the dark snowhouse without food for themselves or seal oil for their lamps. Hunger stirred within him. He knew he must find a way to help them.

The young Eskimo climbed carefully down from his high place on the ice through the great pieces that surrounded him like sharp white teeth. The sea ice that lay before him had been broken many times. It had opened and closed and frozen again until he did not know where to place his feet for fear of falling through. In some places, the ice was much thicker than the height of a man; in other spots, it was thinner than his little finger. A light layer of new snow covered everything, hiding the danger from his eyes.

Before each step, Tikta'liktak felt the ice in front of him with the chisel on the end of his harpoon. Many times the sharp point broke through the thick surface and water flooded over the snow at his feet. He was forced to try one way and then another before finding ice strong enough to hold his weight. He moved forward cautiously, so that it took a long time to travel even a short distance.

Tikta'liktak was lean and strong for his age, with a handsome tanned face, wide cheekbones, and a fine hawklike nose. Like all the people of his race, he possessed quick dark eyes with the lids drawn narrow for protection against long winters on the treeless plain, where they hunted in the wind and sun and snow. He wore narrow-slitted sun goggles.

His square white teeth flashed when he smiled, and his jaw muscles, strong from eating meat, showed clearly. His hair hung straight and black almost to his shoulders. It glistened in the cold morning sunlight like the bright new wings of an arctic butterfly, and the butterfly was Tikta'liktak's namesake.

Tikta'liktak wished most of all to be a good hunter. He could already throw a harpoon with great skill and drive an arrow straight to its mark. He thrilled at the songs and chanting and the great whirling and drumming of the hunters as they performed the autumn and midwinter dances before the hunt.

But the magic of the dancers, and all their hunts, had failed them this year.

As he moved slowly forward testing the ice, Tikta'liktak saw before him the trail made by a huge white bear. Each of its paws had left a mark in the snow as large as if a man had sat down. Looking closely, Tikta'liktak could see that the tracks were fresh and new, for the print of each pad was still sharp and clear.

The bear must have been hungry, too, for its track led away from the land, which meant it had been forced to make the long crossing in search of new hunting grounds. Tikta'liktak hoped that the bear had not seen him, for he did not wish to fight on this thin ice. Farther along, he could see where the bear's immense weight had broken through the ice, but this meant nothing to the huge beast with its thick waterproof fur. It had crawled out of the freezing water and continued on its way.

Tikta'liktak traveled until late afternoon. Ahead of him lay the dark stretch of sea water beyond the ice. Half hidden in the winter fog above the water flew thousands of seabirds in thick black flocks. They gave the young hunter new strength, for he knew that there must also be

423

seals in the dark water, and the birds and seals would
provide food and oil for the lamps of his people.

Small icebergs caught and frozen fast towered above his
head, offering him shelter in their weird shadowy blue
caves. In the haze beyond them, water and ice and sky
seemed to blend into one. The pale orange sun was
surrounded by a great circle of light. In this circle
appeared four false suns and beyond them four more.
These reflections, called sun dogs, were seldom seen, and
Tikta'liktak knew they were a warning of storms to come.

424

His people believed them to be the team of dogs pulling the sun on its endless journey through the sky.

When Tikta'liktak reached the edge of the sea ice, he saw many flocks of birds upon the water. Excitedly, he began to plan the hunt. He would hide downwind of the birds, behind a large piece of upturned ice near the water's edge. The rafts of birds would drift near enough for his arrows to reach them, and when hit, the birds would float in to him.

Nearer and nearer drifted the birds, in countless screaming numbers. Tikta'liktak's arrows flew straight, and the birds they hit floated in as he had hoped, all save one small seabird that floated past the point where he was hiding and was blown by the wind to the far edge of the ice.

When his last arrow was gone, Tikta'liktak stood up. A few birds took off in panic, and then the others followed in great flights. They flew down the coast beyond his sight.

Tikta'liktak picked the soft warm feathered birds out of the water, and after recovering his arrows, he piled them on the ice and started out after the small bird that had drifted beyond him. With much difficulty, he finally reached it with his harpoon and pulled it to the edge of the ice. When he turned to retrace his steps to the pile of birds, a huge crack had opened in the ice, barring his path. It was too wide to jump. Tikta'liktak realized with horror that he could not return. He was drifting out to sea on a large pan of ice, carried by the rising wind and tide.

It was growing colder and soon would be dark. Tikta'liktak squatted on the ice and ate the small seabird, thinking of the precious pile of food only a short distance away. He would never see it again, nor perhaps his home.

He felt somewhat better after eating the bird and with his short knife tried to pry loose some ice to build a small snowhouse. But all he could manage was to stand some flat pieces upright, leaning them together like a tent. The cracks between the ice he filled with snow to complete a rough protection against the night wind. Curled up in this tiny shelter, he dared not sleep for fear of freezing.

All through the night, the small ice island moved with the tide. It sighed and groaned, and he wondered if it would break apart and cast him into the freezing sea.

When dawn came, he walked around his tiny frozen island, waving his arms to warm himself. He wondered about his family and what they must be thinking.

The open water around his moving ice floe sent moisture into the freezing air. It rose as a dark fog against the pale light of morning and fell back into the leaden sea, covering his ice floe with countless frost crystals that turned it into a silent, shimmering magic place.

Suddenly, a seal's dark head came up through the water close to the edge of the ice. Tikta'liktak was ready with his harpoon, but the seal was frightened at finding itself so near a human and quickly ducked beneath the surface before the sharp point could reach him. To bring the seal back, Tikta'liktak began to call the words, "Kilee, kilee, kilee," (Come, come, come). Then he lay on the edge of the ice floe and, with the end of his knife, reached over and gently scratched just below the surface of the freezing water, imitating the sound of a seal's front claws opening a

426

breathing hole in the ice. This sound often makes a curious seal come near. But not this one, nor did any other appear, though Tikta'liktak continued with magic words and scratching until well past midday.

In the afternoon, he walked around his small floating ice island, trying to keep warm, until a new cold wind came out of the northeast, chilling his very bones and changing the direction of his drifting home.

He improved his icehouse as much as he could and spread fresh snow on the floor to serve as a bed, for he would be warmer lying on snow than on ice. Before he lay down, he put one of his sealskin mitts beneath his hip and the other beneath his shoulder.

That night, Tikta'liktak drew his arms inside his fur parka, hugging them close to his body so they would not freeze, and he breathed into his hood to help warm himself. In this way, he managed to sleep, dreaming all night of eating rich haunches of caribou, fat young loons, and the sweet summer eggs of snow geese.

As the first light of dawn crept around his tiny house, Tikta'liktak felt a gentle bump and then another. Rising quickly, he went outside the ice shelter.

His island had drifted against another much larger ice pan. Gathering his precious harpoon, bow and arrows, and his short knife, he ran lightly to the edge of the ice. First he tested the strength of the larger pan with the end of his harpoon; then he leaped across the narrow opening just as the two pieces began to draw apart.

This second drifting island felt much stronger as he walked carefully over it, feeling beneath the snow

428

covering with his ice chisel. It did not have as many cracks
or thin dangerous places as the first pan.

Through the narrow slits of his snow goggles,
Tikta'liktak saw something dark spread out on the snow
before him. As he hurried toward it, a huge black raven
rose up and flew away. The dark stain was a patch of blood
on the snow where, as the tracks leading up to it showed,
a white bear had killed a seal. But, alas, the bear and
almost all the seal meat were gone. Only one small fatty
scrap remained, for the hungry raven had carefully
cleaned away everything else left by the bear.

429

Nearby, Tikta'liktak found some large flat pieces of ice and started to build a new shelter. He soon tired because he was so hungry, but he continued to work until his house was completed. Then he placed the scrap of meat beside a small hole in the roof and crawled inside to wait.

Before long, he heard the swish of wings as the raven returned. The sleek black bird landed on the spot where the seal had been and, finding nothing, rose up with an angry croak. It landed again, this time on top of Tikta'liktak's house, ready to snatch the last remaining morsel of seal fat.

In an instant, Tikta'liktak's hand shot up through the hole, grasped the raven's leg, and pulled it down into the house. Some say ravens are not good to eat; they are wrong. The raven was thin but delicious, and Tikta'liktak felt much better after this fine breakfast.

For three days and three nights, he walked about on his floe to warm himself and slept when he could. The winds and strong tides moved his island back and forth, sometimes out to sea, sometimes toward the land. He found nothing more to eat and felt he would surely die on this lonely ice island.

On the fourth day, Tikta'liktak awoke and sensed that something had changed. He looked out of his house, and there before him was the most welcome sight he had ever seen. In the distance, like a gigantic stony cloud, lay the island called Sakkiak, its raw granite hills piercing through the surrounding shore ice. These hills were swept entirely free of snow by the wind. Tikta'liktak knew that no man dared to live on Sakkiak, but it was solid rock, and

he longed to leave his ice island and place his foot upon it,
though it was a bleak and lonely place.

He judged the drift of his ice pan with great care and
saw that he would come close to the shore ice surrounding
the large island. He realized, too, that his ice floe might
not touch it and might be swept forever out into the open sea.

431

Tikta'liktak planned now to try a desperate trick he had once heard of. If it failed, he would surely die.

He ran to the thinnest corner of his floating island where he had noticed a piece of ice that had cracked off and then partly refrozen. It was not much larger than a walrus, but if he could break it loose, it might keep him afloat and serve as a clumsy boat. He worked frantically with his chisel, trying to free the corner as he drew nearer and nearer to the long floe of loose ice stretching out from the island. He could see now that he would pass the long floe without touching.

Suddenly, the small piece of ice broke beneath his chisel and was free. With a quick jump, he landed upon it and, kneeling down, paddled desperately with his hands in the freezing water. The ice boat was moving, and in a short

432

time he touched against the loose ice that stretched in a wide broken path to the island.

Now came the most daring part of the trick. Arranging his bow and arrow quiver so they hung straight down his back and holding his harpoon with both hands before him at the level of his chest to steady his balance, Tikta'liktak started running and jumping from pan to pan with every bit of skill he possessed.

If he dared to stop even for a moment, the small pieces of ice would roll or sink in the icy water and he would fall. He moved with the balance and delicacy of a sandpiper skirting a wave on a beach until he made a final leap onto the strong shore ice surrounding the island. There he lay, gasping.

As his breath returned to him, Tikta'liktak could scarcely believe that he had reached solid ice and was still alive. Slowly he walked toward the sheltering hills of the great barren island that rose before him, grateful to be on land once more.

He chose a valley that formed a long sheltered passage leading upward to the top of the island. In this valley, under the protecting hills, he built a small strong snowhouse and slept he knew not how long. After this, he lost all track of time.

Tikta'liktak awoke with raging pangs of hunger and hurried out to see what treasures his new island might provide. Weak as he was from lack of food, it took a full day to walk the length of the island. Although Sakkiak was fairly narrow, it also took him a day to cross it because of the steep rocky spine of hills that ran its whole length.

The beaches were blown almost clear. Snow had been driven against the hills in hard wind-packed drifts many times the height of a man. Tikta'liktak walked along the frozen beaches, searching them for any kind of food and peering out hopefully over the shore ice for seals.

Nothing did he see but snow and rock and sometimes bleached white bones or hard dry scraps of bird skins eaten out a season before by foxes. The lemmings, small rodents without tails, seemed not to be on the island, for he saw no tracks. The fat eider ducks had left evidence everywhere, in the form of old nesting places, of their summer occupation of the island. But by the time they returned to lay their eggs, he would surely be dead of hunger.

434

Often he gazed out across the straits, where the white ice floes churned past in the dangerous rip tides. He could see the mainland hanging blue and serene like a dream of some far-off place. There was his home, his family, his friends. All of them must think that he was dead. The mainland seemed near, and yet to Tikta'liktak, without food or materials or a boat, it was an impossible distance.

Staggering from hunger and fatigue, he returned to the snowhouse that evening and had terrible dreams until he awoke in the morning in the cold gray igloo scarcely knowing whether he was truly awake or still in some dark nightmare.

When he climbed the hill the next day, Tikta'liktak used his harpoon for support, like an old man. He had to tell himself again and again that he had lived fewer than twenty summers.

From the top of the rocky hill, Tikta'liktak saw far out on the drifting ice many walrus, fat, sleek, and brown, lying together motionless like great stones, their tusks showing white in the sunlight. The wind was carrying them away, out to sea, and he could never hope to take one.

Sitting there in the cold wind, with no help, he said aloud, over and over again, "This island is my grave. This island is my grave. I shall never leave this place. I shall never leave this place." The idea obsessed him, and at last, in fright, he hurriedly stumbled downward, falling many times, until he came to the snowhouse and slept again for a very long while.

When he awoke, Tikta'liktak cut small strips from the
tops of his boots and chewed them to ease his hunger.
This seemed to give him some strength. Then, slowly, as if
drawn by magic, he started again up the long hill.

It was warmer now. True spring was coming to the land.
But it helped him not at all, for there was nothing living
on the island, nor would there be until the birds came to
nest again, and that would be too late for him.

On top of the hill once more, Tikta'liktak scanned the
sea and saw nothing but water and glaring ice. Again a
distant voice seemed to say, "This island is your grave."
He stood up slowly and looked around. There were many
great flat rocks, and Tikta'liktak decided they would be his
final resting place. Two of the largest ones lay near each
other, offering him a sheltered bed, and with his failing
strength, he dragged two more large stones to make the

437

ends, at head and foot. Another large one placed on top covered the lower half. The stones now formed a rough coffin.

He searched until he found a large flat piece to cover his head. Half laughing and half crying, he climbed into his stony grave. After one last look at the wide blue sky and the sea around him, he lay down with his harpoon, knife, and bow arranged neatly by his side. He hoped that his relatives would someday find his bones and know him by his weapons and know what had happened to him.

Tikta'liktak did not know how long he slept. When he awoke, he was numb with cold. Slowly, a new idea started to form in his mind. "I will not die, I will not die, I will not die." With a great effort, he pushed away the stone that formed the top half of the coffin. Painfully, he arose and staggered out of that self-made grave.

Holding himself as straight as he could with the aid of his harpoon, Tikta'liktak staggered down the side of the hill to the beach. He lay there to rest and again fell asleep. This time he dreamed of many strange things: skin boats rising up from their moorings, haunches of fat year-old caribou, rich dark walrus meat, young ducks with delicious yellow fat, juicy seals, and the warm eggs of a snow owl.

He could not tell if he was asleep or awake, but again and again the head of a seal appeared. It seemed so real in the dream that he took up his harpoon and cast it blindly before him. He felt a great jerk that fully awakened him, and, behold, he had a true seal firmly harpooned. He lay

back with his feet against a rock and held onto the
harpoon line until the seal's spirit left him.

With his last strength, Tikta'liktak drew the seal out of
the water and across the edge of the ice until he had all
this richness in his hands. He knew that the seal had been
sent to him by the sea spirit and that this gift would give
him back his life.

After some food and sleep, and more food and sleep
again, he soon felt well. Using his bow, he whirled an
arrow swiftly into a hollow scrap of driftwood and dried
shavings until they grew hot, smoked, and burst into
flames. The seal fat burned nicely in a hollow stone in his
snowhouse, making it warm and bright. The spring sun
helped to restore his health and strength, and Tikta'liktak
remembered once more that he was young.

He kept the meat of the seal in the igloo and prepared

the fat for use in the stone lamp. The sealskin he turned inside out without splitting it open and scraped it with a flattened bone in the special way that he had seen his mother teach his sister.

One day, he found the tracks of a white fox that had come to the island. After that, the fox came to visit his dwelling every day. It always came along the same way, and that was its mistake. Tikta'liktak built a falling-stone trap across its path, baited with a scrap of seal meat.

The next morning, the fox was in the trap, and after skinning it, Tikta'liktak drew from the tail long strong sinews that make the finest thread. That evening he ate the fox meat and placed the fine white skin above his oil lamp to dry. Tikta'liktak also made a good needle by sharpening a thin splinter of bone on a rock, and with this, he mended his clothes.

After his work was done, he stepped out through the entrance of the small igloo to look at the great night sky. It was filled with stars beyond counting that formed patterns familiar to all his people, who used them for guidance when traveling.

Off to the north, great green and yellow lights soared up, slowly faded, then soared again in their magic way. Tikta'liktak's people knew that these were caused by the night spirits playing the kicking game in the sky. In the way his father had taught him, he whistled and pushed his hands up to the sky, marveling as the lights ebbed and flowed with his movements as though he controlled them.

Life on the island was better now, but still Tikta'liktak longed to return home to his own people.

440

Half of another moon passed, and now the spring sun hung just below the horizon each night and would not let the sky grow dark. Two seals appeared in the open waters of the bay in front of the snowhouse, and by good fortune, Tikta'liktak managed to harpoon first one and then the other. This gave him an abundance of food and of oil to heat his igloo. He again carefully drew the meat out of the seals, without cutting them open in the usual method, and scraped and dried the skins.

Tikta'liktak sat before his small house thinking and making plans. An idea for building a kind of boat without any tools or driftwood for the frame had finally come to him.

He began to prepare one of the three sealskins. First, he tied the skin tightly and carefully where the back flippers had been so that no water could enter. Then where the seal's neck had been, he bound in a piece of bone, hollow through the middle. When he had finished, he put his mouth to the hole and, with many strong breaths, blew the skin up so that it looked again like a fat seal. Next, he fitted a small piece of driftwood in the bone to act as a plug and hold in the air.

The sun was warm on his back as he worked with his floats on that bright spring morning. His stomach was full, his clothes were mended, and he began to make a song inside himself, hoping that someday he might return to his people on the mainland. The song had magic in it. It spoke of fear and wonder and of life and hope. The words came well. There was joy in Tikta'liktak and yet a warning of danger, too.

441

He looked up from his work as a huge shadow loomed over him. Tikta'liktak threw himself sideways, rolling toward his harpoon, which he caught hold of as he sprang to his feet. Before him, between his small house and the sea, stood a huge white bear. The bear's mouth was half open, and its blue-black tongue lolled between its strong teeth. Its little eyes were watching him warily as it decided how best to kill him.

Fear stirred the hair on the back of Tikta'liktak's neck and reached down into his stomach. His harpoon was small for a beast such as this one, and although he had often heard of encounters with bears, Tikta'liktak had never met one face to face.

Remembering the wise words of his father, Tikta'liktak carefully studied every movement of the bear. He tried to think like a bear to understand what the great beast would do next. He slowly knelt down and felt with the chisel end of the harpoon for a crack between two rocks. Finding this, he wedged it in firmly and leveled the pointed end at the bear's throat. He had not long to wait for the attack.

The bear lunged forward, and the harpoon pierced the white fur and went deep into its throat. Tikta'liktak held the harpoon as long as he could, then rolled away, but not before he felt the bear's great claws rake the side of his face. He scrambled to his feet and ran uphill.

The huge beast tried to follow, but the harpoon caught and caught again in the rocks, forcing the point more deeply inward. The harpoon found its life, and with a great sigh, the bear's spirit rushed out and it was dead.

Tikta'liktak's face was numb at first. Then it started to throb with pain. He made his way slowly to a small

443

hillside stream that flowed from the melting snow down to the sea. There he washed his face in the clear icy water.

Returning to his snowhouse, he took a patch of foxskin the size of his hand, scraped and scrubbed it clean, and set it squarely over the terrible wound. As it dried, the clean patch of foxskin tightened and grew smaller. It drew the open wounds together almost forming a new skin on his face.

Tikta'liktak was weak after his fight with the bear and nervous of every shadow. Also, he feared that his wound might fester, so he washed the foxskin dressing often. In time, his face showed signs of healing, and the pain ceased to bother him.

Then Tikta'liktak set about making a little stone and sod house for the summer like the ancient houses of his forefathers. He had no material to make the kind of sealskin tent now used by his people.

Inside the new house, it was warm and comfortable, and the light from his small lamp glowed brightly. The new bearskin was warm to sleep on and the meat good to eat. At this time, another seal came to him one evening in the half dark of spring before the moon had fully risen. It did not see Tikta'liktak until his harpoon reached it.

Cutting this seal open in the usual way, from the rear flippers to the throat, Tikta'liktak then scraped and stretched the skin. With the skin, he made new hip-length boot tops to sew above his own. These bound with drawstrings and packed with dried moss were quite waterproof.

He had placed the two shoulder blades of the white bear

under a stone in the water so that the sea lice would pick
them clean as snow. He now bound them firmly with seal
thongs to each end of his harpoon. In this way, he made a
strong double-bladed paddle.

On a windless day, he tied the three blown-up sealskins
together and placed them in the shallow water. Sitting
astride them, he balanced himself and floated. It took
some practice before he was able to hold steady and
paddle and control this strange craft, but a boat of any
kind seemed his only chance of reaching the mainland
again.

By day, Tikta'liktak would look out over the great
expanse of water with its treacherous tides and wonder if
he had lived through this terrible spring only to drown. At

night, he would dream of his mother, his father, and his sisters. He wondered if they had starved or had found food as he had and were still alive.

He must try to make the crossing. First, he gathered a small parcel of meat, which he wrapped in seal fat so it would float and covered with sealskin so that it would be protected from the salt of the sea. Tikta'liktak tied the package to his waist with a thong, and it floated nicely behind him like a small duck. He filled two seal bladder pouches with fresh water, and these he hung around his neck.

The next morning was gray with fog, but the wind was down, and he decided this would be the day to start the dangerous journey. Pushing the inflated sealskin floats into the water, Tikta'liktak carefully climbed onto the strange watercraft. Then he started out, with only one glance back at his island home and upward to his open grave on top of the hill.

Cautiously, he began to use the bone paddle to steer out into the current, which swirled away from the island and carried him into the open water of the strait. With alarm, he noticed the great strength of the tide as it swept him eastward instead of north to the mainland as he had hoped. Tikta'liktak paddled very gently, careful not to upset his frail craft, learning as he went to guide it with his feet, which hung down awkwardly like those of a young snow goose trying to swim for the first time.

Tikta'liktak tried not to look down, for he could see far below him in the clear gray water great fronds of seaweed waving mysteriously, moved by powerful underwater

446

currents. A light breeze rippled over the surface of the water, sending him out toward the center of the strait. He could see the rip-tides now pressing down or swelling upward in a smooth icy rush. His feet and legs began to feel the freezing grip of the water, although they stayed dry. The chill of the sea drove through his boots, moss packing, and heavy fur socks, leaving him numb with cold.

Slowly, the hills of Sakkiak grew smaller and turned blue in the distance. Tikta'liktak judged himself to be halfway to the mainland. He paddled gently to give himself direction in the fast-moving current and was carried on the tide through gray patches of mist that hung over the water. Now stiff with cold and thirsty, he managed to drink a little of the fresh water from one of the pouches that hung around his neck and paddled on through the eerie silence.

Suddenly, Tikta'liktak heard a familiar sound, a sound he feared. It boomed across the water again and again, the great grunting roar of a huge bull walrus. The tide was carrying him straight into the herd the walrus was jealously protecting.

Dark heads appeared as the large herd grouped together, peering weak-eyed at this new intruder. Almost all of them showed the long thin tusks of female walrus.

The old bull separated from the herd, ready for combat. It started to rear up in the water, trying to see and also to frighten the new enemy, while working itself into a fury. Tikta'liktak knew that to the poor eyesight of the beast he would look like another walrus trying to enter the herd.

With a roaring bellow, the great bull, flashing its white tusks, dove beneath the surface and went straight at Tikta'liktak. He braced himself, expecting to be lifted from the water, when to his surprise the old bull rose up before him locked in combat with a powerful young male walrus.

Tikta'liktak watched them struggle, their tusks ripping and locking, their eyes rolling. The water around them frothed white and then turned red with blood.

By good fortune, helped by the tide and steady. paddling, Tikta'liktak was carried safely away. The huge struggling beasts thrashed in the sea, never noticing that he had drifted onward.

Seabirds screamed around him, and he felt the welcome pull of the tide as it drew him at last toward the shores of the mainland. The dark granite cliffs seemed to tower over him when he drifted into their shadows. Delicate lacings of snow on the cliffs glowed in the long rays of the evening sun.

Suddenly, with a bump that almost upset him, Tikta'liktak felt solid rock beneath his feet. He stumbled ashore, scarcely able to stand on his numb, nearly frozen legs. Looking back over the waters he had crossed, he was filled with gratitude that the spirits who guard the land and sea and sky had allowed him to make his dangerous journey.

Dragging behind him the three inflated sealskins, Tikta'liktak struggled over the rocky beach while the first shower of summer rain beat against his face. With his knife, he cut the thongs that held the bone paddle blades to his harpoon, and it again became his weapon. He then

cut the three skin floats open from end to end, and placing the dry inside of one beneath himself, he stretched the other two over himself and fell deeply asleep.

He was awakened by the damp cold the next morning. The mists of early summer hung down everywhere, obscuring the cliffs and the seabirds that cried above him.

Joyful at the thought of being once again on the mainland after so many moons, he jumped up, ate some of the meat in his small package, drank some fresh water from a nearby stream, and set out along the coast toward the west. Although Tikta'liktak had never traveled in this part of the country before, he knew it would be easier and safer to stay on the coast than to risk a straighter path across the mountains. Climbing would use up his strength, and perhaps he would lose his way.

Tikta'liktak walked for two long days and slept at night under rock ledges like a wild animal. Then he came to a narrow inlet that he had never seen before, but he recognized it from his grandfather's description as the bay called "The Place of Beautiful Stones."

Walking fearfully along the edge of the small half-hidden cove, it did indeed seem like a place from another world. The gray rock cliffs that stood above him had the weird forms of ancient giants. At the end of the small bay, a well-worn path led up to the mouth of a dark cave in the crumbling rock wall.

Tikta'liktak stood before it in the gloom of the late afternoon listening for some sound, almost afraid to enter, yet eager to see for himself the inside of this strange place.

450

Hearing nothing save the dripping of water, he bent down and stepped quickly into the cave. Its entrance was small, but the cave was large inside and rose to a great height. When his eyes grew accustomed to the half darkness, he knelt down and examined the floor of the cave.

It was covered with smooth round white pebbles, and among them lay a number of shining red stones. These were so sharply cut that Tikta'liktak's people believed they could only have been shaped by strange men or spirits. There were also other stones cut in this wondrous way, and as clear as water, they glowed like the waning moon even in the half darkness.

Tikta'liktak looked to the wall on his left, and there, just as his grandfather had said, were two neat rows of holes, exactly as many as he had fingers and toes, each

451

containing a fox skull bleached white with age. Near these, embedded in the walls, were more red stones that seemed to wink like eyes in the fading light.

Some said that this was an ancient secret place of the little people who used to rule the land. It was here they came to collect and cut the precious stones they loved to have and to trade sometimes with other people.

Tikta'liktak gathered a few stones and would have taken more, but he heard a tapping sound deep in the cave and hurried out. He walked quickly all of that night, glad to be away from the strange place.

Throughout the next day, he slept peacefully on a moss-covered ledge above the sea. Before he fell asleep, he watched a rough-legged hawk circling high above him and heard brown female eider ducks cooing below as they plucked the soft down from their breasts to line the warm nests they were building for their young.

That evening as Tikta'liktak strode along the coast in the soft twilight of the Arctic summer, he saw the rugged coastal mountains sloping gently into the great inland plain. Crossing the foothills, he finally reached the immense plain that stood before his homeland. Now his feet welcomed every step forward in the soft tundra.

The warm sun the next morning followed its course through the eastern sky, and small bright flowers burst into bloom everywhere. The edge of each pond was made beautiful by patches of white Arctic cotton that swayed in the light breeze. Best of all, his namesake, the butterfly, traveled in a straight line before him and seemed to guide him on the long journey homeward.

Now he saw many caribou lying on the hillside with their brown backs blending into the land itself, their antlers covered in thick summer velvet. Tikta'liktak ran for joy to think that he was once again in a place of plenty.

He waded straight across wide shallow lakes, whose water came no higher than his knees, and through streams where every step sent fat sea trout darting away like silver arrows. As he traveled, he crossed high sandy beaches covered with shells, where the sea had washed in ancient times.

At last, he looked across the valley and recognized the three familiar hills that stood before his home—Telik, Egalalik, and Ashivak. Soon he would be among his own people. Were they alive? He was almost afraid to know.

He hurried down the gravel slope, across the boulder-strewn floor of the valley that had once been the bed of an immense river, up through the mossy pass between Egalalik and Ashivak, and up the rise past the small lake where his family took their water for drinking. There lay his sister's sealskin water bucket beside a freshly worn path. They must be living still.

Tikta'liktak sat down beside the path and thought. "If I appear before them quickly, they will think I am a ghost or spirit, for they must surely believe I am dead."

Getting up, he peered around a large rock down into that beloved valley. There was the big sealskin tent of his family, and beyond it the tent of his uncle, and a little farther up the valley, the family tents of Tauki and Kungo. Tikta'liktak saw his mother bending over at the entrance to their tent with her head deep in her hood, as was the

454

custom of his people when sad. He saw his sister Sharni carrying something that looked like clothing. She took this to her mother, who placed it on a small pile before her. A moment later, Tikta'liktak saw his father step out of their tent and gaze toward the sea.

In the long shadows of early morning, he saw Kungo and his family, soon followed by the others, walk down toward his father's tent. Although it was not cold, they all had their hoods drawn over their heads in sadness and wore their oldest clothes. Tikta'liktak wondered how he could let them know he had returned without frightening them.

He walked back until he reached the edge of the hill behind the camp, where he knew his figure would be seen easily against the morning sky. Now he moved slowly. Kungo's sharp eyes saw him first. Tikta'liktak watched him point and call to the others in a low hunter's voice. In a moment, they were all looking at him on the skyline.

"Who is that?" said Kungo's daughter.

"Can it be?" asked his sister.

"That person has the shape of Tikta'liktak and his way of walking," said Tauki.

Tikta'liktak coughed twice, and they all said, "That is his cough. He coughs in that way."

Then someone said, "Ghost," and another said, "Spirit," and he could see they were all about to run away.

"Relatives," he called in a soft, ordinary voice. "I have returned. I am glad to see you all again." And he sat down on a rock and started to chant and sing a funny little song his mother had taught them as children.

Sharni, his sister, called, "Brother of mine, that must be the real you singing that song and no ghost!"

Tikta'liktak answered, "Sister of mine, it is really me. May I come down to you and visit?"

They all began to talk at once. Then Tikta'liktak's father called to him, "Come forward," and he walked out bravely, alone, to meet this ghost, or perhaps his returning son, halfway between the hill and camp.

Tikta'liktak's father looked frightened and suspicious. But coming up to his son, he reached out timidly, touched his arm, and tenderly ran his hand over the great new scars on his son's face. He then passed his hand across his eyes, and feeling tears in them, he leaned forward and gave Tikta'liktak a hug that nearly broke his bones.

In a voice ringing with joy, his father called to his wife and daughters and all the others, saying that this was no ghost but a real person and that, on the very day that they were to give his clothes away, their son at long last had returned home to them.

457

Tikta'liktak's mother and sisters led him gently into the dark skin tent and seated him on their wide bed made of sweet-smelling summer heather covered with soft, thick winter caribou skins.

They drew off the long worn-out sealskin boots that he had made and replaced them with warm fur slippers. Slowly, they fed him many of the good things he had dreamed of during his long adventure.

When Tikta'liktak could eat no more, he lay back on the rich warm skins, feeling full of food and contentment. His family was well, and he was overjoyed to be alive and once again in the tent of his father. He closed his eyes and drifted peacefully toward sleep.

In his mind's eye, there arose a shining vision of his island home. Sakkiak now seemed to him a warm and friendly place, for it had become a part of his life, a part of himself.

Tikta'liktak's song floated down to him from the sky. Each word had found its proper place. He could feel himself swaying to the rhythm of the big drum that beat inside him, and he heard the long answering chorus of women's voices in some distant dance house. His mind, knowing the words, started softly:

Ayii, yaii,
Ayii, yaii,
The great sea
Has set me in motion,
Set me adrift,
And I moved
As a weed moves
In the river.
The arch of sky
And mightiness of storms
Encompassed me,
And I am left
Trembling with joy,
Ayii, yaii,
Ayii, yaii.

—James Houston

Key to Pronunciation

Glossary

ac•cu•sa•tion (ak-yoo-ZAY-shən) *noun.* A charge of wrongdoing.

aisle (IGHL) *noun.* The space for walking between rows of seats in a classroom, auditorium, or church.

a•lert (ə-LERT) *verb.* To warn, caution. **alerted, alerting.** —*adjective.* Wide-awake, watchful.

Al•lah (AH-lə) *noun.* Name of God in the Mohammedan or Moslem religion.

Alp *noun.* A high mountain. —**Swiss Alps.** *noun.* A mountain range in south-central Europe.

al•tar (AWL-tər) *noun.* A raised block or table, usually at the front of a church, at which religious services are held.

am•a•teur (AM-ə-chər) *noun.* 1. A person who uses his or her skill for fun and not to make money. 2. An athlete who has never received money for playing.

am•ber (AM-bər) *noun.* 1. A substance of yellow-brown color used in costume jewelry. 2. (Also *adjective*). A yellow-brown color.

am•e•thyst (AM-ə-thist) *noun.* A violet or purple quartz used in jewelry.

An•ky•lo•sau•rus (an-ki-lə-SAWR-uhss) *noun.* A plant-eating dinosaur. Since its body was covered with plates that were thick and bony, it is sometimes called the "armored dinosaur."

an•noy (ə-NOI) *verb.* To bother, irritate, make displeased: The buzzing of that fly annoys me. **annoyed, annoying.**

The pronunciation system and word entries are adapted from *The Ginn Intermediate Dictionary*, © Copyright, 1977, 1974, 1973, by Xerox Corporation, published by Ginn and Company (Xerox Corporation).

ap•pre•hen•sive (ap-ri-HEN-siv) *adjective*. Uneasy or worried about the future.

ar•chae•ol•o•gist (ahr-kee-OL-ə-jist) *noun*. A person who studies ancient people and cultures by examining tools, pottery, pictures, clothing, and other relics.

arc•tic (AHRK-tik or AHR-tik) *noun*. 1. [Often capital A] The geographic area around the North Pole. 2. [Capital A] The Arctic Ocean. —*adjective*. 1. Related to, from, or of the area around the North Pole: An *arctic* fox turns white in winter. 2. Very cold; frigid: Joe feared an *arctic* winter.

as•cend (ə-SEND) *verb*. 1. To rise to a higher rank or position: Herb *ascended* to the rank of Eagle Scout. 2. To travel upward: The climbers *ascended* the mountain. **ascended, ascending.**

as•phalt (ASS-fawlt) *noun*. A dark substance similar to tar that is used with sand or gravel to pave roads and cover roofs. —*verb*. To cover with asphalt. **asphalted, asphalting.**

ath•lete (ATH-leet) *noun*. A trained, skilled person who competes seriously in sports that require qualities like speed and endurance. **athletes.** —**athletic** *adjective*.

at•ten•tive (ə-TEN-tiv) *adjective*. 1. Alert; paying attention: The student was *attentive* during the history lesson. 2. Considerate of the needs and desires of others. —**attentively** *adverb*.

awk•ward (AWK-wərd) *adjective*. 1. Clumsy; not graceful. 2. Not easily managed.

ax•le (AK-sl) *noun*. A rod on which a wheel turns or is turned. **axles.**

bal•lad (BAL-əd) *noun*. 1. A simple song, usually romantic or sad. 2. A poem or song that tells a story, popular legends in particular, in simple verse form.

ban•di•coot (BAN-di-koot) *noun*. A small, ratlike Australian animal.

bane (BAYN) *noun*. 1. A person or thing that harms or ruins something: The destructive dog was the *bane* of Mildred's existence. 2. A poison.

bane•ber•ry (BAYN-ber-ee) *noun*. 1. A plant with small black poisonous berries. 2. Berries from this plant.

ban•nis•ter Also **banister** (BAN-i-stər) *noun*. A railing with supports, usually running alongside a stairway.

ban•yan (BAN-yən) *noun*. A kind of fig tree, found in East India, with branches that grow down to the earth and take root.

ba•sic (BAY-sik) *adjective*. Main; essential; necessary or required: Food and water are *basic* needs for human life. —**basically** *adverb*.

ba•zaar (bə-ZAHR) Also **bazar** *noun*. 1. A fair or a festive occasion at which goods are sold and entertainment is provided to raise money for a special purpose. 2. A section of a town, especially in countries of the Orient, where goods are sold at shops or marketplaces.

be•drag•gled (bi-DRAG-əld) *adjective*. Worn-out; soiled; limp, as with wetness: Bob's clothes looked *bedraggled* after his hike in the rain.

be•rate (bee-RAYT) *verb*. To rebuke or scold harshly. **berated, berating.**

be•seech (bi-SEECH) *verb*. To plead with; to beg for. **besought** or **beseeched, beseeching.**

be•wil•der (bi-WIL-dər) *verb*. To confuse: The difficult instructions on the machine *bewildered* my cousin. **bewildered, bewildering.**

bil•lion (BIL-yən) *noun*. The cardinal number 1,000,000,000 in Canada or 1,000,000,000,000 in Great Britain.

bi•son (BIGH-sn) *noun*. A large animal of the ox family with short horns and a shaggy head; the American buffalo. —**bison** *plural*.

bluff (BLUHF) *noun*. A high steep bank with straight sides.

461

bor•der (BOR-dər) *noun*. 1. The edge or rim of anything. 2. The line which separates political divisions or private property.

boul•der (BOHL-dər) *noun*. A large, rounded, smooth rock: There was a huge *boulder* in front of the cave.

boun•ty (BOWN-tee) *noun*. 1. Generosity. 2. A reward: There was a bounty for capturing the killer. **bounties.** —**bountiful** *adjective*. —**bountifully** *adverb*.

bread•fruit (BRED-froot) *noun*. A large eatable fruit that grows on a tree found in tropical regions.

bur•eau (BYUR-oh) *noun*. 1. A chest of drawers used for storing clothes. 2. A business office that performs a special duty: a travel *bureau*. 3. A department of the government.

bur•noose (ber-NOOSS) *noun*. A long cloak with a hood: *Burnooses* are worn by the Arabs. **burnooses.**

bus•tle (BUHSS-l) *verb*. To walk or hurry busily or noisily. **bustled, bustling.**

calm (KAHM) *noun*. Stillness; quiet; freedom from noise or bustle. —*verb*. To make still or relaxed. —**calmly** *adverb*.

car•go (KAHR-goh) *noun*. The load of goods carried by a ship or airplane; freight. The *cargo* was loaded into the hold of the ship.

carve (KAHRV) *verb*. 1. To form or decorate by cutting: The artist *carved* a statue of marble. 2. To slice; cut into slices. **carved, carving.**

cas•se•role (KASS-ə-rohl) *noun*. 1. A dish usually with a cover, in which foods are baked. 2. Food baked and served in a deep dish. **casseroles.**

cau•tious (KAW-shəss) *adjective*. Careful; watchful. —**cautiously** *adverb*.

cha•grin (shə-GRIN) *noun*. A feeling of shame or disappointment.

chal•lenge (CHAL-ənj) *noun*. 1. An offer to take part in a fight or contest: a *challenge* to a chess game. 2. A questioning; a demand for evidence or proof. **challenges.** —*verb*. 1. To offer to engage in a contest of any type. 2. To question the correctness of or to demand evidence for. **challenged, challenging.**

cham•ber (CHAYM-bər) *noun*. 1. A room, especially a bedroom. 2. Any enclosed space. •

chan•de•lier (shan-də-LIHR) *noun*. A lighting fixture that hangs from a ceiling.

char•ac•ter (KA-rik-tər) *noun*. 1. A person's individual manner of thinking and acting; the qualities of a person or thing that make it different from another. 2. A person in a novel, play, or other work. 3. Moral or spiritual quality; moral strength: It takes *character* to face problems. 4. (Informal) An odd or unusual person.

chord (KORD) *noun*. 1. A combination of musical tones made in harmony. 2. A feeling or emotion: The bitter remark struck a sensitive *chord*.

chore (CHOR) *noun*. 1. An odd job or task. 2. A burden or difficulty: Studying is a *chore* for some students. **chores.**

chute (SHOOT) *noun*. 1. A slope or channel down which things may flow, slide, or be rolled. 2. (Informal) A parachute. **chutes.**

cin•der (SIN-dər) *noun*. 1. A small burned piece of wood or other material. 2. **cinders** plural. ashes.

cit•a•del (SIT-ə-dl) *noun*. A fort, especially one protecting a city: Foot soldiers defended the *citadel*.

clash (KLASH) *noun*. 1. A conflict, as of ideas or opinions. 2. A battle or collision. **clashes.** —*verb*. 1. To conflict: Jim's desire to leave the party *clashed* with Tom's wish to stay. 2. To collide or to do battle with. **clashed, clashing.**

clutch (KLUHCH) *verb*. 1. To grip or hold tightly. 2. To snatch or catch hold of: The drowning sailor *clutched* at pieces of driftwood. **clutched, clutching.** —*noun*. A grip or grasp.

co•coon (kə-KOON) *noun*. A silky case or covering spun by some insects when they are in the larval or early stage of their development.

comb (KOHM) *noun*. 1. A device with a row of teeth or prongs, used to arrange or clean the hair. 2. Any device used to clean, untangle, or arrange fibers, hair, or fur. 3. A crest or outgrowth on the head of a rooster or other bird. 4. A honeycomb. —*verb*. 1. To untangle, clean, or arrange with a comb or similar device. 2. To search or look through thoroughly: Doris *combed* the library to find a special book. **combed, combing.**

com•pas•sion•ate (kəm-PASH-ən-it) *adjective*. Showing pity; sympathetic. —**compassionately** *adverb*.

con•ceit (kən-SEET) *noun*. 1. A vain or too-high opinion of one's own ability, attractiveness, or importance. 2. A whim or imaginary notion.

con•cen•tra•tion (kon-sən-TRAY-shən) *noun*. 1. Undivided attention: To understand the intructions requires *concentration*. 2. The act or process of concentrating.

con•dor (KON-dor) *noun*. A large vulture found in South America and in parts of California.

con•fuse (kən-FYOOZ) *verb*. 1. To bewilder, perplex. 2. To mistake for another; fail to see a difference. **confused, confusing.**

con•quer (KONG-kər) *verb*. 1. To get control of by force, as in winning a war. The army set out to *conquer* the neighboring country. 2. To overcome, to get the better of.

con•sole (kən-SOHL) *verb*. To give comfort, relief, or encouragement. **consoled, consoling.**

con•stant (KON-stənt) *adjective*. 1. Not stopping; continual. 2. Faithful; loyal: David was *constant* in his friendship with Jonathan. 3. Not changing; regular. —*noun*. Something that does not change. —**constantly** *adverb*.

con•ti•nent (KON-tə-nənt) *noun*. 1. One of the seven major masses of land areas on earth. 2. [Capital C] The mainland of Europe; Europe not including the British Isles.

con•tra•dict (kon-trə-DIKT) *verb*. 1. To state the opposite of something already stated: The witness *contradicted* the story of the accused person. 2. To be contrary or opposed to. **contradicted, contradicting.**

con•trite (kən-TRIGHT or KON-tright) *adjective*. Having or showing sorrow or regret. —**contritely** *adverb*. —**contrition** (kən-TRISH-ən) *noun*.

con•ven•ience (kən-VEEN-yənss) *noun*. Comfort; ease; assistance. **conveniences.**

con•ver•sa•tion (kon-vər-SAY-shən) *noun*. Talking, especially in an informal way.

co•pal (KOH-pəl) *noun*. A hard resin that comes from the sap of any of several tropical trees.

cor•ral (kər-KƏL) *noun*. An enclosed space for keeping horses or other animals.

coun•cil (KOWN-sl) *noun*. 1. A group of people who meet to discuss problems or give advice. 2. A law-making body.

coun•cil•or (KOWN-sl-ər) *noun*. A member of a council. **councilors.**

count•less (KOWNT-liss) *adjective*. More than anyone can or will count; innumerable.

cour•age (KER-ij) *noun*. Bravery when faced with something frightening or dangerous.

cove (KOV) *noun*. 1. A small bay or inlet. 2. A sheltered nook. 3. The mouth of a creek.

cray•fish (KRAY-fish) Also **craw-fish** *noun*. 1. A shellfish similar to a lobster but smaller in size. 2. A small, spiny lobster. **—crayfish** or **crayfishes** *plural*.

crease (KREESS) *noun*. 1. A fold, line, ridge, or wrinkle: The old man's face was lined with *creases* of age. 2. The fold pressed into clothing. **creases.** *—verb*. 1. To make a fold or ridge. 2. To graze or wound slightly. **creased, creasing.**

cred•it (KRED-it) *noun*. 1. Honor, recognition, or praise for some deed, quality, or accomplishment. 2. A source of honor or praise: Sue is a *credit* to her Girl Guide troop. 3. Belief in a person's promise to pay a debt: Al bought a coat on *credit*.

crit•i•cism (KRIT-ə-siz-əm) *noun*. 1. The act of judging or testing something, particularly a performance, a piece of writing, or a work of art: The newspaper's *criticism* of the new play was favorable. 2. The act of making an unfair or rash judgment.

Cro-Mag•non (kroh-MAG-non) *noun*. 1. A prehistoric form of human beings who lived in the Stone Age. 2. The village where some Cro-Magnon skeletons were found.

crum•ple (KRUM-pəl) 1. To crush together. 2. To fall down. **crum•pled, crum•pling.**

cul•ti•vate (KUL-tə-vāt) 1. Loosen ground around plants. 2. Prepare soil for planting.

Czech•o•slo•va•ki•a (chek-ə-sloh-VAH-kee-ə) *noun*. A country in Central Europe.

dan•gle (DANG-gəl) *verb*. 1. To swing or hang loosely: A broken wire *dangled* from the telephone pole. 2. To hold (something) so that it hangs loosely. **dangled, dangling.**

de•i•ty (DEE-ə-tee) *noun*. 1. A god or goddess: Apollo was considered a *deity* by the Greeks. 2. [Capital D] God. **deities.**

de•jec•tion (di-JEK-shən) *noun*. Low spirits, discouragement, unhappiness. **—dejected** *adjective*.

de•lir•i•ous (di-LIHR-ee-əss) *adjective*. Hysterical, not making sense (as often happens with a high fever).

de•scend•ant (di-SEN-dənt) *noun*. An offspring. The princess is a *descendant* of the king.

des•ti•na•tion (dess-tə-NAY-shən) *noun*. The place to which someone or something is going: Mars may be the *destination* of future space travelers.

de•tail (di-TAYL or DEE-tayl) *noun*. 1. One small part of a whole. 2. Many or all of the small parts of something.

de•ter•min•a•tion (dee-tər-min-AY-shən) *noun*. Strength of purpose; firmness of decision.

di•ag•no•sis (DI-əg-NO-sis) *noun*. The act or process of finding out what disease a person or animal has by examination and careful study of the symptoms.

di•nar (də-NAHR) *noun*. The money used in several Middle East and Eastern European countries.

dis•col•or•a•tion (dis-KUL-ər-A-shen) *noun*. The act of changing or spoiling the color of; staining.

dis•guise (diss-GIGHZ) *verb*. 1. To change so as to appear to be something else: The robbers *disguised* themselves as window washers.

2. To hide or conceal: Tim tried to *disguise* the fact that he had broken a lamp. **disguised, disguising.** *—noun.* A make-up or costume used to change one's appearance. **disguises.**

dis•in•te•grate (diss-IN-tə-grayt) *verb.* To come apart, separate into pieces. **disintegrated, disintegrating.** **—disintegration** *noun.*

dis•may (diss-MAY) *noun.* Loss of courage, a troubled feeling. *—verb.* To alarm or cause fear. **dismayed, dismaying.**

dis•po•si•tion (diss-pə-ZISH-ən) *noun.* 1. Placement; arrangement. 2. The power to use or manage as one wishes: All the boats were at the captain's *disposition.* 3. Basic or general nature.

dor•mi•to•ry (DOR-mə-tor-ee) *noun.* 1. A large room with many beds. 2. A building with a number of rooms for sleeping and living, especially for students.

down•heart•ed (DOWN-HAHR-tid) *adjective.* Dejected, sad, depressed. **—downheartedly** *adverb.*

drake (DRAYK) *noun.* A male duck, **drakes.**

dra•ma (DRAH-mə or DRAM-ə) *noun.* 1. A story or poem written to be acted out on the stage; a play. 2. The art of writing or presenting plays. 3. An exciting or moving experience in real life.

duck•ling (DUHK-ling) *noun.* A young or baby duck.

dy•nam•ic (digh-NAM-ik) *adjective.* Having power and force: a *dynamic* personality. **—dynamically** *adverb.*

ea•ger (EE-gər) *adjective.* Having a great desire or wanting something. **—eagerly** *adverb.* **—eagerness** *noun.*

earth•en•ware (ERTH-ən-wair) *noun.* (and *adjective*). Any article made of baked clay.

ef•fect (ə-FECT) *noun.* A result: The *effect* of so much rain was a flood. *—verb.* To make happen; bring about: The rain will *effect* a change in the temperature. **effected, effecting. —in effect.** In use or active: The rules have been *in effect* since last week.

e•ko (EK-KAW) *noun.* A solid food made from cooked cornmeal, like cornmeal mush.

el•dest (EL-dəst) *adjective.* The oldest one of more than two persons or things.

el•e•gant (EL-ə-gənt) *adjective.* Having or showing refined grace and taste combined with richness and simplicity.

em•brace (em-BRAYSS) *verb.* 1. To hug or hold in the arms. 2. To take up eagerly: Marion *embraced* the fight against pollution. 3. To include: The school recreation program *embraces* many different sports and activities. **embraced, embracing.** *—noun.* A hug. **embraces.**

em•per•or (EM-pər-ər) *noun.* The ruler of an empire.

en•cir•cle (en-SER-kəl or in-SER-kəl) *verb.* To form a ring around or move around in a circle. The children *encircled* the May Pole. **encircled, encircling.**

en•cour•age (en-KER-ij) *verb.* 1. To give hope or confidence to. 2. To help; to support: Cold weather *encourages* the sale of warm clothing. **encouraged, encouraging.**

en•ter•tain (en-tər-TAYN) *verb.* 1. To amuse. 2. To have as guests. 3. To consider. **entertained, entertaining.**

en•vy (EN-vee) *verb.* To be jealous of. **envied, envying.** *—noun.* 1. Jealousy. 2. Something that causes jealousy.

es•cape (eh-SKAYP or ih-SKAYP) *verb.* 1. To get away; get out; get free: The prisoner *escaped* three times but was always caught. 2. To avoid; keep free from: Susan was the only one to *escape* the measles. 3. To leak out:

465

The gas *escaped* from the balloon. **escaped, escaping.** —*noun.* 1. The act of getting away. 2. A way of escaping. **escapes.**

Es•ki•mo (ESS-kə-moh) *noun.* One of a people who live in the Arctic regions of North America.

ev•i•dent (EV-ə-DENT) *adjective.* Plain to see; easy to understand; obvious. —**evidently** (ev-ə-DENT-ly) *adverb.*

ex•pen•sive (ek-SPEN-siv) *adjective.* Very costly; high in price. —**expensively** *adverb.*

ex•pert (EK-spərt) *noun.* A person who knows a lot about a particular subject. —*adjective.* Highly skilled or trained. —**expertly** *adverb.*

ex•pla•na•tion (ek-splə-NAH-shən) *noun.* 1. Act of explaining; what is said or written that explains. 2. Meaning, reason.

ex•pose (ek-SPOHZ) *verb.* 1. To reveal; uncover; open. 2. To leave open to the effects of sun, wind, or rain. 3. To tell or reveal something that was secret or unknown. **exposed, exposing.**

ex•pres•sion (eks-PRESH-ən) *noun.* 1. Act of expressing: an *expression* of opinion. 2. Show of emotion on the face: Pete's *expression* showed how sad he was. 3. Words of explanation: I know how I feel but I can't give it *expression.* 4. The act of showing or representing feeling: An actor must be a master of *expression.* 5. A special word or words: "23 skidoo" was a popular *expression* around 1900.

ex•tinct (ek-STINGKT) *adjective.* 1. Having died out completely. 2. Burned out; dead.

ex•traor•di•nar•y (ek-STROR-də-nair-ee) *adjective.* More than ordinary; unusual; special. —**extraordinarily** *adverb.*

fas•ci•nate (FASS-ə-nayt) *verb.* 1. To hold the interest of (someone); captivate or charm. 2. To awe or make

powerless. **fascinated, fascinating.**

fawn *noun.* 1. A light brownish color. 2. A young deer. —*verb.* 1. To show affection or fondness. 2. To act like a slave. **fawned, fawning.**

fer•ti•li•zer (FERT-l-igh-zər) *noun.* Manure, chemical compound, or anything worked into the soil to make it produce more richly.

fes•ti•val (FESS-tə-vəl) *noun.* 1. A special occasion or time marked by feasting, celebration, and rejoicing. 2. A group of related events, exhibits, entertainments: an arts and crafts *festival.*

fes•tiv•i•ty (fess-TIV-ə-tee) *noun.* 1. A joyous party or festive occasion. 2. The joyousness of a festival or party. **festivities.**

fez *noun.* A man's hat, of Turkish origin, and usually made of red felt. —**fezzes** (FEZ-iz) *plural.*

fil•ter (FIL-tər) *noun.* 1. A device or substance used to strain out bits of solid matter from a gas or liquid. —*verb.* 1. To pass through a device used to strain out particles of solid matter. 2. To move through a screen: The sunlight *filtered* through the thin drapes. **filtered, filtering.**

flat•ter•y (FLAT-ər-ee) *noun.* Untrue or insincere praise usually given in hope of gaining favor.

flick•er (FLIK-ər) *verb.* To burn or shine unevenly; to make an unsteady flame or light. **flickered, flickering.**

flint *noun.* 1. A hard, dull-colored stone. 2. A piece of this stone used for making sparks by friction. **flints.**

fore•see (for-SEE) *verb.* To expect, know something before it happens. **foresaw, forseeing.**

for•tress (FOR-triss) *noun.* 1. A fort; a place built to be defended. 2. Any protection or safe place. **fortresses.**

for•tu•nate (FOR-chə-nit) *adjective.* Lucky. —*noun.* Those who have good luck. —**fortunately** *adverb*.

foun•da•tion (fown-DAY-shən) *noun*. 1. The base or ground on which something is built: The *foundation* of their friendship is trust. 2. The lowest part of a building, set in or on the ground.

frank (FRANGK) *adjective*. 1. Honest and open in speech; forthright. 2. Without cover, disguise, or hidden motive: Her *frank* report did not omit a single detail.

fres•co (FRESS-koh) *noun*. 1. A painting done on wet plaster (walls or ceiling). 2. The method of painting on wet plaster. — **frescoes** or **frescos** *plural*. —*verb*. To paint on wet plaster. **frescoed, frescoing.**

fringe (FRINJ) *noun*. 1. A trimming of loose or bunched threads on the edge of clothing, curtains, tablecloths, and the like. 2. (Plural) Borders: People are moving to the *fringes* of big cities. **fringes.**

froth•y (FRAWTH-ee) *adjective*. Filled with foam; with many small bubbles.

fu•ner•al (FYOO-nər-əl) *noun*. A ceremony in honor of a dead person followed by burial or cremation of the body.

fun•gus (FUHNG-gəss) *noun*. Any of several plants, such as mushrooms and molds, that do not have green color, leaves, or flowers. —**fungi** (FUHN-jigh) or **funguses** *plural*.

gam•bol (GAM-bəl) *verb*. To frolic about playfully. **gamboled, gamboling.**

gape (GAYP) *verb*. 1. To open the mouth wide. 2. To stare or gaze with the mouth open. 3. To become wide open. **gaped, gaping.**

gap-toothed (GAP-tootht) *adjective*. Having spaces between the teeth.

gar•ment GAHR-mənt) *noun*. Anything worn as clothing.

gen•er•os•i•ty (jen-ə-ROSS-ə-tee) *noun*. 1. Willingness to give or share; unselfishness. 2. Abundance; Nature's *generosity*.

gen•ial (JEEN-yəl or JEE-nee-əl) *adjective*. 1. Cheerful, kindly. 2. Healthy; favorable for growth. —**geniality** *noun*. —**genially** *adverb*.

ge•ol•o•gist (jee-OL-ə-just) *noun*. A person whose field of study is geology, the science of the history and structure of the earth's crust.

ges•ture (JESS-chər) *noun*. 1. A motion of the hand or other part of the body that expresses a feeling or emphasizes something spoken: The girl shook her fist in a *gesture* of anger. 2. An action, often only for effect, performed as a sign or token or some attitude or feeling. **gestures.** —*verb*. To indicate or show (something) with a gesture. **gestured, gesturing.**

gnarled (NAHRLD) *adjective*. Twisted and knotted.

gouge (GOWJ) *verb*. 1. To cut into with a digging motion; to dig with a gouge. **gouged, gouging.** —*noun*. 1. A tool with a curved blade used for digging into wood. 2. A hole or mark made by gouging.

gri•mace (gri-MAYSS or GRIM-iss) *noun*. A twisting of the face to show dislike.

ground sloth (GROUND-slohth) *noun*. An extinct animal that lived on the ground: It is thought to be an ancestor of the modern tree sloth.

guard•ed (GAHR-did) *adjective*. 1. Protected or watched. 2. Very careful and cautious: *guarded* answers. —**guardedly** *adverb*.

gust (GHUST) *noun*. 1. A sudden and forceful rush of wind: A violent *gust* tipped over the small sailboat. 2. A sudden rush of emotion: Maria felt a *gust* of anger over the insult. *—verb.* To rush or flow suddenly, as a wind or strong feeling, **gusted, gusting.**

hab•it (HAB-it) *noun.* 1. A usual or regular practice or action: Getting up early is one of my *habits.* 2. A special outfit, such as that worn by some nuns.

har•bor (HAHR-bər) *noun.* 1. A port or sheltered water for boats and ships. 2. A protected inlet of a lake or ocean.

harsh (HAHRSH) *adjective.* 1. Cruel or unkind; demanding. 2. Unpleasant to the senses. **harsher, harshest.** **—harshly** *adverb.*

head•band (HED-band) *noun.* A strip of material worn around the head.

hemp *noun.* 1. A tall plant with strong, tough fibers. 2. Fibers used to make rope and heavy cloth. 3. A drug made from the flowers and the leaves of some kinds of hemp.

hes•i•tant (HEZ-ə-tənt) *adjective.* Undecided; holding back; tending to hesitate. **—hesitantly** *adverb.*

hinge (HINJ) *noun.* The movable jointed device by which a door, gate, or lid is joined to a frame. *—verb.* 1. To install or apply a hinge or hinges. 2. To depend (on): The success of the team *hinged* on the hard work of all. **hinged, hinging.**

hoax (HOHX) *noun.* Something that tricks or deceives. **hoaxes.** *—verb.* To cheat, deceive, or mislead. **hoaxed, hoaxing.**

hon•est (ON-ist) *adjective.* Honorable; truthful; fair. 2. Sincere; open: an *honest* smile. 3. Genuine; pure: *honest* merchandise. **—honestly** *adverb.* **—honesty** *noun.*

hy•e•na (high-EE-nə) *noun.* A wild dog or wolf of Africa and Asia that has a shrill, laugh-like bark: A *hyena* looks like a wolf.

ig•nore (ig-NOR) *verb.* To pay no attention to; disregard on purpose. **ignored, ignoring.**

im•age (IM-ij) *noun.* 1. A picture or statue. 2. Something seen through a lens or reflected as in a mirror.

im•ag•i•na•tion (ih-MAJ-ə-nay-shən) *noun.* The ability or act of creating in the mind. **—imaginative** *adjective.*

im•ag•in•a•tive (im-A-jin-ə-tiv) *adjective.* 1. Having the ability to picture or invent vividly. 1. Original, creative: an *imaginative* painting.

Im•pe•ri•al Pal•ace (im-PIHR-ee-əl PAL-iss) *noun.* A building that is the official dwelling of an emperor or empress. **palaces.**

imp•ish (IMP-ish) *adjective.* Mischievous; playful.

im•pres•sion (im-PRESH-ən) *noun.* 1. Imprint made by pressing: The FBI keeps files of fingerprint *impressions.* 2. A feeling: I got the impression Al didn't like me. 3. An effect made on someone: Politeness makes a good *impression.*

in•cense (IN-senss) *noun.* 1. A substance such as gum or spices that gives a sweet or fragrant smell when burned. 2. A pleasing smell or perfume. **incenses.**

in•dig•na•tion (in-dig-NAY-shən) *noun.* An angry reaction to unjust acts. **—indignant** (in-DIG-nənt) *adjective.* **—indignantly** *adverb.*

in•i•ti•ate (ih-NISH-ee-ayt) *verb.* 1. To begin; start: The school will *initiate* a hot lunch program. 2. To introduce or teach the basics of a subject. 3. To admit a person into a club, organization, or society, often by a secret ceremony. **—initiated, initiating. —initiation** (ih-nish-ee-AY-shən) *noun.*

in•scribe (in-SKRIGHB) *verb.* 1. To write or engrave (letters, words, numbers) upon a surface: My identification bracelet is *inscribed* with my name and address. 2. To write a brief message in a book, on a photograph, etc. 3. To make a lasting impression, especially on the mind: The scene of the accident was *inscribed* on her memory. **inscribed, inscribing.**

in•scrip•tion (in-SKRIP-shən) *noun.* Words, usually only a few lines or less, written or carved on something like a memorial stone.

in•sist (in-SIST) *verb.* To be firm about a demand or wish; refuse to give in. **insisted, insisting.**

in•stinct (IN-stingkt) *noun.* 1. An inner force that moves one to action: *instinct* guides animals to places where they can find food and water. 2. A natural inner trait: an artistic *instinct.*

in•tro•duce (in-trə-DOOSS or in-trə-DYOOSS) *verb.* 1. To make known or acquaint, as one person to another: Sally *introduced* me to her cousin from Ottawa. 2. To make (someone) aware of for the first time. 3. Insert; include. 4. To begin; start off with: The minister *introduced* his sermon with a reading from the Bible. **introduced, introducing.**

itch (ICH) *noun.* 1. A prickling sensation of the skin that makes one want to scratch. 2. Any of various skin diseases that make one want to scratch. 3. A restless urge or feeling: Bill had an *itch* to do something. —*verb.* To feel an itch.

in•ves•ti•gate (in-VESS-tə-gayt) *verb.* To look into or examine closely. **investigated, investigating. —investigation** *noun.*

jag•ged (JAG-əd) *adjective.* Rough; having sharp points: I cut my foot on the *jagged* rocks.

jag•uar (JAG-wahr or JAG-yoo-ahr) *noun.* A large wildcat found in the jungles of South America.

jew•el•er (JOO-ə-lər) *noun.* A person who sells, makes, or repairs jewelry.

jos•tle (JOSS-l) *verb.* To move or push aside in a clumsy or rude way. **jostled, jostling.**

jo•vi•al (JOH-vee-əl) *adjective.* Joyous; merry. **—jovially** *adverb.*

land•slide (LAND-slighd) *noun.* 1. The sliding of a mass of earth and rocks down a mountain or hillside. 2. A great victory, especially in an election. **landslides.**

lark (LAHRK) *noun.* 1. Any of several types of songbirds. 2. (Informal) Something done just for fun; a carefree adventure.

lob•ster (LOB-stər) *noun.* An edible shellfish with ten legs, two of them big claws in front, a hard outer covering and no backbone. **lobsters.**

mam•mal (MAM-əl) *noun.* Any animal, including a human, that has a backbone and some hair and, in the female, feeds its young with breast or udder milk.

mam•moth (MAM-əth) *noun.* A type of huge elephant, no longer existing, that had a hairy body and very long, curved tusks. —*adjective.* Huge; gigantic.

man•da•rin . (MAN-də-rin) *noun.* 1. A high official in the former Chinese Empire. 2. (Capital M) A major dialect of the Chinese language.

mar•ga•rine (MAHR-ja-rin) *noun.* A

blend of edible vegetable oils used as a butter substitute.

marsh (MA-RSH) *noun*. A swamp or bog. **marshes.**

mass *noun*. 1. A shapeless lump: a *mass* of clay. 2. A large number of things considered as a whole: a *mass* of people. 3. The greater part or majority: The *mass* of the residents favors the new playground.

mas•sive (MASS-iv) *adjective*. Solid, large, or heavy: *massive* legs of the dinosaur. —**massively** *adverb*.

med•i•ta•tion (med-i-TAY-shən) *noun*. Deep thought, often as a kind of prayer.

mer•ri•ment (MER-i-mənt) *noun*. Mirth; fun or laughter; celebration.

midge (MIJ) *noun*. A small insect, as a gnat or fly. **midges.**

mile•stone (MIGHL-stohn) *noun*. 1. A stone or marker by the side of a road that shows the distance in miles to a particular place. 2. An important event: a *milestone* in space exploration. **milestones.**

mi•ser (MIGH-zər) *noun*. A greedy person who loves money for its own sake —**miserly** *adjective*.

mon•as•ter•y (MON-ə-stehr-ee) *noun*. A building in which monks live. **monasteries.**

mor•sel (MOR-sl) *noun*. A small piece or quantity.

mor•tal (MORT-l) *noun*. A human being. —*adjective*. 1. Causing death; fatal. 2. Certain to die. 3. Lasting until death. 4. Causing death of the soul or spirit.

mu•si•cal (MYOO-zi-kəl) *adjective*. 1. Having to do with music: The piano is a *musical* instrument. 2. Having a pleasant sound: a *musical* voice. 3. Being accompanied by music: a *musical* comedy. 4. Fond of or skilled in music. —*noun*. A play with music and dance. —**musically** *adverb*.

musk (MUHSK) *noun*. 1. A strong-smelling substance taken from a gland in the musk ox and used for making perfume. 2. The smell of musk.

—**musky** *adjective*.

mus•sel (MUHSS-l) *noun*. A bluish-black shellfish, somewhat like a clam, which is found in both fresh and salt water **mussels.**

na•tion•al•i•ty (nash-ə-NAL-ə-tee) *noun*. 1. The state of being part of a nation; citizenship: My *nationality* is French. 2. Existence as a separate nation or country. 3. A group of people organized under the same government and usually within the same country. **nationalities.**

nat•u•ral•ly (NACH-ər-ə-lee or NACH-rə-lee) *adverb*. 1. In a natural way: pose for the picture *naturally*. 2. By or through an inborn talent; by or through nature: Pat is a *naturally* good athlete. 3. Of course, surely.

nes•tle (NESS-l) *verb*. 1. To settle comfortably: "The children were *nestled* all snug in their beds…" (C. C. Moore). 2. To hold close with pleasant feelings: Bobby *nestled* his teddy bear in his arms. **nestled, nestling.**

no•bil•i•ty (noh-BIL-ə-tee) *noun*. 1. Nobles as a class. 2. The noble rank. Generosity; greatness of character. **nobilities.**

none•the•less (nuhn-the-LESS) *adverb*. However; nevertheless: in spite of that.

nu•mer•ous (NOO-mər-əss or NYOO-mər-əss) *adjective*. Many in number: Stanley has *numerous* friends. —**numerously** *adverb*.

ob•sti•nate (OB-stə-nit) *adjective*. 1. Stubborn; pigheaded; unwilling to change one's mind or do what someone else wants: The *obstinate* dog won't obey. 2. Hard to treat, remove, or bring under control: an *obstinate* pain. **—obstinacy** *noun*. **—obstinately** *adverb*.

of•fend (ə-FEND) *verb*. 1. To insult; annoy: The speaker *offended* the audience. **offended, offending.**

O•jib•wa (O-JIB-wa) *noun*. A member of an Indian tribe that lived on the shores of Lake Superior.

out•come (OWT-kuhm) *noun*. The result; the way a thing comes out.

pack•et (PAK-it) *noun*. 1. A small package. 2. A boat that carries passengers or goods on a regular schedule, usually on a river.

pa•go•da (pə-GOH-də) *noun*. A temple, common in most Oriental countries, that is shaped like a tower of many tiers.

pa•le•on•tol•o•gist (pay-lee-on-TOL-ə-jist) *noun*. A scientist who studies fossils and ancient forms of life: The *paleontologist* discovered a dinosaur bone in the cave.

par•tic•u•lar (pər-TIK-yə-lər) *adjective*. 1. Of or belonging to one person or group: Ruth is a *particular* friend of mine. 2. One apart from all others: I do not like that *particular* garment. 3. Careful, exact: He was *particular* about his appearance. —*noun*. (Plural) Details: The *particulars* of a trip. **—in particular.** Especially.

pas•ty (PAYSS-tee) *adjective*. Like a paste; moist and thick, often with a lumpy or grainy texture.

pa•tient (PAY-shənt) *adjective*. 1. Calm, kind, tolerant. 2. Willing to keep on trying: *patient* training. 3. Long-suffering, willing to put up with: We have been *patient* too long with our enemies. —*noun*. One who is under a doctor's care. **—patiently** *adverb*.

pe•cu•liar (pi-KYOOL-yər) *adjective*. 1. Odd; strange: a *peculiar* look. 2. Belonging solely to; distinctive. **—peculiarity** (pi-kyoo-lee-AIR-ə-tee) *noun*. **—peculiarly** *adverb*.

pee•vish (PEE-vish) *adjective*. Easily irritated. **—peevishly** *adverb*.

perch *noun*. 1. A place for a bird to nest. 2. A place to rest. **perches.** —*verb*. To sit, rest, or alight on a particular place. **perched, perching.**

phy•si•cian (fi-ZISH-ən) *noun*. A doctor; one who is duly qualified to practice medicine: The *physician* examined her patient and said he was in good health.

plait (PLAYT OR PLAT) *noun*. 1. A braid. 2. A fold of cloth; a pleat. —*verb*. 1. To braid. 2. To fold into a pleat or pleats. **plaited, plaiting.**

pli•ers (PLIGH-ərz) *noun, plural*. A tool, hinged somewhat like scissors, that is used to hold, twist, or cut small objects and wire.

plough *verb*. 1. To cut into and turn over soil with a plow. 2 To push aside or lift snow, dirt, or some other substance. **plowed, plowing.**

por•tion (POR-shən) *noun*. A part or section of a larger whole. —*verb*. To cut or divide into sections or shares. **portioned, portioning.**

por•trait (POR-trit or POR-trayt) *noun*. A painting or photograph of a person.

pos•ses•sion (pə-ZESH-ən) *noun*. 1. Something that is owned or controlled. Ownership or control: *possession* of wealth.

po•tion (POH-shən) *noun*. A special drink, as for curing illness.

pov•er•ty (POV-ər-tee) *noun*. 1. The condition of being poor or in need. 2. A poor or small quality, amount, or degree: a *poverty* of ideas.

pre•cious (pre-SHASS) *adjective*. 1. Valuable; of great worth. 2. Much loved.

pre•his•tor•i•ans (pree-hiss-TOR-ee-ənz) *noun*. Scholars who study the earth's distant past, or the time before human beings left written records.

pre•his•tor•ic (pree-hiss-TOR-ik) *adjective*. Referring to a time before events were written down.

pre•serve (pri-ZERV) *verb*. 1. To keep from harm or injury. 2. To keep whole, free from damage. 3. To keep from spoiling or decaying by applying a solution or other material. **preserved, preserving.**

pre•text (PREE-tekst) *noun*. A false reason; an excuse.

prey (PRAY) *noun*. 1. A hunted animal sought for food: The tiger stalked its *prey*. 2. A victim of an attack (by a person or misfortune). —*verb*. 1. To seize (animals) for food. 2. To rob or attack. 3. To worry, pre-occupy:*prey* on the mind. **preyed, preying.**

prim *adjective*. Overly proper or demure. **primmer, primmest. —primly** *adverb*.

pris•on•er (PRIZ-n-ər) or PRIZ-nər) *noun*. A person who is locked up in a prison or is kept somewhere against his or her will.

pro•ces•sion (prə-SESH-ən)*noun*. A group that moves along in an orderly way: graduation *procession*.

pro•file (PROH-fighl) *noun*. 1. A view of a person's face from the side; a picture of such a view. 2. The outline of anything seen from the side. 3. A short article about a person. **profiles.**

prong *noun*. A long projecting part: the *prongs* of a fork.

pros•per (PROSS-pər) *verb*. 1. To gain success or wealth, etc. 2. To grow or live vibrantly; to thrive. **prospered, prospering.**

pro•test (prə-TEST, proh-TEST or PROH-test) *verb*. 1. To oppose or resist with strong statements; to object. 2. To state strongly; declare: The man *protested* his innocence. **protested, protesting.**

quar•ry (KWOR-ee) *noun*. An open mine or pit from which stone or gravel is removed. **quarries.**

quilt (KWILT) *noun*. 1. A bed cover made of two layers of cloth filled with a soft filling, held in place with stitches in patterns. 2. A bed cover.

quiv•er (KWIV-ər) *verb*. To shake or cause to shake slightly; tremble: The leaves began to *quiver* in the breeze. **quivered, quivering.** —*noun*. 1. A slight shaking. 2. A case used to hold arrows.

rave (RAYV) *verb*. 1. To speak in a wild and senseless manner. 2. To speak about very favorably or with great enthusiasm: Dave *raved* about the new movie. **raved, raving.**

re•cov•er (ri-KUHV-ər) *verb*. 1. To get well. 2. To get back something taken away or lost. 3. To make up for: Can the time I spent away from school be *recovered*? **recovered, recovering.** —**recovery** (ri-KUHV-ə-ree) *noun*.

reed *noun*. 1. A tall straight grass with a hollow stem, found in marshy places. 2. A musical pipe made from a reed.

re•gal•ia (ri-GAYL-yə) *plural noun*. 1. The emblems or decorations of any society. 2. Splendid clothes; finery.

re•gret (ri-GRET) *verb*. To feel sorry about; be disappointed about: "I *regret* that I have but one life to lose for my country." (Nathan Hale). —*noun*. 1. A feeling of distress, disappointment, or sorrow. 2. (Plural) A message that one will not accept an invitation: I sent my *regrets* that I could not attend the play.

re•lease (ri-LEESS) *verb*. 1.To free; *release* from jail. 2. To give up: Vera *released* her claim to the property. **released, releasing.**

re•lieve (ri-LEEV) *verb*. 1. To ease or make less, as pain or worry. 2. To give aid or assistance.

re•new (ri-NOO or ri-NYOO) *verb*. 1. To restore, make like new. 2. To start (efforts) again: He *renewed* his attempt to force the door open. 3. To continue or get again: *renew* a magazine subscription. **renewed, renewing. —renewal** *noun*.

res•cue (RESS-kyoo) *noun*. Deliverance from danger. **rescues.** *—verb*. To save from danger. **rescued, rescuing.**

res•er•va•tion (rez-ər-VAY-shən) *noun*. Land set aside by the government for a special purpose, for example, for people to live on.

re•spect (ri-SPEKT) *noun*. 1. Honor; regard, consideration: *respect* for the rights of others. 2. (Plural) A polite expression of regard or honor: I'd like to pay my *respects* to your parents. *—verb*. To show or have regard or consideration for: The students respected the excellent teacher. **respected, respecting.**

re•spon•si•ble (ri-SPON-sə-bəl) *adjective*. 1. Having an obligation or duty regarding: Parents are *responsible* for their children. 2. Being the cause of: The broken machine was *responsible* for the loud noise. 3. Able to accept duties; worthy of trust: The manager gave the important job to the most *responsible* worker. **—responsibly** *adverb*.

rest•less (REST-liss) *adjective*. 1. Not able to relax or be still: The *restless* man paced up and down the hall. 2. Without rest or sleep: The tourist spent a *restless* night in the noisy hotel. **—restlessly** *adverb*.

re•treat (ri-TREET) *verb*. To withdraw; pull back. **retreated, retreating.**

re•ward (ri-WOHRHD) *verb*. To give something in return for an action or service. **rewarded, rewarding.** *—noun*. 1. Something earned or given in return for an action or service. 2. Money or something else of value offered for the capture of a criminal.

rheu•ma•tism (ROO-mə-tiz-əm) *noun*. A disease that affects the muscles and joints with stiffness and pain.

rhi•noc•er•os (righ-NOSS-ər-əss) *noun*. A very large mammal, found in Africa and Asia, that has thick folds of skin and one or two large horns on its snout. **—rhinoceros** or **rhinoceroses** *plural*.

rhythm (RITH-əm) *noun*. 1. Any movement that shows a regular pattern, as of rise and fall, short and long beats, or similar combinations: the *rhythm* of the waves, the *rhythm* of heartbeats. 2. A pattern of beats or stressed sounds, as in music or poetry.

rock•er (ROCK-ər) *noun*. 1. A rocking chair. 2. A curved section on which a rocking chair or cradle rocks.

rug•ged (RUHG-id) *adjective*. 1. Sturdy: tough and strong: *rugged* fullback. 2. Having a very rough, uneven surface: *rugged* mountains. 3. Difficult; harsh: *rugged* voyage. 4. Not smooth: a *rugged* face. **—ruggedly** *adverb*.

ruin (ROO-in) *noun*. 1. (Often plural) The remains of something that has decayed or been destroyed: the *ruins* of an old castle. **ruins.**

saber-toothed tiger (SAY-bər-toothd TIGH-gər) *noun*. A prehistoric animal with long and sharp canine teeth or fangs.

salve (SAV or SAHV) *noun.* A cream or oil used to soothe the pain of a wound or burn.

sap•ling (SAP-ling) *noun.* A young tree.

sat•is•fy (SAT-iss-figh) *verb.* 1. To fill (a need or wish): The ice cream *satisfied* my hunger. 2. To give assurance to; to answer. 3. To pay or fulfill. **satisfied, satisfying.**

scuff (SKUHF) *verb.* 1. To scrape or drag the feet when walking. 2. To cause a scraped or rough spot on: Tim *scuffed* his new shoes when he tripped. **scuffed, scuffing.** —*noun.* A scraped or rough spot.

seed•ling (SEED-ling) *noun.* A young plant grown from a seed. **seedlings.**

shaggy-coated (SHAG-ee-KOHT-əd) *adjective.* Having long or coarse hair.

sha•man (SHAH-mən) *noun.* A member of an early tribe who practiced magic by means of spells, dances, and so forth.

sher•bet (SHER-bit) *noun.* A sweet frozen dessert made with fruit juice, milk or water, and gelatin or egg white.

shield (SHEELD) *noun.* 1. A large piece of metal or wood held in front of the body to protect it in combat. 2. Anything that serves to protect. 3. Something shaped like a shield, as a police officer's badge. —*verb.* To defend or protect. **shielded, shielding.**

shim•mer (SHIM-ər) *verb.* To shine with a faint unsteady sparkle; gleam faintly. **shimmered, shimmering.** —*noun.* A faint gleam or sparkle.

shrine (SHRIGHN) *noun.* A place considered sacred because of a person or event associated with it: The Lincoln Memorial is an American *shrine.* **shrines.**

shrink (SHRINGK) *verb.* 1. To make or become smaller or less. 2. To draw back; shy away (from): *shrink* from a dog. **shrank** or **shrunk, shrunk** or **shrunken, shrinking.**

sift *verb.* 1. To separate big or coarse parts from little or fine ones by passing through a sieve: *sift* flour. 2. To pass (through): The sunlight *sifts* through the branches. 3. To examine with care: I must *sift* all he tells me. **sifted, sifting.**

singe (SINJ) *verb.* To burn slightly, especially hair or feathers. **singed, singeing.**

site (SIGHT) *noun.* A place where something is, will be, or was: Somme was the *site* of great World War I battles. **sites.**

siz•zle (SIZ-l) *verb.* To make a hissing sound like fat over a fire: Bacon *sizzles* in the pan. **sizzled, sizzling.**

skull (SKUHL) *noun.* The part of the skeleton that forms the head.

sky•line (SKY-lighn) *noun.* 1. The line where the earth and the sky seem to meet; horizon. 2. The forms of buildings as seen against the sky. **skylines.**

smol•der (SMOHL-dər) *verb.* To burn and smoke without flame. **smoldered, smoldering.**

snork•el (SNOR-kəl) *noun.* 1. A tube or tubes permitting a submarine to take in fresh air while it is under the water. 2. A tube used by a swimmer to get air when his head is under the water. —*verb.* To swim under the water while using a snorkel. Also called "snorkel dive." **snorkeled, snorkeling.**

snuf•fle (SNUF-l) *verb.* To sniff repeatedly, as when one is crying or has a cold. **snuffled, snuffling.**

snug•gle (SNUHG-əl) *verb.* To cuddle; press close or lie close (to) in a loving way. **snuggled, snuggling.**

so•ber•ness (SOH-bər-ness) *noun.* The state of being quiet or serious.

spear•head (SPIHR-hed) *noun.* 1. The pointed end of a spear. 2. The forward line of a military attack. —*verb.* To lead a military attack or any movement or project. **spearheaded, spearheading.**

spin•dly (SPIN-dlee) *adjective.* Very long and thin: *spindly* legs.

splotch (SPLOCH) *noun.* A smear or spot of a color or material different from that of the surface or background.

stab *verb.* 1. To wound or pierce with a knife or other pointed object. 2. To offend deeply; hurt the feelings of.

stabbed, stabbing. —*noun.* 1. A wound made by stabbing. 2. A thrust; a poking into. 3. (Informal) A quick try; attempt: Janet took a *stab* at water skiing.

stage•coach (STAYJ-kohch) *noun.* A horse-drawn coach or enclosed wagon used in former times to carry passengers and mail. **stagecoaches.**

stain (STAYN) *noun.* 1. A spot or mark. 2. A liquid used to dye or color something. —*verb.* 1. To spoil or make a spot or mark on. 2. To blemish or spoil, as one's honor or character; dishonor. 3. To color, as with a dye. **stained, staining.**

sta•lag•mite (stə-LAG-might or STAL-əg - might) *noun.* A mineral deposit that is built up from the floors of caves. **stalag-mites.**

stam•pede (stam-PEED) *noun.* A sudden and widespread rush or running. —*verb.* To run suddenly in a large group. **stampeded, stampeding.**

stif•fen (STIF-ən) *verb.* To make or become thick, rigid, or tense. **stiffened, stiffening.**

strain (STRAYN) *verb.* 1. To injure by too much effort: Ralph *strained* his back when he lifted the log. 2. To make a great effort: The movers *strained* to lift the piano. 3. To force through a sieve or screen to separate small from large pieces or solid from liquid parts. **strained, straining.**

streak (STREEK) *noun.* 1. A narrow stripe that is different from the surrounding area: Mother's hair has *streaks* of gray. 2. A particular quality: a mean *streak.* 3. A series of events: a winning *streak.* —*verb.* 1. To make

lines or streaks. 2. To move quickly. **streaked, streaking.**

stroll (STROHL) *verb.* To walk slowly. **strolled, strolling.** —*noun.* A slow walk.

stub•by (STUHB-ee) *adjective.* 1. Short and thick: *stubby* fingers. 2. Covered with or made up of stubs. **stubbier, stubbiest.**

stu•di•o (STOO-dee-oh or STYOO-dee-oh) *noun.* 1. The workshop of a painter, musician, photographer, or other artist. 2. A place for broadcasting radio or TV programs, or for making movies. **studios.**

sulk•y (SUHL-kee) *adjective.* Sullen; quiet because of bad temper. —**sulkily** *adverb.*

sum•mit (SUHM-it) *noun.* The highest point; peak; top.

sur•vey (sər-VAY or SER-vay) *verb.* 1. To look over carefully: inspect. 2. To collect information about: study. 3. To make exact land measurements. **surveyed, surveying.**

swag•ger (SWAG-ər) *verb.* 1. To walk or behave in a bold, rude, or showy way; to strut. 2. To brag or boast. **swaggered, swaggering.** —*noun.* A showy way of behaving: a strut.

swamp (SWAHMP or SWAWMP) *verb.* 1. To sink; flood; fill with water: A big wave *swamped* our boat. 2. To put into deep water; to cover with water. 3. To overcome; flood: Molly's new shop is *swamped* with business. **swamped, swamping.** —*noun.* A marsh; soft, wet land. —**swampy** *adjective.*

sweet•meat (SWEET-meet) *noun.* A candy.

Swiss *adjective.* Having to do with the country of Switzerland.

tangy *adjective.* Having a sharp, biting flavor or odor.

tart (TAHRT) *adjective.* 1. Sour; sharp: Cherries have a *tart* flavor.

2. Cutting, biting, as a sharp remark. **tarter, tartest.** —*noun*. A small open pie. —**tartly** *adverb*.

tas•sel (TASS-l) *noun*. 1. A hanging decoration made up of a tuft or bunch of thread or string fastened together at one end. 2. Something like this: Corn has *tassels*.

tem•per (TEM-pər) *noun*. 1. The state of one's feelings or attitudes: a gentle *temper*. 2. A state of anger; rage. 3. Control of one's feelings: The coach lost his *temper*. —*verb*. 1. To treat a metal to make it hard or flexible. 2. To modify, make less severe. **tempered, tempering.**

tempt *verb*. 1. To encourage to do something, especially something unwise or improper. 2. To dare; to test: *tempt* your luck. 3. To be inclined: *tempted* to quit the team. **tempted, tempting.** —**temptation** (tem-TAY-shən) *noun*.

ten•sion (TEN-shən) *noun*. 1. The act or condition of stretching or being stretched: When a fish bites, there is *tension* on the fishing line. 2. Mental strain; nervousness. 3. An uneasy, unfriendly feeling or state.

three-fourths (three-FORTHS) *noun*. A part of a whole, when the whole is considered to be four fourths.

thresh•old (THRESH-ohld) *noun*. 1. A doorsill. 2. The beginning: the *threshold* of adventure.

throb *noun*. A quivering feeling or movement, as a strong beat of the heart. —*verb*. To move, beat, or vibrate in a steady, pulsing way. **throbbed, throbbing.**

tin•der (TIN-dər) *noun*. Dry material that will start to burn easily and quickly, as paper and twigs; any material that is very flammable.

tis•sue (TISH-oo) *noun*. 1. A very light, thin fabric or paper. 2. (Biology) Similar cells in a part of the body or plant: muscle *tissue*.

tod•dler (TOD-lər) *noun*. A child just learning to walk. **toddlers.**

tol•er•ance (TOL-ər-ənss) *noun*. 1. The ability to be fair to those whose views, customs, or actions are different from one's own. 2. (Medicine) The natural or acquired ability to resist the effect of (an element, as a drug).

torch *noun*. 1. A flaming light, usually carried by hand. 2. (British) A flashlight. 3. A tool that burns gas to produce a hot flame, used to melt metals and remove paint; a blowtorch. **torches.**

trag•e•dy (TRAJ-ə-dee) *noun*. 1. A very sad event; a piece of extreme bad luck. 2. A serious play, novel, or other work with an unhappy ending; such writing in general.

tri•al (TRIGH-əl or TRIGHL) *noun*. 1. A trying or testing. 2. (Law) An examination of facts, conducted in court, to determine the truth of charges or claims. 3. A person or thing that causes hardship.

tu•pe•lo (TOO-pə-loh) *noun*. A large tree that grows in swamps. Its soft, light wood is used for making wooden shoes, and pieces of its root are used to float fishing nets.

tur•ban (TER-bən) *noun*. 1. A Moslem head covering made by winding a long cloth or scarf around the head. 2. A hat that looks similar to a turban.

tusk (TUHSK) *noun*. A long, curved tooth (usually one of a pair) of an animal such as the elephant.

twine (TWIGHN) *noun*. Strong cord or string made of two or more strands twisted together. **binder twine.** Cord used to bind up grain.

ty•rant (TIGH-rənt) *noun*. 1. A ruler who exercises complete control or authority; a cruel ruler. 2. Anyone who dominates other persons cruelly or unfairly.

un•earth•ly (uhn-ERTH-lee) *adjective*. 1. Apparently not from the earth: an *unearthly* being. 2. Frightening: an *unearthly* scream. 3. Strange: odd: an *unearthly* hairdo.

un•pop•u•lar (uhn-POP-yə-lər) *adjective.* Not well liked; not favored or approved of. **—unpopularity** (uhn-pop-yə-LA-rə-tee) *noun.*

un•rea•son•a•ble (uhn-REE-zn-ə-bəl) *adjective.* 1. Not having or showing sense or clear thought. 2. More than is right or sensible. **—unreasonably** *adverb.*

urge (ERJ) *verb.* 1. To encourage earnestly; to push (someone) to action: We *urged* Dad to buy a new car. 2. To present (an idea, plan, or such) strongly; to recommend strongly. 3. To push or drive forward: the farmer *urged* the oxen into the field. **urged, urging.**

ven•ture (VEN-chər) *verb.* 1. To risk; take a chance. 2. To take the chance of going: *venture* into the cave. 3. To dare (to give an opinion): I *ventured* to tell Augustus that he was wrong. **ventured, venturing. —noun.** An enterprise that is risky or unsure. **ventures.**

vi•brate (VIGH-brayt) *verb.* 1. To move or make move up and down or back and forth quickly. 2. To make a wavering sound: Tarzan's voice *vibrated* when he pounded his chest. **vibrated, vibrating. —vibration** (vigh-BRAY-shən) *noun.*

vic•tim (VIK-tim) *noun.* 1. One who is hurt or killed. 2. One who is fooled, cheated, or hurt: the *victim* of our pranks. 3. An animal offered as a sacrifice. **—victimize** *verb.*

vul•ture (VUHL-chər) *noun.* 1. A bird in the hawk family that lives by eating the carcasses of dead animals. 2. A person who feeds on or profits from the mistakes or bad luck of others.

waft (WAHFT or WAFT) *verb.* To float or move gently through the air or on the water. **wafted, wafting. —noun.** A

gentle puff of air.

ware•house (WAIR-howss) *noun.* A large storage building. **warehouses. —verb.** To store or put into a warehouse. **warehoused, warehousing.**

wat•tle (WOT-l) *noun.* The red skin hanging down from the neck of a chicken or turkey. **wattles.**

wa•ver (WAY-vər) *verb.* 1. To sway; move back and forth. 2. To incline first toward one thing and then toward another. 3. To lose strength. **wavered, wavering.**

weave (WEEV) *verb.* 1. To make fabric by interlacing or overlapping threads or strips of material. 2. To travel or move by winding in and out: *weave* through traffic. **wove** or **weaved, weaving.**

whiff (HWIF) *noun.* 1. A puff or light current of air. 2. A sniff or quick breath, as of an odor. 3. The odor itself, moving through the air: a *whiff* of newly cut grass.

wig•wam (WIG-WOM) *noun.* An Indian tent; a tepee.

wilt *verb.* 1. To droop or cause to droop: Cut flowers *wilt* without water. 2. To weaken; lose courage or strength. **wilted, wilting.**

wince (WINSS) *verb.* To pull back, as if in pain. **winced, wincing. —noun.** The act of drawing back.

woo *verb.* 1. To try to gain the love of. 2. To seek: Both candidates will *woo* the labor vote. **wooed, wooing.**

wor•ri•some (WUHR-ee-səm) *adjective.* 1. Causing worry or concern. 2. With a tendency to worry.

yoke (YOHK) *noun.* A wooden frame used to fasten two work animals together, as for plowing. **—verb.** To fasten together. **yoked.**